# PRAISE FOR THIS MORTAL COIL

"*This Mortal Coil* redefines 'unputdownable.' A thrilling, exhilarating read that's crackling with intelligence. Compelling characters and incredible twists come together perfectly—I loved this book. This is brilliant science fiction." —Amie Kaufman, *New York Times* bestselling author of *Illuminae*

"I was thrilled; I was shocked; I have so many questions. I want to know what happens next." —NPR

"A smart, page-turning thriller that gave me chills. I couldn't put this book down." —Laini Taylor, *New York Times* bestselling author of *Strange the Dreamer* and the Daughter of Smoke and Bone trilogy

"I can't remember the last time I was so hooked by a book. Relentlessly paced, expertly plotted, and with a romance as tense and as captivating as her wicked twists, Emily Suvada has crafted an unputdownable story. I loved every terrifying page." —Stephanie Garber, *New York Times* bestselling author of *Caraval*

★ "Stunning twists and turns." —*BCCB*, starred review

"Suvada's debut novel balances characterization and action with an intensity that readers of dystopian fantasy will find infectious." —*VOYA*

## ALSO BY EMILY SUVADA

*This Cruel Design*

# THIS
# MORTAL
# COIL

EMILY SUVADA

**SIMON PULSE**

New York  London  Toronto  Sydney  New Delhi

SIMON PULSE

An imprint of Simon & Schuster Children's Publishing Division

1230 Avenue of the Americas, New York, New York 10020

First Simon Pulse paperback edition September 2018

Text copyright © 2017 by Emily Suvada

Cover photograph copyright © 2017 by Sunny/Getty Images

Also available in a Simon Pulse hardcover edition.

All rights reserved, including the right of reproduction in whole or in part in any form.

SIMON PULSE and colophon are registered trademarks of Simon & Schuster, Inc.

For information about special discounts for bulk purchases, please contact Simon & Schuster Special Sales at 1-866-506-1949 or business@simonandschuster.com.

The Simon & Schuster Speakers Bureau can bring authors to your live event.

For more information or to book an event, contact the Simon & Schuster Speakers Bureau at 1-866-248-3049 or visit our website at www.simonspeakers.com.

Cover designed by Regina Flath

Interior designed by Mike Rosamilia

The text of this book was set in Minion Pro.

Manufactured in the United States of America

2 4 6 8 10 9 7 5 3 1

The Library of Congress has cataloged the hardcover edition as follows:

Names: Suvada, Emily, author.

Title: This mortal coil / by Emily Suvada.

Description: First Simon Pulse hardcover edition. | New York : Simon Pulse, 2017. |

Summary: "In a world where people are implanted with technology to recode their DNA, gene-hacking genius Cat must decrypt her late father's message concealing a vaccine to a horrifying plague"—Provided by publisher.

Identifiers: LCCN 2016056177 (print) | LCCN 2017027758 (eBook) |

ISBN 9781481496353 (eBook) | ISBN 9781481496339 (hc)

Subjects: | CYAC: Hackers—Fiction. | Genetic engineering—Fiction. | Plague—Fiction. |

Fathers and daughters—Fiction. | Science fiction.

Classification: LCC PZ7.1.S886 (eBook) | LCC PZ7.1.S886 Thi 2017 (print) | DDC [Fic]—dc23

LC record available at https://lccn.loc.gov/2016056177

ISBN 9781481496346 (pbk)

*To Edward:*
*my best friend, my love, my inspiration.*
*You are the shining focus of the locus of my heart.*

# CHAPTER 1

IT'S SUNSET, AND THE SKY IS AFLAME, NOT WITH clouds or dust, but with the iridescent feathers of a million genehacked passenger pigeons. They soar across the sky like a live impressionist painting in brilliant swirling arcs of tangerine and gold. Their strange cries sound like pebbles tossed against a window, and they move in perfect unison, blocking out the sun.

Amateur coders in Nevada rebuilt the long-extinct pigeon's DNA, then spliced it into something new and bold. Razor-tipped beaks. Metabolic hijacks. Color-shifting feathers to signal danger to the flock with a single muscle twitch.

Through years of work, they crafted the pigeons to be stronger than their ancestors. They're leaner, smarter, fiercer.

And they made them look like *fire*.

I lean out over the cabin's porch railing, my hips pressed into the wood, squinting through the scope of my father's rifle. Without magnification, the flock is just a blur of stippled color, but through the scope, with my ocular tech sharpening my vision, the colors resolve into the wings and chests of individual birds.

"Come on, little birdy," I breathe, squeezing the trigger. The shot echoes off the mountains, and the scent of gunpowder fills the air. That's homemade powder. Low sulfur, fine grade, nanoprinted in the basement, rigged to fire a tranquilizer dart and bring me down a bird without killing it.

The dart whistles through the air, a mere blur even with my tech. My audio filters peg it at Mach 2, which is far too high. My calculations were wrong again. I look away too late and see the dart hit a pigeon, blowing it into a puff of colored feathers.

"Dammit," I snap, dropping the rifle, not bothering to flick on the safety. It's now a thirty-pound paperweight, since I'm officially out of ammo. Well, not if you count the bullet swinging from the chain around my neck. But that's my insurance bullet, and it only comes off as a last resort.

The dead bird drops like a stone, tumbling down to land on the rocky shore of the cabin's tiny private lake. The flock shifts direction instantly, letting out a deafening warning cry that echoes off the steep mountain slopes like a hail of gunfire.

"I know, I know," I mutter. The flock scatters angrily, their plumage twitching to crimson, telegraphing the attack. I didn't *want* to hurt it. The bird was supposed to be a present. A little genehacked pet for my neighbor, Agnes, to keep her company. Now I'll have to bury it, because I sure as hell won't eat it. Barely anyone eats meat anymore, not since the outbreak.

The last two years have taught us what we could not forget: that animals taste a lot like people.

The porch's wooden railing squeaks as I launch myself over it and jog through the yard to the circle of feathers near the lake. A breeze dances through the knee-high grass, sweeping in across the water, carrying the cries of the pigeons, the chill of the evening, and the rich, deep scent of the forest.

It's wild out here. This secluded valley nestled deep in the Black Hills has been my home for the last three years and my sanctuary from the outbreak. Steep, forested mountains rise on either side of the lake, and my ramshackle log cabin sits just a short walk back from the shore. It's so well-hidden that you almost have to know where it is to find it, but it's close enough to town that I can ride in on my bike. All things considered, it's a perfect place to spend the apocalypse, with only one down side: The comm reception sucks.

"Hey, Bobcat. This . . . Agnes . . ."

I tilt my head as Agnes's elderly voice crackles in my ears, blasting through my subdermal comm-link. She checks up on me nearly every day but refuses to text me. Always calls, even though I can't hear her. I close my eyes, drawing up the mental interface to send a text, but her voice breaks through in a burst of static.

"Urgent . . . danger . . ."

Her voice cuts out. No static, nothing.

I spin around, bolting straight up the side of the mountain.

"Agnes?" I shout. Damn Russian satellites. They're a century old, but they're all we can use now that Cartaxus has taken over every other network on the planet. My comm-link can get texts in the cabin, but every time I want to take a call, I have to run half a mile uphill.

Static fills my ears. ". . . reading me . . . Bobcat?"

"Hang on!" I yell, racing up the rocky slope. The path between the trees is still wet from last night's rain. I skid as I race around a switchback, scrambling to keep myself upright.

She might be hurt. She's all alone. The old girl is armed and tough as nails, but there are things in this world you can't fight. Things that have no cure.

"Almost there!" I shout, forcing myself up the final stretch. I burst into the clearing at the summit and double over. "Agnes? Are you okay? Can you hear me?"

A beat of satellite-lag silence hangs in my ears, and then Agnes's voice returns. "I'm fine, Bobcat. Didn't mean to scare you."

I drop to my knees in the grass, trying to catch my breath. "You nearly gave me a heart attack."

"Sorry. But I guess I figured out how to make you answer your comm."

I roll my eyes and push the sweat-soaked hair from my face. "What's so urgent?"

"You up on your hill?"

"Well, I am *now*."

She chuckles, her voice popping with static. "I just got a call from one of the locals. They spotted a jeep out near your place. Big black thing. You see anything from up there?"

I push myself to my feet and scan the forest. From this outlook, on a clear day, I can see for miles. The Black Hills roll out before me, tumbling granite draped with pines, dotted with the flash of lakes and a web of leaf-strewn roads. This time of day two years ago, the highway to the east would have been lit up with a steady stream of headlights from the evening commute. There would have been planes flying into Rapid and the glow of houses through the trees, but instead the hills are dark, and the highway is an empty stretch of black.

All the houses are shuttered, and the land is dotted with craters. It always makes me sick to see it like this, but it's the only place I can get reception.

"No headlights," I mutter. "They might be using infrared. You sure it was a jeep?"

"Brand-new, they said. Has to be Cartaxus."

The hair on the back of my neck rises. I've never seen a jeep out here before. Cartaxus always sends its troops out in camouflaged trucks, with whining drones for air support. I scan the forest again, straining my ocular tech until my vision starts to glitch.

"I tried calling you," Agnes says. "A few times, the last couple of days."

"I've been in the lab," I mutter, scanning the roads. "Trying to make gunpowder."

"That sounds dangerous."

A half smile tugs at my lips, and my fingers twitch instinctively, running over the sensitive, newly regrown skin on my palms. "There were some minor explosions. Nothing my healing tech couldn't handle."

Agnes clicks her tongue. "*Bobcat.* When did you last eat?"

"Um . . . yesterday?"

"Do you have clean clothes?"

I glance down at my filthy sweater, my dirt-encrusted jeans. "Uhh . . ."

"Get yourself over here right now, young lady. I don't like the sound of this jeep, and you need to get out of that godforsaken lab for a night. Right now, you hear me?"

I bite back a laugh. "Okay, Yaya. I'll be there soon."

"Damn straight you will. And bring your dirty clothes with you."

The connection clicks off in my ears with a kiss, leaving me grinning. Agnes isn't really my *yaya*, though she certainly acts like it. We don't share DNA, but we've shared food and tears, and ever since the outbreak, that's all that really counts. Sometimes I think the only reason either of us is still alive is that we can't bear the thought of leaving the other alone.

I stretch my arms over my head, scanning the forest one last time before dialing my ocular tech back down. The embedded panel in my forearm that powers my tech chews through a few hundred calories a day even on standby, and food isn't exactly plentiful anymore. My vision blurs as my eyes refocus, and it takes me a second to realize there's a plume on the horizon that wasn't there before.

"Uh-oh."

I freeze, counting the seconds until the *crack* hits my ears. The plume rises before spreading, mushrooming out across the sky. The flock of pigeons fragments into wild, panicked streams, racing away from the billowing cloud. The sound takes fifteen seconds to hit me, which tells me it's three miles away. Too far to make out the details, but I can tell the cloud is a sickly shade of pink.

That's the color of a human body when its cells are ripped open, blown into mist, and spat into the air.

A Hydra cloud.

My stomach lurches. Depending on which way the wind is blowing, this distant cloud just might kill me. One breath is all it takes. One lungful of swirling, airborne virus particles that will swarm through every cell in your body. You'll get a fever; you'll incubate; then two weeks later you'll go off like a grenade, infecting everyone in a mile-wide radius.

There's no cure, no treatment. There's one way to get immunity, but it's been twenty-six days since I last took a dose.

Agnes's voice crackles in my ears. "That . . . near you?"

I close my eyes, using a mental command to switch my comm over to text mode. It's slower—I have to focus harder, bringing up each word separately in my mind—but it doesn't need a clear signal.

3 miles, I send. Blowing further east. Probably out of infection radius.

haul out quick, she replies.

I will. She doesn't need to tell me twice.

I pause as I turn back to the trail, watching the cloud drift. It's twice as big as the clouds I first saw in the outbreak, two years ago. The virus is evolving, and the blasts are getting stronger. If they keep growing, pretty soon there won't be anywhere left to hide.

I push the thought away, jogging back down the mountain, trying to dodge the worst of the mud. There's no need to panic about a cloud as far away as this, but without immunity, I can't help but feel a little nervous.

I glance back as I descend into the trees, telling myself that it's miles away, that I'll be fine. I'll go to Agnes's place, and she'll feed me lentils and her disgusting licorice candies like she always does. We'll fire up her woodstove and play a game of cards. Simple. Easy. But just as the cabin comes into view, another *crack* tears through the air, and I jerk to a stop.

A second plume shoots up, pink and leaf strewn and terrifying. Close enough that I forget to count the seconds that pass until I hear it. The mist billows into the air like a living, heaving thing, unfurling through the forest, sending the pigeons scattering. The wind is dragging it away from me, but the wind can change in a heartbeat.

This cloud is far too close. I'm going to have to run.

Agnes's name pops up in my vision as I race down the mountain.

another one

I KNOW, I reply, skidding to the bottom of the hill.

dont like this bobcat, she says. shdnt let ur immunity lapse.

There's nothing I can say to that because I know she's right; it was reckless to let myself run out of doses. There was a reason, but thinking about it now makes my cheeks burn with its sheer stupidity.

I bolt up the cabin's stairs to the porch and grab my rucksack and knife, picking up the rifle before throwing it back down. Dead weight. I race out to my bike, an old BMX with a rusted frame that can handle dirt trails like nobody's business. I sling my rucksack over my shoulder, slip my knife into my belt, and haul the bike out from the bushes I keep it hidden in. One leg is over it, my grip tight on the handlebars, when an alert from my audio tech sends me flying into a crouch.

Rustling. Nearby. An unenhanced ear wouldn't hear it, but my filters sharpen the sound into slow, heavy footsteps. Labored and staggering. The way people move when they're infected.

They're just beyond me, in the trees, and they're coming my way.

"Oh shit," I breathe, my hands shaking.

near me, I send to Agnes, my mind spinning so fast that I can barely form the words.

HIDE NOW, she replies.

The command is so unlike her, so frantic and bizarre that I don't even pause to question it. I just drop my bike and run.

The cabin is too far, but there's a willow near the lake, and I haul myself up through the branches, my newly healed palms scraping against the bark. I kick and claw my way to a high branch in a matter of seconds, flying up the tree on sheer adrenaline. As soon as I find my balance, a man crashes through the bushes, and I hold my nose at the exact moment he splashes into the lake.

It's a blower, no doubt about it. He falls to his knees in the shallows, sucking in a wet, labored breath. He's badly wounded. Scarlet rivers run down his arms, trickling from innumerable gashes and bite marks covering his skin. It looks like a mob got him. I can see his teeth through the stringy hole in one cheek, and his eyes are swollen shut, his ears reduced to stumps of cartilage.

He's bleeding out and feverish. Definitely infected. Second stage, probably a day away from detonating. Even with my fingers clamped over my nose, I can still feel my body starting to shake in response to his scent.

There's nothing quite like the scent of infection. No odor or perfume matches the sharp, sulfurous clouds that roll off a Hydra victim's skin. Some people liken it to the scent of burning plastic or the air after a lightning strike. I've always thought it smelled like the hot springs I visited as a child. Whatever the comparison, nobody gets much time to think about it, because as soon as the scent hits you, it takes your breath away.

And that's not all it does.

I grit my teeth, fighting the response building inside me. My fingers curl instinctively, clawing into the bark of the tree. Breathing the scent won't hurt me—blowers aren't infectious until they detonate—but the scent will crawl into my mind, igniting a response that's impossible to control. Even forcing myself to breathe through my mouth, I can still feel it whispering, rising inside me like a curse. It wants me to grab the knife sheathed at my thigh, to drop from my perch in the tree.

To unleash the monster that wakes in me at the merest whiff of infection.

But I don't want to yield to it. I tighten my grip on the tree, shake my head, and invoke my comm-link. In . . . tree . . . above him, I send to Agnes.

The man tries to get up, but he's too weak. He falls to his knees, letting out a moan. The wind lifts his scent into the branches, and it hits me like a punch.

u must do it, Agnes replies.

I blink the words away. My chest is shuddering, my vision starting to blur.

no choice bobcat. its the only way

I won't, I write, then delete it, because she's right. Or maybe it's because the scent has me by the throat, shattering my self-control. Either way, there's a cloud less than a mile from me, and there's only one way to guarantee that I'll make it out of this alive. I need immunity, or I'll die. The math is simple. I draw my knife, my stomach turning at the thought of what I have to do.

The man below me starts to cry, oblivious to my presence. The blood flowing from the bite marks on his skin forms swirls of scarlet in the lake's clear water. A single mouthful of his flesh, choked down in the next few minutes, will give me immunity from the virus for the next two weeks. This is the Hydra virus's cruelest side: It forces the healthy to eat the sick. To hunt and kill and feed on each other to save ourselves. Nature designed this plague as a double-edged sword: It either takes your life, or it takes your humanity.

I shift on the branch, staring down at the man, my knuckles white on the knife. My other hand is still locked on my nose, holding back the scent in a desperate attempt to fight it for just a moment more. My comm-link hisses wildly in my ears. Agnes knows me well enough to guess that I'm hesitating, and she's trying to call me, screaming that he'll be dead soon anyway, that he'd *want* me to do it.

But I don't want to hear it. I don't want to justify this, to keep the circle of death going. This is why I stopped taking doses, why I let my immunity lapse. I just wanted a few precious weeks of something like a normal life, without someone else's blood itching in my veins. I wanted to keep the monster locked away, to rise above my instincts.

But deeper down, the hunger is growing.

This man's sharp, sulfurous scent has clawed its way into my lungs, and my hands are already shaking. It's a neurological response. The scent pounds against my mind like fists against a cracking wall until I can't hold it back anymore.

When I finally drop my hand from my nose and let the smell sweep into my lungs, it feels like drawing breath for the first time.

For a moment I'm free, weightless and euphoric, like the moment at the top of a roller coaster before you hurtle down.

Then it hits. A jolt. A cataclysm of rage, rocketing through my muscles, curling my lips back in a snarl.

My eyes snap down to the man below me, the knife gripped in my hands.

The world blinks to scarlet, and I launch myself into gravity's arms.

# CHAPTER 2

Two Years Earlier

"THIS LOOKS LIKE FUN," DAX SAYS. "WHAT ARE YOU up to, Princess?"

"If you call me Princess one more time, I'm going to shoot *you* instead."

The sky is a clear, cerulean blue, the sun pitched high above me, its light catching the feathers of a flock of passenger pigeons. They shimmer gold and white, dazzling as they loop and swirl, filling the air with their strange, percussive cries. I've been standing on the cabin's front porch, aiming my father's rifle at them for the last five minutes, but I just can't pull the trigger.

"You know, Princess, you're holding it wrong."

I groan and spin around, but find Dax standing right behind me, and the barrel of the rifle swings into his chest. He grabs it in a flash, flicking on the safety before I can blink. "Well," he says. "I suppose I should have learned to take an Agatta at their word."

"Sorry," I blurt out, staring at the rifle. "I . . . I wasn't thinking."

"Not thinking? Now *that* would be a first." He leans the rifle against the cabin's side and crosses his arms, giving me a playful smile that sends my heart rate skyrocketing.

Dax is my father's lab assistant, and he's lived at the cabin ever since he showed up alone, begging to work with the *great* Dr. Lachlan Agatta. He's just seventeen, two years older than me, and he had no references, no degree, but Dax is the kind of guy who's impossible to refuse.

He also happened to be the author of a hepatitis app that my father said was one of the most beautiful pieces of code he'd ever seen.

"I've had some issues with my genkit," he says, stepping closer. "Someone's reprogrammed it to play videos of porpoises whenever I type a command."

"Oh?" I ask, leaning back against the railing. "That's odd."

"Yes," he says, moving forward until I can feel his breath on my skin. "They seem to have some strong opinions about my coding abilities in relation to yours. Quite disparaging. They suggested saving my work to */dev/null*."

I stifle a smile. "Clever porpoises."

"Indeed." He steps away and glances at the rifle. "Doing a little hunting?"

I shrug. "I was trying to distract myself from this whole end-of-the-world thing."

From the broadcasts on every channel. From the hourly reports of new infections, and the video of Patient Zero they keep replaying, showing him throwing his head back, showing him *detonating*, showing the clouds of pink mist racing through the streets of Punta Arenas.

"Right," Dax says, nodding seriously. "And we're taking it out on the pigeons, are we? Fair enough. I've never liked their beady little eyes."

I can't help but smile. "I was trying to get a sample to sequence. This flock looks like a new strain. I think they might have the rest of the poem."

The poem is a sonnet. I already have the three quatrains, and I've been waiting four months for the couplet to arrive.

"Ah," he says, snatching up the rifle. "No time to waste, then. We have some birds to shoot."

When the genehacked pigeons first appeared in our skies six months ago, it was my father who shot one down to take a look at their DNA. Their genes were expertly coded, except for one tiny section, a messy string of DNA that didn't seem to fit. My father said it was junk, but it bugged me, so I took a sample to analyze on my own. I ran it through my trusty laptop genkit, a portable genetic sequencer, but none of the built-in search algorithms could find a pattern. Finally on a whim, I translated the base pairs into binary, then ASCII, and into a string of alphanumeric letters.

Then it all made sense. It wasn't a gene—it was a message. That odd patch of G, T, C, and A was hiding the words of a poem.

That's the beautiful thing about gentech—the science of genetic coding. You can get lost in the minutiae, but then you step back sometimes, and patterns appear like sunlight bursting through clouds. Reading the genetic code behind a feather or a cell can make you feel like you're reading poetry written by God.

Unfortunately, the poem in the pigeons was written by amateur genehackers, and it's not the best thing I've ever read, but I still want to know how it ends.

"One or two? Big or little?" Dax squints through the rifle's scope at the swirling flock of birds above us. His shoulder-length red hair is tied back in a low ponytail, a few loose strands hanging around his face. One streak is white blond, more a boast of his coding prowess than a fashion statement. A whole head of hair is easy to hack, but you have to be a coding wizard to zero in on just a few strands.

I cross my arms, looking up at the birds. "You really think you can just hit one?"

"I know I can."

I roll my eyes, but he's probably right. Dax's ocular tech is state-of-the-art, along with every other app running from the panel embedded in his arm. It stretches from his wrist to his elbow, a soft layer of nanocoded silicone glowing in a stripe of cobalt light beneath his skin. Inside it, tiny processors run gentech code, packaged up as individual apps to alter his DNA and change his body. Those apps govern everything from his implanted sensory upgrades to his metabolism, even the streak in his hair.

The computers that can handle manipulations on DNA were once the size of a room, but they eventually became small enough to bury inside your body. The gentech panel is a perfect combination of hardware, software, and *wetware*, generating constant streams of algorithmically designed nanites. Those nanites move through a network of cables inside your body, then bleed through your cells, building and destroying coils of synthetic DNA. Gentech can grow wires and circuits the same way your body grows bone, or it can grow your hair in perfect ringlets even if you were born with it straight. Almost everyone has a panel, budded at birth to grow inside them, and most people carry hundreds, even thousands, of apps.

My wrist holds just six lonely dots. My hypergenesis, an allergy to the nanites that run most gentech, means the panel in my arm is little more than a glorified phone. I have standard healing and sensory tech, and a glitchy twelve-kilobyte comm that my father personally coded for me. But if I download anything else, even the simplest of apps, the nanites will shred through my cells and kill me within hours.

It's ironic, really. I'm the daughter of the world's greatest gentech coder, but I'll never be able to experience most of his work.

Dax fires the rifle. A shot rings out, and feathers puff through the air. A single bird arcs up parabolically, then tumbles to the ground. He lowers the rifle, leaning it back against the wall, and arches an eyebrow. "What do you say, first one to the bird gets to finish the poem?"

My jaw drops. "No, this is my project. You can't finish it. That's not fair."

He launches himself over the porch and lands in the grass with cat-like grace, then tilts his head to smile up at me. "Life isn't fair, *Princess*."

"Oh," I breathe, cracking my knuckles. "You are so in for it now."

I bolt down the stairs and race through the grass, my long dark hair streaming out behind me, veering left as Dax tries to block my path. He's stronger, but I'm faster, and I dart past him, skidding to a stop on the lake's pebbled shore, snatching up the bird with one outstretched hand.

I'm fast, but not fast enough. Dax hurtles into me, knocking me to the ground, yanking the pigeon from my hand. I roll over on the grass and scramble up just in time to grab a fistful of his hair.

I yank it back, hard. He lets out a cry, dropping the pigeon, and spins to face me with a wild look in his eyes.

A few seconds ago we were two coders discussing DNA, but now we're like wolves, circling each other, fighting over something neither of us need. The pigeon doesn't matter. Any one of the feathers littering the ground could yield its DNA, but this isn't really about the bird, or even about the poem. This is about Dax and me, and the tension that's been building between us since he kissed me last week when my father was away. We haven't talked about it since. I tried to pretend it didn't happen, too frightened that my overprotective father would find out and fire Dax. We've spent the week trying to work together, to ignore the energy crackling between us, like two humming electrodes just waiting for a spark.

My eyes drop to the pigeon. I make the slightest move toward it, and

Dax's arm whips around my waist, lifting me clean off my feet. My heart pounds at the feeling of his chest against my back, but his feet slip, and for a heartbeat we sway together before tumbling into the lake.

"Dax, no!" I shriek, scrambling away, shoving my sopping hair from my face.

He just laughs. He flicks his head back, sending up a glistening Mohawk of water. "I wasn't going to take the damn bird."

"Then why did you *start* this? How are we going to explain this to my father?"

He grins. "That's what I came to tell you. He knows, Princess. We had a chat, and he's okay with it, but he kept telling me that some things are better when you *wait* for them."

I almost choke. "Are you kidding me?"

"Nope. I don't know if it's the whole apocalypse thing or not, but I got the Agatta stamp of approval. I hope you know that when we get married, I'm taking your name, and then we're calling all our future children Lachlan, after your father. It might be hard on the girls, but I'm sure they'll understand, and—"

"Catarina!"

We both spin around as my father throws open the front door.

I glance at Dax, whose face has paled. My stomach drops. He was lying. There was no conversation, no Agatta stamp of approval, and now the two of us are dead. I'm fifteen. It's reckless. I should have known better than to let us get so close, and now everything is going to be ruined.

Dax will be sent away. I'll go back to boarding school. The brightest, happiest time of my life will be over before it's begun.

"Both of you in here, now!" my father shouts.

"We were just . . . I shot a pigeon," I say. "The poem . . ."

"I know," my father says. "Forget about the damn bird and get inside."

17

Dax and I exchange nervous glances as we hurry up to the cabin. My father only curses when he's angry, but it doesn't sound like he's angry at us. Dax hops on one leg to pull his sneakers off while I unzip my wet sweater and drop it on the porch.

Inside, my father is standing in the center of the living room, dressed immaculately in his lab coat, staring at the walls. Only he's not really staring at the walls. He's not even really *staring*. He's back in a virtual reality session, watching something through his panel. A live feed of images, sent from his panel through fiber cabling inside his body, pulsed directly into his optic nerve. To his brain, there's no difference. The feed from his panel and his eyes merge and intersect, creating a single, seamless image. When my father stares at the wall, he could see a screen with video footage, or a painting, or a scrolling stream of headlines.

Or he could see something else entirely. A beach. The stars. His panel could thrust him from the cabin into a fully rendered world. At least that's what I'm told. I've never tried it myself. The only graphics card that works with my panel is too weak to render VR. All I have is an ancient chip that can run basic ocular filters and sketch a few lines of text in my vision. That's enough to send messages through my comm, but not enough to watch movies, play games, or even *code* the way the rest of the world does.

One sleeve of my father's lab coat is rolled to his elbow, and his crypto cuff is strapped around his forearm. It's a sleek sheath of chrome that scrambles the transmissions from his panel's wireless chip, and he only wears it for important calls, to stop Cartaxus from listening to his conversations.

I stare at the cuff, my stomach lurching. My father wasn't angry at Dax and me. He's been talking to someone about the outbreak. Whatever he heard, it's left him practically shaking.

"What's going on?" I touch his elbow to let him know I'm here. His eyes are glazed; his vision is probably 360 degrees of pure VR.

"The virus has swept through Nicaragua," he says. "Now that it's past the canal, there's nothing left to stop it. They're planning airstrikes."

"On *civilians*?" I glance at Dax. "Who's considering that?"

My father blinks out of his session. His eyes refocus, and he turns to me. "Everyone, darling. Every government in the world is considering it."

I swallow, taking in my father's bloodshot eyes, the strain in his face. Everything about this outbreak is terrifying, but none of it worries me as much as the lines etched into his brow. He's the world's greatest gentech coder. He wrote the cure for Influenza X, and I've never seen him like this.

We must be in serious danger.

"Nicaragua," Dax repeats, his brow furrowed. "That's close. It only broke out two days ago. If it keeps spreading that fast, it could be here within days."

"Hours," my father says. "It's spreading exponentially. It's going to be chaos when it hits the cities. There'll be panic until a vaccine is released, and I fear that might take a very long time." He takes my hands. "There's food in the basement, clean water in the lake, and new solars on the roof, and you can always hide in the old mine shafts in the mountains."

"What . . . what are you saying?" My eyes drop to the crypto cuff. "Who have you been talking to?"

As if in response, a low thumping sound starts up in the distance, and the cries of the pigeons crescendo into a roar. But it's not the pigeons I'm listening to. It's the sound of helicopter blades growing louder with each passing second until the windows shake. Through the glass, I can make out two black Comox quadcopters swooping into the valley, their bellies slashed with a white logo.

I'd know that symbol anywhere. I've seen it in my nightmares.

Stylized white crossed antlers.

It's Cartaxus.

Not the military, and not a corporation, but a massive international amalgam of technology and violence. A mix of public and private interests that has become the world's biggest provider and controller of gentech. My father worked with Cartaxus for twenty years, until he couldn't take it anymore and finally wrenched himself free of their iron grip. He told me this day might come, that they might show up and drag him away even though he swore he'd never work for them again. Not after the horrors he saw. The horrors that keep him awake at night, that he still can't bring himself to talk about.

Now they've come for him, just like he said they would. He turns to me, resignation traced into every line of his face.

"No," I blurt out, my voice breaking. "They can't just *take* you."

"They can, and they will. This isn't influenza, darling. They're rounding up everyone they think can help."

"But you can hide," I plead. "We can *run*."

He shakes his head. "No, Catarina, they'll find me wherever I go. They think Dax and I can write a vaccine for this virus. We have no choice but to go with them."

Dax steps back. "They want *me*? I'm not going anywhere."

"You mustn't fight them," my father urges. "I worked for Cartaxus, and I know what they're capable of. They want your brain, but they don't need your legs."

Dax blanches. The copter rotors grow louder, the vibrations sending puffs of dust drifting down from the ceiling. They're already landing on the grass outside, sending up frothy waves from the lake. The windows rattle as a storm of grass and dust hits the cabin, the front door slamming shut in the gale.

My father grips my hands in his. "Get in the panic room, Catarina. You have to stay here. I know you can do this."

"No!" I yank my hands away. "I'm coming with you. I can help with the vaccine. Nobody knows your work better than me."

"I know that, but you can't come, darling. It's not safe. You don't know what these people are like. They'll torture you if they think it will make me work faster. They'll *kill* you to break me if I try to resist them. You must stay away from them."

"But you can't *leave* me."

"Oh, my darling. I wish I didn't have to, but I have no choice. I know you can take care of yourself, but you must promise that you will never let them take you. No matter what happens, you have to stay away from Cartaxus. Promise me you'll do that."

"No," I choke out, starting to cry. "No, I'm coming with you."

The sound of shouting voices cuts through the roar of the copters. My father turns to Dax. "Hide her," he snaps. "Quickly, they're coming."

"No!" I grab my father's coat, but Dax wrestles me away. I kick and thrash, but his grip is tight as he jogs to the back of the house with me clutched against him.

It's no use. I can't fight. All I can do is cry. Cartaxus is going to take my father, and I didn't even get to say good-bye.

The voices outside grow louder. Heavy boots stomp across the porch. Dax drops me and yanks open the panic room door.

"Be safe, Princess," he whispers. He shoves me into the cramped, padded closet, then kisses me urgently, crushing his lips to mine.

The last thing I see is his face, white with fear, as soldiers burst into the house.

Then he slams the door on me, and everything goes silent.

I know there are Cartaxus soldiers outside, and I know they're shouting, smashing, swarming into the cabin, but I can't hear a thing. The only sound I hear is my heart as it pounds against my ribs, loud enough that the padded walls and their interference circuits can't possibly be enough to hide me. The soldiers must hear me. I clutch my hands over my mouth to muffle my breathing, waiting for a black-gloved fist to yank open the door.

But nobody does.

Ten minutes pass in blank, terrified silence, until my traitorous heart begins to slow of its own accord. There's only so much adrenaline your body can manufacture while you're standing in complete sensory deprivation. An hour passes, then two. Finally, I can't wait anymore and force myself to flick the pressure lock on the panic room's wall and swing open the door.

Night has fallen, and the cabin's lights are out. The living room window has been shattered, but the glass is regrowing already in snowflake-like crystals that split the moonlight into rainbows. The room is a mess. Dead shards of glass are strewn across the floor, along with scattered gold feathers, muddy boot prints, and a pool of glistening blood.

I stand on shaking legs above it, gripped with a fiercer anger than I have ever known.

They shot him. I know it without checking. Cartaxus burst in here, and they shot my father and dragged him away.

My genkit confirms that the blood belongs to my father, and I find no bullet casings even after scouring the room. My rudimentary panel can't show me the VR feed from the security cameras, and they don't convert easily into 2-D, but I finally manage to coax out a grainy, black-and-white feed on my little laptop genkit's screen. It shows my father kneeling on the floor beside Dax, both their heads lowered, their hands raised as twelve soldiers storm into the room.

Orders are shouted. Twelve semiautomatic rifles are aimed at two unarmed men—two scientists Cartaxus needs to build them a vaccine. My father turns his head and stands suddenly to reach for something on the wall, and when I see this on the video, I start to cry. I know what he's reaching for. He wants the photograph of my mother, from when I was nothing more than a gentle curve beneath her dress. As my father stands, he barely manages to take a step before a soldier fires two bullets, the flashes saturating the feed.

One bullet in the thigh, another in the bicep, avoiding the femoral artery, doing musculature damage that healing tech will fix in a week.

In the grainy, stuttering video, my father slumps to the floor, and Dax screams. It's silent, but I can *hear* him screaming. The soldiers drag him and my father out of the cabin, and the copters send a hurricane of feathers through the windows as they leave.

The night burns into morning. I sit alone in the empty cabin as the viewscreen reports a steady stream of outbreaks around the world. I kneel on the floor with the photograph of my mother in my hands, beside a pool of my father's blood, and make him a promise I intend to keep.

No matter what happens, I will do what he told me. I will stay safe, and stay free.

I will never let them take me.

# CHAPTER 3

Present Day—Two Years
after the Outbreak

THE SUNSET IS A SINGLE HYPHEN OF LIGHT ON THE
horizon by the time I'm done with the infected man's body. The glimmer
of moonlight on the lake's surface guides me to the shore, where I shove
my filthy sleeves back and scrub the dirt and blood from my hands. The
water is icy against my skin. Stray feathers dot the surface, fallen from
the pigeons that are still overhead, silhouetted against the stars.

I'll sequence this flock's DNA tomorrow, but I already know that
all I'll find are lines from the same poem, growing more garbled as the
birds mutate. Each new generation brings more typos. Whole words
collapse into nonsense. I'm starting to think that was the poet's message all along.

My hands shake in the water, jittery in the aftermath of the trigger
response to the infected man's scent. Its official name is intermittent
acute psychotic anthropophagy, facilitated by the neurotransmitter
epinephrine-gamma-2. Most people just call it the Wrath. The beast
that claws into your mind, taking your humanity. It's hard to remember the details of what happens when you yield to it. Everything blurs
into a fog of teeth and flesh and instinct. Some people don't realize

they've succumbed to it until they stumble away and see the blood on their hands.

you okay bobcat?

Agnes's text burns white in my vision. Blocky Courier script, the only font my measly graphics card has built in. The words swing across the lake's surface as I tilt my head, moving with my vision until I blink them away. Fine, I reply, focusing on the word until my panel detects the thought. It ripples into my vision. I'll be there soon . . . maybe an hour.

want me to get you

No. I splash my face. Going to drop into the market on the way. Got some slices to trade for ammo.

Slices of flesh, that is. There's an immunity market in town where the locals gather to trade doses for food and bullets. I dragged the body as far from the cabin as I could, cut fifty doses from it and shoved them in my last freezepak, then smacked them against a tree until they froze. That's enough to keep a person immune for years. Half will go to the market, and the rest will sit in the cabin's solar freezer as my own personal supply. I won't let myself run out again, not after tonight. This might have been the closest call I've had since the outbreak.

A herd of deer melts through the trees on the other side of the lake, coming down from the mountains for an evening drink. They approach the water cautiously, watching me with wide, reflective eyes, lifting their noses, confused by my scent. It wafts from my skin like a too-strong perfume. Sulfur and wood smoke—almost the same scent as the infected man, but missing a crucial note. My skin and hair, my clothes and breath, all stink of the plague, but I'm not infected.

I'm immune.

The fictonimbus virus, commonly known as Hydra, passes through two distinct stages before sending its victims into the sky. First, it injects triggers into a victim's cells, throwing them into a fever, painting a mosaic of black-and-blue bruises across their skin. After a week they pass into the second stage, where it wraps every cell in their body with a layer of proteins, like the casing around a bomb. It's that casing that gives off the scent that sparks the Wrath in anyone standing nearby, and it's also the only thing that can stop the virus from entering your cells.

That's how the immunity works. If you eat the flesh of a second-stage victim, the virus doesn't realize it's changed hosts. Within an hour of taking a dose, it'll wrap all your cells up, forming the only barrier strong enough to keep the virus from burrowing into them. You have to be careful, though. An early dose, taken from someone in the first stage, will infect you with the virus too. A late dose, taken from a second-stager on the brink of detonation, could blow a hole right through you before you digest it. The dose I took tonight was late stage, but didn't have the warning signs—speckles of blood from burst capillaries that hint at imminent detonation.

That's lucky, because after the scent of infection hit me, I don't know if I could have stopped myself.

The deer lower their heads to drink, their ears twitching as I scrub my face and hands with the lake's icy water. Every time I blink, I see the dead man's face behind my eyes, a constant reminder of what I've just done to stay alive. To be honest, I can live with the killing, and I can even live with the *eating*, even though before the plague I would have sworn that I'd rather die.

It's funny, that saying—*I'd rather die*. It's funny because nobody means it. The truth is that when you're facing death, there's no telling what you'll do. When you're killing people who are dying anyway, it almost makes it too easy.

Almost.

No, it's not the killing that haunts me, or the immunity itching in my blood. It's the fact that every time I do this, part of me *likes* it.

Whenever the Wrath hits you, it comes on like an *instinct,* as powerful as survival and as basic as hunger. And when you yield to that instinct, it's like nothing you've known. Endorphins. Fireworks. Your body's entire arsenal of neurochemicals, all hurled into your brain as a staggering reward. Your body tries to convince you that murdering someone is the best thing you've ever done.

It's like a drug, and a dangerous one. The Wrath is so consuming that sometimes people lose themselves in it and never come back. We call them Lurkers. They travel in packs, hunting like wolves, locked in a constant state of hunger and bloodlust.

I wipe my hands on my jeans, gather my things, and follow the gravel path up to the cabin. Night is falling fast, and I can barely see my way. My ocular tech makes a weak attempt to help me, multiplying the moonlight, turning my world into a pixelated mess. Before the outbreak, I begged my father to write me cosmetic apps like skinSmooth and luster, but he always said it was a waste of his time. These days I wish I'd asked him for ultraview or echolocation, or even the clunky kind of night vision that leaves scars around your eyes.

I dump my bag on the cabin's porch and wave my forearm over a sensor near the door, waiting for an LED to blink by the handle. You wouldn't see it if you weren't looking. You also wouldn't see the electromagnets bolted inside the frame, not until it was too late. When panels are first budded, they grow networks of cables inside you, like a subway system to transport nanites throughout your body. The cables use metal sockets in your shoulders and knees, so I wired up two electromagnets inside the door to wrench the knee sockets out of anyone who might try to break in.

It's not a perfect security system, but it's better than nothing. Especially when all I have left is one bullet.

The door clicks open, and the cabin's lights blink on, casting a jaundiced glow across the living room. My sleeping bag is crumpled on a mattress near the fireplace, where a pile of last night's embers smolders silently. The walls are bare, with the exception of a single photograph that Dax took of me and my father just before the outbreak. My father has his arm around my shoulders, and my hand is halfway to my face, pushing the windblown hair from my eyes.

We look so alike. I have his gray eyes, his long, thin nose. Our chins are neat and tapered, like the bottom of a heart. In the photograph, my father's mouth is curved in a rare smile—we'd just finished a piece of code we'd been working on for months. He never used words like "love," but the day the photograph was taken, he told me he was proud of my work, which was close enough for me.

I pick up my dirty clothes from the living room floor, shoving them into my rucksack to bring to Agnes's. My long-suffering genkit is hidden under a pair of jeans—an old laptop model with a needle wire to jack into panels. Genkits are coding tools, used to access and edit gentech software and tweak or install apps and run maintenance. They're not technically computers, but mine will act like one if you ask it nicely, and it's been my trusty sidekick for the last two years.

I flick it open, trying to decide whether to bring it with me. Ninety-five percent of the cracked screen blinks to life. A chat request pops up in the menu, and a woman's face appears on the screen. Dr. Anya Novak. Scarlet hair, rhodium fingernails, and a trademark smile she blasts around the world three times a day. She's the leader of the Skies, the loosely formed group of survivors that sprang up after Cartaxus used the outbreak to take over what was left of the world.

They only took over to *help* us, of course. Cartaxus is always trying to help. They tried to help my father into a chopper by shooting him twice. They tried to help us after the outbreak by dissolving the world's governments, seizing the media, and urging people into their massive underground bunkers.

It seemed like a good idea at the time. If I hadn't known better, I would have lined up with most of the locals for a place at the closest bunker, Homestake. Food, shelter, airlocks. Protection from the virus. Most people couldn't think of a single reason not to go.

But I could. My father's words were fresh in my ears, and they still echo there two years later. *Never let them take you.* Sure enough, even though the bunkers were faradayed and guarded, rumors drifted out of deplorable conditions. People were living in dark, dirty cells. Cartaxus had taken control of their panels, wiping nonstandard apps and code. Security was brutal. Families were ripped apart.

The choice was clear: risk your life on the surface, or swap your rights for an airlocked cell.

Needless to say, not everyone made that trade. That's when the Skies began.

Novak waves at me from the genkit's cracked screen. Most people make calls in VR, so I had to resurrect some old-school video code so I could talk to her. Her face pixelates for a moment into green and purple static, garbled by the weak satellite connection. The genkit gets a better signal in the cabin than my comm-link does, but the lag is still ridiculous.

She smiles. "Good evening, Catarina."

I flinch. The Skies network is encrypted, but I still don't like using my real name. As far as Cartaxus knows, I died in the outbreak, and I'd like to keep it that way.

"Sorry, *Bobcat*," she says. "I got the asthma code you forwarded. A little boy in Montana is breathing on his own again, thanks to you. I've got a segment ready to broadcast. I'd love to put you on air."

"No," I say, waving my hands. "Absolutely not."

Novak pauses as my words bounce between satellites, reaching her a long, lagged moment after I speak. She sighs. We have this argument every time I steal a piece of code from Cartaxus's servers and release it to the Skies. That's another way Cartaxus is trying to *help* us—by withholding medical code and giving it only to the people in their bunkers. If you get hurt or sick, you can't just download an app like you used to. You have to hand yourself in to a bunker, or suffer on your own.

Or you can try Novak and her people. They maintain the last independent network, run on the old Russian satellites. They have libraries of code—open source, as free as the skies—but it's glitchy and mostly written by amateurs. I write occasional apps and patches, but my biggest contributions come from the assaults I launch against Cartaxus's servers. Basic smash-and-grab jobs. Busting into their databases, stealing any scraps of code I can find. Sometimes it's antibiotics, sometimes it's comm patches, and sometimes it's a piece of code written by Dax or my father.

Every time I find one of their files, it's like a beam of light. Suddenly the years have been rolled back, and they're downstairs in the lab again. There's no virus, no Cartaxus soldiers. For a single, weightless moment there is only Dax's stupid variable names and my father's love of Fibonacci search. The lonely years spent learning, coding, and hacking are worth it just for that. Just to find scraps of their work and know they're still alive.

"I'm going to get you on air one of these days," Novak says, arching a scarlet eyebrow. "But that's not why I called. Something big's going down at Cartaxus. We heard your name in the scuttlebutt."

"My name?"

"Yes, your *real* name. Couldn't make out many details, but your father was mentioned too. I don't know what's going on, but I don't like it. You might want to lay low for a while."

My chest tightens. "When was this?"

"An hour ago. I just got the report now and called as soon as I could."

I glance at the window. That was around the time Agnes warned me about a jeep near the property. It can't be a coincidence.

"Everything okay there?" Novak asks. "Catarina, can you hear me?"

Her voice rises, but I stay silent, the back of my neck prickling. My hand slides to the genkit's mute key. Through the living room window I can see the last spots of light on the lake and a herd of scattering deer.

They're running from the water, wide-eyed and skittish, as the pigeons above them cry and swirl, twitching to crimson. Something's spooked them. Something close. There's nothing on my scans, but I feel it in my stomach.

Someone's *here.*

"Gotta go," I whisper, closing the genkit on Novak's worried face. If I run, I might get into the woods before they reach the cabin. I stand, grabbing my rucksack, then bolt through the front door, across the porch, and down the stairs.

My bike is on its side in the grass. I grab it and drag it with me, racing away from the cabin and into the cover of the trees. Still nothing on my scans. I run along the path, dodging branches, following a dirt trail through the forest.

My ocular tech scrambles to adjust to the dim light, filtering the signals from my retina and pulsing them into my optic nerve. If I had better tech, I'd be able to see clearly in pitch blackness, but all my rudimentary panel can show me is a slightly brighter, pixelated view of the trees. It's just enough to let me run, my knuckles white on the handlebars of my bike, weaving through the trees, skirting the edge of the lake. I reach a thicket on the far side and pause, throwing a glance over my shoulder. For a second all I see is darkness, and then the cabin's lines resolve, and I throw myself behind the closest tree.

They're here. A black jeep, just like Agnes said, is crunching down the driveway. My tech chirps, finally picking up the engine's whine. The windows are obsidian black, the sides clearly armored. It looks like the love child of a Ferrari and a tank.

The engine cuts out as the jeep pulls up beside the cabin, and the driver's door swings open, throwing a slice of light across the porch. A single man steps out. His face is a blur of pixels until my tech locks in on him, drawing his features into focus.

He's young. Eighteen, maybe. Tall, with jacked-up muscles, dressed in a black tank top with the Cartaxus antlers stamped in white on his chest. His hair is dark and close-cropped, framing a stubble-dusted jaw and a nose that looks like it's been broken a dozen times. Black leylines stretch up from his panel and frame the edges of his face, branching into the outer corners of his eyes and under his jaw. They're matte and sleek, tattoolike, a conduit for code that's too unpredictable to run beneath the skin.

He steps toward the cabin, holding a semiautomatic, and turns his head slowly to scan the trees. My curiosity spikes. One soldier. That's all they sent. He's not a normal soldier, though; I've never seen one like this before. The troops from Homestake all look the same—armored jackets and fatigues, with HEPA-filtered masks and weapons wired right into their arms. They're always fidgeting, jumpy with stimulants, snapping their heads around to let their visor's AI scan their surroundings for them.

But not this man.

His clothing isn't even bulletproof, and he stands eerily still as he scans the trees, his face expressionless. He has no backup, no drones, no shouted instructions. He's just a kid, barely older than me, with a gun and a fancy car.

What the hell is Cartaxus up to?

I lean forward, squinting, when a *crack* echoes through the forest like a gunshot. The soldier spins around, searching for the origin of the sound. I flinch instinctively, drawing back behind the tree. My vision zooms in and out, and my hand comes down on a dry branch as I try to steady myself.

It snaps beneath my fingers.

Such a little sound that might as well be a firecracker for the way it slices through the air, echoing off the mountains. I shoot a glance back at the soldier and find him staring right at me. His hands tighten on his weapon.

I grab my bike and run.

Through the trees, back along the creek that feeds the lake, bolting for the fire trail that cuts between the mountains. Leaves and branches whip my skin. More shots ring out behind me, echoing from the slopes until the night air sings with violence. I hit the fire trail, throw my leg over my bike and pedal blindly down the pitch-black, rock-studded slope.

My ocular tech kicks into overdrive, burning calories I can't afford to lose. Hints of light become lines of fire that guide my way. My audio filters amplify the footsteps in the distance into thunder, punctuated by the crack of gunshots. The soldier must be chasing me, shooting in the dark. Each gunshot rattles my breathing, its acoustic fingerprint multiplied in my ears. . . .

Only those aren't gunshots.

It hits me like a punch. I skid to a stop, scrambling off my bike, wrenching my sweater over my head. That wasn't a shot that startled the soldier; it was a piece of the infected man's body. The man I killed for immunity. The man I took a dose from. His body is detonating, but I could have sworn I checked his flesh for warning markers. I thought he had at least a day, but I must have missed the signs. Now he's blowing, every single cell bursting into scalding gas, including the blood soaked into my clothes.

Patches hiss on my jeans, erupting into tiny plumes. A hundred points of fire, a hundred lit cigarettes. I fall to my knees, tearing at the fabric, crying out as they sizzle across my skin.

My healing tech kicks in, sucking the energy from my panel, and my ocular tech sputters out, plunging me into darkness. Footsteps pound somewhere nearby, crashing through the trees, but I can't track them on my own, and I can't see well enough to run.

I'm trapped.

He's coming. He'll be here any minute, and there's nowhere I can run to, nowhere to hide.

"Agnes," I gasp, scrambling for a comm-link, hearing only static. "He's coming. Yaya, can you hear me?"

If Agnes can hear, she doesn't reply. The footsteps pound closer, somewhere along the fire trail. I crawl forward in my tattered clothing, grasping blindly for my bike even though there's no way I'll be able to ride like this. Another *crack* echoes from the hills, and the breath rushes from my lungs as something *lurches* inside me.

I scream, clutching my stomach, and tumble into the dirt. A ribbon of fire coils up into my throat.

The dose I ate, it's not digested yet. And what's left of it just blew inside me.

# CHAPTER 4

I LAND HARD ON MY SIDE, CURLING INTO A BALL, biting my fist to stop myself from crying out. My stomach is aflame, the pain streaking up my back, arcing along the curve of my ribs and swallowing me whole. The footsteps grow closer, pounding up the fire trail until they're right on top of me, but I can't get up or run away. All I can do is scrunch my eyes shut, hoping that if the soldier wants to kill me, he'll have the decency to make it quick.

"Bobcat, is that you?"

Strong hands roll me to my back. I blink, expecting the soldier, but instead see a woman's face framed by a halo of gray hair. Agnes gapes down at me, her eyes wide and frantic. "Oh, Bobcat. Oh, my poor girl."

"Yaya," I choke out, shaking with relief. "You found me. How did you get here so fast?"

She wipes the dirt from my face. "Novak called me, said she was worried."

"Th-the soldier," I say, coughing. It feels like there's a knife in my stomach. Every breath, every movement just drives it deeper. "Cartaxus is *here*."

"I know." She drops her voice, glancing over her shoulder. "We're gonna get out of here, but you have to get up. I can't carry you."

I force myself to take her hands, summoning the strength to rise to my feet. Somehow we stagger down the hill to where her car is waiting. There's a door, then light, then I'm lying in the back, curled on my side. Agnes's breath comes short and fast as she races around to the front and throws herself into the driver's seat. Her skin is flushed and damp, wisps of gray hair plastered to her cheeks.

She wrenches the car's joystick. The engine spins up with a high-pitched whine, and we lurch along the fire trail. "What happened to you?" she asks.

I cough again, the movement sending pain stabbing through me. "The dose was too late. Thought I checked it, but it was dark. . . ."

"Ohh," she cries out, leaning around to look me up and down, letting the autodriver follow the trail on its own. She reaches out to yank up what's left of my sweater. The fabric is in tatters after the spots of blood on it detonated. Her eyes rise to mine slowly, her voice falling to a whisper. "You immune?"

I nod. She lets out a sigh of relief.

"I took the dose an hour ago." That's not long enough to fully digest it, but it's enough time for the immunity to spread through my cells. I won't get *infected*, but that doesn't mean I'm coming out of this alive.

"You must be hurting, Bobcat," she says. "Heard it's been happening a lot lately. I swear they're blowing faster than they used to. The damn plague keeps getting smarter. But don't worry, this ain't hard to treat. The doc will have you better in no time."

"No he won't." I scrunch my eyes shut, clutching my stomach. "Hypergenesis, remember?"

Gentech has been around for thirty years, and people have already forgotten how medicine used to work without it. The local doctor can set a broken bone or dig a bullet out, but he cures most of his patients by optimizing apps for their DNA. Standard healing tech does the rest. Agnes could come back from almost any injury without so much as a scar, but my tech can't handle major trauma. It can't stop heavy internal bleeding or hypovolemic shock. It'll heal me, but it'll do it so slowly I might die before it's finished.

"So what do you want me to do?" Agnes's brow furrows. The autodriver swings us onto the dirt road that circles the edge of the property.

"We need to get somewhere safe." I cough into my hand. The pain is like a living, clawing beast inside me. "You need to lower my body temperature, give my tech more time to work. And I need calories. I'm running on empty right now."

She turns back to the front. "Okay, I can do that. I'll call Novak. She'll know what to do. You're gonna be just fine, Bobcat."

I cough again, clutching my stomach. I wish I had her optimism. The only time I've been hurt this badly before, I had my father there to save me. To jack into my panel and run a live stream of hypergenesis-friendly nanites, writing the kind of code that made Cartaxus so desperate to take him.

Now I'm on my own, with tech in my arm that took a week to heal a broken finger. I'd have a better chance if I had my genkit, but I left it back at the cabin, along with all my files, and my code. The photograph of me and my father. Now that Cartaxus knows I'm here, I might never be able to go home again.

Branches smack against the windows as we veer onto an overgrown road, heading for the highway that leads into what's left of town. Agnes tilts the rearview until her eyes meet mine. "Why did you let your immunity lapse?"

I snort. "Because I'm an idiot."

She grabs the joystick to swing us around a bend. "You're not an idiot. You're a genius, if I recall."

"Well, I'm feeling pretty stupid right now."

She presses her lips together. "You'll come back from this, Bobcat. Remember the shape you were in when I found you?"

"Yeah," I mutter. "But I don't think soup is going to save me this time, Yaya."

Agnes and I met when she showed up at the cabin a few months after the outbreak. The temperature was diving with the start of a bitter winter, and I wasn't prepared, not by a long shot. My food supplies were gone, and the solars on the cabin's roof kept getting blocked by snow, killing my only source of power. I was spending my days huddled in blankets, shivering and hungry, not knowing if my father and Dax were even still alive. When Agnes arrived, searching for supplies, she found me feverish and shaking, passed out beside the fireplace.

I woke two days later, scrubbed clean, with a stomach full of soup she'd fed me when I was too delirious to remember. She nursed me back to health and said that she'd seen the footage on my genkit of Cartaxus storming the cabin. She had no love for Cartaxus either and had just joined a group determined to stop them from taking over the world.

She asked me if I'd thought about working for the Skies.

That day was a turning point for me. It's almost as though I died beside the fireplace and woke the next day as someone else. One of those moments that split your life in two, letting the weakest parts of yourself fall away so you can emerge as something stronger. I promised that day that I would live to see my father again.

But tonight, I don't know if I'll be able to keep that promise.

We speed up as we hit the highway. The acceleration throws me back into the seat, and I cough wetly. Something dribbles from my lips. When I touch it, my fingers come away dark. Agnes turns back to me, her face paling.

"You're bleeding. Bobcat, it's worse than I thought. We need to . . ."

She trails off as headlights splash through the rear window. I pull myself up, gritting my teeth against the pain to look behind us. The hulking black jeep is hurtling through the forest. It skids onto the road, sending a spray of rocks and dust flying out from its tires.

"He followed me," I whisper. "You shouldn't have come, Yaya. Now you're in danger too."

"Nonsense," Agnes snaps. "Is it just the one soldier?"

I nod, swallowing. My mouth tastes like acid and rust.

"Then we'll scare him off. He'll stop and call for backup. They always do. My gun's on the floor back there, but it's not loaded. Ammo should be in a box somewhere."

I tear my eyes away from the jeep and grope around the floor, fighting back a surge of pain from the movement. My fingers close on the wooden butt of Agnes's rifle, and I haul it up and into my lap. Still need ammo. I grit my teeth, searching for the box.

A shot rings through the air. Agnes swerves, startled.

"They've never shot at me before," she says, her face lit up by the jeep's headlights.

Another shot rings out. This time it takes off Agnes's side mirror, forcing the autodriver into an emergency stop.

"No, you idiot, come *on*," she growls, struggling with the car's controls.

We finally surge forward again, but now the jeep is right behind us. I throw a desperate glance through the rear window. No time to find the ammo. My hand rises to the insurance bullet on the chain around my neck.

I yank it off, loading it with shaking hands. The rifle lifts easily, swinging to my shoulder in a well-practiced arc. I take aim through the rear window, squinting in the headlights, and the jeep screeches to a stop, swinging around.

Its window opens suddenly, showing me a glimpse of the soldier's face. There's a weapon on his shoulder aimed directly at me. The world lurches into slow motion. Agnes's rear window shatters, and something flies into the car. A small cylinder, painted military green. It bounces through the back and lands on the passenger seat. A series of high-pitched beeps cut the air, then a burst of light and pressure blows out the car's windows.

I fly back into my seat. Agnes screams, jerking at the car's controls as we spin wildly into the trees. I throw my arms over my face instinctively, and the next thing I know, I'm lying on the ground.

Dirt. Grass. Blood in my mouth. My stomach is a tight mass of pain. Thick, acrid smoke chokes the air, spilling from the wreckage of Agnes's car.

"Agnes!" I shout, squinting through the smoke. The blurriness at the edges of my vision is growing, shrinking my world down to a speck. "Where are you?"

"Here, Bobcat," she croaks, limping from the car. Her hair is wild, her pants bloodied. She has the rifle in one hand. She staggers over to me. "Stay down. I'll draw him away."

"No," I choke out, coughing. "He's after me! Get out of here."

She gives me a crinkled smile, blood dripping from a gash on her forehead. "After all this time, you think I would leave you?"

"Please, Yaya, you have to get away."

"Ain't no point in living alone," she says, peering back through the smoke. "The only damn thing that makes life worthwhile is people looking after each other."

"No," I beg. I don't want to hear these words. This is the kind of thing people say to each other before they die.

The jeep stops in the middle of the road, its doors flying open. The soldier rushes out so fast he's barely more than a blur.

Agnes lifts the rifle. "I love you, Catarina."

"No!" I scream as two shots echo from the hills.

Time stutters and slows. My vision wavers. The soldier stumbles back, and Agnes disappears into the grass.

But that's not right.

I saw it wrong. It's a trick of the light. She can't be down. Agnes is the toughest woman alive.

"Agnes!" I cry out, not caring if the soldier hears me. I try to push myself up, dragging myself through the grass, but a hand grabs my shoulder, flipping me over. I blink and find myself staring into twin pools of perfect blackness.

It takes me a horrified second to realize that they're the soldier's *eyes*.

"Catarina Agatta?" he shouts, shaking me.

"Help!" I scream, fighting his grip. His hands are like steel. I claw for his eyes, and he grabs me around the neck. I try to scream again, but my voice is nothing more than a whimper.

The smoke and wreckage fade into a speck that sputters and disappears.

# CHAPTER 5

*POP . . . POP.*

I wake with a pounding headache to a sound that feels like nails being driven into my skull. Beyond the throbbing in my temples, there's a fuzziness to my thoughts that tells me I'm getting another migraine. They come every few months, pounding at the base of my skull, tracing glowing silver scotomas across my vision. I ran out of pills last year, so now they leave me crippled for days. Another thing my panel doesn't do: synthesize painkillers.

*Pop.*

Wincing through the pain, I take a slow breath and open my eyes, searching for the source of the sound. Wooden beams ripple into view on the ceiling above me. Real wood, not the cultured stuff where the knots and carefully engineered imperfections repeat at regular intervals. This wood is old and ragged, coated in thick spiderwebs that stretch down to moldy boards nailed over a window. It suddenly occurs to me that I don't know how I got here.

Perhaps more concerning: I don't know where I am.

Bladelike shafts of light slant obliquely through the boards nailed over the window, so it's either late afternoon or early morning. I'm lying on a wrought-iron bed in a small room with a heavy woolen blanket draped over me, facing a row of dusty bookshelves. A portrait hangs on the far wall, a framed sketch of a little girl with long dark hair. Her pursed mouth is captured with sparse, confident strokes, her eyes lifted, as though she has been asked a difficult question and is contemplating her response.

Her image is frustratingly familiar. A name on the tip of my tongue, held aloft and out of reach by the pain at the base of my skull. I dig my fingernails into my palms. An old trick my father taught me. Wrestle the pain into a spike, force it under your control. The fog in my mind clears, and I sit bolt upright on the bed.

The little girl in the sketch is me. My father drew it when I was a child. I'm on his bed, staring at his books, sitting in his room in the cabin. I twist to look around, gripped by the sudden, insane hope that he's home, that he's here, but the movement sends a stab of pain through me, and it all comes hurtling back.

The plumes, the jeep. The dose blowing in my stomach. The soldier shaking me, shouting my name before I passed out. Was he the one who brought me here? My breath catches at the thought, and I stare wildly around the room, sending my tech into overdrive.

My audio tech spins up, but I can't hear the popping sound that woke me from my sleep. I can hear my own breathing, my heart pounding inside me, and a sudden blare of scrambled noise rushing in from the forest. It grows louder as my tech isolates and amplifies each source. The rustle of the pine trees. The cries of a distant flock of pigeons. A steady *thump*, somewhere below me.

The footsteps of a man on the front porch, pacing back and forth in heavy boots.

My heart slams against my ribs. It has to be the soldier. The memory of his black eyes sends a chill through me. I need to find a way to get out of here, to call Agnes . . .

Shit. I completely forgot about Agnes.

I invoke my comm-link, closing my eyes. I don't have enough reception in the cabin to make a call, but I can usually send a text.

Agnes. Where. Are you. Soldier . . . took me.

The pixelated words appear in my vision slower than usual. My mind is racing, making it hard for my panel to detect the shape of my thoughts. I focus on Agnes, on the command to send. The text disappears, but her username shows her as offline.

Agnes, I send again, struggling to form the words. Agnes. You okay? Please respond.

A network icon spins in my vision next to Agnes's username, pinging her to connect, but she's still offline. She's always responded in seconds before. The icon stops spinning, and Agnes's username appears above a line of gray text.

This user either does not exist or is out of range.

A gasp escapes my lips before I can clamp my hands over my mouth, and the footsteps on the front porch stop. The soldier. He heard me. I hold my breath, frozen.

Every time I've seen this comm-link message, it meant the user was dead.

But that's not possible. My mind spins with alternatives: Maybe she turned off her panel; maybe she's faradayed, and her signal is being blocked. There's no way Agnes is dead. Downstairs, the front door swings open, its rusted hinges squealing. I scrunch my eyes shut.

*Get yourself together, Bobcat.*

The voice rears up, sharp as a whip. It's not Agnes, but I know that's what she'd say. The old girl would probably yell at me for sitting here like this. *Quit your moping*, she'd say, *and get back on your damn feet.*

Footsteps thud across the living room below me. I push myself up from the bed, swallowing hard against the pain. I don't know why the soldier brought me back here, but I know it can't be good. I clutch my stomach, scanning the room for something I can use to get away.

One of my father's silver fountain pens gleams on the mahogany bedside table atop a stack of dusty, handwritten notes. I pick it up, turn it in my hand. The ink-stained nib is flimsy, but it's sharp and metal, and it's better than nothing. I grip it in one fist and run to the far wall, where my rucksack has been dumped on the floor. I slump to my knees and rifle through it, finding the dirty clothes I was bringing to Agnes's, a water filter, bandages . . .

And thirty-five ounces of frozen infected flesh

My breath rushes from me. The freezepak is soft, completely thawed. I pull it from the rucksack and flip it over, checking the meat. It shudders in my hands, letting out a *pop* as a bubble of gas forms at one end. The sound that woke me from my sleep. The meat is starting to detonate, cell by cell, and it could blow at any minute. When it does, it could take out half the room.

My eyes slide to the boarded-up window, a rough plan forming in my mind. It's dangerous, and crazy as hell, but it just might get me out of here.

Footsteps creak up the stairs. I hold the fountain pen in my teeth and lurch to the window, squeezing the freezepak between the boards. It catches on the splinters, but I manage to shove it through and spin around, hiding the pen behind me just as the door swings open.

The soldier stands in the doorway, looking me up and down with ice-blue eyes that I could swear were black when he attacked me. He steps forward slowly, his eyes darting to the corners of the room, and the hair on the back of my neck bristles.

This isn't just a soldier. He is a *weapon*.

That fact is written in the leylines stamped around his face, in the fierce alertness of his sparkling blue eyes. He's unarmed, but every movement seems threatening. Every footstep is a steel spring coiling, the flash of a razor's edge. There's an air about him that speaks to a lifetime of military training, of shouting and drills and cleaning weapons. His hands are empty, slightly open, and I have a flash of them closing on my neck.

"Good evening, Catarina." He reaches out one hand. "I'm Lieutenant Cole Franklin."

"Don't touch me," I say, backing away. "Don't come any closer."

He looks puzzled by my fear. Of course he is. He probably doesn't know what it is to be afraid, to be as hopelessly outmatched as this. A rabbit cornered by a wolf. The fountain pen in my fist suddenly feels like a child's toy. I could stab him in the side, and he'd probably just pull it out and laugh.

"I'm not going to hurt you." His voice is low and calm.

"What did you do to Agnes?"

"What do you mean?" He steps closer, and I back into the bookshelf. Nowhere to go, no way to fight. Not until the slice blows, which could be any second. Or it could be far too late.

"My friend," I say. "You shot her."

"No I didn't." He steps closer. "I shot the gun out of her hands, but I didn't hurt her."

"Liar."

His eyebrows rise. "If I killed her, then who do you think braided your hair and changed your clothes? It certainly wasn't me."

I raise one hand to the back of my head, where my waist-length dark hair has been washed, brushed, and knotted into a fishtail braid. My skin is clean, and I'm dressed in a black cotton T-shirt and shorts with the Cartaxus logo printed across them.

I didn't even notice.

I open my mouth but don't know what to say. Last summer Agnes taught me how to do a fishtail braid when I said I was sick of my hair and planning to shave it off. She's braided it like this a dozen times, nimble fingers drawing my unruly dark hair into clean, glossy knots. My skin and hair are scented lightly with her lavender soap, the kind I helped her make a batch of last month in her basement.

The soldier isn't lying. Agnes must have survived. So why the hell isn't she responding to my comm?

"Wh-what happened after I passed out?"

The soldier smiles. He's handsome when he smiles, but it doesn't make me less afraid of him.

"We put you in an ice bath in her basement," he says. "We had to lower your temperature for twenty-four hours to let the healing tech work. She washed you and changed you into those clothes. She cooked me soup, and we decided you'd feel better waking up somewhere familiar, so I brought you here."

"Then why won't she answer her comm?"

"I have no idea. She was packing when I left. It looked like she was leaving."

I grit my teeth. That must be a lie. Agnes would never leave without telling me. She'd leave me a note, a comm, a message. She wouldn't *abandon* me.

*Pop.*

I let my eyes dart to the window, where the freezepak lies hidden.

47

There are still no signs of heat, no jets of gas. I need to stall the soldier longer. His head is turned to the window, his brow furrowed.

"Who are you?" I blurt out, trying to distract him. "Why are you here?"

He narrows his eyes, staring at the window a moment longer, before turning his gaze to me. "My name is Lieutenant Cole Franklin. I'm here because a week ago your father's laboratory and research files were hacked by the terrorist organization known as the Skies."

I almost laugh. *Terrorist organization.* We're not the ones with the drones and soldiers, with screaming jets and long-range missiles. We don't bury landmines around our bases or shoot people who come begging for food. Hacking Cartaxus's servers is the most aggressive thing we do, and we're not even particularly good at that.

"I don't know anything about that," I say.

"Your father was in the laboratory—"

"He hasn't talked to me in years. I told you—I don't know anything."

"Miss Agatta, your father is dead."

I freeze. The words hang in the air. My heart gives a single panicked thump before I grab hold of myself.

"You must think I'm an idiot if you expect me to believe that."

The soldier tilts his head. "Whether you believe it or not, I'm telling you the truth. The terrorists infected our servers with a virus that caused the genkits in your father's lab to self-destruct. Your father was caught in the explosion along with most of his staff. I'm very sorry for your loss, Miss Agatta."

I swallow, scanning the soldier's face, searching for a sign that he's lying. There's nothing—no nervousness, no flickers of guilt. But that doesn't mean anything. He's a trained Cartaxus soldier, so lying must be second nature to him. I straighten, squaring my shoulders. "You said the Skies did this?"

He nods. "The attack used a sophisticated computer virus that infected most of our systems. Some of them have been permanently corrupted."

I let out a long, slow breath. He's definitely lying. I've launched hundreds of hacks with the Skies, and our attempts were anything but *sophisticated*. They were smash-and-grab jobs. Kick down the doors and steal everything shiny. We never came close to destroying genkits or corrupting files.

"So you're a messenger?" I ask. "That's very kind of Cartaxus, to send someone out to deliver the news in person."

"That's not why I'm here."

Of course it's not. Novak told me something big was going down at Cartaxus—something involving me. Maybe my father tried to escape, maybe he refused to follow their orders, and they've sent someone out here to see if they can find some leverage.

But I won't give it to them. My grip tightens on the fountain pen. It won't do much harm, but it might buy me some time if I jam it in the soldier's face. I shift my weight, preparing to swing my arm around, but before I can move, the soldier's hands fly out.

The room spins. There is pressure on my arms, a sudden blur of light. In the time it takes me to register what's happening, I have been picked up and spun around, and the fountain pen is gone.

"What the . . . ," I gasp, grabbing the bookshelf to steady myself. I've never seen anyone move that fast I didn't even know it was *possible*. I blink, shaking my head, waiting for my vision to stop spinning.

The soldier throws the pen across the room. "I wouldn't try that again if I were you. I don't want to hurt you, Miss Agatta, but if you don't cooperate, I'll be forced to improvise."

*I don't want to hurt you.* Another lie. That's all Cartaxus does. They lie and crush anyone who tries to resist them. Anger bleeds through me I step closer, glaring at the soldier. "You can threaten me all you like, but you're a fool if you think I'm going without a fight."

The soldier's brow creases. He opens his mouth just as a hiss starts up beside me, followed by a rapid series of pops.

The sound of human cells beginning to blow inside the slice of flesh hidden in the window.

There's my escape, right on time. The soldier turns to the boarded-up window. We're close enough that I can see the spark of panic in his eyes and smell the air wafting from his skin. He smells only of soap and sweat and laundry detergent, without a single hint of sulfur.

My captor is not immune.

I'd smell it if he was. That sharp, sour scent that clings to your skin as long as you're protected from the virus. The soldier is going to get infected unless he turns and runs. Judging by the sound of the slice, he needs to run *fast*.

"You'd better go," I say.

His eyes blink wide. "Catarina, what are you doing?"

I raise an eyebrow. *"Improvising."*

The window starts to rattle. The freezepak is swelling now, the meat shuddering and frothing as it prepares to blow. I lurch away, hoping to take cover behind the bed, but the soldier's weight crashes into me, and the slice blows with the force of a thunderclap.

# CHAPTER 6

THE BEDROOM'S OUTER WALL EXPLODES, BLASTING
into splinters and shards of glass that slash my skin as they hurtle
through the air. The bookshelves fly across the room, sending out a
flurry of paper, and a jet of mist slams against the plaster ceiling. The air
is hot and choking, stinking of blood and plague. I cough, scrunching
my eyes shut, my hands bunched in the soldier's shirt. We land hard on
the mattress, with his body above me, curled around me.

Protecting me from the blast.

I scramble back, coughing. The soldier falls to his knees, doubled
over, the skin on his shoulders sliced to ribbons. His eyes are midnight
black, but they quickly change to blue, an ocular upgrade that I've never
seen before. I stare at his eyes for a full, stunned beat before I realize he's
staring back at me.

"Are you okay, Catarina?"

I blink. I should be jumping through the hole in the wall and bolting
through the woods, but I can't move. Everything about this is wrong.
He's not supposed to ask if I'm okay, not after I just murdered him. Not
after I infected him with a Hydra cloud.

"Your leg," he says, reaching for my ankle, where I took the blast straight on. Fat droplets of blood are welling on my skin, mixing with the pink, foamy sheen of the cloud. Jagged splinters jut from my ankle, and scratches arc across my calf, but it's nothing compared to the shredded skin on the soldier's arms.

"You got hit," he says. "I need to clean this."

"Soldier, you . . . You're not immune." I wait for his eyes to widen, for the realization to set in, but he only seems interested in the wounds on my leg.

"You can call me Cole." He tilts his body to look down the length of my leg, his eyes pausing on a few deep scratches. His own skin is bloody and raw, with splinters and glass embedded in his shoulders, but he doesn't seem to notice, or maybe his implants have dulled the pain. He pulls a yellow plastic packet from his pants and tears it open with his teeth. The scent of disinfectant cuts through the haze as he swipes my ankle with a stinging towelette.

"Don't touch me," I whisper, scrambling back on the bed. A trickle of foam runs down my cheek. I wipe it with the back of my hand. "You're *infected*. Are you even listening to me?"

"Please, I'm not going to hurt you. I've been programmed to protect you."

That makes me pause. You can't program someone's mind, not even with gentech, but that's not what's bothering me about what Cole just said. "Why would you be programmed to protect *me*?"

"Because your life is important. Please, Catarina. I need to clean this wound."

At this point I'm too confused to resist. I let him clean my ankle and barely wince at the sting of the disinfectant. Cole seems utterly calm despite the scarlet mist swirling in the air, the countless Hydra particles sweeping into his lungs. He's completely unconcerned, but I *know* he's not immune. I would have smelled it on his skin, I would have . . .

"Oh shit," I breathe. "You're not infected, are you?"

He shakes his head, his eyes meeting mine through the wafting clouds of mist. It clicks inside me like the tumblers in a lock.

"There's a vaccine."

"Yes, Catarina," he says. "There's a Hydra vaccine."

The words are like a jolt. I stand up, pushing the foam-slicked hair back from my face. My hands are shaking with the thought that this could all be over. No more blood on my hands. No more nights spent alone. With a vaccine, people could leave the bunkers. We could finally start to rebuild. The nightmare of the last two years could fade to a distant memory.

I could have a *life* again; the world could go back to normal. . . .

But that still doesn't explain why there's a Cartaxus soldier sitting in my father's bedroom.

"I haven't heard anything about a vaccine." I gesture to the ruined wall. "You could have planted that meat, or it could have been faked somehow. This could all be a setup."

Cole sighs, folding the bloodied towelette into a square on his knee. "Now why would I want to do that?"

I don't have an answer to that, just a growing sense of unease. I cross my arms over my chest, limping to the toppled bookshelves. The floor is slick with greasy foam, littered with splinters, glass, and paper. If Cole is telling the truth about the vaccine, does that mean he's telling the truth about my father?

"If there's a vaccine," I ask, "then why hasn't Cartaxus released it?"

"Because they don't have it anymore."

I spin around. "Then who does?"

"Nobody. The hack that destroyed your father's lab corrupted most of his work. I'm one of a handful of trial subjects who received the code in a test a few days before the attack. We have fragments backed up, but the attack was complex. Most of your father's work is unrecoverable."

I just stare at him. "That's ridiculous. The Skies are amateurs—they couldn't pull off a hack like that. And besides, how could the code be lost? Didn't you just say you had it in your arm?"

Cole's face darkens, and he turns his forearm so his panel shines up at me. It's a bar of solid blue, even bigger than Dax's. The silicone that forms his panel's body is a grid with spaces for thousands of separate function cores—individual processors that run each of his apps. The bigger the panel, the more function cores, the more cobalt dots on his skin representing the apps running inside him, altering his body. But I've never seen a panel as big as Cole's before. What the hell does he have in that thing?

"The vaccine works as a special implant," he says. "Once it's installed, it becomes locked to each user's DNA, so even if I ejected the function core out of my arm and put it into yours, it wouldn't work. The only way to share it is to get the original code, but that's heavily encrypted."

I nod. A lot of the code I stole from Cartaxus to release on the Skies network was encrypted like that. We had to crack it before we could release it, something I've never been good at. I have natural talents for hacking networks and stealing files, but cracking and decrypting takes a whole different set of skills. The Skies have a team dedicated to it. Most of Cartaxus's code is easy to unlock, but some files are so well encrypted that we've never come close to cracking them.

"But Cartaxus would have the key," I say, speaking to Cole like I would a child. "Or they'd be able to guess it. They have standard encryptions. They have backup procedures for data breaches."

Cole frowns. "You know a lot about this."

"Not really." I drop my eyes. "I just picked up a few things from my father."

This is dangerous ground. It's a miracle Cole hasn't already put it together that I'm one of the Skies hackers he's talking about. My genkit is downstairs, and it would only take a moment for someone who knows what they're doing to open it up and log in to Novak's network.

From what I've been able to determine from my time hacking their servers, Cartaxus would very much like to see the hacker known as Bobcat disappear from the face of the planet.

Cole watches me carefully. "Our scientists are working on unlocking the code, but they estimate that it'll take six months to crack it with brute force."

"Six months?" My head spins. That's an eternity. "What insane kind of encryption algorithm did they use on it?"

"I don't know, except that it was encrypted by your father."

I look up sharply. That doesn't make sense. My father hates gentech encryption—he always said that medical code should be released to anyone who needs it. He'd never lock up the vaccine—he'd shout it from the rooftops. He'd give it away for free.

"If my father encrypted it," I say, "it's because Cartaxus forced him to."

"I don't care *who* encrypted it," Cole snaps. "The problem is that it's locked."

I flinch at the sudden edge in his voice, reminded of the way he moved when he grabbed the fountain pen from my hands. He's a Cartaxus weapon, tightly strung. It might not be the best idea to get into an argument with him.

"If you don't trust me, that's fine," he says, scowling. "I shouldn't be surprised. You're a damn Agatta, after all. But I'm not here to fight." He wipes his hand on his shirt and slides a slip of plastic from his pocket.

"I'm here because before he died, your father left me this."

He hands me the slip. It's white and scratched, with a burn mark along one side and a faint image of a scythe etched on the front. A ghost memo. An encrypted chip that displays messages when the person who left them behind has died. People use them to confess their sins and store their secrets. Sentimental stuff. The kind of thing my father would never do.

I press the button on the side. Glowing letters appear on the plastic, flickering faintly, lit by a dying battery.

> Cole—If required, my daughter Catarina can unlock the
> vaccine. You must find her, and protect her with your life.
> She may be our only chance to save humanity.

A gust of wind sweeps through the hole in the bedroom wall. I shiver in my foam-streaked clothes, staring at the words. The note means nothing to me, but that doesn't stop a chill from settling in my stomach. It's probably a fake. Something put together by Cartaxus. I press the button again, but the message doesn't change.

"So will you help?" Cole asks.

I glance up at him, then back down to the memo, turning it over. No ports, no access. It must connect wirelessly. "Help with what?"

"With decrypting the vaccine."

I press the memo to my forearm on the off chance my panel will register it, but nothing appears in my vision. "I don't know anything about that. I wouldn't even know where to start."

It's true. I don't know the first thing about decryption; my job is purely hacking. If Cole's telling the truth about the vaccine, and Cartaxus's scientists can't crack the code, I don't see how I can help.

"But Lachlan *said* you could."

"Well, I'm sorry to disappoint you." I run my fingernail along a crease in the edge of the memo, splitting the plastic apart. It falls open neatly in my hands. Inside is a tiny screen—LCD, old-school, with two stubby buttons wired up to it. I look up, scanning the room, searching for the fountain pen, and settle for a splinter of wood on the floor beside me.

"What are you doing?" Cole leans in to watch me jab at the buttons with the splinter. The tiny screen flickers with green text as I make my way into the ghost memo's operating system. "You've broken it."

"I haven't broken it. I'm trying to see who it's registered to."

To figure out if it's really linked to my father's panel, or just part of some elaborate Cartaxus lie.

Cole watches me use the memo's buttons to navigate through its file system. "How do you know how to do that?"

"You said it yourself. I'm an Agatta. I know how to do a lot of things."

"Fair enough."

Honestly, I've never used a ghost memo before, but it's only taken me a few moments to figure it out. That's how I've always been with software. Learning new programming languages has always felt like relearning words and concepts that I already knew. Like I was born with the knowledge inside me and just had to remember it. That's how my father always described the way he felt about DNA.

The memo's display blinks, showing me the registration details, the log of people who've had access to the chip. I navigate into the memory. The message Cole showed me was recorded in the last two weeks and activated just three days ago. It was set off by a death notice from the panel it's paired to. I jab the button one last time, my chest tightening.

The ID flashes on the screen. A hundred hexadecimal digits I know by heart, that I've searched for every time I've hacked Cartaxus's servers. A void inside me opens up. A yawning, empty chasm.

It's there on the screen. Cole wasn't lying.

My father is dead.

The pieces of the memo tumble through my fingers. *My father is dead.* The words circle inside me, over and over, the dimensions of my universe shifting to accommodate this truth.

"Catarina?"

"It's true."

"Yes."

"The vaccine, the encryption . . ."

He just nods. I double over, clutching my chest. My ribs feel like iron bars, unyielding. I can't breathe. My heart can barely beat.

My father's lab was attacked. His work was destroyed, his staff were killed . . .

"Wait, what about Dax?" My head snaps up. "Dax Crick? He worked with my father. Is he alive?"

Cole nods, and the breath rushes from my lungs. I reach for the wall, fighting a wave of dizziness.

"Crick is fine," Cole says. "He was one of the few who made it out of the lab before the genkits self-destructed. Your father left instructions for both of us. We're working on this together, and he's going to try to join us out here."

"He's coming here?"

Cole nods. I shut my eyes, the thought of Dax breaking through something inside me, a door that I'm now struggling to close. The plague has taught me to handle grief, and my father's death is an ember in my fist—I know to crush it, let it burn into my palm, shrinking it down until it morphs into something hard and cold. A diamond. But this is more than grief. This is too much to take in—the vaccine, the attack on my father's lab, the thought of seeing Dax again. It's a rush of oxygen, making the ember of my father's death burst into flames that threaten to engulf me.

"There must be some instructions we're missing," Cole says, but I barely hear him over the thudding of my pulse in my ears.

Joy and grief are battling inside me. The last two years of pent-up emotion are rushing for the open door in my heart, fighting to make their way out.

But I can't let them. I can't break. My father left a mission for me. I look down for the plastic pieces of the ghost memo, but I can't see through the tears in my eyes.

"Catarina?"

I rub my eyes. "I'm sorry," I blurt out. "I . . . I can't handle this."

I turn away, pushing through the bedroom door. My shoulder hits the frame as I stumble blindly into the hall. I can't think about vaccines or viruses. I can't think about my father. I need air, and light, and space. I need to get out of here.

My feet find the stairs, and one foam-streaked hand grips the banister as I run down to the living room and race to the front door. Military bags and weapons blur past in my peripheral vision, stacked in piles against the walls. I see disassembled rifles, the tube of a rocket launcher, a pair of silver handcuffs on the living room table.

Somewhere behind me, Cole shouts my name. I burst through the front door and run outside, expecting him to chase me down.

But he lets me go.

# CHAPTER 7

TWO HOURS, FOUR HOURS PASS; I DON'T KNOW. IT'S dark and the moon has risen by the time I make it back to the lake. My throat is sore, my eyes are swollen, and I'm still coated in filth from the blast of the infected flesh, so the icy waters are a revelation against my skin. I wade in until they lap at my throat, and arch my back to soak my hair, unbraiding it underwater.

Overhead, a thick band of stars glitters in a cloud-streaked sky. A flock of pigeons call to one another as they flap across the lake. They skim the water, dropping their beaks to drink.

How can the world keep spinning when its brightest star is dead?

The cabin door swings open, throwing a slice of yellow light across the grass. Cole emerges carrying a towel and a fresh pile of clothes. He's shirtless, with a bandage wrapped around his shoulders—a blue transparent film that looks vaguely like plastic wrap.

"Thank you for coming back," he says. The gravel on the path crunches under his boots. "I should have waited to tell you everything. It was too much to take in at once."

"I'm fine." I swipe a handful of water up to splash my eyes. And I *am* fine. I'm strong, the way my father taught me to be. Take the pain under your control, wrestle it into a spike. There are bloody half-moons etched into my palms, but the doors in my heart are locked. "I'm ready to talk."

"Okay," Cole says, sitting down on the lake's rocky shore, putting the clothes and towel down behind him. He must have bathed while I was gone. The light from the cabin falls across his back, catching the curves of his shoulders, leaving his face in shadow.

I sink into the water, watching him. I still don't know what to think about Cole. He's been honest enough so far, but he's a Cartaxus soldier. My father made it clear that nobody wearing the antlers could be trusted, but I don't know how to reconcile that with the message he left Cole.

Now, more than ever, I'm desperate for Agnes's advice. She met Cole, she must have spent time with him, but now she's disappeared. When I ran into the woods, I commed her over and over, but the same message kept flashing up. Out of range. Out of range. My mind spun to the worst-case scenario—that Cole had killed her—but when I slumped on the ground at the foot of a tree, I felt the weight of something in my pocket. A licorice drop.

One of Agnes's horrible homemade candies that I've turned down so many times before. I'd spend a night at her house every week or two, eating lentils, playing cards, until I found myself itching to get back to the lab. She always slid a licorice drop into my pocket as a farewell gesture, even though she knew I hated them. The fact that she put one in my pocket when Cole brought me to the cabin means that she must have been alive and trusted him to take care of me. But it makes no *sense*. He's a Cartaxus soldier, armed and dangerous. We've spent the last two years hiding from people just like him.

"Why did Agnes trust you?" I ask.

"She didn't at first." Cole's shadow ripples across the rocks on the lake's shore, dipping into the water. "After you passed out, she realized I was trying to help you, and you were hurt so badly that we didn't have time to talk. She told me how to get to her house, and kept a gun trained on me while I drove, while I put you in the ice bath, and for a few hours after that. I think the frostbite changed her mind."

I blink. "Frostbite?"

Cole stretches out one hand, the movement crinkling the bandage around his shoulders. "We ran out of ice from her freezer, and the bath you were in kept heating up. I had some freezepaks in the jeep. I used them to make more ice, but after a few uses they started to split."

I close my eyes, empathic pain shooting through my fingers. I've split a freezepak before, and it wasn't fun. The chemicals in the freezepak's lining undergo an intensely endothermic reaction when they're agitated. It's strong enough to freeze whatever's inside, and if the lining splits and the chemicals land on you, it's enough to freeze your skin as well.

Cole bunches his outstretched hand into a fist, as though testing it. He unfurls his fingers slowly and drops it to his side. "She started to trust me after the first one split. After the tenth, she knew I hadn't come here to hurt you."

I swallow hard, trying to imagine the state his hands must have been in. Even with healing tech and anesthetic, it must have been excruciating. No wonder Agnes warmed to him. Made him soup, let him stay. It still doesn't explain why she left, but it's enough to quiet my unease.

"You didn't call for help," I say. "Cartaxus could have sent a Comox. There's a bunker just a few miles from here."

"I know."

I scrub my hands across my neck, wiping away the streaks of dried foam. "You said my father left a message for Dax, too. He told him to keep this a secret, didn't he? Cartaxus doesn't know you're here."

Cole leans back, watching me. The light from the cabin catches on a pattern of ridges on his chest. It looks like some kind of upgrade, but I can't make out the details. "You figured that out fast."

"I'm an Agatta. I thought we went over that."

"Of course," Cole mutters dryly. "How could I forget?"

"I think I'm starting to understand what my father wanted me to do." I push back in the water, scrubbing my hands over my arms, trying to wipe away every last trace of blood and foam. "My father was a genius, but he wasn't psychic. He couldn't have predicted that his lab would be hacked, or that the vaccine's source code would be destroyed. So why would he give you that note?"

Cole pauses. "I . . . I haven't really thought about that."

"Well, I have. He gave you that note because he'd just finished the vaccine, and he knew that Cartaxus wasn't going to release it to the survivors on the surface. They were going to restrict it like they do with everything else. My father would have tried to release it freely, but in case he died, he left a backup plan for us to do it instead."

Cole sits forward. "That's crazy. Cartaxus would never hold back the vaccine."

"Oh yeah?" I run my hands through my hair, flicking away splinters tangled up in the long dark strands. "They hold back everything else—antibiotics, medical code. People out here are living with illnesses that were solved twenty years ago. If you want to use Cartaxus code, you have to join one of the bunkers."

Cole snorts. "That's because the bunkers are *safe*. They want people to join so they're protected from the virus. But once the vaccine is released, we won't need the bunkers anymore."

I turn my arm in the water, rubbing tracks of foam off the lights of my panel. "So Cartaxus will give the vaccine to everyone, free of charge, no requirements? They'll let anyone use it, even people with nonstandard tech?"

For the first time, Cole sounds hesitant. "I'm sure they would."

"Yeah," I say, splashing my face. "That's what I thought."

When Cartaxus opened their bunkers, most survivors of the initial outbreak flocked to them, with only a few choosing to remain on the surface. Almost everyone who stayed behind did so because they couldn't bear to lose control over their panels. Human gene editing has been around for over fifty years, but it was Cartaxus who invented the first implantable panels. They perfected the technology, copyrighted it, and released budding kits freely around the world.

Panel buds only cost a few cents to make. They start the size of a grain of rice, injected into your arm to grow inside you like a tree growing from a seed. The cables, the metal sockets, the processors all grow in place, one molecule at a time, branching out from that first bud. Even the poorest countries distributed them, and within a few years the uptake rate was almost 100 percent, thanks to the first detox app. Over the last century mountains of nanowaste used in everything from plastics to fertilizer had leached into the soil and water, until the planet was swimming with toxins. No matter how careful a mother was, her baby would still be born with hundreds of artificial chemicals floating in its blood.

Panels changed all that. Mortality rates plummeted. The number of lights on a person's arm told you how healthy they were. Cartaxus opened up their software market to approved providers, and soon there were apps for asthma and weight loss, then hair growth, self-tanners. People could download the solutions to their weaknesses. The industry exploded overnight.

Then the genehackers arrived, and they wanted to be more than *pretty*. They wanted to be ten feet tall, with prehensile tails and retractable claws. They wanted to grow a winter coat and shed it in the spring. To feel the earth's magnetic field the way migratory birds do.

The genehackers had glimpsed the future, and they saw a day when people would be defined by the limitations of their imagination, not their DNA. My father loved them. They represented pure creation.

Cartaxus tried to sue them all for copyright infringement.

Even before the outbreak, the war over the definition of "human" was raging between Cartaxus and the genehackers. When the virus hit, and Cartaxus opened their bunkers, I wasn't surprised that the only condition of entry was letting them control your panel.

No hacks, no nonstandard apps, no open-source code. People entering the bunker agreed to let Cartaxus wipe it all. The problem was that for a lot of people, that code is what *defined* them, and for some people it was also keeping them alive. Every app in my measly panel is technically nonstandard, since it was written by my father and never approved by Cartaxus. If I went into a bunker, they'd make me wipe the whole thing. My sensory and healing tech, all nonstandard. All gone.

Cartaxus says these rules are to keep people *safe*, but my father would have seen the truth, and that's why he left this plan. He knew they'd withhold the vaccine and use it as blackmail to crush the genehackers once and for all.

"Look," Cole says, rubbing his face. "Cartaxus's line on nonstandard tech is firm, but—"

"*Firm?*" I ask. "They tried to make it a crime to own a genkit. They've cut access to their code for anyone living on the surface, and they'll do the same thing with the vaccine."

"That's ridiculous. They want to vaccinate as many people as possible—that's the only way to kill the virus. They won't risk losing another vaccine."

The water around me seems to freeze. The sounds of the forest die away. All I can hear is that little word, echoing. Thundering.

"What do you mean, *another* vaccine?"

But he doesn't need to say it. My mind is already clicking into gear, running through my father's lessons on viruses. In our first summer at the cabin, he showed me the code that made him famous—the gentech vaccine for Influenza X.

It was *robust*, he said. Previously, flu vaccines would work for a year before Influenza evolved, mutating like the poem in the pigeons. The code would lose its effectiveness, and the vaccine would become obsolete. That's called *fragile* code. It uses strategies that nature will shrug off in a few years, flicking them aside in its endless march of evolution. But my father's code was different. It acted like a knife, unstoppable and true, aimed at the virus's heart. It would work forever, and once enough people downloaded it, Influenza X simply ceased to exist.

"You had one, didn't you?" My voice wavers. "There was a vaccine, but it was fragile."

He nods. "Your father developed one in the first months of the outbreak, but the virus evolved too quickly. The code was useless within weeks."

The thought makes me sway. Fragile code. We had it, but nature swept right past it.

Nature *laughed* at us.

"That's why Cartaxus won't hold back the vaccine," Cole says. "They'll give it to as many people as they can. They'll broadcast it day and night to make sure we crush the virus. They don't care about non-standard tech, not anymore. They only care about the fact that if we take too long to decrypt it, we could lose the vaccine. We couldn't have written it without your father, and now . . ."

"Now he's gone."

The full weight of it hits me. The last vaccine was useless within weeks, and Cole said this one might take six months to decrypt. If we wait that long, the virus will evolve, until there's a chance the code won't even work anymore. The vaccine could be useless, and without my father, it could take years to write another one.

By that time, everyone on the surface could be dead.

"You said your father left a plan for us," Cole says, leaning forward. The light from the cabin catches on the ridges on his chest, but I still can't make out the pattern. "All he left was the ghost memo. No instructions, nothing. He must have been sure that you could figure it out on your own."

"I know." I sink into the water. "But how am I supposed to do that?"

"I thought you were an Agatta."

"Very funny." I roll my eyes, but Cole's right—my father left this to me because I'm his daughter, and because I knew him better than anyone. There has to be something I'm missing. Some clue, some instructions he's hidden so Cartaxus won't find them, but I will. Something he *knew* I'd pick up on.

Cole scratches at his bandage, twisting his body into the light spilling from the cabin. The ridges on his chest fall into sharp relief, and I stand up in the shallows, covering my mouth.

"What the hell?"

Cole's entire chest, from his navel to his collarbone, is completely covered with scars. Lines of puckered skin stretch up and down, from one side to the other, crisscrossing his body like a human circuit board.

"What happened to you?" I step out of the water. "Why didn't they heal your scars?"

He looks down and runs a hand over his chest as though he's

forgotten they were there. "They could have, but I keep them as a reminder."

"A reminder of *what*?"

"Of what they did to me. I'm a black-out agent. Do you know what that means?"

I shake my head. I've heard the term whispered on the Skies networks—reports of half-machine soldiers given superhuman skills. I thought it was just another rumor, but maybe it wasn't. *Black-out agent*. The words bring up a flash of Cole's midnight eyes, of him racing out of his jeep with inhuman speed. The way he threw himself over me, immune to the pain of his wounds.

How he said he'd been *programmed* to protect me.

Cole extends his arm, showing me the full stripe of his panel. Three leylines trace their way up his arm from the glowing cobalt light. They look like tattoos, but they're not. They're micrometer-thick tubes, the width of a single layer of human cells, lying flush with his skin. Most gentech nanites are transported from your panel through the cabling *inside* your body to make their way to where they're supposed to run. Your muscles, your eyes, your stomach. The nanites could just drift through your cells, but the cables act like a railway system, transporting them instantly.

Leylines are for dangerous code. Some nanites can't be trusted to play nicely with the rest of your tech. The black lines streaking up Cole's arms might be carrying toxic nanites, or experimental tech pushing the limits of what the human body can take.

He turns his arm until his panel faces up. The glow lights up the scars across his chest. "Being a black-out agent means Cartaxus has given me tech that's above my security clearance. I don't have access to my panel, and I can't remember most of my training. They wiped it, leaving behind just enough for me to act on it instinctively. The only thing I was allowed to keep were these scars, so I did."

My eyes widen. It's hard to take in the horror of what he's saying, especially when he talks so easily about being sliced open. I can't imagine the pain he must have suffered, but I can read the story of misery etched into his skin. A testament to Cartaxus's cruelty. A record of the military tech he's not even allowed to know he's carrying.

Cole gets to his feet. "Sometimes I don't even know what's inside me until it kicks in, like the protection protocol. Or the jeep. The moment my hands touched the wheel, I—"

"Wait." I cut him off. "What did you just say?"

"About the jeep?"

"No, before that."

"Sometimes I don't know what's inside me until it kicks in?"

My heart stills. Suddenly it all makes sense. Staring at the scars on Cole's chest, I can finally see what my father has been trying to show me. It's so utterly, painfully simple. He sent me instructions to unlock the vaccine, but they aren't in the ghost memo at all.

They're standing right in front of me, hiding in plain sight, like the sonnet in the pigeons.

They're inside *Cole*.

# CHAPTER 8

"I NEED MY GENKIT," I SAY, SPLASHING OUT OF THE water.

Seeing Cole's scars and hearing the story behind them is the scientific equivalent of waving a flag in front of a bull. My father must have known I'd be itching to jack Cole into my genkit and see what's inside him, and that *has* to be what he wants me to do. The one thing my father knew I could do better than anyone else is hack panels. I did it to my own panel when I was fifteen, nearly killing myself in the process.

Now I just need to do it to Cole. He's already carrying the encrypted code for the vaccine. What if he's also carrying the key?

"Where are you going?" Cole holds out the towel he brought down for me.

I spin back to him. "Th-the lab," I stutter, too excited to speak. Goose bumps prickle my skin. "I need to jack you in. I think I just figured it out."

He raises an eyebrow. "And?"

"I think there's a message inside you. Well, inside your panel. Or maybe in your chest, I don't know, but I think I—"

"Of course," he says, tilting his head back. "That's classic Lachlan. But like I said, I don't have access to most of my tech. My firewalls are military grade."

"I can g-get through," I say, shivering, "I know I can. L-let's go down to the lab, we can—"

"Seriously?" Cole cuts me off, shaking his head. "You're just like Lachlan, you know that? Your blood sugar is plummeting, you're freezing, you just woke up after being in a healing coma for days, and all you want to do is code. You need to *rest*."

"We don't have *time* to rest. The v-virus is evolving as we speak, and I'm fine. I'm j-just excited."

"That's not excitement, Catarina. It's called shock, and it'll knock you out if you're not careful. Hold out your hand."

I lift one hand. "I'm f-fine, see . . ."

Only, I'm not. My hand is trembling like a leaf, and the harder I try to keep it still, the more wildly it seems to shake.

He gives me a level stare. "I know we need to hurry, but you won't be able to do anything if you crash. Dinner first, then you can jack me in."

I slump, dropping my shaking hand. "Okay, fine. After dinner, then."

Cole sends me into the downstairs bathroom to get changed and gives me a plastic packet of disinfectant wipes to clean the scratches on my leg. The wipes smell like the soap I used at boarding school—something close to vanilla, but cheaper and sharper, with a hint of ammonia. I've always hated the scent. It reminds me too much of those lonely years at school, which I've done my best to forget.

I spent most of my childhood at boarding school, after my mother died and Cartaxus stationed my father at a remote research lab. He tried to quit, but it took him over a decade to get out. When he did, he bought the cabin and pulled me out of school, and we had a single year together before the outbreak.

That year feels like a lifetime ago. Days spent coding, talking, reading. My years at boarding school are so distant now they're barely more than a blur.

I sit on the bathroom floor, running the wipes over the scratches on my calf and ankle. Pots clatter in the kitchen.

"I hope you like pasta," Cole calls out.

My stomach growls at the thought. All I've been eating for the last six months are floury, stale nutriBars from a stash I found in a garage outside town. They're nutritious, but they're designed to be eaten while using a taste-bud-hacking app that you can download flavors for. To me, they just taste like dust. "Pasta sounds great."

"Okay," Cole replies. "Ready in five."

I give my face and hands a rub with the last of the wipes for good measure, and pick up the clothes Cole gave me to wear. Every piece of clothing I own was stuffed in my rucksack when I blew out the wall in my father's room, and now they're all ruined. Cole brought a few sets of clothes in various sizes in case I might need them, and they're all stamped with the Cartaxus logo, but otherwise they're not too bad. Black cargo pants like the ones he's wearing and a gray tank top that's cool to the touch. The fabric is soft, but I have a feeling it's pseudometallic, the kind of fiber that's made by genehacked bacteria in industrial vats. It won't stop a bullet, but it'll probably stop a knife. I tug it on over a black sports bra and turn to the mirror.

A single glance reminds me why I don't look in mirrors anymore.

My face is pockmarked and thin, my gaunt cheeks traced with scars from where I face-planted out of a tree last summer. My hair is wild and tangled, my right canine tooth badly chipped. I'm completely and undeniably hideous.

I don't usually care what I look like, but despite all logic and reason, having a male presence around stirs up old feelings of insecurity. Like, despite the apocalypse, I'm somehow supposed to be *pretty*. It feels stupid even thinking about it, but I still find myself tilting my head back and forth in the light from the naked bulb overhead, searching for an angle that makes me look good. All I see is sun-damaged skin, chapped lips, and untamed eyebrows over my father's piercing gray eyes.

The longer I look at myself, the more I see him in my features, until it hurts too much and I have to look away.

"Okay, I'm out," I say, leaving the bathroom, running my hands through my still-damp hair.

"Just another minute," Cole calls from the kitchen.

I wander through the living room, glancing at the front door, where the frame has been splintered apart on either side at knee height. That's where I hooked up the electromagnetic trap to yank out the sockets from an intruder's knees. It looks like Cole got to the trap before it got to him. The broken pieces lie on the floor. I let out a sigh. It took me a whole *week* to set it up.

The room is littered with Cartaxus-branded equipment that Cole must have brought here with him. There are two sleeping bags and air mattresses, a bag of clothes, a box of food, and a terrifying assortment of weapons. Guns, knives, lasers, and darts are laid out across the coffee table in the living room, along with a leather-bound book. I pick it up, check the spine for a title, and flip it open without thinking. The pages fall open to a sketch of a young girl.

Black glossy hair, a wide smile, and delicate features shine out of the paper, rendered in simple, elegant lines. I flick through the pages, seeing a dozen more portraits of the same girl. Running, laughing, sleeping. She's stunningly beautiful. In one picture, her cheeks are tracked with tears, her distress practically screaming through the paper. I glance at the kitchen nervously. The sketches are signed with Cole's name, and it's clear that he must have been in love with her.

Her name is printed in careful script beneath each portrait: *Jun Bei*. She looks like she was around his age when the sketches were done. Most are dated from before the plague, and as I flip through the pages, I see the tone of the sketches suddenly change. They grow softer, more refined. As though the girl herself has been distilled and condensed, scraped back to her very essence.

It's like the earlier sketches were drawn from life, and the later ones from memory.

"Don't touch that."

I spin around to find Cole standing in the doorway wearing a fresh tank top over his bandages, two steaming plates of pasta in his hands.

A chill races through me at the look on his face. "I-I'm sorry, I didn't mean—"

"Put it down now." His voice is like ice. He sets the plates on the dining table and strides across the room, his movements inhumanly fast. He grabs the book in a blur, sending fear skittering down my spine. A second ago he was a boy cooking dinner, but now he's transformed back into a trained Cartaxus weapon.

He yanks the sketchbook from my hands. The pages slide open to the drawing of the girl with tears glistening on her cheeks. He stares at it for a moment, then snaps the sketchbook shut and sets it on the table beside the gleaming knives.

"I-I'm sorry," I say again, then stop myself when I realize how pathetic I sound.

I've spent two years on my own, dodging blowers and protecting the cabin, doing whatever it took to keep myself alive. I just found out my father is dead, that there's a Hydra vaccine, and that its fate has been left in my hands. I'm grieving and tired, but I'm not weak, and I'm not going to let a jacked-up Cartaxus soldier order me around in my own home.

I cross my arms. "No, you know what? You're in *my* house, soldier. You showed up uninvited, and you have no right to fill up my living room and then snap at me when I touch something. Maybe you shouldn't have brought the book with you if you didn't want me to see it. What the hell do you need it for on this mission, anyway?"

He meets my eyes, a muscle twitching in his jaw. "It's all I have left. You think Cartaxus will let me back if they find out why I'm really here? They'll court-martial me for this. They'll destroy everything I own. I've left my whole life behind on the back of a single note from your father, so I'm sorry if you're a little put out by having my things in your living room."

I open my mouth, then close it. I don't know what to say to that. I hadn't considered what Cole might be risking by coming here like this. Of course Cartaxus will court-martial him if they find out why he's here. I'd be surprised if they didn't *kill* him.

That fact alone should convince me that Cole is on my side, but for some reason it just makes me more nervous.

He looks me up and down, then turns and walks to the dining table. "Come on. We're both tired, and you need to eat. I've cooked you a double serving. It looks like you could use it. Your healing tech must be using a lot of calories." He pulls out a chair at the table for me.

I hesitate for a moment, then walk over slowly and sit down. A heaping plate of herbed, creamy spaghetti lies waiting. The sight makes my stomach rumble. I pick up a fork and lean over the plate, drawing in a slow breath.

"This might be the best meal I've seen in a year."

75

He looks up. "What have you been eating?"

I jerk my thumb at a stack of foil-wrapped nutriBars in the corner. "Those, mostly. There isn't much else around."

He twirls his fork in the spaghetti. "Really? I drove past a farm just north of here that looked like it went for miles. Soybeans, vegetables . . ."

"Um-mh," I say, through a mouthful of spaghetti. "That stuff's proprietary. You can't digest it without their app's synthetic enzymes. It tastes good going down, but it'll leave you sick for days. There's a special place in hell for whoever came up with DRM for *food*."

"So you've been living on nutriBars?"

I swallow a mouthful. "I wouldn't call it *living*. I nearly lost my mind eating them every day last winter. It's better than starving, though."

He pauses with his fork mid-twirl. "So why didn't you go to a bunker? Homestake isn't far, and Cartaxus would have come to pick you up. Hell, you're an Agatta. They would have sent a chopper."

My shoulders tighten. "I know. They sent one for my father. They put two bullets in him too. I wasn't going to let myself become their prisoner."

"Your father wasn't mistreated, Catarina."

I dig my fingernails into my palm again, but the pain is becoming meaningless. "If he wasn't mistreated, then why would he make me promise to stay out here?"

Cole raises an eyebrow. "I'd like to know that myself."

I lean forward. "I'll tell you why—it's because he knew he was walking into a cell he'd never escape from. He wanted me to live on my own terms."

Cole looks around the room, at the spiderwebs on the ceiling, at the bare walls and dusty kitchen. "Yeah, you're really knocking it out of the park."

I scowl. "At least I can leave anytime I want. Cartaxus threatened my father's life when he tried to quit. It took him years to get out."

"He quit? I thought Lachlan was fired over the influenza crisis."

"Fired?" I freeze with a forkful of spaghetti midway to my mouth. "No, that's ridiculous."

"Thirty thousand people died."

"I know. That was *Cartaxus's* fault."

Cole chews silently, and the condescending look on his face makes me want to stab him with my fork. Influenza X was the most lethal virus in human history, before Hydra came along and shot straight to the top of the list. My father coded a vaccine that should have won him a Nobel prize, but Cartaxus encrypted it and refused to release the source code. Soon people started guessing at what might be hidden inside it. One rumor caught hold—that the code was *impure*, that it was based on canine DNA.

My father said there were a lot of rumors like that in the early days of gentech—that innocuous-looking apps were based on the genes of animals that many religions believed to be unclean. Pigs, dogs, insects. Genes that people didn't want swimming around inside their cells. The concern was well-founded, since many early apps were derived from the previous decades scientists had spent studying *rats*. It was estimated that almost 60 percent of early gentech code contained at least one rodent gene. That changed as time went on, and people like my father invented new and superior genes that were entirely synthetic. When he wrote the code for Influenza X, there was no need to lift genes from nature's encyclopedia—he could write better code himself.

The rumors about the Influenza X vaccine were false, but that didn't stop them spreading, and Cartaxus refused to release the code and put them to rest. Hundreds of thousands of religious objectors refused to download the vaccine, and thousands of them died.

"If Cartaxus had learned from Influenza, we wouldn't be in this mess," I say. "The whole idea of *encrypting* gentech code is unconscionable. People need to know what their code is doing to them, which means they need to read it. But Cartaxus doesn't care about people. They just care about copyright."

Cole snorts. "Encrypting the Influenza vaccine had nothing to do with copyright. You can't pander to extremists about code they don't understand while a virus is killing millions of people."

"It's not pandering! It's open, honest debate. People have a right to choose what goes into their bodies."

"What about their children's bodies? Who chooses for them when the alternative is death?"

I throw my fork down. "I don't know, but it sure as hell shouldn't be Cartaxus. All they care about is power. My father knew that, and that's why he quit."

"Is that what he told you?"

"He wasn't lying."

Cole picks up my plate. "Then he shouldn't have based the Influenza vaccine on canine DNA."

I push back from the table, biting back the urge to yell at him. He just told me my father is dead, and now he's trashing him in front of me. I'm so worked up I can barely keep my voice level, but I'm not going to let him disrespect my father like that. "You don't know what you're talking about, soldier," I say. "My father wouldn't do that. He would have found an alternative, or even if he couldn't, he would never have lied about it. He wasn't ashamed of his work."

Cole's eyes meet mine, flintlike and cold. "Believe what you want to believe, Catarina. Let me know when you're ready for the truth."

He stands and walks into the kitchen, leaving me in a storm of grief, with a trickle of blood weaving from the palm of my left hand.

# CHAPTER 9

BY THE TIME COLE IS DONE WITH THE DISHES, I'VE tugged a comb through my hair, cleaned my nails, and am pacing back and forth across the living room. Cole's words are spinning through my mind—but it's not what he said that's worrying me. It's the cold, angry tone in his voice when he talked about my father.

He sounded like a perfect Cartaxus soldier. A true believer, loyal to the conglomerate that has taken over the planet. He didn't sound like a renegade gone AWOL on the back of a single note from a man whose word he's ready to risk his life on.

If anything, it sounds like Cole didn't like my father at all.

So why the hell is he here?

Doubt has taken hold inside me, a fire that first sparked when Cole told me that the Skies hacked Cartaxus and destroyed the vaccine's code. That's ridiculous. I'm probably the best coder the Skies have, and I'm nowhere near good enough to pull off a hack like that. But if not the Skies, then who? Part of me feels like Cartaxus is playing some larger game that I can't yet grasp. All I know is that my father is dead, and he left a message for Cole.

I saw the proof of that, at least. I held it in my hands.

What I have to decide now is what to do with Cole. My eyes glide across the gleaming handcuffs on the living room table. For all I know, he's waiting for me to unlock the vaccine so he can drag me back to Cartaxus, and they can control the code again. I've spent the last two years hiding from people like him. How could my father possibly expect me to work with him now?

"Are you ready?"

I jump as Cole walks back from the kitchen with my little battered genkit in his hands. "Where did you get that?"

"It was on the floor." He hands it to me. "I moved it out of the way when I brought my gear in. I'm guessing you'll need it to get into my arm."

I take the genkit carefully, a wild idea sparking in my mind. This machine holds backups of every piece of code I've ever written. Every algorithm, every firewall-busting script I've developed with the Skies. But that's not all it holds. There are viruses in here, malware that can be triggered remotely, with a vocal command. If I can dump one of those viruses into Cole's panel, it'll give me a chance at getting away from him if he turns on me.

Maybe that's what my father wanted—not for me to work with Cole, but to fight him. To control him. To hold my own against this living, breathing weapon.

"Are you ready to do this?" Cole asks.

I nod swiftly, turning away. "Yeah, I'm ready. Let's go down to the lab."

A set of dank concrete steps at the back of the house leads down to the laboratory my father built in the basement. The motion sensors at the door trip as I step through, and the ancient fluorescent bars on the ceiling blink to life.

It's a mess down here. Sheaths of musty paper lie spilled across the floor, a testament to my father's love of old-fashioned notes. The black lab counter runs the length of the room, cluttered with dirty beakers and metal canisters of proteins ready to be laser-coded. A pile of broken petri dishes and test tubes fills one corner, and the frayed wiring of a disemboweled genkit takes up most of the floor.

It's a minefield of broken glass and toxic chemicals, just the way it's always been. It's my favorite place in the cabin.

"This place is a death trap," Cole says, scanning the room.

I nod to the broom hanging on the far wall. "I'm going to need a few minutes to get ready. Feel free to clean up."

He raises an eyebrow at me and leans against the door frame. "Not a chance, Catarina."

I smile, walking to the counter, and set my genkit down. Its screen is dim, cracked in one corner and mended badly with duct tape. It's just a basic laptop model: the kind of thing someone would buy if they were getting into coding but didn't want to spend too much money. The higher-end genkits can take up an entire room, designed to run calculations on every possible permutation of the human genome. My genkit has a screen and keyboard, which most people use when they're learning before upgrading to the smoother, faster VR interface. I tried hooking up my panel's low-tech graphics card to the genkit's VR stream a dozen times, but all it did was crash my tech. One day I'll find a way to upgrade my panel's processors, but until then I'm stuck using a basic, clunky, entry-level genkit.

A slow, broken, taped-up genkit that I love with all my heart.

The screen glows blue as it boots up. I glance over my shoulder at Cole and run a quick scan through my files for a virus I can hide in his arm. Most of them are for attacking computer systems, but a handful are straight-up malicious gentech code. Biocryptic warfare. I wrote them after the outbreak, while the world was going to hell and I was alone and terrified. The only weapon I had was my father's rifle, and I barely knew how to use it.

But I knew how to code.

A forty-kilobyte Trojan catches my eye—a command that should short-circuit Cole's wiring and knock him out if I say a trigger word: recumbentibus. It's perfect. Small enough to slip past his security scanner, and it'll give me time to run the hell away from him if it comes to that.

I pull out the genkit's I/O wire, a three-foot-long cable coiled into the back of the device, and wave it at Cole. A chrome-plated, inch-long needle gleams on the end. "Okay, soldier. Let's get you jacked in."

His shoulders tighten. "With a needle?"

"Don't be a baby. Give me your arm."

He eyes the gleaming needle, shifting uncomfortably. He's not alone in his discomfort—most people hate the wire. Panels can usually be updated or checked through their wireless connection, but there are some apps that need to be physically budded through a brand-new stream of nanites, and that's where the wire comes in. Its needle tip is hollow, ready to send in a microscopic drop of saline teeming with nanites. Whenever I'm coding, I always use the wire. Hardwired connections are faster, and you don't have to worry so much about electromagnetic interference.

Cole steps closer reluctantly, his gaze hovering on the duct tape holding the genkit's screen in. "Are you sure this thing is safe?"

"The machine is fine. It's just old, and a little slow."

He doesn't look convinced. "And you're sure you know what you're doing?"

I stare at him. If I didn't know better, I'd think he was afraid, which is ridiculous coming from a man who could kill me in seconds with his bare hands.

At least, it would be ridiculous if I wasn't planning on dumping a Trojan into his arm as soon as I get in.

"Of course I know what I'm doing," I say. "How many times do I have to—"

"Yeah, yeah," he says, cutting me off. "You're a smart-ass Agatta, I get it. I still don't think you'll be able to get past the firewalls."

"We'll see." I flick the machine into reading mode and pull Cole's arm toward me, turning it so his panel faces up. It glows beneath his skin, an oblong of soft blue light stretching from his wrist almost all the way to the crease in his elbow. There's a thick, soft layer of silicone in there, just above the muscles, grown from the bud Cole would have been injected with a few days after birth. The function cores inside the silicone each act as tiny factories, producing nanites that build and destroy ribbons of synthetic DNA. They can also build structures out of metal or plastic to create implants inside your body. Titanium wrapped around your bones to make them unbreakable. Fiber-optic wires to pass commands to your fingers at the speed of light.

With the knowledge I have of coding and hacking, using the genkit humming beside me, there's almost nothing I couldn't do to Cole's body if I wanted to. Stop his heart. Cut his oxygen supply. Shut down everything in his panel.

It's really no surprise that he looks so uncomfortable right now.

I hold the needle end of the wire against Cole's panel. It flashes for a second, and the probe jerks free of my grasp, burying itself in his arm. He flinches as it dives beneath his skin, and the genkit's screen flashes white.

*ALERT. Unauthorized use of this software is prohibited. Password required.*

"See?" Cole says, reaching for the wire. "I don't know the password. You're not going to be able to get through."

"Hush now," I say, slapping his hand away. "I need to concentrate. No more talking."

My fingers dance across the keyboard as I start to work, loading up libraries, feeling out the basic structure of Cole's security. I'm not going to dump the Trojan in just yet. My first priority is blasting open his fire-walls and getting access to his memory. Once I'm in and we're scanning his panel for files left by my father, it should be easy to dump the Trojan and hide the keystrokes in a harmless-looking command. The *hard* part is getting in—figuring out which scripts to run, trying to remember the best methods of attack.

It's been a long time since I've done this. The last panel I hacked was my own, and that was almost three years ago. Dax had been at the cabin for a month, I'd fallen head-over-heels for him, and although we'd flirted constantly, we'd never actually kissed. In retrospect, it was because I was fifteen and he was afraid of my father, but at the time I thought it was because I wasn't pretty enough.

The other girls I'd known at boarding school had satin, colortrue skin. They had fingernails that grew in pink, and quad-follicle eyelashes that grew until they cut them. Next to them, I felt like a common gray pigeon—dull and obsolete—so I modified a cosmetic app to be hypergenesis-friendly. My father refused to test it. Too dangerous, he said. When I pushed him, he'd always tell me how my mother died. How the well-meaning doctor gave her a syringe of healing tech, and she took just fourteen seconds to die. How her cells fragmented, splitting apart like a billion screaming mouths, until she choked to death on the bloody pulp of her own lungs.

My father wouldn't help me, but I thought that I knew better. I sat down one night, hacked my panel, and uploaded the app myself.

It took thirty-seven seconds until the burning started.

The rest of the night is a blur. My father hauled me downstairs and jacked me into his industrial-grade genkit, jumping my panel to keep me alive. He stopped and restarted my heart, flushing my system, wiping any trace of the rogue nanites as he knelt on the floor beside me. With Dax's help, I survived, lying in the basement while the skin on my back bubbled up, sloughing off in chunks.

That was the last time I disobeyed my father, and the last time I hacked my panel. I learned the hard way that there are some things in life you're not supposed to change. I was left with an ugly track of scar tissue along my spine, but Dax didn't seem to care. He told me that night was when he realized he was in love with me.

The memory makes the scar tissue on my back prickle as I weave past Cole's security, feeling out his hardware. Hacking my panel's firewalls took days of preparation and testing, and the actual attack took over an hour. But if I'm lucky, hacking Cole's panel should only take a few minutes. When I broke through the firewalls in my arm, I discovered a weakness in the way the panel's power is distributed. Exploiting that weakness will mean running a serious electric current into Cole's arm, but it should also give me a shortcut to get in.

First up: distract his security scanner. Cole has a miniature AI in his arm that's always watching for attacks, learning how to protect his code. I throw a virus at his wireless chip and watch as the AI responds, its primary defenses surging around it.

Now I'm free to attack his battery.

Every panel has a power system somewhere in the body—sometimes deeper in the forearm, sometimes inside the chest. They charge up using a mixture of your body's kinetic energy and your metabolism, gaining energy as you digest food. That means guilt-free hamburgers when you're running power-intensive VR sessions, but it also wastes a lot of food when all you have is nutriBars. With the AI scanner distracted, I prepare the genkit's cable to send a series of electric pulses into Cole's arm.

"Uh, hold on for a second," I say. "This might hurt. . . ."

"What?" Cole asks, his eyes flaring. "Is this safe? I'm not sure you should—"

His arm goes tense as he cuts off, his whole body jerking against the counter, his eyes flashing to black for a split second.

"What the . . . ," he breathes, a vein on his forehead popping up. He reaches for the genkit's cable, but I smack his hand away again.

"It worked," I say. "Hold on, I need to do it one more time."

"No—" he starts, but it's too late. I've already run the command. His eyes fly wide as it surges through him, his mouth opening silently.

He doubles over, his muscles twitching furiously. It's probably not good for his heart to take this kind of stress, and I'm sure he's got a dozen implants that are close to shorting out, but the last shock brought down one of his firewalls, and the final barrier is toppling before my eyes. . . .

And it's down. One second. That's all I get, but it's all the time I need to drop a single command and run. The AI surges back from the wireless chip, furious, and I flick the genkit off before it races inside to corrupt it.

Cole's forehead glistens with sweat. "What the hell are you doing, Catarina?"

"Just wait," I say. "It takes a while for your security to reset."

"You couldn't do it." He reaches for the wire in his arm. "I'm not letting you shock me again."

I grab his wrist, meeting his gaze with all the steel I can muster. I can't let him pull the wire out. Not until I've logged in and checked his files for the vaccine. Not until I've bought myself an edge by dumping the Trojan into his arm.

"I said *wait*, soldier." I reach out with my free hand to flick the genkit on.

*ALERT. Unauthorized use of this software is prohibited. Password required.*

"See?" he says. "You couldn't do it. I *told* you."

I ignore him, typing with my free hand, letting my hand slide from his wrist. "I just typed in your new password, which I reset for you. It's my name—Catarina."

He stares at me for a second, then drops his eyes to the screen. "Holy shit," he breathes. "You did it."

The genkit beeps, and his panel's menu unfolds. A list of Cartaxus apps scrolls across the screen, almost too fast to read. Most are standard upgrades I recognize, but some are apps I've never heard of. Toxic aorta shielding. Neocell mesh. One is labeled *Hydra Vaccine*, and the sight of it makes my heart skip, but it's encrypted. I can't click on it. I can't even see its size, or how it's running.

Cracking that file would take more than a few electric shocks.

"What about hidden files?" Cole's skin is flushed, beaded with sweat after what I just put him through.

"Just a second," I say, my fingers flying across the keyboard. I throw together a command to dump the Trojan into his arm, wrap it up in the best camouflage I can think of, and send it to his panel. His security is down, but it starts spooling up as I type, and my stomach tightens, waiting for the code to transfer.

"What are you doing?" There's an edge to Cole's voice.

"I'm running a scan. Chill out." I stare at the screen. His security is racing now, but it doesn't seem to be going after the Trojan. It's scanning his memory, probably running a routine check after the password change.

"A scan on what?"

I swallow hard, bang out a frantic command, and spin the screen around to face Cole. "A scan for hidden files, like you asked for. It's coming back now."

Cole's eyes drop to the screen. It flashes as the scan returns, and half a dozen text documents appear in a list.

One is titled *To_Catarina*. The sight sends a chill through me. I click on it, and the screen fills with text.

> *Catarina,*
>
> *My darling girl, if you're reading this, it means I am dead. I know you want to grieve, but there is something I need you to do. I have completed a Hydra vaccine that may be our last chance at survival. The code is strong, but it is not without weaknesses, and it is essential that as many people as possible receive it.*
>
> *Unfortunately, there are those at Cartaxus who plan to withhold the vaccine and deploy it only to those who will submit to their rules and ideology. This will not only result in the preventable deaths of millions of people, it may threaten the vaccine itself. You, my darling girl, must not allow this to happen.*
>
> *Cartaxus forced me to encrypt the vaccine so that they could control it, but I have done it in a way that you will be able to unlock. You must decrypt it as soon as possible. You'll need to use the notes I left with you and run them through a clonebox. There is an abandoned laboratory in Canada with all the additional equipment you will need. You must travel there, and once you arrive and unlock the vaccine, you must release it freely to all survivors. It is of utmost importance that you remain hidden from Cartaxus—you must never let them take*

*you, my darling girl. If they find you, they will take the*
*vaccine back under their control. Lt. Franklin will protect*
*you, but he is a weapon of considerable power, and you will*
*need to find a way to work together to unlock the vaccine.*
    *All my love,*
    *Lachlan*

I step back, swaying, the words racing through my mind. "Did you
see that?" I turn to Cole. His eyes are glazed over, his brow furrowed in
concentration. "Cole? Are you reading this?"

He shudders and blinks, coming out of a VR session.

"Did you see it?" I ask, breathless. "I know what my father wants us
to do."

His eyes narrow. He barely glances at the screen before ripping the
wire from his panel with a sickening screech of metal.

"Jesus," I gasp, backing away. "What happened?"

"What happened? My security scanner just sent me a report."

I close my eyes. The Trojan. His scanner must have found it, and
now he looks like he wants to break me in half. My father said the two of
us would have to work together, and I've just destroyed what little trust
we've managed to build so far.

I step back, raising my hands. "Cole, I'll take it out. I'm sorry, I was
just—"

He cuts me off, slicing his hand through the air. "I don't want to hear
it, Catarina. Or maybe I should call you *Bobcat*."

The air stills. My Skies codename. "Wait, what are you talking about?"

"My scanner checked your genkit, and it sent me a report. You're the
hacker, the one they're always talking about."

Oh no. This isn't about my stupid little Trojan. He knows I'm part
of the Skies.

This is far, far worse.

"Cole, I can explain—"

"You're the one who dumped the virus that killed Lachlan. You're the one who destroyed everything."

*"What?"* I step back, and my shoulder hits the wall. "No, that wasn't me, and it wasn't the Skies, I swear. How could you think I'd hurt my own father?"

"Because you're a terrorist."

"We're not *terrorists.* We had nothing to do with the attack on the lab." I take a stumbling step to the side, but he grabs my shoulder and shoves me back against the wall.

"Listen!" I yell, shrinking away. "Just listen, okay? My father left a plan for us. You need to read his note."

"You hacked our base," he growls, "and you killed your own father. I'm taking you back to Cartaxus, and I'll let them decide how to deal with you."

"Wait," I say, clawing at his arm. He pulls the pair of silver handcuffs from his pocket and flicks one open. He must have taken them when I wasn't looking. "Just check your panel," I say. "There's a file—"

"I don't want to hear any more lies." His hand shoots out in a blur, grabbing my wrist.

I have only a heartbeat of time left before I'm trapped, before he locks those cuffs around my wrists and drags me back to a Cartaxus cell. I dumped the Trojan into his arm, and I don't know if it installed, but this seems like as good a time as any to test it out.

"Recumbentibus," I whisper, praying the code works.

The lights on Cole's panel fade, and he drops to the floor.

# CHAPTER 10

IT TAKES FIFTEEN MINUTES UNTIL COLE STARTS TO stir, his skin pale and clammy. I've hauled him up so he's sitting on the floor, his hands cuffed behind him to the lab counter's frame. Once I'd made sure he wasn't going to choke on his own tongue, I sat down with my genkit, plugged him in, and started reading through his panel.

Cole has some seriously strange, seriously *dangerous* tech inside him.

The protective protocol that kicks in and makes his eyes go black is single-handedly the most complicated code I've ever seen. On one level, it's simple. His panel has been fed a photograph of me, probably from my father. It recognizes me by reading the signals from Cole's retina and constantly scans me and my surroundings. Whenever I'm in danger of being injured or killed, the AI shows Cole the threats in red through his VR interface, then pumps him full of adrenaline. The end result is that he's so terrified and disoriented that he wants to attack anything that might hurt me.

But there's a whole other level I don't understand. Pages of code I can't figure out, linking to other files that look like gibberish to me. It's my father's code, I can tell by the notation, but it's not like anything else he's ever written.

It's not like anything *anyone* has ever written.

The thing is, gentech doesn't change your DNA. It doesn't *splice*—cutting genes out and replacing them with new ones—even though most people think that's what it does. Before gentech was invented, people thought splicing was the only way to change DNA, but it was problematic. Your body *remembers* how it was made. Splicing rogue genes into your DNA can corrupt it, which can lead to a sudden, painful death.

Instead, most gentech uses ribbons of protein that cover your DNA like clothing covers your body. Underneath, you're still the same naked person you always were, but you can dress yourself up or down to make yourself look different. That's why you need a panel—your DNA keeps trying to take off its clothes and go au naturel, and your panel keeps forcing it to dress up.

But Cole's *underlying* DNA, beneath the layers of gentech, looks altered, which should be impossible. It's hard to tell if I'm reading the output from his panel correctly, and maybe I'm not, but something tells me that whatever gave Cole the scars across his chest left him with even bigger scars on his DNA.

"What . . . ," he murmurs, stirring. "Where am I?"

I look up from the screen. "You're in South Dakota, last time I checked."

He tries to lift his hands, but the handcuffs stop him. He jerks forward, making the whole counter shudder, but it doesn't move. It's steel frame, fire-resistant, bolted into the wall. He growls. "What the hell did you do to me?"

"I knocked you out with a piece of code. I don't think it's good for your nervous system, so please don't make me do it again."

"I knew I shouldn't have let you touch my panel." His eyes drop to the genkit, following the cable all the way to his forearm. He tenses. "What are you doing?"

"Reading."

"Take it out."

"I'm not going to hurt you."

"Just take the cable out." His voice is strained, his forehead glistening.

"Okay, okay." I type a command. The cable slithers out of his arm and flips around on the floor, reeling itself into the back of the genkit.

He closes his eyes. "Thank you."

I raise an eyebrow, staring at him. "I'm sorry I knocked you out, but you were about to handcuff me. I didn't have a choice. There's no reason to be afraid."

"Yeah, right." He shakes his head. "And you're probably afraid of *me*."

"Well . . . ," I mutter. "Have you *seen* yourself?"

He smiles bitterly. "I'm just a soldier, Catarina. I'm muscle and train-ing, but you're a coder, like Lachlan. Most people are afraid of the guy with the gun, but the person they should be afraid of is the one with a genkit cable. It's software that runs the show in this world, not hardware. People like you are *always* in control."

I drop my eyes, remembering Cole's face when I first jacked him into my genkit. He was nervous, sweating. He flinched when the cable connected. I didn't think about it, but it should have been obvious that he was afraid of what I'd do to him. I've seen the scars on his chest. He didn't get those from combat.

He got them in a *lab*.

Guilt settles in my stomach. I've been afraid of Cole since he arrived, but he hasn't even come close to hurting me. And what have I done? I used a dose to blow out a window and slice his shoulders to

shreds. I jacked him into a genkit and ran electricity through his body.
I dumped a Trojan into his panel and knocked him out with a *word*.

Of course he's afraid of me.

I chew my lip. "I'm sorry. I guess we haven't got off to a good start."

"That's a hell of an understatement."

I hold his gaze. "Look, my father left a plan to release the vaccine.
There's a note in your panel that explains everything. Read it, you'll see."

His eyes glaze over, flitting back and forth as he drops into a VR
session. He doesn't say anything for a long time, and then his eyes focus
on mine. "It says all we need is your father's notes and a clonebox."

I pause, recalling the note. Cloneboxes are rare machines for studying code that's running inside live cells, and they're not easy to find. But
that's not all my father told us to do. "No, he said we need a lab. He said
there was one left set up for us, somewhere in Canada. He didn't leave
the directions, but there must be something to tell us where it is."

"I know where it is," Cole mutters.

"How?"

"There's a Cartaxus lab in Canada. A place he used to work that's
abandoned now. That must be what he's talking about."

"Okay," I say, nodding. "So we just need to gather all of my father's
notes that we can, find the lab and drive there, and pick up a clonebox
on the way."

Cole just watches me. "There's no *we*, Catarina. Cartaxus has cloneboxes and labs, and I don't think they're going to restrict the vaccine. I
don't see why I can't copy the notes, bring them back to Cartaxus, and
leave you to follow this plan on your own."

I sigh. "I need the copy of the vaccine that's in your arm. And besides,
I can't make it to Canada on my bike."

"Why don't you ask your terrorist friends for help?"

I bunch my hands into fists. "I told you, they're not terrorists. All they do is distribute medical code."

"*Someone* attacked your father's lab."

"I know, and I meant it when I said it wasn't the Skies, but that doesn't mean I trust them with this. They're disorganized, their code is sloppy, and Cartaxus is probably listening in on their network, anyway. If my father wanted their help, he would have said so, but he didn't. All he said was that you and I have to work on this together."

Cole leans back against the counter, sighing. "Well, we're off to a fine start."

I scrape my hands over my face. He's right—this is ridiculous. How am I supposed to drive with him across the country when I can't even bring myself to uncuff him?

There has to be a way for us to work on this together. My father's plan relies on it. The whole *world* relies on it.

I shift on the floor until I'm sitting cross-legged on the concrete, facing him. "Why are you even here, Cole?"

He lifts an eyebrow. "I thought we went over that. Looming apocalypse, unlocking the vaccine, remember?"

"No, I mean—why *you*? You were safe in a base with airlocks and food, and it's clear that you don't want any part of this plan. My father must have chosen you for a reason, and I need to know what it is."

He tilts his head back, watching me. "Why should I tell you?"

"Looming apocalypse, unlocking the vaccine. Remember?"

His lips curl in the faintest of smiles. He looks me up and down, his ice-blue eyes bloodshot after the command I used to knock him out. "I'm not the heartless soldier you think I am, and I'm not an idiot either. We're doomed if we lose this vaccine. Of course I'm going to do everything I can to unlock it."

"So my father knew you'd pack up and go AWOL because you're a *hero*?"

He presses his lips together. "There's another reason too."

"Go on."

"How about you uncuff me, and we can talk?"

I let out a snort. "Not a chance, soldier. Nice try, though."

He grimaces, shifting on the floor, the handcuffs rattling against the lab counter's leg. "I was planning to leave Cartaxus anyway. Someone I cared about went missing and might be on the surface, and I want to find them. Your father knew that. He was going to help me get out so I could look for them."

"Oh," I say. "Is it someone he knew too?"

Cole nods, then pauses, as though he hadn't meant to tell me that. His tone and the tight look in his eyes tell me he doesn't want to talk about whoever it is he wants to find. It's obviously personal, and it might be irrelevant, but I can't rule out the chance that it's important somehow—another clue my father left for me.

My mind spins back over the conversations we've had. I don't think Cole ever mentioned any family or friends, but there was that girl in the sketchbook. I glance up at the ceiling, trying to remember the name written in careful script beneath each drawing.

"Is it Jun Bei?"

He stiffens. He doesn't need to answer—it's clear from his response that I've guessed correctly. He had the same fierce reaction when he found me flipping through the sketchbook, as though seeing her face or saying her name was an intrusion into his privacy. Whatever happened between him and this girl clearly isn't over. The look in his eyes when I said her name was like an open wound.

After a long, tense moment, Cole nods. "Yes, it's her. We were separated years ago, and she's not in the Cartaxus system, so I know the chances of her being alive are low. But she could have survived out here, holed up somewhere, like you."

I nod, lacing my fingers together, this new piece of the puzzle sliding into place. I'm starting to understand why Cole was such a perfect choice by my father. He's capable of protecting me, that much I'm sure of, but it's what he's driven by that makes him special.

It's his *hope*.

Even after two straight years of horror and death, Cole still believes that a girl he once knew might still be alive. In this world, that's a *wild* hope. Barely more than a prayer. He was willing to leave the safety of Cartaxus to risk his life on the most impossible of chances. If I can find a way to link Cole's hope to the plan my father left us, something tells me nothing will stand in our way.

I unfold my hands, staring at Cole. "If Jun Bei is on the surface, Cartaxus isn't going to give her the vaccine. She's vulnerable every minute we waste arguing here. The only way you can protect her is by helping me release the code freely to everyone, not let Cartaxus keep it to themselves. *That's* why my father chose you for this mission."

He shakes his head. "I don't think Cartaxus is going to restrict access to the vaccine."

"Are you willing to bet Jun Bei's life on that?"

A muscle in his jaw twitches. "I don't even know if she's alive."

I sit back. He's right. I can practically see a candle of hope glowing inside him, but it's not enough to justify going against everything he's been trained for. There has to be something more than this. If my father was going to help Cole find this girl, he must have had some faith that she was alive, as well.

I slide my genkit closer. "Do you know her panel's ID?"

"I've already searched for it everywhere. If she's connected to a server, she'll be masking it."

"Oh, a *mask*," I say, flipping my genkit open. "How could I ever hope to get past that? What's her ID?"

He stares at me silently, unimpressed by my sarcasm.

I sigh. "Look, I'm just trying to help. Maybe I can find her."

He closes his eyes and starts reciting the hexadecimal code linked to Jun Bei's panel. I type it into a file in my genkit, then ping the Skies network, logging in. If Jun Bei is on the surface, she'll probably be using the Skies' satellites. My genkit's screen fades to black with a single, blinking cursor, and my fingers drop to the keyboard, punching out commands.

First, I have to navigate through the ancient systems the Skies uses to control their satellites. Jun Bei's ID has never pinged the network as far as I can tell from a quick scan, but if she's masking it, I'd need to run a recursive check across the most common encryptions. I load up a handful of scripts, grabbing scraps of code, running them until my genkit's fan whines with the effort. Millions of users, millions of IDs, thousands of them masked. Countless pings across the network every second of every day . . .

"Oh," I say, freezing.

Cole draws in a sharp breath. I look up to see his face paling. "What? What did you find?"

I spin the screen around. "I don't know if she's alive right *now*, but it looks like she pinged a server in Australia three days ago."

Cole turns to stone. I spin the genkit back around, trying to get a better lock on her location. A week ago she hit a server in Zimbabwe. But that can't be right. Even Cartaxus officials don't fly around the world like that these days.

I race through another scan, finding results faster now that I know the masking method she's been using. Her technique unfurls in the results, and it's brilliant. She's bouncing her location all around the world continually. Moscow, Beijing, Antarctica. Outposts in the Sahara. Wherever this girl is, she doesn't want to be found.

"Wait, not Australia," I say, hunting through the data. "I think she might be in the US, but that's the best I can do, sorry."

I look up. Cole's jaw is clenched, and his eyes are squeezed shut. His shoulders are twitching. . . .

Oh shit. He's crying.

I look away. This feels wrong. He shouldn't be handcuffed to the counter, not like this. He's just found out the girl he loves is still alive. "I, uh . . . let me find the key to the handcuffs." I pat around on the floor, avoiding looking at him. "I'm sorry, I don't know where I dropped—"

He pushes himself up from the floor, rubbing his wrists. The handcuffs lie split on the concrete, the glinting steel twisted and bent. He wipes his eyes with the back of his hand. "I'll help you," he says, holding his hand out. "I'm in, Catarina, for whatever it takes to unlock the vaccine."

"Oh," I breathe, nerves kicking inside me. I take his hand cautiously and let him help me up. "Are you sure?"

He nods. "She's *alive*." His eyes are blazing. The candle of hope I saw in him before has leaped into a roaring fire. "She's alive, and she's out there somewhere, which means you're right. She's vulnerable until we release the vaccine. Whatever you want me to do, I'll do it. We won't go to Cartaxus. I'll hide you from them. I'll take you wherever you need to go. I can't risk losing her again."

"Okay," I whisper, the hair on the back of my neck rising. A low, thrumming power is rolling off Cole. The cluttered laboratory seems to shrink around him. It's like looking at the sun. Like he could tear the world apart with his hands if he wanted to.

*He is a weapon of considerable power.* That's what my father said. For the first time, I think I know what he meant by that.

"We'll leave tomorrow," Cole says, scanning the room. "We'll take all of Lachlan's notes and go through them on the way. We'll find a clonebox—we can steal one if we have to. There's no time to waste. We can make it to that lab in a day if the roads are clear."

"Sure," I say, still staring at him. He's not even listening to me. I can see the plans for the journey to the lab forming in his mind.

Twenty minutes ago he was ready to slap a pair of handcuffs on me and drag me back to a Cartaxus cell. Now he's pledging his allegiance, promising to do anything to help me, all because a girl he loved years ago is still alive. The change is so abrupt and deep, it's left me spinning, and at the core of my confusion is a single, burning thought: My father knew all of this would happen.

He knew Cole would come to me, that I would find these clues, and that I would find Jun Bei to convince him to help me. The pieces of my father's jigsaw puzzle have interlocked and now stand before me, a Cartaxus weapon allied to my cause.

It's *terrifying*.

This is blackmail. I'm using Cole's feelings to force him to help me, and I know that my father planned this; he played Cole with perfect pitch. I should be proud I heard enough of the melody to carry the song alone, but for some reason it's left me feeling shaken.

My father was distant sometimes, even cold. He could lose himself in his work for weeks and forget to speak to me. He was blunt, he was eccentric, and he was sometimes hard to live with, but my love for him never wavered because deep down I believed that he was *good*.

He spent his life writing vaccines. Crafting medical code. His mind was a razor, but he only wielded it to fight suffering and disease. Never like this—as a weapon. As a way to control people. Standing here, watching Cole pace across the lab, I suddenly feel like I'm in a stranger's house.

Cole turns to me. "You know, you look a lot like your father when you do that."

My heart twists. "When I do what?"

"When you look at someone like they're a problem you're trying to solve."

"My father looked at you like that?"

"He looked at everyone like that, Catarina." He blinks, still distracted. "Come on, let's go upstairs. We need to pack and plan out a route to the lab, and you need to get a good night's sleep before we hit the road. Are you ready to do this?"

I wrap my arms around myself, nodding. "Of course."

Cole turns and heads up the concrete stairs to the living room. I follow dumbly. We finally have a chance to end the nightmare of this plague. I should be thrilled, I should want to celebrate, but all I feel is a growing sense of unease.

I'm beginning to realize that the father I remember isn't the one Cole seems to know.

# CHAPTER 11

THE NEXT MORNING I WAKE TO THE FAMILIAR sounds of the forest, with the last remnants of sleep still heavy in my bones. For a few precious moments I float in a state of half alertness, snuggling deeper into the warmth of the blankets, hiding from the dawn. Just as I start slipping under, the squeak of floorboards sends me sitting bolt upright, falling into my body so hard it drives the breath from my lungs.

My father. The vaccine. It all slams into me in a gut-wrenching wave of grief that leaves me trembling. I push the tangled strands of hair from my face, pulling in a breath to steady myself as I take in my surroundings.

I'm on an air mattress on the living room floor, my legs tangled in a silver Cartaxus sleeping bag Cole gave me when he ordered me to rest. The front door is open, and there's no trace of the bags and weapons that filled the cabin when I fell asleep. My father's notes are gone too. We hauled up all the paper files we could find in the basement, to bring them with us on our journey. Two tattered cardboard boxes of handwritten notes and a few dozen sticks of memory.

Now they're gone, and there's no sign of Cole. My breath catches.

Motes of dust rise from the bare floorboards, forming swirling patterns in the air. I scramble out of my sleeping bag and race barefoot through the front door, skidding across the front porch and down the steps to the driveway.

The chill of the morning hits me like a hand across my face. The bare skin on my arms prickles with goose bumps. I spin around, ratcheting up my tech to search for Cole, and find him leaning against his jeep, his arms crossed, smirking at me.

My hand flies to my heart, relief flooding me. "Dammit, Cole. I thought you'd taken off with the files."

His smirk grows into a smile. He's wearing a black tank top and cargo pants with a teched-up rifle slung across one shoulder. The bandage from last night is gone—the skin across his shoulders that was shredded is now flushed and puckered, but his injuries are healed. His jaw is dusted with a day's worth of dark stubble that makes him look older, and more interesting, somehow. My eyes linger on him longer than I intend them to.

"I made you breakfast," he says. "I want to get on the road this morning." He reaches into the open window of the jeep and pulls out a metal flask, tossing it to me. The Cartaxus antlers are stamped on one side, but my name is etched into the other in the careful script I recognize from his sketchbook. I look up to see him swigging from an identical flask. Steam curls from the top when he lowers it.

I turn the flask in my hand, feeling liquid slosh inside it. "Did you engrave this?"

"I don't want to get them mixed up."

"What, you don't want girl germs?" I unscrew the top, sniffing it. Coffee and hazelnut. The scent makes my stomach growl. "Having spent years studying biochemistry, I can assure you they're not real."

"I'm more worried about *you*." He taps one of the black leylines curved around his face. "Agnes said you had hypergenesis, and my tech isn't always stable. I don't want to contaminate anything and make you sick."

"Oh." That's thoughtful. I take a sip of the coffee, picking up the chalky taste of nutrient powder mixed in with it. I hadn't thought about nanite contamination. It's probably not a concern unless Cole were to *kiss* me, which isn't something either of us needs to worry about.

The thought makes my eyes stray again to his face, until heat prickles at my cheeks.

"Are you . . . okay?" he asks.

I almost spit out the coffee. He can see me blushing. Of course he can—his tech probably has biosensors to check my heart rate and skin temperature. "Yeah, I-I burned my mouth," I stutter.

He frowns. "I'm sorry. I didn't think I made it that hot."

"It's fine," I say quickly, turning back up the steps, the coffee gripped in my hands. "I'm going to get changed and check the cabin again."

He nods but doesn't reply. I hurry inside, feeling his eyes burning into my back as I go.

After I've changed into fresh clothes and finished the coffee, I check the cabin over one last time. All the doors are thrown open, each room rifled through for anything we might need on the trip. I won't lock it when I leave. That's basic courtesy in a post-apocalyptic world: An empty house belongs to no one. I don't even know if I'll come back. These walls hold too many memories of the last two years, of the things I've done to stay alive. I look back at the boarded-up windows, stepping away from the porch, giving the cabin a silent good-bye before I turn away.

Cole is waiting beside the jeep with his hands stuffed in his pockets, his brow pinched as he squints up at the mountains. The lines of his face are smooth; he must have shaved while I was double-checking the rooms. The scent of his aftershave wafts around him in a haze of ice and pine.

"Is that everything?" he asks.

I glance down at a folder clutched to my chest, filled with every scrap of paper I could find. "Yeah. This is probably all junk, but I didn't want to risk leaving anything behind. The rest of the notes are in the storage rooms in the mine shafts."

He blinks. "*Mine* shafts?"

I smile. "That's why my father bought this property. The family who used to own it secretly dug a bunch of shafts into the mountains, hoping to strike gold. I don't know if they found any, but they left a whole network of tunnels. We get forest fires here sometimes, and the mines are a good place to hide. My father stored a lot of things in them, including most of his notes. The best entrance is up a hiking path on the other side of the mountain. We can take the fire trail there."

"You're telling me Lachlan stored his genetic research notes in amateur-built, illegal mine shafts? That's . . . eccentric."

"Did you *meet* my father?"

His face softens. "You're right. I don't even know why I'm surprised."

The moment hangs in the air, and I let it linger, analyzing the way it feels to joke about my father. The same avalanche of grief I woke up to is still there, heaped against the forged-steel walls in my heart, but there's more than that. The wound of his death aches, but he was too complex a man to feel just one emotion for. Part of me is furious with him for tasking me with this—for throwing me together with a stranger and putting the world's fate on my shoulders. But part of me is overjoyed, too. I want to shout his name, to laugh and celebrate the fact that he coded a *vaccine*.

Then, deeper down but refusing to be silent, part of me is curious about the man I spent so little time with. Cole seems to have known him well, and I want to ask him everything—how he knew my father, when they met, if he knew what his room at Cartaxus looked like. The questions spin around inside me, but every time I think about asking them, I see flashes of the scars on Cole's chest, the terrifying code in his panel. I'm not sure if I'm ready to find out just how closely my father worked with Cole.

"So we'll get the notes," Cole says, patting the side of the jeep. The rear doors swing closed, locking with the hiss of an airtight seal. "Then we can hit the road. I want to reach the border by nightfall." He pulls open the passenger-side door, gesturing for me to get in.

I walk over, admiring the jeep. It's a beast of a machine. Black and hulking, with a roof of gleaming nanosolar sheeting. Diamond-dusted tires glint beneath the armored side panels, and the windows are dark and nonreflective. The interior is finished in the standard Cartaxus palette: black trimmed with more black, and subtle hints of gold.

"This is a nice machine," I say, climbing in, setting the folder on my lap.

Cole snorts. "You don't know the half of it."

He climbs into the driver's side and pulls his door closed. The tires send out a spray of gravel as we lurch up the driveway, swinging onto the fire trail that winds around the outside of the mountain. The jeep seems to be doing most of the driving, but it still has a steering wheel, and Cole keeps one hand resting on it constantly.

"What about the clonebox?" I ask as the cabin disappears into the trees behind us. My father said we needed two things—his notes and a clonebox—to unlock the vaccine.

"I have a few ideas about where to find one."

I raise an eyebrow. Hospitals sometimes have cloneboxes, but they're usually only found in research facilities. They're rare machines, though it's debatable that you can call them machines, since, technically speaking, cloneboxes are *alive*.

If you're testing brand-new gentech code, it's not safe to try it on a person. Badly programmed code can be lethal, so scientists test their ideas on cloneboxes instead. They're two-foot cubes of steel and glass, filled with cylinders holding millions of synthetic cells in liquefied form. The cells are able to be recoded to match the DNA of whoever jacks their panel into one—to *clone* them, effectively. Only, the cells you're cloning aren't in the form of a person—they're a soup of blood and muscle and brain tissue.

It makes sense that we'd need a clonebox to study the vaccine, because the code running inside Cole is locked to his panel. When we jack him into one, the cells inside the box will act like an extension of his body, and the vaccine should spread to them. That solves the problem of getting the live code out of Cole's arm, but it doesn't help with the problem of how to *decrypt* it. The answer to that should be in my father's notes, and once we have both, we should be able to release the vaccine.

Cole leans forward, peering up at the mountains through the windshield. "Do you have neighbors?"

"Not anymore. Why?"

He squints. "I've been getting strange readings from that mountain ever since I got here. I think it might be people, but I can't tell where they are, and I'm not catching any words."

My skin prickles. "Maybe they're not talking."

"For two days?"

"They might not talk at all anymore if they're Lurkers."

Cole looks confused by the word. Of course he does. He's spent the last two years in airlocked comfort, with HEPA visors and decontamination chambers. He's probably never killed for immunity, never had to choke down a dose or see a child, lost in the Wrath, turn on their own mother.

I rub my arms, looking out the window as the trees fly past. "You know about the Wrath, right? How the scent of second-stagers makes people crazy? How it . . ."

"Makes them eat infected people?"

I nod, suddenly aware of the scent of immunity wafting from my skin and of what I did to get it. I force the thought away. "That's a neurological response, like psychosis. When the Wrath takes over, people lose themselves, and some of them never come back. We call them Lurkers. They travel in packs, and they'll kill and eat you whether or not you're infected."

Cole raises his eyebrows. "I've heard stories about people like that, but I always thought it was Cartaxus propaganda: Don't leave the bunkers or you'll get murdered by people who kill for sport."

I shake my head. "It's not like that. They're more like wild animals, like bears or wolves. It's like they've regressed to their basic instincts. They seem to recognize each other, and form packs to hunt together, but they tend to stay in the woods like animals do. That's why we call them Lurkers. Don't get me wrong—they're bloodthirsty, and if you run across a pack, they'll try to kill you, but they're not hard to avoid."

"That's good," Cole says, speeding up when we hit an open stretch of the trail. "Because I'd like to avoid them *completely.*"

The trail rises through the forest, winding closer to the entrance to the mines. Cole keeps peering through the windshield, frowning, as though trying to see something hidden in the trees on the mountain.

I open the folder on my lap. He glances over. "Where did you find that?" he asks. "I thought I checked everywhere."

"In the basement, behind the cabinets." I flip through the loose mix of stained papers. Most are scribbled diagrams and calculations, nothing that can help us. My father must have used a kind of encryption on the vaccine that he's used before, maybe in his time at the cabin. There must be instructions somewhere in his notes, but nothing I've seen so far is helpful. I shuffle through the rest of the papers in the folder, pausing when I reach a watermarked sheet with gold-embossed lettering at the top.

Cole glances over, raising an eyebrow. "You got into the biomath program at Cambridge?"

I nod, reading the letter, remembering how excited I was when it arrived. We'd only been at the cabin a few months, and I applied in secret to a special program for minors, hoping to impress my father. I sent a portfolio of my code, and they offered me a full-ride scholarship for the next year. Cambridge was where my father had studied, and I thought he'd be proud of me, but we ended up having a fight about it when he found out.

Too young, he said, and too far away. He promised to teach me more than they could. I locked myself in my room and fumed about it for days. Then Dax showed up, with his tilted smile and easy charm, and I began to see the advantages of studying at home.

I drop the letter back in the pile, staring out the window as we drive up the side of the mountain. "My father wouldn't let me go. I'd just gotten out of boarding school. I think he wanted me here for a while longer."

"Boarding school?"

"Yeah," I say. "Saint Lucia's, up in Canada. It was awful. Everyone spent all their time in VR, so I didn't have any friends. Gave me plenty of time to learn to code, though. What about you? Where did you go to school?"

Something passes across Cole's face—a wall coming down. "Military academy."

Of course. I should have guessed. There's a precision to Cole's movements, a calculated alertness in his eyes that tells me he isn't a new recruit. Most of the Cartaxus troops I've seen rely heavily on their tech and weapons, but Cole seems to have been trained for years.

"What about college?" I point to the Cambridge letter. "What were you going to study before the world ended?"

His eyes go distant for a moment, and then he shifts uncomfortably. "I don't know. I never really thought about it."

"There must have been *something*."

He shakes his head. "It's not worth thinking about."

"If you don't tell me, I'm going to start guessing. Right now, I'm thinking professional clown."

He sighs, slowing the jeep to pull us around a bend. "I wanted to study art."

"Oh." Of course. I've seen his sketches, but I didn't think about it. It's hard to reconcile the leylined soldier with the boy who wanted to draw. "Why art?"

"Why *biomath*?" he asks sarcastically.

I roll my eyes. "I'm just trying to get to know you. We're going to be stuck in this jeep all the way to Canada."

He spots the base of the hiking trail that leads to the mine's entrance before I can point it out and pulls us off the gravel road. The jeep crunches to a stop, its dash dimming. He opens his door to get out but pauses and turns to me instead. His hand picks nervously at the fabric of his pants. He doesn't *look* nervous, but that same energy I've glimpsed before is rolling off him, changing the pitch and the feel of the air. He meets my gaze and holds it so long I have to fight the urge to look away.

For the first time, I feel like I'm really seeing *him* instead of the Cartaxus soldier. He's younger than I thought, probably my age. His ice-blue eyes catch the morning light. There are a handful of tiny freckles scattered across his nose.

"You're the coder," he says finally. "What genes make someone an artist?"

I raise an eyebrow. That's a trick question, and he knows it. Most of human behavior and its relationship to DNA is still undiscovered territory. We know what genes make rats afraid of eagles, and we know why birds fly south in the winter, but the complexities of human nature are still a mystery to science.

"There's no gene for art," I say. "At least, not that anyone's been able to find so far."

He nods, with what almost looks like pain in his eyes. "*That's* why I wanted to be an artist."

He slides from his seat before I can reply and shuts the door behind him, leaving me alone in the jeep's airlocked silence with the lingering scent of his aftershave.

# CHAPTER 12

WHEN I GET OUT OF THE JEEP, COLE IS STRIDING
back up the road we just came down, his arm held aloft as if trying to
get reception. The landscape is rocky, the trees scraggly and sparse, and
from here the trail to the mine's entrance is so narrow and winding it
needs to be hiked on foot.

"Should have guessed," he says, walking to the jeep. "Come on, let's
make this quick."

"What's wrong?"

"I'm running blind, that's what's wrong. I've been setting off scans
ever since we started driving, but they're all coming back glitched. I
think it's the same thing that was giving me those strange readings in the
cabin. There's something in this mountain that's throwing off my tech."

"What, like mineral deposits?"

"No, like top-secret Cartaxus tech that shouldn't be here. Lachlan
must have stolen it when he left."

"Oh. Yeah, that sounds familiar. He wired up something in the mines to
keep the bats out of the main cavern, some kind of ultrasonic . . . thing. . . ."

"It's called a black dome." Cole knocks on the jeep's rear doors. They open with a hiss, and he climbs in, rummaging through the back. "It creates a dead zone for transmissions."

"Well, it works on bats, too."

"Great. I'll be sure to tell Cartaxus."

I glance at the mine's entrance, invoking my comm-link. There are so many places on the property without reception that I hadn't noticed it was bad near the mines. I try to load my message bank, hoping for something from Agnes, but all I get is a spinning icon. Still no calls or texts. The only thing I can think of is that she figured out that Cole was carrying the vaccine. He said the freezepaks split when they were keeping me in the ice bath, so he would have lost skin and blood. Maybe she grabbed a sample and drove straight to the Skies.

Cole shuffles out of the jeep with a backpack in his hands. He tosses it to me, and I catch it warily, stumbling with the weight. It's nanoweave, flexible but bulletproof, with the white Cartaxus antlers stitched on the back.

I look up. "What's this for?"

"It's got a medkit, a water filter, and an emergency beacon in it. I need you to wear it everywhere you go."

I roll my eyes but swing the backpack on. "Where's my gun?"

"You're not getting one."

"You're kidding, right? I thought we were working together."

"We are, but you're still not getting a gun. It's too dangerous. Let me handle the security."

"This is bullshit," I mutter, buckling the hip strap, shifting the backpack's weight. "I should have a gun, and this pack might be the most uncomfortable thing I've ever worn."

"Let me do it." He grabs the strap from me and slides one hand around the side of my waist, then holds me in place while he yanks the strap until it's snug around my hips. "How's that?"

I look up. He's suddenly right next to me, the light catching his eye-lashes, his scent wafting in the morning air. I meet his eyes for a moment, and something wordless passes between us, until I realize that his hand is still curled around my waist.

He realizes it at the same moment and pulls it back, stepping away from me. A guilty look flashes across his face.

Oh, no. Absolutely not. He did not just let his hand *linger* on my waist. I'm not sleeping in the same car as some muscle-bound jerk who thinks he can put his hands on me whenever he wants.

"Hands off, soldier," I snap, "or I'll break your fingers."

I expect him to recoil, to bluster excuses and tell me I'm overreacting, but he drops his head. "I'm sorry, I didn't mean to. I just . . ."

"Just what?" I cross my arms.

He scratches his head, embarrassed. "I just can't stop thinking about Jun Bei. You remind me a bit of her, so whenever I talk to you, I can't help but imagine how it'll feel to talk to her." He pauses. "Sorry, this is probably making you more uncomfortable. . . ."

I watch him, keeping the hardness in my gaze until I'm sure he's not just making up an excuse, then blow out a sigh. He isn't trying to make a move—he's just lovesick. I can't imagine how he feels, finding out his girlfriend is alive after so long. He must be a wreck.

"No," I say. "I get it. I just thought you were a creep."

"I know it's crazy to still care about her. She hasn't contacted me in years. You must think I'm an idiot."

"If you're an idiot, then so am I. I haven't heard from Dax since the outbreak, and I still think about him every day."

"Dax?" Cole looks up, stunned. "You're in love with *Crick*?"

He looks so shocked it makes my shoulders tighten. "We were, sort of . . . Why, is he dating someone else?"

It's been years. Of course he's moved on. I've told myself a hundred times that he would, but some stupid part of myself still pictured us getting back together when this was over.

An unreadable expression passes across Cole's face. "No, he's not. I just . . . I didn't think you'd be his *type*. But Jesus, that's perfect. Agatta and Crick. What a couple you two would make. You must have the combined IQ of a small planet."

The tension in my shoulders releases. "A medium-size planet, surely."

A beat passes, and then Cole's lips curl. "Fine, then. Medium-size."

I grin, shifting the backpack, starting up the hiking trail. "I meant what I said, just so you know. I'll break your fingers if you touch me."

He laughs, following me up the trail. "Yeah, so would Jun Bei."

"Oh, I *like* this girl. Tell me more."

He chuckles. "Well, she's tough. She could beat me up any day of the week."

I glance back, clambering over a boulder. "Really? She must be strong."

"Yeah, but she's mostly fast, and kind of vicious. She isn't above biting people, or poking them in the eye."

"Okay, I *definitely* like her." I grab a branch, pulling myself up a steep, rocky scramble and pause at the top to watch Cole climb up. He moves across the rocks with a mixture of grace and strength that makes me think of a lion.

"So did you two get separated in the outbreak?" I ask.

His smile freezes. "No, it was before that."

"Oh." I straighten. *Before* the outbreak. For some reason I assumed Cole and Jun Bei were at Cartaxus together, but that doesn't make sense. They would have been sixteen during the outbreak, and Cartaxus doesn't recruit minors. "So how did you two meet?"

He wipes a trickle of sweat from his forehead. "We were friends since we were kids."

"But how did my father know you? You said he knew Jun Bei, too. He must have met you both before the outbreak."

Something flashes across his face. A look that reminds me of the scars on his chest, of how he begged me to jack out of his panel. It lasts only a heartbeat, before a wall slams down and his eyes go flat. "Let's talk about this later," he says. "Like I said, I'm running blind without my tech. We need to find these notes and get out of here."

He heads up the trail, leaving me behind him with my intuition buzzing. I don't know what I just hit on, but something tells me it's not good. Some link between Cole, my father, and Jun Bei. Something from before the plague. I shift the backpack again and follow him up the trail, a growing sense of unease prickling inside me.

We don't speak again until we reach the entrance to the mine—a square, fortified slice of blackness cut into the mountain's side. Cole pauses at the edge of the darkness and pulls two headlamps from his pocket. Inch-wide FIPEL strips on black elastic, gold-stamped with the Cartaxus antlers. He tosses one to me, and I slip my braid through, flicking it on. The steel rails set into the rocky floor catch the light as I step into the mine. The temperature drops instantly, and my nostrils burn with a hit of ammonia and decay.

"Oh man," I whisper, choking. The bare granite walls are spotted with a thick layer of bat guano. The floor is coated with sawdust to soak up the worst of it, but it doesn't stop the smell. "You're lucky it's early. This place is unbearable in the heat."

Overhead, countless brown-furred bats squeak and jostle as we enter. Cole swings his headlamp up, but I motion for him to kill it. The flash of light makes the bats scatter, their chittering rising into a roar.

"Keep quiet unless you want a thousand of them in your face," I say. "Come on, the main storeroom is along that shaft. There aren't any bats up there, so it doesn't smell so bad."

We hurry down a narrow, sawdust-coated shaft with boxes of broken tech lining one side. My father used these mines the way most people use their garage—to store old, dusty equipment and crates of junk. The shaft climbs into the mountain until it reaches a giant, natural cave the miners must have stumbled on. White cardboard boxes are stacked on one side, and a network of shadowy, smaller caves branches off from the other. I point the boxes out to Cole, catching my breath.

"Those are his notes. There might be some in the smaller rooms, though. We should check."

Cole's eyes drift to the far wall, which is split by a foot-wide crack in the rock. "Is there a cave through that gap?"

I nod. "Yeah, a little alcove. I stored some things there. I thought it would be a good place to hide out if I ever had to leave the cabin."

"When were you last here?" Cole slings his rifle over his shoulder, walking to the edge of the cavern, glancing through the crack.

I drop my backpack on the floor. "I stayed up here for a few nights last winter. Why?"

He pulls a handful of yellow glow sticks from his pocket, cracking them to fill the room with light, and gestures to a pile of ash on the floor. "There was a fire here. Can't have been more than a few days ago."

I peer at the remains of the fire. A few charred sticks and pine needles are scattered around it. Half buried in the ash, a slender, blackened bone juts out.

It's a human fibula.

"Lurkers," I breathe. "You're right. They've been here."

Cole stares at the remains of the fire, his shoulders tensing. "Okay, let's find these notes and get out of here. I don't like this at all."

I nod quickly. "I'll look in the smaller caverns."

A narrow, twisting passageway takes me to a cavern with a towering, stalactite-covered ceiling. It's empty except for a box of unused flares leaning against an orange kayak. Cole follows me in with his rifle in his hands, his eyes flitting over the dark corners of the room, checking for Lurkers.

"Just a kayak," I say. "I have no idea why it's here."

He nods. "Check it out. I'm going to start carrying these boxes down to the jeep."

The kayak is coated in a layer of dust. I've seen it here before but don't remember using it. We had a canoe for a while at the lake, but I have no memories of anything else. I hoist it to the floor and spot a hint of something buried deeper in the cavern's wall. A cardboard box is stuffed in a narrow crevice behind the kayak.

"I found another one," I yell, dragging the box from the crevice. The cardboard is old and water stained, with only a few moldy manila folders stashed inside. I squat down and slide one out. The pages have Cartaxus letterheads and are dated from a few years after I was born.

"This is from years ago," I call out. "It's from when he was working with Cartaxus."

"Bring it," Cole shouts back, his voice echoing through the caves. "Bring anything you think might help. I'll be back in a minute."

I flip through the file, frowning. This isn't gentech research. It seems to be a diary of psychological experiments. I flip the pages, trying to understand what my father was working on, when the file falls open to a black-and-white photograph of a little boy.

He's shirtless and skinny, his arms hanging limp beside a bandaged torso, a purple-black bruise creeping down the side of his face. An IV tube is taped into his neck, and his hair has been shaved down to the skin, where a circle of stitches winds around his head.

I drop the file in the dust, choking back a cry.

The name printed across the bottom reads *Subject 5, Cole Franklin.*

# CHAPTER 13

"OH SHIT," I WHISPER, SINKING TO MY KNEES, staring at the photograph. I can see Cole's features so clearly in the little boy's face. He can't be more than five, with dark scars peeking out from the bandages across his chest, and he looks desperately unhappy. A medical report tagged behind the photograph lists his injuries: broken fingers, contusions, a detached cornea, and a pierced lung. Selective mutism, tendencies to violence, chronic insomnia.

Dozens of notes are scrawled in the margins of his DNA profile, and every single comment is in my father's handwriting. It takes me a long, sickening moment to realize what that means.

My father was experimenting on Cole when he was just a boy. The scars on his chest, the experimental code . . .

My father did that to a *child*.

I flip through the rest of the file, trying to find something that could have justified this work, but there's nothing. I can't imagine any excuse for doing this kind of research on children. It's totally unethical, highly illegal. Another photograph of Cole is stapled to a sequencing report in the back, along with a single scrawled comment from my father.

*No pain response while beta-6 is triggered! Tolerance off the charts!*

"Catarina?" Cole appears over my shoulder, wiping his forehead with a cloth.

I slam the file shut, burying it in the box. "I'm fine. I was just seeing what was in here."

"I'll take it out to the jeep, then we can go. This place is creeping me out."

"I'll take it," I blurt out, picking up the box.

"Wait a second."

I freeze, expecting Cole to grab the box and pull his file out, to explain that this is how he knew my father from before the plague. I want the truth, but I'm not ready to hear it. My hands are shaking. Every time I blink, I see a flash of Cole's scarred, bandaged chest.

He lifts up my backpack. "Can you put this on? I mean it when I say I need you to wear this all the time."

"Oh," I say quietly. I set the box down and sling on the backpack, not bothering to buckle the hip strap. I grab the box and shuffle along the passageway, clutching the moldy cardboard to my chest. The bats screech as I hurry through the entrance and down the trail, my feet somehow finding each step on autopilot.

*No pain response,* the file said. *Tolerance off the charts!*

What was my father doing measuring a little boy's response to pain?

The back of the jeep is open, and I push the moldy box in, pausing to yank out Cole's file and flip it open again. The little boy stares up at me, gaunt and terrified.

Scarred and stitched up by my father's own hands.

The box holds four more files identical to Cole's. In a snap decision, I grab them all and shove them into my backpack, then scramble up the trail and back into the mines. When I emerge from the passageways,

Cole stands hunched in the main room. I can barely bring myself to look at him.

"I've double-checked all the rooms except the little alcove," he says. "I can't get through that crack."

"There are no files in there."

"Can you make sure?"

I nod, dropping the backpack, happy for any excuse to avoid talking to him face-to-face until I can pull myself together. I duck into the foot-wide crack in the rock face, angling my hips into a channel I have to stand on tiptoe to reach. My chin grazes against the stone, and the rough sides bruise my ribs every time I inhale, shuffling sideways an inch at a time.

"I've changed my mind," Cole calls out. "I don't like this. Come back, please."

"It's fine, I'm almost there." I reach for the edge of the gap and drag myself the last few inches, stumbling into the alcove. My headlamp dances across the walls, lighting up a stack of nutriBars and my crumpled sleeping bag. I brought supplies in here a few times, setting myself up with an emergency shelter to hide in if a fire came through the hills.

I lift the sleeping bag with the toe of my boot. A bundle of under-wear spills out, revealing a couple of yellowed books and the dull sheen of an antique revolver.

Mother-of-pearl handle, ivy-leaf molding. I'd forgotten all about this gun. Agnes gave it to me, but I always preferred the rifle. Longer range, better accuracy, easier to snipe from cover. The revolver's cylinder still holds two bullets. I lift it slowly and turn it in my hand, wondering whether to keep it.

Cole won't give me a gun, but that doesn't mean I can't bring my own. I briefly consider hiding it in my waistband, but I know that's a stupid idea. He'll notice it in a heartbeat, and two bullets won't get me far, anyway. I set it back down on the floor again, still trying to make up my mind.

"There's nothing here," I call out. "No notes, at least."

A beat of silence hangs in the air, but Cole doesn't reply.

"Cole?" I call, looking back through the crack. The main room is empty, and all I can hear are the bats' shrieks, louder than they should be. Louder than they were when we came in. My audio implants tick up, searching for Cole through the roar of the bats.

The sound of muffled laughter echoes off the walls.

I flick off my headlamp and dive into cover. A man's footsteps pound into the main room, then turn and retreat again. I catch the barest glimpse in the yellow light of the glow sticks, but it's all I need to know that we're in serious trouble.

Dirt-crusted skin. Blackened nails. Tattered, blood-smeared clothing. The Lurkers must have hidden when they saw the jeep.

Now they've come for us.

"Catarina?" Cole's voice is a whisper through the roar of the bats. "Can you hear me?"

"Yes," I breathe, pressed flat against the wall.

"There are four of them. They might not know you're here, and they might not be able to get to you through that crack. I need you to stay in there, whatever happens."

"Okay."

"Keep quiet." Cole runs out of the main room, his footsteps echoing through the shafts. The sound bounces off the walls, merging with the hurricane of leather wings until I can't track him anymore.

A sudden shout of surprise from one of the Lurkers echoes wildly, followed by a burst of gunfire that saturates my audio tech. I wince, the blare of static fading just in time for me to hear the thuds of three bodies slumping to the floor.

Cole said there were four of them. Three down, one to go. I close my eyes, focusing on the sounds, trying to hear what's happening.

Footsteps echo in the main shaft, and the last Lurker lets out a roar. He's running fast, spraying the walls with bullets. Cole's rifle is almost silent, but I can hear him firing regular, careful shots. Both are getting closer, moving into the main room. A burst of gunfire bites into the walls, and I catch a glimpse of Cole racing into one of the side tunnels.

The gunshots cease. I can hear two sets of lungs, both panting, both in cover on the edges of the room. I don't think the Lurker can see me from where he is, but my eyes dart to the mother-of-pearl revolver on the floor.

It's lying in the middle of the crack, in plain sight of the main cavern. The silver is dull, but it still catches the gleam of the glow sticks. I must have kicked it into the crack when I scrambled to the wall, and now it could lead the Lurker straight to me. I drop to my knees and reach forward to grab it just as another burst of gunfire erupts.

A wild spray of bullets slams into the cave walls. One hits the back of the alcove, and I throw myself backward, the gun clutched in my hands. Chips of rock spray out from the impact, slicing a gash across my wrist. A puff of sawdust floats through the crack as something hits the floor outside.

Without looking, without listening, I already know what's happened. I can feel it like a kick to the stomach.

Cole's been hit.

In a moment of panic, I jerk my head to the crack, catching a glimpse of the Lurker. He's in a tattered leather jacket, his hair in matted clumps.

He picks up Cole's rifle in one filthy hand. Cole is lying on his back in front of the alcove, but I can't see where he was shot.

I slide back out of sight, pressing myself against the wall. Cole is hurt. He needs my help. I look down at the revolver in my hands.

"Tried to hurt me," the Lurker growls, pacing around the room. He's limping, breathing heavily. "Shouldn't have *come* here." His words have a strange inflection, his cadence off-kilter. All the Lurkers I've come across sound like that—the ones who can still speak, that is. Some talk only in snarls, abandoning language as they descend into pure savagery.

Cole doesn't reply.

I risk another glance through the crack. In the dim light of the glow sticks, I can see his hand pressed to his stomach. He's alive, but he's badly wounded. His shirt is soaked with blood. The Lurker ambles past, and I dart back into cover.

"Going to kill you now," the Lurker says. I can hear the sneer in his voice.

"G-go on, then," Cole stutters. "Take your best shot."

"Reckon I will."

"I reckon . . . ," Cole starts, then groans with pain. He sucks in a breath. "I reckon you're batshit."

The Lurker chuckles, a deep sound that echoes off the walls. He stops pacing, coming to a stop on the other side of Cole. A metallic click rings out as he cocks Cole's rifle.

There is no conscious thought in my mind as I stand and swing around.

I pull the trigger. The bullet flies through the crack and catches the Lurker square in the chest.

In the space of a breath, my world splits into choppy, broken frames. The Lurker howls, his bloodshot gaze snapping to me. He swings the rifle up, and Cole's head snaps around, shouting for me to hide. But his voice is lost in a roar of static. There is only me and my target. I exhale and fire my final bullet.

The Lurker's skull explodes. Blood splatters the walls. His body slumps into a crumpled heap on the floor.

I drop the gun, swaying on my feet.

"Catarina!" Cole roars.

"I'm coming!" I shout, scrambling through the gap in the rock. I fall to my knees beside him and grab the medkit from my backpack. I tear open a packet of gauze with my teeth and press it to the gaping wound in his stomach.

"Oh, Jesus," I whisper as his blood bubbles up between my fingers.

"Th-the bullet," he gasps. "It's nanite rigged. You need to get it out and cauterize the wound to stop the spread. It's interfering with my healing tech."

I lift the gauze. There's nothing but torn flesh and oozing, pulsing blood. I don't know how to get the bullet out or cauterize this without killing him. Nanite-rigged bullets are lethal if they're not removed. Cole needs a surgeon, or he'll die.

"I can do better," I breathe. "You just need to hang on a few minutes. There's a doctor in town, a friend of Agnes's—he can help you. Do you think you can get to the jeep?"

Cole nods stiffly, his eyes still black, then moans as he staggers to his feet. I throw the backpack on and duck under his arm to help him down the shaft. He drags his rifle through the sawdust with one shaking hand.

"Okay, you're doing great," I whisper. We burst into the sunlight, stumbling down the trail and back to the jeep.

Cole falls into the passenger seat and tosses his gun into the back. "You're going to have to drive. My tech is glitching out."

I scramble in and grab the steering wheel. The seat is made for a body bigger than mine, and the dashboard is a smooth, curved LED screen. There are a thousand icons about weather and perimeter scans, but nothing to start the engine. Nothing to tell me how to *drive*.

Cole grunts, leaning forward to press his forearm to the dash. The display changes to a map of our surroundings, and the engine growls to life.

"Thanks," I say, pulling the seat belt around me. If I had a better panel, I could just mentally picture where to go, and the autodriver would take us there. But I can't even see an icon to load the GPS or enter a destination. I'm going to have to get us to the doctor's on my own.

"I haven't really done this before." I shoot a nervous glance at Cole. "We're going to make it, I promise, but you should probably still hang on."

A hint of pressure on the accelerator is all I need to send the jeep surging forward, snapping a sapling in half as we plow into a copse of trees. The brakes kick in automatically, and I twist in the seat to reverse, then send us speeding back down the fire trail, racing toward the cabin.

An alert on the dash picks me up as an untrained driver, and the autodriver kicks in, following the curves of the fire trail for me. It seems to sense my urgency, and maybe it even knows Cole is hurt, because we take the turns at a terrifying speed. I keep turning the wheel and using the pedals, but the jeep is an alien beast, hauling itself around the bends as it attunes itself to my driving. Valves hiss on the floor and the seat shudders as it folds and shrinks, rising slowly until it hugs my body perfectly.

"Where did you get that gun?" Cole asks. His face is ashen and streaked with sweat. The pad of gauze on his stomach is already soaked with blood.

"In the alcove, I'd forgotten about it."

He grits his teeth. "I told you to let me handle the security."

"Seriously?" I swing the jeep across a hill, cutting cross-country to the road at the edge of the property. "I just saved your life, as I recall."

"I had it under control."

"Didn't look like it from where I was standing. That bastard was getting ready to shoot you with your own gun."

"That was the plan."

I let out a choked laugh. "Getting shot? I think you're losing too much blood."

He lets out a grunt of pain. "The gun wouldn't work for him. It's coded to my panel."

"What do you mean, *coded*?"

Cole winces as we swerve around a boulder, flying full speed toward the fence at the edge of the property. "It's locked to my panel. I set it to defensive mode, which means if he tried to shoot me with it, it would have backfired and killed him instead."

The jeep crashes through the fence and hurtles onto the road, its tires screeching as we spin around to head south.

"Oh," I murmur. "I didn't realize."

Cole lifts the gauze to peek at his wound and presses it back, closing his eyes. "I need you to stay in cover when I tell you to."

"I don't take *orders* from you," I say, flooring the accelerator. "We're in this together. That's the only way this works."

"You staying alive is how this works, Catarina. I'm not giving you *orders*. I'm trying to protect you, like I've been trained to. You're my responsibility."

*My responsibility.* Who the hell does he think he is? I spin the jeep around a bend, rocks and dust flying into the trees. "You know, a simple thank-you would suffice."

"If you had stayed behind cover like I *told* you, then none of this would have happened."

"What do you mean? The only time I came out of cover was to shoot the Lurker, and you were already shot . . ."

My voice falls away as I realize that's not true. I replay the scene in my mind. I was pressed against the wall when Cole killed the first three Lurkers, and then . . .

Then I crawled out of cover to grab the gun right as the Lurker started firing.

"You took that bullet because it was going to hit me."

Cole doesn't reply. His face is white, his fingers tight on the gauze.

"Cole, was that bullet going to hit me?"

He rolls his head away from me, his eyelashes beaded with sweat. "There was a forty percent chance of it hitting you, according to my equipment."

I choke, flooring the accelerator, my hands shaking on the wheel. "Forty percent? Jesus, Cole. Why did you trade that for a hundred percent chance of being shot?"

He swallows. "I didn't. Black-out agent, remember? I'm not always in control."

I glance over at his stomach, at the wash of blood across his shirt. He took a bullet for me. He saved my life, and here I was thinking I'd saved *him*.

"This is my job, Catarina. This is what I'm trained to do."

"I know," I say, my eyes fixed on the road. I have no doubt of Cole's need to protect me, not anymore. I just don't want to be the cause of his death.

I veer the jeep off the road and through a gap in the trees, hauling us up a rocky, overgrown driveway. This is the doctor Agnes and I were going to the night Cole arrived. He was a neurosurgeon back before the plague. I used to babysit his daughters. His wife bred prize-winning horses, showed them all around the country.

They ate the last mare over the winter.

"This is it," I say as we hurtle down the driveway. "Just a couple more minutes and the doc will have you back to normal."

Cole doesn't reply. His hand is still lying on his stomach, but his fingers are hanging loosely and his forehead is shiny with sweat.

"Come on!" I yell, elbowing him as we swing around a corner. "Stay with me, asshole." He doesn't have much longer if he keeps bleeding like this. Not long enough to haul him inside and get the bullet out.

I let the autodriver take over, twisting in my seat to reach into the back.

"What are you doing?" Cole whispers.

"Just hang on." I haul out my genkit. There's a piece of code my father used on the night I hacked my panel, when I was bleeding out on the cabin floor. It's called a jump, and it releases a violent surge of synthetic hormones and chemicals that swarm through the body, shocking the nervous system. It's painful, and it's dangerous. There's a chance it'll kill Cole, but he's on the verge of death right now, and I don't have much of a choice.

I flip the genkit open and jam the wire into his panel, urging the hard drive to spin up as the jeep barrels down the driveway. The screen blinks to life, and my fingers race across the keyboard, navigating through my stored files, searching for the code. Cole's panel lets me in using its new password, and the genkit's screen flashes with a burst of emergency messages.

"I know," I growl. I know his blood pressure is dropping. I know his vitals are low. What I don't know is whether jumping him will save or kill him.

"What . . . ," Cole whispers again, just as I find the file.

My fingers hover over the keyboard. I don't know how this code is going to work. My father wrote it specifically for me. It might clash with whatever tech they put inside Cole and kill him instantly.

"I'm sorry," I say as blood trickles from beneath the gauze, spilling over his belt. His lips form a word, but no sound comes out. In that moment he looks so close to death that I can feel his life rising from his chest, unfurling in the slow breath he exhales. For a moment I pause, lost in doubt.

Then his eyes flutter, and I realize that he's dying, truly *dying*.

My fingers blur across the keys as I send the command.

# CHAPTER 14

FOR A MOMENT COLE SITS BESIDE ME, PALE AND deathly still, as the jeep bounces across the potholes in the doctor's driveway.

"Come on," I whisper, but he's not breathing. He's not moving. Maybe his body couldn't handle the jump.

"Cole!" I urge, grabbing his face. "You can't die, dammit!"

His body jerks suddenly, his head slamming back into the seat. The cobalt dots of his panel flash wildly. The genkit lets out a series of high-pitched beeps, and his eyes blink wide, his body shaking with violent spasms. He throws his head back, letting out a roar, and his hand shoots up, hitting my chest hard enough to slam me against the window.

"Cole!" I shout, jerking into a ball, one leg caught below the steering wheel. The jeep's dash flashes red, and it shudders to a stop. "Cole, stop it!"

But his expression doesn't change. His eyes are sharklike, glassy and blank. He's staring at me like he doesn't even know who I am.

I bat at his arm, and his lips curl back. I scramble behind me for the door handle, wrench it open, and tumble out into the grass.

"Stop it, you psychopath. You're hurt!" I struggle to my feet.

He pauses, swaying in the seat, the pad of gauze slipping from his wound. "Catarina?" Recognition flickers in his eyes. "I feel . . . I feel cold."

"That's because I jumped your panel. You're dying, Cole. I need you to sit down so I can take you to the doctor."

He looks down at his hands, bloodied and shaking, and blinks slowly at the gaping wound in his stomach. "Oh shit," he whispers, falling into the passenger seat. He grabs another pad of gauze as I climb back into the jeep.

"I must be crazy," I mutter. We surge forward again. "I thought you were programmed to *protect* me."

"I glitched out."

"Yeah? That's one hell of a glitch."

"How much time do I have?" He unfurls an IV from the medkit, holding the saline bag in his teeth. He slides the cannula into his arm. His panel is still flashing, resetting itself as the jump's nanites race through his cells. He stares at his forearm, blinking repeatedly as though trying to turn it back on.

"A few minutes," I say. "You're running on some seriously unholy tech. We're almost at the doc's. You just need to hang on a little longer."

"Who is this doctor?"

"A friend." I grab the steering wheel, trying to dodge the worst of the potholes.

"Do you trust him?"

I glance over at Cole. Marcus, the doctor, is a member of the Skies, and he hates Cartaxus even more than I do. Cole is clearly one of their soldiers, and we're arriving in one of their jeeps, but I have to believe that Marcus will help us.

"Yes," I say, flooring the accelerator. "I trust this man completely."

The driveway rises, disappearing into a grove of towering cedars whose shadows race across the hood as Marcus's house inches out of the trees. It's a two-story log cabin, its windows boarded over. The yard is overgrown, littered with trash. Marcus's car is gone.

"Come on . . . ," I breathe, scanning the house. We skid to a stop. "Where are they?"

"I don't know. It looks . . ." I can't bring myself to say it. It looks abandoned. Hopeless.

"They're gone," Cole says. He closes his eyes. The color is already draining from his face. "It's okay, Cat."

The calmness in his voice stuns me. Something inside me tightens. "No," I say, swinging the door open. "I'm going to find them."

He grabs my wrist before I can get out. "They're gone. This isn't your fault, but you need to work fast. Go into the back and get some paper to mark down the route to the lab. You'll need to cut my panel out and freeze it, or you'll lose the vaccine. Then you just have to make it to the lab. You can do this."

"Cole, please," I whisper. "Maybe I can stop the bleeding. Let's go inside."

"There's not enough time." His eyes soften. "It's important you keep going. Now get some paper, hurry."

I back out of the jeep, my eyes swimming with tears, stumbling blindly to the back. When I swing the rear doors open, something whistles past my ear, hitting a tree behind me with a crack.

Cole swings around, staring at me. I notice with a shock that his eyes are blue. The jump rebooted his panel, which means his implants aren't working yet. We could be surrounded by Lurkers, and neither of us would know. He's running blind without his tech. He grabs his gun and lurches from the jeep, letting the blood-soaked bandage fall to the ground.

"Cole, no!" I shout, but I have no plan, no options, just a dying man and a stranger's gunfire from the trees. It could be Marcus, or it could be Lurkers. Either way, if I wait much longer, Cole is going to bleed out.

"Marcus!" I scream, running into the driveway, my hands held high. "Marcus, please! We're not with Cartaxus. Please, we need your help!"

A moment of silence stretches out. Cole's eyes are wide and frantic. He grits his teeth, scanning the trees.

A figure steps into the driveway, staring down the barrel of a rifle. "Catarina? Is that really you?"

"Yes!" I shout, laughing with relief. "I'm so glad you're here, Marcus. I thought you were gone."

Marcus lowers the rifle, looking warily at Cole. His two daughters emerge from the trees behind him. The younger, Eloise, has pink ribbons in her hair, and her face lights up as soon as she sees me. Her older sister, Chelsea, watches Cole suspiciously. Deep shadows hang beneath her darting, cautious eyes.

"I know how this looks, Marcus," I call out. "The jeep, the gear, I *know*. But I need you to trust me. This man is a friend of my father."

Marcus looks down at Cole's wound and gives me a tight smile. "Then he's a friend of mine, whoever he works for. Let's get him inside."

Marcus sends his daughters in to get his surgical bag, and he slips under one of Cole's arms to help him into the house. Cole's face goes ghostly white, his feet dragging as we haul him into Marcus's kitchen. The wooden table is crosshatched with scratches, the windows splattered with blood that Marcus and his wife, Amy, must have given up cleaning long ago.

"The bullet was nanite rigged," I say, helping Cole up to the table. "It's interfering with his healing tech. I jumped his panel a few minutes ago. I was losing him on the way here. I didn't have a choice."

Marcus rips Cole's shirt open to pull the fabric from the wound. "That's probably the only thing keeping him alive, but you've taken a hell of a risk. His healing tech has completely stalled. We're going to have to fight to keep him stable until we can get the bullet out and get his tech running again." He turns from the table and pours a bottle of disinfectant into the sink, then scrubs his hands up to his elbows.

Chelsea runs into the kitchen with Marcus's briefcase, a battered portmanteau filled with scalpels and a gleaming saw. She swaps out Cole's IV, hooking a bag of anesthetic into his arm. "I'll scrub up, Daddy," she says, rolling up her sleeves.

I raise my eyebrows. Chelsea's just a kid. "Doesn't your mom normally help with surgeries?"

"She's not feeling well," Chelsea says, dunking her hands in the sink. She lifts them out slowly, scrubbing with the careful motions of a professional. "Don't worry. I know what I'm doing."

"Yeah, I guess you do."

"I think we might get lucky." Marcus pulls out a scalpel. "His tech is coming back online, and he looks like a strong lad."

"Good," I say, swallowing. This kind of scene doesn't usually bother me, but for some reason the sight of Cole on Marcus's table is hitting me hard. His skin is pale, dotted with sweat, his blood trickling to the floor. He looks so weak, and so *vulnerable*. I can't stop staring at his chest, watching it rise and fall, my stomach tightening every time there's a pause in his breathing. Chelsea drives a long, gleaming syringe into his stomach, and the sight makes me sway, grabbing the wall for support.

I dig my fingernails into my palm, trying to tell myself that my response is rational, that I'm just worried about Cole because I need him to unlock the vaccine. But I know it's more than that. I've known him less than two days, but there's already a bond between us, forged in blood and urgency. Part of me feels like we know each other now on some fundamental level.

I guess seeing someone take a bullet to save your life will do that.

Chelsea looks up at me, her hands still gripped on the syringe. "You don't look so good, Cattie. You want to wait in the living room?"

I pause. My instinct is to stay, but my stomach is turning over, and I don't know if I can stand here and watch much longer. "I . . . ," I start, but Marcus slides a pair of tweezers into Cole's wound, and that's it. That's all I can take.

"I'll wait out there," I murmur, backing into the living room. Cole is in Marcus's hands now. There's nothing I can do for him.

Two hours later, I'm sitting cross-legged on the couch with Eloise asleep with her head in my lap. A headache is pounding at the base of my skull. It's the migraine that I've known was coming ever since I woke up in the cabin yesterday. They always build up slowly and then bring days of pain that I have no escape from, not since I ran out of painkillers. I sit as still as is humanly possible to minimize the spikes of pain that flood my senses with every beat of Cole's heart.

It's all I can hear. My audio implants are maxed out, tracking every clink of steel in the kitchen, every word, every breath. Cole is still alive, and the bleeding has stopped. It sounds like he's stabilizing. Marcus thinks his tech is taking over the healing process.

It's hard for me to admit to myself just how relieved that makes me.

Eloise murmurs in her sleep. I run one hand absently through her hair, watching her eyelashes flutter on her cheeks. She gets the occasional tremor, but they're not nearly as bad as they used to be when I first met her, years ago. She's the reason Marcus's family joined the Skies, and she's why they're still out here, instead of in a bunker. She was born with nucleatoxis disease, a genetic disorder that has no cure, no treatment, and is essentially a death sentence. It's so rare that Cartaxus and the other pharmacoders never bothered to develop a cure, even though the disease is easy to treat with gentech. Faced with no other option, desperate families like Marcus's started writing cures of their own, pooling their knowledge. They built a database of open-source gentech code for thousands of rare diseases that eventually grew into the Skies.

Novak was their leader, even before the plague. She had Creutzfeldt-Jakob disease and hacked a Cartaxus concussion app into a cure to save her own life. It was a brilliant piece of code, but Cartaxus sued her for copyright infringement. She fought them for the right to keep using it, and the community rallied around her. A group of ordinary people who refused to watch helplessly as their loved ones died. Self-taught, self-tested, self-financed. Some of them started writing impressive code and giving it away for free.

They scared the hell out of Cartaxus.

That was before Hydra. In the pre-outbreak days it seemed like almost everyone had at least one amateur app on their panel. An aesthetic tweak, a stimulant. But Cartaxus wiped that code from the panels of everyone who entered their bunkers, so if Marcus and his family showed up at Homestake, they'd have to delete the hacked code keeping Eloise alive. It's a ridiculous requirement. What use are airlocks and protection from the virus when your ten-year-old daughter is dead?

I look up as my audio tech picks up Amy stirring in her bedroom down the hall. Footsteps pad across her room, and something heavy scrapes the floor. Her door creaks open, and her figure appears in the hallway, hunched and trembling.

"Hello?" she calls out, her voice low and rasping.

"Amy?" I ask. "It's Catarina Agatta. Chelsea said you weren't feeling well."

She shuffles closer, her face hidden in shadow. A thick gray blanket is slung over her shoulders. She's shivering, her breath coming in painful gasps.

"Amy?" I shift Eloise off my lap. "Amy, are you okay?"

"Voices," she says. "I heard voices."

"That's Marcus and Chelsea. They're doing a surgery. . . ." I trail off, stunned into silence as she steps into the light.

Her eyes are sunken, her mouth twisted down horribly on one side, her skin dotted with open, weeping sores. Her scalp is almost bare, a few stringy white strands falling from a scabbed, bleeding skull that sports rudimentary horns.

She looks like a *monster.*

"Amy?" I choke out. The mutated wraith in the hallway is nothing like the laughing, pretty woman I remember. Her spine is twisted, her hands stretched and curved horribly by some butchered chimpanzee gene shoved in the wrong place. My eyes race across her body, spotting the signs of at least a dozen rogue genes. Python, rat, bovine—all hacked and shoved together without any understanding of what they'd do to her.

In all my life, all my time with the Skies, I've never seen anyone so mutated.

Eloise scrambles up. "Mommy, you're not supposed to be up. You're sick."

"I heard voices," she says. She steps forward, and the blanket slips from her shoulders. Iron manacles gleam around her wrists, chained to a ring around her waist.

"Amy," I whisper. "What happened to you?"

Her eyes snap to mine, and I step back instinctively. She looks *wild* suddenly. She stalks closer, her mouth curling up in a sneer.

"Amy?"

She lunges for me, snarling, revealing a mouth of yellowed fangs.

I skitter back into the couch, scrambling over it to the wall. The chain around her waist snags tight, jerking her body back. She growls, twisting in the restraints like an animal caught in a trap. Her eyes are flat and inhuman, locked on my neck.

"Stop it, Mommy!" Eloise shouts.

"She's a Lurker," I gasp, grabbing Eloise's shoulders. "You can't keep her here. It's not safe, sweetheart. This is the Wrath."

"No, Mommy's just sick," Eloise says. "She's getting better, but she needs to rest."

"Stay away from her, Eloise." My eyes dart to the heavy chain slung between Amy's hands. "Who did this to her?"

Marcus swings open the kitchen door. His face gleams with sweat, his plastic apron splattered with blood. "Your friend has stabilized," he says, wiping his forehead with the back of his wrist. "I removed the bullet and cauterized the wound." His eyes cut to his snarling wife. He stiffens. "Chelsea, Eloise," he barks. "Get your mother back into her room and lock the door."

The girls guide their mother back down the hallway. Somehow Amy doesn't seem to want to attack her daughters like she did me. She's still talking, so she hasn't lost herself completely to the madness yet, but the slide is inevitable. It won't be safe to keep her here for long, even chained up and locked away.

Marcus wipes his bloodied hands on his apron. I just stare at him, my heart pounding. "Did you do that to her, Marcus? Mutate her like that?"

"No," he says, his face falling. "No, child, I didn't do that. She downloaded the code herself when she realized she was slipping. It worked, but the cost to her body was too high, and the Wrath started coming through anyway, so I turned the damned cure off and chained her up to keep us safe. Now I'm just trying to heal her, waiting for safer code."

My head spins. "What *code*? There's no cure for the Wrath."

"There are several," Marcus says, "but none are guaranteed, and as you can see, they have their side effects. People are working on this all over the world, Catarina. We're not the only family that's seen a loved one slip."

"But that's crazy." I rub my forehead, wincing through the migraine. "The Wrath is a *neurological* condition—you can't cure it with code. Gentech doesn't change people's brains."

"Not yet," Marcus says, "but it will one day. You of all people should know that. People said it was impossible to code robust antivirals until your father did it. It just takes time and research. We're getting closer every day. The code Amy downloaded was written by thousands of families, all trying to save their loved ones from the Wrath."

I slump back down on the couch, letting my head drop into my hands. This kind of coding is the essence of the Skies—no rules, no trials, no safeguards—but I haven't seen it mutate anyone as badly as this before. Science has a long history of self-experimentation, and I'm sure Amy knew the risks she was taking, but the sight of her scabbed horns sets my teeth on edge.

It's butchery. It's inhumane. But Cartaxus is no better. The photograph of a five-year-old Cole with scars on his chest is proof of that. Did my father really do that to him? My skull pounds with pain. I just want to wake up and start this day over again.

"You have a migraine, don't you? Are you still getting them?"

"Yeah," I say, rubbing the back of my head. I visited Marcus a while back when I ran out of painkillers. He didn't have any pills, only gentech code I couldn't use. "It's probably just stress, but it's the worst I've had in ages."

"Seeing someone get shot tends to be stressful, yes," Marcus says, swinging open a cupboard beside the couch. "Chelsea and I did a supply run recently, and . . . Ah, here we go." He pulls out a tray of syringes, lifting one up triumphantly. "Analgesic, basic dose. I only have the injectable kind, because it's formulated for arthritis, but it should take the edge off your migraine."

I eye the syringes warily, but pull my sleeve up over my shoulder. With painkillers, I'll be able to drive. The jeep can do most of the work, and Cole can sleep in the back. We might not make it far, but we can get on the road tonight.

"Thank you, Marcus. You don't know how much this is going to help."

He slides the needle into my shoulder. It kicks in instantly—a bucket of water tossed over a fire, extinguishing the blaze in my skull. I close my eyes, tilting my head back, lost in the sudden joyous weightlessness that comes with the absence of pain.

"That's great . . . ," I murmur, sinking into the couch. All over my body, my nerves are flickering off, falling silent, like a blackout spreading through a city. My lips tingle, my eyelids strangely heavy as I try to open them, to push myself up from the couch . . .

But I can't move.

"Marcus," I breathe, confused, my vision growing foggy. I see him standing over me, his two daughters appearing at his side.

"This is what we've been praying for, girls," he murmurs, his voice growing distant.

"Good work, Daddy," Chelsea says. "I'll go and get a scalpel."

# CHAPTER 15

I WAKE DRENCHED IN SWEAT, STARING WILDLY around me. My breath, rushing from my lips, sounds rough and unfamiliar. Everything looks blurry and strange. My eyes flit around the room, my heart rate pitching higher as I realize what's different.

I'm seeing the world through natural, unfiltered eyes.

My lungs empty in a gasp. My sensory tech is gone. It's been years since my implants have been switched off like this. I've always had their base levels in the background, fine-tuning my reality.

Now everything feels wrong.

My breathing sounds rasping and foreign, and my skin is a vague, blurry tan. I'm used to glancing at my hands and seeing every pore, but now my brain has to scramble to recognize them as *hands*. It's like seeing the world upside down, with all the colors switched around.

What the hell did Marcus do to me?

My eyes drop to my forearm, my vision spinning. All the glowing dots of my panel are gone, with a row of stitches in their place. A three-inch gash throbs along my arm, swabbed with yellow antiseptic.

The bastard knocked me out, then cut open my arm.

The thought makes me want to be sick. I press my fingers around the stitches, searching desperately, making out the soft edges of the silicone beneath my skin. I let out a sigh of relief. I don't know what Marcus did to me, but at least my panel is still there.

I stand up shakily, but my arm snags and I fall back to the couch, finding a cannula in my wrist with an IV curling out of it.

"Marcus!" I yell, yanking at the IV, hissing as it slides from my vein. "Marcus, what the hell have you done?"

"Shh," he whispers, running in from the hallway. He makes a gesture with his hands, but the movement just makes my head spin.

My brain isn't used to following moving objects without my panel. My ocular tech is primitive compared to most people's, but I never realized how much it streamlined my sense of reality. With my implants running, everything in my peripheral vision was sharpened. Now I feel like I'm looking through a narrow, blurry tunnel.

"You're fine," Marcus says, dropping down beside me. "You're more than fine, my dear. You've saved our family is what you've done. I'm sorry about the incision, but I had to take it. The firewalls wouldn't let me transfer the code."

"What do you mean, *take it*?"

It suddenly hits me, and my blood runs cold. My fingers slide to my wrist, to a divot in the silicone of my panel, right where one of my function cores is supposed to be.

My healing tech. He took it. I stare at my arm, my stomach heaving. He cut out my healing tech's function core to steal the code. There is no method of transferring gentech that's more brutal than that.

The grid of silicone that forms a panel's body has spaces for thousands of apps, each kept separately in its own function core. The cores are designed to be removable, like cards in an old-school computer, but you can't just *cut* them out like this. You're supposed to eject them slowly, retracting the interconnecting wires, balancing the panel's delicate operating system. Cutting one out like this could damage my tech permanently. My panel might never turn on again.

I grab Marcus's collar, yanking him closer. "What the hell have you done?"

"Easy, easy," he says, backing away. "I needed the neural code your father left you. I knew if there was anything that could help us, he would have been the one to write it, and might have left it with you. Turns out he did. It was just what we needed for Amy."

I drop my hands from his collar, speechless. This can't be happening. There's no such thing as neural code—apps that can change the brain—it's just a myth. Gentech can't do that, and it can't turn Lurkers who've lost their minds, like Marcus's wife, back into the people they were before.

"I didn't have any goddamn *neural* code," I say. "You cut out my healing tech, Marcus. I only had six apps, and now none of them are working."

"They'll be fine. Your panel will regenerate the core in no time."

"No it won't," I spit. "I don't even have a backup node." I press my hands to my face. A backup node is a compressed version of your panel's code, backed up every day so you can regrow it if it's damaged. Most people have one or two lodged somewhere in their bodies, but my father never designed one to work with my hypergenesis-friendly tech.

That means my healing code is gone, forever. Maybe the rest of my apps will recover, but there's a chance Marcus has damaged them beyond repair. He's lost his mind. He drugged me, sliced me open . . .

I look up suddenly. "Where's Cole?"

"He's fine. He's waking up now."

"Then we don't have much time." I look down at my arm, the fire of my anger quelled with a rush of fear. I don't know how Cole's black-out tech will respond when he finds out that Marcus did this, but I know it won't be good.

"Look, Catarina, I know you're angry—"

"You're damn right I'm angry, but I happen to care about your daughters, and I don't want them to get hurt. We need to cover these stitches."

"Why, what's wrong?"

I grope around the couch for my jacket. "Didn't you see Cole's implants, Marcus? Did you see his leylines? He's a Cartaxus *black-out agent*, and he's been tasked with protecting me. You need to bandage my arm, and I'll get him out of here before he realizes what you've done."

The color drains from Marcus's face. He turns and hurries into the kitchen, leaving the door swinging behind him. I catch a glimpse of Cole—bandaged and bleary, rubbing his eyes, sitting up on the kitchen table.

"Catarina," he calls, his voice slurred. "Where are you?"

Marcus darts back through the door, unrolling a bundle of gauze with fumbling hands. I snatch it from him and wind it around my forearm.

"I'm okay!" I shout. "Marcus is bandaging my wrist."

"What's wrong with your wrist?" Cole's voice is suddenly sharp.

"Nothing, just a scratch. I got hit by a chip of rock in the mines. Marcus cleaned it for me."

Marcus takes the end of the gauze to wrap it around my wrist, sweat beading on his forehead.

"You were hurt?" Cole's voice is softer now. He shuffles across the room and pulls the door open, leaning his shoulder against the frame.

His torso is smeared with yellow antiseptic, and there's a patch of gauze taped to his stomach. He looks thinner, somehow, as though his body has chewed itself up to heal his wound.

"I'm fine," I say, my teeth gritted. "It's just a scratch."

Marcus ties off the gauze and steps back, his hands trembling. "Looks like you're all set. Let me help you to your vehicle."

"Could we stay for a while?" Cole asks, rubbing his eyes. "I'm not sure I'm ready to get back on the road."

"No, let's go," I say, stepping to Cole, taking his arm. "I can drive. Don't worry, I'll get us to the lab. I feel fine."

It's the truth. Despite the anger boiling inside me, I *do* feel fine. Whatever Marcus knocked me out with, it's wiped away every last trace of my migraine. My head is clear, despite the fact that my eyes seem unable to stay focused without my tech.

"What lab?" Amy emerges from the hallway, with Chelsea and Eloise on either side of her.

My jaw drops. She looks *lucid*.

Her scabbed, horned skull is wrapped in a towel, and a pink bath-robe hangs from her shoulders, covering the worst of her mutations. Her face is still strained and lined, her eyes horribly sunken, but there's no trace of the Wrath I saw before. She walks up to Cole. "You're Cartaxus, aren't you? Are your people getting close to a vaccine?"

"We're very close, ma'am," Cole says. "Catarina is helping us."

Amy nods, twitching. Her left arm hangs limp and bandaged by her side, which means Marcus cut my healing tech core out of me and sewed it straight into her. It's a reckless, dangerous move, but as I watch Amy hobble into the living room, it actually looks like it *worked*.

But that's not possible. My healing tech core was barely strong enough to repair skin-deep scratches. Amy seems rational now, but it must be the placebo effect. She'll turn back into a snarling monster soon, and Marcus will regret letting her out of those restraints.

"We should go," I say, nudging Cole. "Come on, we need to hurry. We need to get to the lab."

"The lab?" Amy asks again. Her eyes narrow. I can see her fighting back the Wrath, her teeth grinding with the effort to keep it under control.

She steps closer. I stiffen, waiting for her to lunge, and for Cole to respond and unleash the carnage I've been trying to avoid.

Instead, she just stares at me. "Please take the girls," she whispers.

"No," Marcus gasps. "You're not thinking straight, you're—"

"This is the sanest I've been in months," she snaps. "They're not safe here, not for long. You think you can protect them when a pack of Lurkers finds this place?"

"Ma'am, I'm afraid we can't do that," Cole says.

"Chelsea can shoot," Amy says quickly, "and Eloise is helpful. They'll do anything you tell them. Please, they'll be safe with Lachlan."

"I'm sorry, ma'am. Lachlan is dead."

Amy sucks in a breath, and Marcus's face blanches. "If he's dead, then God help us," he whispers.

Eloise starts crying. I grab Cole's hand. "Let's just go," I say. "Come on, we need to keep moving."

"Okay," Cole murmurs, eyeing Amy, as though he's finally sensing the danger that lurks beneath her shaking facade.

We head through the kitchen. Cole's footsteps are slow and labored. Marcus follows close behind, offering suggestions. "Make sure he rests for the next few hours, and keep him warm," he says.

"I will," I mutter, fighting the urge to yell at him.

I climb into the jeep, and Cole settles in beside me. My eyes cut to

Marcus's as I swing us around, sending out a spray of gravel. He looks guilty, as he should. He clearly thinks the function core he took from my arm will help Amy, but he doesn't understand—my father wrote all my apps himself. Every app was as bland and generic as it could be to stop it triggering my hypergenesis. There was nothing in there that could help her. If Marcus had just *asked* me, I would have showed him that myself.

The jeep speeds us back down the driveway. I keep my eyes on the rearview, where Marcus is watching us leave, with his broken, mutated wife at his side. Chelsea has her arms around Eloise, who's crying into her hands. Marcus is a butcher, and his wife is a monster.

Maybe we should have taken the girls.

Two hours later, a light starts blinking in the corner of the jeep's dashboard. We're in Wyoming, after taking a detour to avoid Homestake and its soldiers. Now we're deep in overgrown farmland, surrounded by sprawling fields and the occasional herd of buffalo. Houses are few and far between, most of them boarded up or burned to the ground. It's only been two years since the outbreak, but everything looks like it's been abandoned for decades thanks to the acidic nature of Hydra's corrosive clouds. Every building has paint hanging in strips from the walls or blistering off the concrete, and fingers of rust creep around the edges of the road signs. Even the highways are cracked. It used to make riding my bike difficult, but the jeep flies over the potholes as though there's nothing there.

Cole is asleep, his seat reclined as far as the boxes in the back will allow, and his eyelashes flutter every so often when a tremor shakes his body. He's still recovering. The color is back in his face and his breathing is steady, but his body will take time to repair itself. Judging by the flashing lights on his panel, some of his tech needs repairing too.

Those aren't the flashing lights I'm worried about, though. The glowing symbol on the dashboard has blinked to red, showing me a picture of a lightning bolt. I scan the empty fields around us and pull the jeep to the side of the road, chewing my lip nervously.

"What's wrong?" Cole asks, waking as we crunch across the gravel. "Why are we stopping? Are you okay?"

I kill the engine. The dashboard goes blank, but the blinking light remains. "I think we're low on fuel. The jeep has a warning light."

"What?" Cole straightens, rubbing his eyes. "We should be on batteries, not fuel. We had a full cell this morning."

I flick the display, but the light keeps glowing. A cold feeling settles in my stomach.

"We should have plenty of fuel, too," Cole says. "Are you sure you're reading this right?"

"Wait here," I say, swinging my door open. I grab the edge of the roof and haul myself up, but before I even see it, I know they're gone. The roof feels too low, too flat.

Marcus stole the solars while I was unconscious.

*"Dammit!"* I throw myself back into the seat, punching the steering wheel. The jeep's horn blares down the empty road.

"They took them," Cole says.

I nod, my eyes scrunched shut, my hands pressed to my face.

"But there's more," he says slowly. "Catarina, what did they do?"

I let out a sigh, peering out through my fingers. "Marcus cut out one of my function cores. My panel isn't working anymore, and I don't know if it's going to repair itself."

For a moment Cole is deathly silent, and then he swings his door open and jumps to the ground. "Out!" he shouts, striding around the jeep. "Out, Catarina, now!"

"No!" I grip the wheel. "We can't go back!"

He yanks my door open, grabbing me around the waist, and hauls me out onto the road.

"They stole our solars," he shouts, "they *cut* you open, and you're protecting these people? Get in the passenger seat. We're going back there."

"No!" I yell. "We don't have time. We need to keep moving."

"How?" he shouts, whirling around. "How do you propose we get to the lab? We're out of gas and we have no solars. We can't even make it there on what we have left, and we still need to find a clonebox."

"We'll figure something out."

His eyes blaze. "I've already figured something out. We go back there and we take our goddamn solars back."

I run my hands through my hair. He's literally *shaking* with anger, his hands in fists as he stares back down the road. My eyes drop to his bandage, where a spot of blood has seeped through the gauze.

Oh shit. He's not shaking with anger. He's torn his stitches, and now he's going into shock.

"Cole," I say, reaching for his arm. "You're—"

He yanks his arm away. "We need the solars. We have to go back."

"Cole, listen to me. You're bleeding."

Scarlet spots seep through the cotton. A sheen of cold sweat glimmers on his chest.

"I'll be fine," he says.

"No you won't. You're not invincible."

"I'll be *fine*," he says again, then blinks, another tremor racing through his body. His face pales and he stumbles back, falling against the jeep.

"Oh, no, no," I breathe, lunging for him, slipping beneath his arm. His skin is cold and clammy, covered in sweat. "You're freezing, Cole. You shouldn't be moving."

"But we need to—"

"Get in the damn jeep," I say, grabbing his face. "You need to rest. I *need* you. I won't make it there alone."

He glares at me a moment longer, and then the anger fades from his face. "Okay," he whispers finally.

We shuffle to the back with the bulk of his weight on my shoulder, and I somehow manage to pull open the rear doors. He climbs in, swaying, and I shove the boxes aside so there's enough space for him to lie down. He collapses on his side, letting out a grunt of pain. The spots of scarlet on his bandage have spread into a terrifying wash of blood.

"I-I need to get warm," he stutters. "My tech is heat boosted. I need to keep my temperature up for it to heal me."

"Okay." I grab one of the Cartaxus sleeping bags and yank it out of its sack, then climb in behind him, crushing the boxes against the side.

"Just hold still." I throw the sleeping bag over him. "You're going to be fine."

But the calmness in my voice is a lie. Cole's hands are freezing, and his face is white, his pupils narrowed down to specks. I need to warm him up and get his tech running again. Judging by the way he's shaking, I need to do it *fast*.

"Okay, close your eyes." I yank my jacket and tank top off.

"W-what are you d-doing?" His teeth are chattering so badly he can barely form the words, but he still turns his head to look at me.

"I *told* you to close your eyes." I lie down on the floor beside him, slipping underneath the sleeping bag in my bra, pressing my chest to his back.

"Y-you have to buy me a drink before you g-get me into bed."

"Shut up," I whisper, wrapping my arm around his chest.

"A-after this is over, I'm telling C-Crick you came on to me."

I snort, pressing my cheek to the back of his neck. "Yeah, well, just don't tell your girlfriend. It sounds like she'd kick my ass."

He pauses for a moment, still shivering. "I-I don't know, it's been years. She never sent a message, she—"

"Shh," I say, tightening my grip on him. "Don't think about that, okay? Just try to relax."

He nods, sliding his hand up, lacing his fingers through mine. I feel his pulse in his hands and in his neck, where our skin is pressed together. We lie in silence until his tremors slow. His body heat rises, his breathing settling into a slow, steady rhythm that tells me he's asleep.

I keep my cheek pressed to his neck, a hum of pressure rising in my ears. Sparks of electricity seem to dance through me in the places our skin touches. There's nothing romantic about us lying like this, it's simply life and death, but for some reason I can't stop thinking about the way he's holding my hand.

I know it doesn't mean anything. We both have other people, and he's so drunk on anesthetic he probably doesn't know what he's doing. I tell myself this, but all I can smell is his aftershave and the raw, musky fragrance of his skin.

It tugs at something inside me, building like a fire.

*Deep breaths, Catarina.*

This is going to be a problem.

# CHAPTER 16

I FELL ASLEEP BEHIND COLE, BUT WE MUST HAVE moved in the night, because I wake up pressed against his chest, entangled in his arms. His breath is soft on my hair, one hand brushing the back of my neck, and the bare skin of his chest is warm against my cheek.

It's absurdly intimate, but waking like this shouldn't mean anything. It's cold and cramped in the back of the jeep, and it's normal for people to huddle for warmth in the night.

At least, it *would* be normal if I hadn't woken with a sense that some deep, lost part of myself had finally found its way home. It would be normal if I didn't wake up wrapped in Cole's scent, pulling him closer, breathing his name.

His *name*.

I stiffen as soon as the word leaves my lips, and Cole's ice-blue eyes blink open, meeting mine in confusion. I don't know if he heard me, but his arms slide away and he rolls to his back, rubbing his face as though dragging himself from a dream.

This is not good.

I scramble to sit up, pushing the hair from my face, kicking my way out of the sleeping bag covering us. I'm still in my bra. My tank top is wedged under a box, and I yank it out, pulling it on clumsily. My heartbeat is a drum.

Cole must hear it. He can surely read the flush of heat on my cheeks and the goose bumps on my neck. I straighten my top, angling myself away from him, trying to hide behind the dark curtain of my hair.

Outside, the morning light is pale. The jeep's tinted windows show me a landscape of flat, grassy plains all the way to the horizon. My brain is finally starting to adjust to seeing the world without my tech, and it's almost pleasing to let my focus dance across the land outside. There are no houses in sight, no craters or rusted cars, no sign that anyone lived here even before the plague. The dark curve of the highway stretches for miles, empty and black, until my nonenhanced eyes can't track it anymore.

"I shouldn't have parked here overnight," I say "It's not safe to stay near the highways. Lurkers drive along them, hunting people. I should have driven us into cover."

Cole just grunts, sitting up slowly, leaning against the side of the jeep. The bandage over his stomach is dark with blood, and there are rings beneath his eyes, but he looks better than he did last night. His eyes run over me, from the dirty boots I slept in, to the tangled mess of hair puffed out around my face. I brace myself for questions about what just happened—how I ended up in his arms, why I said his name—but he just nods at my wrist.

"How's your arm?"

I look down, surprised. "My arm? It's fine. How are *you*? You're the one who got shot. You took a bullet for me, remember?"

A smile tugs at his lips. "It sounds pretty heroic when you say it like that."

"Yeah, well, let's try to keep the heroics to a minimum from now on. You nearly died on me. You probably shouldn't be moving around."

"I'm fine."

I raise an eyebrow. "Sure you are, soldier."

He shrugs, pulling at the bandage taped over his stomach. "See for yourself."

"Cole, don't . . . ," I start as he peels back the tape, but I trail off as the gauze folds down, falling away from his wound.

It's silver.

The skin around the gunshot has healed over seamlessly, but an inch-wide patch on his stomach now looks like it's made of metal. Iridescent silver streaks that branch like veins stretch across his abdomen, fading as they spread away from the wound. At their center, a glistening patch of pure, reflective silver lies where hours ago all I could see was pulped and bloodied flesh.

It's nanomesh. A myth. An app whispered about in Skies forums, rumored to exist in just a handful of prototypes. A nanoscale mesh capable of being built throughout a person's body, then warped and grown with a single command. The patch on Cole's stomach isn't flesh—it's a lattice that's grown overnight that his own cells will migrate through and fill. The silver will shrink down to a speck, until the patch is made completely of living, breathing tissue.

It'll heal Cole's wound perfectly, but nanomesh isn't just for healing. It could be used for regrowing limbs or adding entirely new ones. With this tech Cole could grow an exoskeleton, or eyes in the back of his head. With the right code, he could grow himself *wings*.

"You have nanomesh?" I breathe. "What the hell *are* you, Cole?"

He looks down at the wound. "I'm a very expensive weapon."

Something in his voice makes me pause. A note of pain—but it has nothing to do with the gleaming wound on his stomach. It's the way he says the word "weapon," like he's a *thing*. A mindless tool instead of a person with his own thoughts and dreams. When we were at the cabin, he said Cartaxus turned him into this, but now I'm not so sure.

I can't help but remember the words my father chose in the message he left for me: *He is a weapon of considerable power.*

What if it was my father who turned him into one?

I lean back against the side of the jeep, running one hand through my hair, teasing out the knots with my fingers. The photograph from Cole's file flits through my mind. It's one thing to turn yourself into a black-out agent, but it's another to have it *forced* on you as a child.

"The nanomesh," I say. "My father gave that to you, didn't he?"

Cole meets my eyes. He doesn't nod, but I already know the answer. It's not even really a question. There's only one geneticist in modern history with the skills to pull off something like this. Maybe another team could have developed it with decades of testing, but Cole's seamless, perfect version is certainly my father's work. It's not that my father was a genius—he was, but there were countless geniuses working on gentech code before the outbreak. His strength lay in the way he thought about DNA, as though it were a language he'd been raised to speak, and everyone else had learned it at school. He knew the subtleties, the hidden rules that even the most sophisticated coding algorithms tended to miss.

That's why my head is spinning, staring at the silver patch on Cole's stomach and the network of scars slashed across his chest. I can't understand what my father could have gained by carrying out painful, intrusive research on a five-year-old boy.

My eyes stray to my backpack, where I've stashed the files I found in the mines. I start to reach for it, but Cole lets out a growl of frustration.

I pause. "Are you okay?"

He covers his face with his hands. "No, I'm not okay. I'm hungry and tired, and I'm still in a lot of pain, so I'd appreciate it if you didn't punch me."

"Why would I punch you?"

He drops his hands, a look of guilt flashing across his face. "Because I think Cartaxus might know we're here."

A long beat passes. *"What?"*

He slumps. "I've been blocking my panel from them, but when I was crashing last night, my tech might have sent out a beacon. I told you—I'm an expensive weapon, and Cartaxus protects its investments. I think they've sent someone out to find us."

I stiffen, looking out the window. If Cartaxus finds us now, they'll drag us into a bunker and seize my father's files. They'll figure out how to decrypt the vaccine, but they'll have complete control over it, which means they won't give it to people on the surface. Millions of people, left to die. Families like Marcus's. My father's plan for us will be ruined.

"How much time do we have?" I pull my hair back into a ponytail, looking along the curve of the highway. We're low on fuel, and we have no solars. We're still a day's drive from the lab my father wanted us to go to, but there might be hope yet. I scan the back of the jeep. Maybe we can make it to a town and find another vehicle, but it might not have room to carry the boxes of my father's notes. I haven't even opened them to see if they have any hints for unlocking the vaccine, and we don't have time to sort through them now.

But maybe I don't need them.

I glance at Cole. My father left a note in his arm, then I found a file from when Cole was a little boy. It can't be a coincidence. Those musty files I found behind the kayak are the ones my father wanted me to use—somehow I'm sure of it.

"How much time, Cole?" I haul my backpack up from the floor and peer in at the folders. Five mold-spotted sheaths of paper, tucked beside my genkit. "Cole, how long? Are you even listening?"

But he isn't. His eyes are glazed over, his head tilted, one hand pressed to the side of the jeep. He's listening to something I can't hear, not without my implants.

My stomach tightens. "They're here, aren't they?"

He nods slowly, blinking out of his session. "A Comox flew past about half an hour ago. Their scan went right over us, so I didn't think they'd noticed the jeep, but now they're circling back. I can't tell who it's carrying, but it could be a whole platoon."

I chew my thumbnail, staring out the window. We can't run. We can't hide.

"Wait, did you say half an hour ago?"

A hint of color bleeds into Cole's cheeks. "Yeah."

I blink. That was when I was still asleep, still curled into his chest. I thought we were both asleep. He had his hand on the back of my neck. . . .

"You were *awake*?"

The color on his cheeks grows deeper, then he freezes, tilting his head again. This time I hear it too. The low, thumping sound of a Comox, racing toward us.

Cartaxus is here.

"Stay inside," Cole says, rolling to his knees.

I yank on my backpack, shaking my head. "I'm coming with you. We don't know how much they know, or what Dax told them. It's better if we act like we have nothing to hide."

He frowns, considering. "Okay, but stay behind me, and get ready to run into the jeep if I tell you to."

"So you can what? Blow them up?"

He pulls a shirt on, wincing. "I don't know yet."

"Yeah, well, the last time you didn't share your plans with me, you ended up getting shot."

He snatches up his gun as the Comox's blades grow louder. "I know, Cat. I screwed this up. You don't need to remind me."

I grab a fistful of his shirt as he reaches for the door. "No, Cole, this isn't over. Even if Cartaxus takes us, there might still be a way to release the vaccine, but we need to work together, now more than ever. Please don't do anything reckless."

He turns back to me, his eyes unreadable, then throws open the rear doors and launches himself outside. The thumping of the Comox's blades rises into a roar as I slide from the back of the jeep, one hand over my eyes.

Cole stands like a statue in the middle of the road, staring up at the sky, where a hulking black quadcopter is dropping toward us. It lands with a thud in the middle of the empty, potholed highway, sending up billowing clouds of dust.

I turn my face away, squinting as the side door opens and a metal ramp extends down to the road. I brace for a rush of soldiers, a unit armed to the teeth like the one that stormed the cabin during the outbreak, but the doorway stays empty. The rotors slow, and through the clouds of dust, a single figure jogs down to the ground.

He has sparkling green eyes. Freckled skin and red hair.

"Hey, Princess," Dax says. "It's been a while."

# CHAPTER 17

THE WORLD TILTS AND SPINS. MY BACKPACK SLIDES from my shoulders.

"Dax," I choke out, running to him.

He catches me in his arms and lifts me. His body is trembling, his breathing coming fast and shallow. "You're really here," he whispers. "You don't know how happy I am to see you."

I pull back, half laughing, half crying, wiping my eyes. "Dax, look at you! You're like a different *person*."

The man before me isn't the Dax I remember from our days in the cabin. His ponytail is gone, along with the white streak in his red hair. He now wears it combed back in a sophisticated cut. The soft lines of his face have grown sharp and refined, graced with a single leyline snaking up his neck, terminating at his temple. His body isn't jacked up like Cole's. He's leaner and taller, with the same subtle elegance in his movements that I remember. He wears a black metal cuff over his forearm, covering his panel. It looks like my father's crypto cuff but has a row of blinking scarlet lights along the side.

"Catarina, look at *you*," he says, stepping back to look me up and down. "You're all grown-up, and you're positively stunning. Lachlan would be so proud if he could see you now."

A lump forms in my throat. Hearing Dax say my father's name hits me harder than I thought it would. It sounds so different from the way Cole says it. So intimate, so raw. Dax loved my father like I did. I have to fight to keep my face straight.

"Oh, Princess," Dax breathes, pulling me back to him. "I'm so sorry. You must be devastated."

"No, I'm fine." I step away, scrubbing at my eyes. "I just . . . I can't think about it right now."

"Of course." Dax nods, taking my hand in his. "We have a lot of work to do."

Cole clears his throat conspicuously. His expression is stony, but it breaks into a grin when another figure appears in the quadcopter's door. It's a soldier with the same smooth, purposeful movements as Cole, the same leylines traced across his arms and the sides of his face. His silhouette is exactly like Cole's—ridiculous shoulders, close-cropped hair, even the same tank top and cargo pants—but the details couldn't be more different. This soldier wears a playful smirk, and his eyes are underlined with a sweep of cobalt shadow. Tattoos of eagles and wolves cover the dark skin of his arms, and his hair is bleached or hacked to a startling white blond.

"Leoben!" Cole shouts, laughing. The two men run to each other and hug fiercely. There's no awkwardness in their movements, no hesitation. Their embrace is deep and real, and a single word springs into my mind as I watch them: brothers.

Cole pulls away, still clutching Leoben's shoulders. "Lee, it's true. Jun Bei is *alive*."

The words burst from Cole with an excitement I haven't heard from him before. His face is lit up, his eyes shining. The reverence in his voice when he says Jun Bei's name makes the skin on the back of my neck prickle.

It's love.

Pure, euphoric, unbridled. The emotion is so clear on Cole's face that it makes me look away. My chest tightens with something that almost feels like jealousy.

But that would be insane.

"What?" Leoben steps back, his eyes growing wide. He balls his hands in fists and lets out a whoop. "What did I tell you? She's invincible, man!"

"Yeah, I guess she is." Cole grins, still shaking with excitement. "What the hell are you guys doing here?"

Leoben glances at Dax. "We intercepted your beacon and came to save your ugly ass. I'm Dax's official bodyguard, effective yesterday. He fed them some bullshit about needing to leave, and they sent me out with him."

I turn to Dax. "Cartaxus knows you're here?"

Dax sweeps the hair back from his forehead. "Yes and no. They think I'm here to pick up Lachlan's notes in case there's something in there to help with the vaccine."

"And they just *let* you go?" I thought Dax was a prisoner, that he and my father were being locked up and tortured. But Dax looks healthy and confident, like he's been living in comfort.

It's been two years. I haven't heard anything from him. If Dax could leave whenever he wanted, why didn't he visit me?

"Princess," Dax says, taking my hands, "there's a lot we need to talk about. You must have a lot of questions, and I do too, but right now we need to focus on unlocking the vaccine. We need your father's notes— anything he left behind that might be related to decryption."

I rub my forehead, trying to focus. "Yeah, I know. We have all his notes in the jeep, and there was a message in Cole's panel."

"Mine too, and Leoben's. Your father liked to cover his bases. I take it you were on your way to the lab in Canada?"

I nod, still trying to stop my head from spinning. Dax flew here. He took a Comox. He's healthy; he looks happy. I spent two years surviving on my own because my father told me it would be safer—that Cartaxus was evil, that they'd hurt me to get to him.

But after seeing the research my father carried out on Cole, I don't know what to believe anymore.

"We still need a clonebox," Cole says. "Did you bring one?"

"Not exactly," Dax says. He and Leoben exchange another glance.

Cole stares at them for a second, then steps back, shaking his head. "No, absolutely not. It's too dangerous."

Leoben grins. "But you've thought about it."

I look between the three of them. "Thought about what?"

Leoben chuckles. "About stealing a clonebox from one of the bunkers. Homestake isn't far from here."

"Are you kidding me?" I ask, stunned. "Go *into* a bunker? I've spent the last two years hiding from Cartaxus, and Cole is AWOL. Why don't we just call them and ask them to lock us up?"

"It won't be like that," Dax says. "I told Cartaxus that I sent Lieutenant Franklin out to find you. I didn't say who you were, just that you were a coder I knew, and there was a chance you'd be able to help us. I've already booked us in to refuel at Homestake. It'll be fine. We'll be able to get out of there easily."

"No we won't," Cole says. "Homestake is a tier-one-secured facility. If we go in and they lock the place down, we could be stuck in there for weeks. We'll have to find a clonebox somewhere else. We can't risk going into a bunker. Lachlan made it clear in his message that we have to keep Cat away from Cartaxus."

Dax crosses his arms. "Listen, Lieutenant. *Cat* will be just fine, don't worry. I don't know if you've noticed, but we're in something of a minor apocalypse, and the chances of finding a living clonebox on the surface are slim to none. We don't have a choice. We have to go to a bunker, and we don't have time to stand around here arguing about it. Homestake is expecting us. We'll restock our supplies, and then we'll take the clone-box and drive to the lab."

"That sounds fine," Cole says, crossing his arms as well, mirroring Dax's pose. "But tell me, Crick, won't Homestake notice when we steal one of their cloneboxes?"

Dax holds Cole's gaze. "Well, they've only got one, so yes, I assume they'll notice, and then they'll institute a lockdown, as you've noted." He taps the black cuff on his arm, glancing at Leoben. "Fortunately, Lachlan gave me access to his personal libraries, and I found a piece of code that should keep them busy long enough for us to get out."

"What code?" I angle myself between Dax and Cole, breaking up their staring match.

"It's a simulation," Leoben says. "We call it a kick, like when you kick the doors down to get into somewhere secure—only we'll be using it to get out. It was written by a friend of ours."

I nod. I've written similar code for the Skies. Blunt attacks to cripple systems. That's how I got into Cole's panel. I've never seen anything like that in my father's work before, though. The only thing he turned his coding skills to was DNA.

"Is this a Cartaxus thing?" I ask.

"Kind of," Leoben says. He runs one hand over his buzzed white-blond hair, frowning. "It was written by Jun Bei, actually. Come to think of it, she could have been the one who got us into this mess. The hack that blew up the lab was all explosions and data corruption. That's classic Jun Bei."

"What?" I spin to Cole. "What is he talking about?"

Cole shifts uncomfortably. "Jun Bei . . . she was a coder, a prodigy. She worked with your father at Cartaxus before the plague, but they never got along."

"Oh, they got along," Leoben mutters. "Like a goddamn house on fire."

My stomach flips. I turn to Dax. "Did you know about this?"

Dax looks as stunned as me. "Jun Bei's name was on a lot of the code I saw, but she left before the outbreak, so I never knew her. Cartaxus said the attack came from the Skies."

Leoben snorts. "Yeah, right. Those guys can't code for shit. There's no way they're the ones who did it."

My head spins. Leoben's right—I've been trying to tell Cole all along that it wasn't the Skies who hacked Cartaxus and destroyed my father's lab. It was someone else, someone better. Someone who knew their way around Cartaxus systems. From the way Leoben's talking, it definitely sounds like it could have been this girl.

"Cole," I say, my voice shaking. "Why didn't you tell me this before?"

"I would have told you if I thought it was important, but it's not. It couldn't have been her."

"My father is *dead*," I say, my hands in fists. "I don't know what could possibly be more important than that. You said she hasn't talked to you in years. How could you know it wasn't her?"

"I know her," Cole says. "She wouldn't have done it."

"Well, maybe you didn't know her as well as you think."

The words are out of my mouth before I can think them through. Pain flashes in Cole's eyes before his face turns to stone.

Leoben lets out a low whistle. "You two have some crazy shit going on."

"Yes," Dax says, looking between Cole and me, frowning. "I'm sure you've both been through a lot. The sooner we get the clonebox, the sooner we can be done with this. I still say Homestake is our best option."

Cole shakes his head, still glaring at me. "It's too risky. You can go in, but Catarina and I are staying here."

"Who put *you* in charge?" I snap.

Cole's jaw clenches. "You're the one who said we couldn't go to Cartaxus. I know you're angry, but this is a bad idea. We've got enough juice to drive to the closest town. We'll find some more solars, and we'll get the jeep working. We can still get to the lab tonight."

I grit my teeth. Cole's damn right I'm angry, but that's only part of it. I'm tired, I'm confused, and I have stitches in my arm. There are files in my backpack that frighten me, I'm on a mission I don't understand, and Dax is standing beside me, with a Comox and a Cartaxus bodyguard.

Part of me still wants to stick to the plan and play this safely. The smartest idea is to drive to the lab and look for a clonebox on the way. But part of me wants to see Homestake, the bunker I've been living an hour away from for the last two years. I want to know exactly what it is that my father kept me away from.

And if I'm really honest, part of me wants to piss off Cole.

"Are you sure you can get us out of there?" I ask Dax.

He nods. "Easily."

"Then let's do it," I say. "Let's go to Homestake."

# CHAPTER 18

DAX, COLE, AND I SIT STRAPPED INTO THE COMOX'S cargo hold while Leoben leans back in the pilot's seat, his feet crossed on the controls. The Comox is a drone, but apparently Leoben knows how to fly it if the onboard AI "goes stupid" in midair.

Cole is *furious*. His arms are crossed, his face is stormy, and he hasn't spoken to me since I agreed to Dax's plan. But that doesn't matter. Once we decrypt the vaccine, he'll go off to find Jun Bei, and I'll never have to see him again.

The thought makes my stomach clench. I don't know if it's some ridiculous, inexplicable jealousy, or the fact that Leoben thinks Jun Bei was the one who killed my father. It sounds like she was a piece of work. I don't understand why Cole was defending her. She *left* him and hasn't contacted him in years.

But that's what Dax and my father did too.

I lean against the Comox's side, watching fields and forests pass below us. The jeep has disappeared into the distance, following behind us on the ground. Leoben transferred one of the batteries from the Comox into it, which should give it enough juice to drive itself to Homestake. It's still stocked with the boxes of my father's notes, but I have the five musty folders I found behind the kayak stashed in my backpack. Something tells me they're the only notes we're going to need.

"Almost there," Dax says, peering through the window. I strain against my harness to get a clearer view. We've reached Homestake's buffer zone—a mile-wide patch of wasteland that circles the bunker to keep blowers from detonating nearby. The perimeter is lined with a deep trench and rolls of razor wire atop a towering concrete wall. Inside it, every building is bulldozed, every tree is gone, and the roads are covered in a dark layer of ash.

It looks like a war zone. Despite this, crowds of people are still huddled on the perimeter, trying to get in. They're probably infected. The blowers love the bunkers—they come from miles away in the desperate hope that Cartaxus can help them. The crowd is being kept away from the checkpoints by gun-bots on arched metal legs that skitter around like giant steel spiders. A low-altitude army of drones hovers above them, ready to incinerate anyone who might break through.

"Think they have enough security?" Leoben calls back. He's joking, but Cartaxus is right to guard the wasteland fiercely. I'm sure Homestake's airlocks are sophisticated, but the buffer zone is still their best defense. No airlock is foolproof, and it only takes a single virus particle to cause infection. Keeping the blowers a mile away from the bunkers is the only way to guarantee the air is safe.

"It won't be enough for much longer," I say, pointing down at a plume on the perimeter. One of the people has detonated, sending the others scattering. The cloud drifts sideways, flattened by the wind, but even from here it still looks enormous. The others follow my gaze, but none of them seem to understand what I'm saying.

Of course they don't. They haven't learned to read the clouds like

I have, to analyze the shape and color and guess how the wind might change. My life has depended on it ever since the outbreak. They've all spent the last two years *inside*.

"That cloud is twice as big as they used to be," I explain. "The virus is evolving, and the detonations are getting stronger. A mile is still a decent radius to keep the air clean, but pretty soon those clouds are going to reach the bunker."

Dax stares down at the cloud. "Hopefully that won't be a concern for much longer."

I nod, watching the cloud drift across the buffer zone. "Yeah, hopefully."

The Comox drops lower. In the center of the wasteland, a single lookout tower juts from the blackened ground. This is Homestake, at least what we can see of it. Almost all of the bunker is underground, built into an enormous abandoned gold mine. I've seen the lookout tower from afar, and I've skirted the perimeter on supply runs with Agnes, but I've never seen it up close like this. The sheer size of the place stuns me, along with the realization that eighty thousand people are currently beneath me. It's hard to get my head around.

Dax taps the black cuff on his forearm. A diagram of the bunker flickers on the Comox's floor, projected by a row of lights on the cuff's side. "The top third of Homestake is military," he says. "The civilian levels are underneath, in a different airlock system. The only point of access to the whole place is the central shaft."

I look over the diagram. The bunker is shaped like a house built entirely underground, with the civilian floors forming a giant rectangular section. The military levels slope in above it like a roof, linked to the ground by an elevator shaft that looks like a chimney.

"The clonebox is here," Dax says, gesturing to a red dot near the top of the bunker. "It's in the main lab, which I have access to, but alarms will sound as soon as it's disconnected. Cartaxus thinks we're here to stay for a few nights, so I've got rooms booked in the military barracks to avoid suspicion. We'll check in, and you can shower and have a meal. The only problem might be your panel. None of the hypergenesis-friendly apps your father wrote for you are on the list of approved Cartaxus tech. I'll talk to the scanning officers, and—"

"There's no need," I say, pulling my sleeve back, showing him the bandage wrapped around my forearm. A few black stitches poke out from between the layers of gauze, and a thin line of blood has seeped through from the incision.

Dax frowns. "What happened?"

"Someone cut out one of my function cores. The panel might repair itself, but I don't know yet. I don't have a backup node, so it could be ruined."

Dax's face darkens. "I'm sorry to hear that. I'll help you fix it once this is over. We'll get it running again, I promise. But in the meantime, I suppose it'll make this easier. You and Leoben can check in to the barracks, but Lieutenant Franklin and I will need to be debriefed on the mission they think I sent him on. That might take a few hours."

"Won't they want to talk to me?"

"They will, but not today. I told them you were a friend of mine, and that you'd be frightened. I convinced them to give you a day to settle in. Don't worry, we'll be in and out in a matter of hours. After Lieutenant Franklin and I are done debriefing, I'll get the clonebox, and we can leave."

"What happens then? How do we get out?"

Dax spins the diagram, zooming in on the top few levels. "Once we start the kick simulation, we'll have control of the elevators and the doors to the parking garage. Homestake will think it's under attack, and we'll evacuate under the pretense of keeping me safe. We'll send the Comox to the Los Angeles bunker while we drive north—you and Cole in his jeep, Leoben and me in another. By the time Cartaxus figures out that we're not in the Comox, we'll be halfway to the lab, and they won't have a hope of finding us."

I stare at the diagram, trying to get a feel for the scale of the bunker. It seems to stretch impossibly far down into the earth. Ever since Homestake opened, I've tried to imagine what it's like. A giant, forbidden fortress whose drone patrols I could sometimes glimpse in the distance. Thousands of people, locked underground. Living, eating, breathing.

I look up at Dax. "I want to see where the civilians live."

He shakes his head. "Like I said, the civilians are in a different airlock system. It's a pain in the ass moving between them."

I cross my arms. "I want to see it."

"Sheesh, talk about a pain in the ass," Leoben yells back.

Cole smirks, the first flicker of emotion I've seen since we took off.

"I mean it," I say. "I want to see where they live."

"Fine," Dax says, sighing. "I'll move the booking to the civilian levels, but you owe me for this. Those airlocks mess up my hair."

"What if I like it better messed up?"

The Comox dips sharply, then rises just as fast, making me jerk against my harness and slam back into the wall.

"What was that?" I mutter, rubbing the back of my head.

"A glitch." There's a slight edge to Leoben's voice. "You better hang on, Agatta."

I glance at Cole, to see if hitting my head activated his protective protocol, but his eyes are still blue. The smirk on his face has grown into a grin. Dax crosses his arms, watching Leoben with a stony expression on his face.

We approach the lookout tower, and the Comox drops smoothly, landing on a black airstrip, sending up clouds of ash and dust. A laser scanner throws a scarlet grid across us, and a row of gleaming gun-bots ambles toward us, forming a line between us and the base.

The Comox's rotors slow. My harness releases automatically, and I stumble forward, grasping my backpack to my chest. This time Cole's arm shoots out instinctively to steady me, grabbing my hand.

His eyes meet mine for the briefest second before he lets go and looks away.

"Welcome to Homestake," Dax says, opening the door, letting in a swirling wall of dust.

I throw my hand over my eyes, coughing, squinting at the gun-bots still lined up around the Comox. "Where do we go now?"

A black-gloved hand takes my elbow, and I look up into deep brown eyes lined with blue shadow. "You're with me, Agatta," Leoben says. His voice is sharp. "These two have to debrief. I'll take you through the airlocks to the civ section."

I sling the backpack on, nerves jumping inside me. Leoben has the same rippling energy as Cole, but it rolls off him in a completely different way. Cole is reserved, focused, controlled, but Leoben looks like he'd kick someone through a wall just for the thrill of it.

The steel in his eyes when he looks at me tells me he doesn't like me at all.

He steps to the door, leading me by the elbow. Cole grabs his arm as we leave, pressing their panels together. Something seems to pass between them, though I've never seen anything like it. It must be a way to transfer messages without Cartaxus listening in.

Leoben's eyes narrow, and he nods. I don't know what Cole told him, but when Leoben pulls me down the ramp, his fingers dig into my skin. He looks back once, meeting Dax's eyes, but doesn't say anything. He just pulls me into the wasteland. I swallow, jogging to keep up with his strides.

He *definitely* doesn't like me.

Dax and Cole stay by the Comox while Leoben leads me past the twitching gun-bots and through an airlocked door in the side of the tower. We pass through a series of dimly lit hallways with sloped floors that I have a feeling are designed in a labyrinth, to make it difficult for anyone to break in. I'm lost after just a few turns, unsure if we've been climbing or dropping underground, if we've been moving forward or walking in circles. Eventually we come to an unmarked elevator that opens as soon as we reach it and closes behind us with a hiss.

Leoben leans against the side of the cab, crossing his arms. A whine starts up above us as we begin to drop.

"You and Dax seem to get along," I say.

He grunts but doesn't reply.

"Has he been . . . okay? In the lab, were he and my father treated well?"

He looks me up and down, taking in the scars on my cheek, my dirty fingernails, the lines of my too-thin shoulders. "Compared to you, they were living like kings. I can't believe you were an hour away from this place. Eating doses to stay alive? You guys on the surface are all insane."

Something tells me he's trying to change the subject, but I can't help rising to his bait. "It's not crazy to want to be free."

Leoben's eyes glitter coldly. "Try telling that to the good people who've been forced to stay down here because murderers like you have kept the plague alive." He steps closer—close enough that I can tell he's trying to intimidate me. It takes all my strength not to shrink away from him. "You people on the surface always talk about freedom," he says, "but you don't see that you're the ones keeping the rest of the world locked away. You're the jailers, not Cartaxus. If we rounded you all up at gunpoint like we should, pretty soon the virus would be gone, and we could all move back up to the surface in safety again."

I hold his gaze. "That's ridiculous. You think the virus would just *disappear* if everyone on the surface joined a bunker? There are millions of frozen doses and bodies out there that could thaw and blow at any time, and every lab in the country has viral samples that could be accidentally released. The only way to protect the people in these bunkers is to release a vaccine."

He leans back again. I can't tell if he's frustrated or impressed that I'm not intimidated by him. "Okay, so the virus wouldn't disappear," he says. "But it wouldn't evolve, either. If we'd rounded everyone up in the outbreak, the first vaccine Lachlan wrote would have worked."

A chill creeps down my spine, and it's not just from the callous way that Leoben keeps talking about rounding up millions of people. It's because this time he has a point. Cole said my father coded a vaccine in the first weeks of the outbreak, but the virus evolved and made it obsolete. If Cartaxus had forced everyone on the surface into a bunker, the virus wouldn't have had a chance to mutate. The vaccine would have been safe—fragile, but safe. There's a chance society could have rebuilt itself after that.

Only, that's not true.

If everyone on the planet had let themselves be rounded up, we wouldn't all have lived to see the rebuilding. Eloise wouldn't have survived. Neither would Novak, or half the people in the Skies whose lives depend on unsanctioned code.

"Cartaxus always talks about *safety*," I say, turning Leoben's words back on him, "but you don't realize that you're the ones forcing us to live in danger. If you dropped your restrictions on unsanctioned code in the bunkers, then millions of people whose lives depend on it wouldn't be forced to live on the surface."

"Is that why you stayed up there?"

"My father told me to stay away from Cartaxus."

He lifts an eyebrow. "You look like him," he says finally. "Same hands, that's weird. I never thought I'd recognize a pair of hands."

"You knew my father?"

"Cole didn't tell you?"

"Tell me what?"

Leoben glances up at a camera in the ceiling, then pulls the bottom of his tank top up.

I gasp. His chest is exactly like Cole's—same size, same shape— except Leoben's is covered with tattoos of eagles, bears, and wolves. That's not what makes me gasp, though. It's the scars rippling beneath the tattoos. The network of slashed, puckered skin covering his chest.

"They did it to you, too—" I start, and then I remember. It wasn't Cartaxus who gave Cole his scars. It was my father. There are five files in my backpack, but I've only opened one. For some reason I assumed they'd all be about Cole.

But that was naive. Of course there's more.

"There were five of you, weren't there?" I ask. "You, Cole . . ." It sud-denly hits me. "And Jun Bei."

Leoben nods, lowering his shirt.

"My father did that to you, didn't he?"

"He did it to all of us. He wanted to see what was inside us, to see how we *worked*."

"But why? What was he trying to do?"

Leoben's eyes narrow. "You want me to justify my own abuse? I was a child, Agatta. Are you really asking me why he did it?"

I turn my head away, stung. He's right. There's no excuse for what my father did. There's no possible reason for torturing five helpless children.

"So he hasn't told you about Jun Bei?" Leoben asks.

"He mentioned her. He said she was smart, she was tough—"

"Tough," he snorts. "Yeah, that's a euphemism. This one time, when we were kids, a nurse was trying to get Cole to swallow a Geiger pill to monitor a radiation treatment. Those things are huge, and she accidentally dislocated his jaw. Jun Bei bounced across the room, cute little thing, and stuck a pair of scissors into the nurse's neck. Took three surgeons to save her. We didn't get scissors after that. They made us eat with plastic knives and forks for the next ten years."

"Jesus," I gasp.

"Yeah, she was a blast," Leoben says, stepping closer. "She'll put you in the ground if she finds out you're sleeping with Cole."

"We're not *sleeping* together. He's just helping me."

"Yeah, helping you into bed. I can smell you all over each other."

"It's not like that," I say, my cheeks burning. "And it's none of your business."

"I'm his brother," Leoben says. "Maybe not through DNA, but through everything that counts. I know him well enough to see that you've got into his head."

"That's the protective protocol—"

"It's more than that," Leoben snaps. "You know it, and so do I. I just want you to know that Cole's been broken before. He doesn't need you playing games with his heart, not now he has a chance of getting Jun Bei back. Those two are meant to be together."

I drop my eyes as the elevator slows. Beneath the sharp scent of my immunity, I can smell it too. Ice and pine. Cole's aftershave on my skin. Just the slightest hint of it brings back the feeling of waking up this morning, locked in the circle of his arms. I didn't mean for it to happen, I don't think either of us did, but that doesn't change the fact that my first reaction when I woke was to pull him closer.

It makes no sense. Leoben's right—Cole has a chance at finding Jun Bei again. No matter what I think of her, I heard the love in his voice when he said her name. Once we've released the vaccine, he'll go looking for her. That's the whole reason he came on this mission. That's why he's doing this.

For her.

Deep down, part of me twists at the thought. A stab of jealousy, even though I know I have no right to feel it.

"I'm not playing games," I whisper. "I never intended for us to get close."

"Of course you didn't," Leoben mutters. "But there's nothing quite as dangerous as an Agatta's best intentions."

# CHAPTER 19

THE ELEVATOR JERKS TO A HALT, AND THE DOORS
slide open to reveal a stark concrete room with a space-grade airlock set
into the wall. The frame is circular, and its gleaming steel doors overlap
like scales, opening out from the center. The words WASH-AND-BLAST
are stenciled in red above it, and the whole room stinks of disinfectant,
that same sharp scent I remember from the soap I used at boarding
school.

I shuffle out of the elevator, following Leoben to a desk beside the
airlock. A guard stands at attention, wearing a mirrored visor and a
black uniform with the Cartaxus antlers stamped in gold across his
chest.

Leoben shoots a grin at the guard. "We're booked in as part of
Dr. Crick's party. Priority alpha, code thirteen." He glances at me. "That
means we're as VIP as it gets."

The guard just nods. "Yes, sir. Your reservation has been processed.
Your entry is approved, but I'll need to scan your personal items and
weapons."

Leoben starts unbuckling his holster. The guard turns to me. "No explosives are permitted in the Wash-and-Blast, ma'am. Your personal items can pass through the vacuum airlock."

"I don't have any explosives," I say, clutching the backpack's straps. My genkit and my father's files are in there, and I can't risk losing them.

"The scanners in the elevator detected a genkit in your personal items, ma'am," the guard says. "Priority thirteen means you can keep it in your possession, but it's not permitted inside the airlocks. If it self-destructs, it'll set off the airlock's pressure-sensing glass and lock the entire facility down."

I stare at him. Genkits don't just randomly *blow up*. They have self-destruct sequences to stop them from being used to hurt people, but it takes a lot of work to make them actually explode. Most of them just belch smoke when they self-destruct. You have to be running dangerous code with the lasers fully primed to get a genkit like mine to truly detonate.

I consider explaining this to the guard, but Leoben looks back at me and shakes his head.

"Hand it over, Agatta. You'll get it back." He lays his holster on the counter. Another handgun is concealed at the small of his back, and a knife comes out of his boot. He empties his pockets, pulling out a packet of chewing gum, a lighter, and a length of wire that I'm guessing is a garrote.

If the guard is surprised, he doesn't show it. He arranges Leoben's arsenal in a plastic tray and slides it through a steel hatch in the wall. I swing my backpack off reluctantly, and he sends it through too, then pulls a black scanning wand from his pocket.

"Panel check."

Leoben holds his forearm out. Five black leylines snake up from his panel, intertwined with his tattoos. The guard swipes the scanner over Leoben's panel, and a light on its handle blinks green.

"All clear. Your panel, ma'am."

I hold out my bandaged arm. "It was damaged, and now it's non-functional. I'll need to get it replaced."

The guard swipes the scanner over my arm, then repeats the motion. "Looks like it's regenerating, should be done soon." The light on the handle of the scanner blinks green, and the guard steps back. He swipes his arm over a sensor on the wall, and the airlock slides open. "All clear. Welcome to Homestake."

"What . . . what do you mean it's clear?" I stare down at my arm.

"He means shut up and go in." Leoben grabs my shoulders, guiding me into the airlock. The tiny steel room is just big enough for the two of us, with a metal grating for a floor and a gaping air vent overhead. The door closes behind us, leaving us in the dim glow of a row of lights built into the floor.

"What did that green light mean?" I ask.

"It means your father found a way to trick our systems into letting in nonstandard tech."

"Oh," I breathe. "Of course."

"What kind of wireless chip do you have?"

"Basic model, K-40 line. It barely connects to anything."

"Easy to tweak, though," Leoben says. "He could have planted a mirror."

I look up at him. "You know how to code?"

He rolls his eyes. "I'm not just a pretty face. I don't know shit about DNA, but my hardware skills are pretty solid."

I raise an eyebrow. "Then you'd know that a mirror won't run on a K-40 encoding. You'd have to use a Joburg echo."

"Ah," he says, tilting his head back. "Of course, that's old-school. Nice."

He looks down, meeting my eyes, the hard lines of his face softening for a second before he looks away.

An electronic voice starts up in the ceiling. *"Air cycling starting now."*

The vent above us opens with a crack, and ice-cold air blasts over us with enough force to make me cower against the wall. I scrunch my eyes shut, huddling with my arms over my face for what feels like an eternity, until the vent slams shut.

The voice starts up again. *"Air cycled. No viral particles detected."*

"Y-you could have warned me," I say through chattering teeth.

Leoben shrugs. "What would be the fun in that?"

I glare at him, clutching my arms around myself as the wall beside us slides open. Beyond it, a long hexagonal corridor stretches out with another circular door set into the far end. The corridor's walls are slick concrete covered with tiny nozzles, and the floor is another metal grating. My eyes water with the sharp scent of disinfectant.

*"Please proceed to airlock two."*

My stomach sinks. "I'm guessing this is the *wash* part."

Leoben nods, pushing me through. "You guessed right."

The door slams shut behind us with a hiss of cold air, and the grating below us starts to shake.

"Anything you want to warn me about this time?" I ask.

Leoben looks me up and down, a low smile on his face. "There's no preparing for this, Agatta, but you might want to close your eyes."

I obey. A humming sound starts up, growing louder until it makes the whole corridor shudder. Thousands of tiny jets of ice-cold liquid hit my skin, choking the air with the harsh vanilla scent. I hold my breath but still get a splash of bitter liquid in my mouth, and cover my face with my hands, coughing. After a few seconds the streams cease, and I suck in a lungful of air that burns lines of fire through my sinuses.

*"Please keep your eyes closed. Stage two is almost complete."*

"Almost complete?" I splutter, opening my eyes just long enough to see a hurricane of air spiraling through the airlock. It's like a horizontal tornado, strong enough to make me stumble until Leoben grabs my wrist, yanking me upright. My wet hair whips around my face, covering my mouth. Something above us clicks and the airflow ceases as suddenly as it began. The third and final steel door opens with a hiss.

*"Thank you,"* the mechanized voice says. *"Welcome to Homestake."*

"I guess I know why Dax was complaining about the airlocks," I say.

Leoben chuckles, dragging me through the door and into another concrete room with a row of doors along the far wall.

"You look hilarious," he says, shaking his hands, splattering the walls with disinfectant. His clothes are dripping, but the fabric must be hydrophobic, because his tank top already looks dry. The blue shadow under his eyes isn't smudged at all, making me think it might be a pigmentation app, and a masterfully well-coded one at that. My backpack is waiting on a scratched steel counter, along with Leoben's gear. He swings his holster back around his shoulders and tucks his weapons away. "You ready to see the civ levels?"

I nod, shivering. My eyes are burning, one ear is blocked, and my hair is strewn across my face in tangled ropes, but I'm ready. I've spent two years wondering what this place looked like on the inside. I want to know what my father told me to stay away from.

I pull my backpack on, shoving the sopping hair from my face. "Okay, let's go."

Leoben leads me through one of the doors and into a cargo-size elevator. It runs sideways, groaning, then drops for what feels like an eternity. When it finally shudders to a stop, I hear a murmur of voices on the other side, and for some reason I can barely breathe.

The doors slide open. I expect to see more concrete, or rows of cells. Instead, I find myself in the middle of a street.

There are trees and flowers. Bright green grass. Cobblestoned paths wind between cafés, shop fronts, and pretty stone buildings. I know there's a ceiling above us, I know we're underground, but all I can see when I look up is a perfect azure sky.

Families are strolling and chatting, all dressed in blue—some in overalls, some in T-shirts with the Cartaxus logo stamped on the front. At a sprawling café across from the elevator, people are sitting on couches drinking what looks like coffee from steaming white mugs. Families are sharing meals. Children are running between tables, playing and shrieking as their parents pass plates of food to one another.

Suddenly I know why nobody who went to Homestake ever came out.

This place isn't a prison. It's a goddamn paradise.

Leoben takes my elbow, leading me out of the elevator, but his touch is gentler than when he led me in. He must sense the shock rolling through me. "You okay, Agatta?"

I nod dumbly, staring at the people. With a single glance, I can tell that none of them have killed for immunity, never lost themselves in the darkest moments of the Wrath. They've never starved through winters or hidden from Lurkers. They've never watched a crying child with bruises on his skin detonate in the middle of the street.

They all rushed into Homestake as soon as it opened, and they've been here ever since—eating muffins, sipping coffee.

I've been dying from the inside out, and why? Because my father told me to? Because he said Cartaxus was evil?

The file about Cole in my backpack looked pretty evil to me too.

A ripple of silence spreads through the crowd. Heads turn slowly, until every eye is locked on me. I see horror in their faces. Snatches of their words echo around me.

"New arrival, just a kid."

"Look how thin she is. I can't believe she made it this long."

"I wonder what she did to survive."

I pull my wet sleeves over my hands, hiding my dirty nails, suddenly seeing myself as the crowd must see me. As a scarred, filthy freak. A monster. Someone who's killed to survive rather than come here.

Why would my father keep me away from *this*?

"You want food or something?" Leoben asks.

I shake my head, staring at the crowd. "I could have been here, but he made me promise to stay away. He never called, he could have told me . . ."

Leoben's eyes narrow.

"I *killed* people," I whisper, my voice breaking. "I didn't want to, but he said . . . He said I had to stay away."

"Oh, goddammit," Leoben mutters, scraping a hand over his face. "Come on, Agatta, let's get you out of here."

He throws his arm around my shoulders and guides me into a building where we follow one hallway after another until I have no idea where we are. An apartment complex of some kind. Numbered white doors are set into the walls, lined with vacuum-style airtight frames. Most are closed, but some have been left open, giving me glimpses of the rooms inside. They're tiny, with beds that fold into the wall and counters with jet-cookers and sinks, the occasional stack of dirty dishes. I see a boy my age sprawled on a beanbag, his eyes glazed over, watching a film in VR. He lets out a snort of laughter as we pass, and it hits me like a punch.

Every glimpse, every smiling face is another open wound.

How could my father keep me away from *this*?

Leoben guides me through an open door. "Dax booked us a couple of rooms, even though we're not staying. This one's marked for you and Cole. It, uh, it should have everything you need, and Dax and I are right down the hall. You can shower, get yourself together before we leave."

I walk inside, looking around. Two bunk beds are set into the back, each with a curtain that slides closed to create a tiny private space. Another fold-down bed forms a couch near the door, opposite a kitchenette, and a tiny bathroom is tucked into the back.

Everything is just a little small, a little cramped, but there's a bed and food and water. I could have been *happy* here.

Leoben shifts uncomfortably, standing in the doorway. "I guess we weren't the only ones Lachlan screwed up. I sure as hell wouldn't want him for a father. I'll send Cole down when he's finished debriefing."

I nod, standing with my arms wrapped tight around my chest, swallowing hard against the rising pressure in my throat. Leoben leaves without another word, letting the door hiss closed behind him.

When he is gone, I finally let myself break.

# CHAPTER 20

BY THE TIME COLE FINDS ME, I'VE EATEN, SHOWERED, and dressed in clean Cartaxus clothes with my hair knotted in a plait down my back. My eyes are red rimmed, despite the ice-cold water I splashed on them in an attempt to hide the fact that I'd been crying.

I'm not crying anymore. I'm *angry*. My shoulders are tight with tension, and I have to fight the urge to get up and run, to break something. I'm sitting cross-legged on the floor with my genkit and the musty folders of my father's notes scattered beside me.

Cole barely glances at me as he hurries in from the hallway, drenched in the airlock's disinfectant. He's still annoyed at me for coming here. He avoids my eyes as he slides the door shut behind him, but his face goes white when he sees the folders on the floor. "Where did you get those?"

"In the mines. Cole, I need you to tell me what my father did to you."

He presses his hands to his eyes, drawing in a long, slow breath. "Okay, but I need to shower first."

He walks silently into the bathroom and shuts the door. I flick open Leoben's file for a moment before closing it again. The notes inside still don't make much sense to me, and seeing the photograph in the back of a young and frightened Leoben feels like an invasion of his privacy. He was just a child. They all were. My stomach churns at the thought.

Why the hell was my father studying them?

Cole soon emerges from the bathroom, dressed in fresh clothes, the sharp vanilla scent of Cartaxus's soap rolling off his skin. He grabs a bottle of water from the kitchenette and sits down on the floor beside me, scanning the folders before picking up his own file. His face is impassive. It's the same mask I've seen on him before, and I recognize it now for what it is: his way of dealing with too much pain.

"I think these might be the notes we need to unlock the vaccine," I say. "The other boxes were just junk. This is the only one that stood out."

Cole nods, staring at the photograph of himself as a boy, then flicks through the other folders, pausing for a long time on Jun Bei's. "These are my family," he says finally. "This is . . . this is her."

He hands me the file, open to a photograph at the back of a little girl glaring at the camera, her mouth twisted with rage. There are bandages across her chest, and scars creeping up her neck. The name below the picture reads *Subject 1, Jun Bei Meng.*

"She was the strongest of us," Cole says. "She escaped three years ago. I never found out if she made it or not until you showed me those server results. I don't know why she didn't tell me, why she didn't ask me to come. We were together. I thought we were in love, but maybe she thought I'd slow her down."

He flips open the other files, arranging the five subjects in order on the table. Subject 2 is a blond-haired girl called Anna, and Subject 3 is Ziana, a bald girl with skin so pale that you can see her veins through it. Subject 4 is Leoben, and Subject 5 is Cole, whose young face has haunted me since I first saw his photograph.

"Ziana escaped during the outbreak," Cole says, rubbing his face.

"And Anna's been at another facility for most of the last year, with almost no contact. Leoben and I were the only ones left at the base in the end. We had nowhere to run, or we might have left too."

I close my eyes. "My father . . . ," I say, trying to keep my voice calm. "What was he doing to you?"

Cole sighs. "I don't know if you need to hear this, Cat. There are things that can't be unheard, and this is getting into dangerous territory."

"It's already dangerous, Cole. My father was experimenting on *children*. If you're worried that I'll hate him for this—"

"That's exactly what I'm worried about."

"Why would that matter to you?"

He reaches for my hand, taking it between his. "It matters because your father is the reason we're doing this. We're following a couple of his notes to do something we don't understand, and it might put us all in danger. If you don't have faith in the man he was, there's no reason we should keep going."

"But you do? After all this, you still have faith in him?"

Cole nods, his face solemn. "More than anyone else on the planet."

I pull my hand away and run it through my hair, leaning back against the lower bunk. "Cole, my father had secrets. I've always known that, and I guess maybe part of me didn't want to know what they were. But I need to know now. I think this might be the key to unlocking the vaccine."

He holds my gaze for a long time, then lets out a sigh. "Well, the first thing you need to know is that we were all born at Cartaxus. I never met my parents. We were raised in a lab and had nurses when we were young, so that was all we ever knew, and I think that made it easier. We didn't join the rest of Cartaxus until the outbreak, but we were soldiers from the start. That was the point of the Zarathustra Initiative."

*The Zarathustra Initiative.* The words send a chill down my spine. I glance at the files, but it's not printed anywhere on them. I almost feel like my father mentioned it once, but I can't dredge up the memory. Maybe something he was talking about with Dax that I overheard.

"So were they making you into supersoldiers? Why would they need children for that?"

Something in Cole's expression makes me pause, and I remember the irregularities I saw in his DNA when I hacked into his panel. I thought my father had changed his genes somehow, splicing new DNA into his, but I should have known better than that.

Splicing doesn't work. Your cells reject the altered DNA, and it kills you. You have to be *born* with those genes.

I flick through Jun Bei's file. Her sequencing report and gene diagrams tell me she's allergic to dairy and that her eyes are green, but they also tell me that several of her chromosomes differ significantly from the average human's.

"What the hell is this?" I flip open the other files. "You can't change this sort of thing with gentech. You can't rewrite this much of someone's DNA without killing them." I point to a circled area in one report. "This is the anthrozone—we don't even have that part of the human genome *mapped*. This isn't splicing, it wouldn't be possible, it would . . ."

I drift off, staring at the files. "They weren't making soldiers, were they? They were making knockout kids."

The thing with genetics is, there's no map to explain how it all works—you just have to figure it out through trial and error, learning along the way. Back when we first sequenced the genome, it was an unintelligible mass of data that scientists broke into smaller chunks—genes—like the words in a sentence. But nobody knew what the words meant, or what the genes did, so they'd knock out one gene at a time in mouse DNA and grow a mouse without it—a *knockout* mouse. If the mouse was blind, the gene they knocked out must control vision. Maybe it wouldn't grow cartilage properly, or its fur would be curly. They made thousands of them, slowly mapping out the mouse genome, and since humans and mice have similar DNA, we learned a lot about ourselves.

But it got messy, like language—if you move the words around in a sentence, you get a different meaning, and that's how genes work too. Eventually, we reached a limit of what we could learn from mice, and we were left with parts of the human genome we still didn't understand. They moved on to rabbits, chimps, bonobos, zeroing in on the anthrozone—a set of gene combinations which are unique to humans. It's against the law to knock genes out in babies, and for good reason. They might be born with horrific mutations or be unable to survive at all. It's the worst kind of ethical violation. The anthrozone is off-limits for experimentation, and it holds thousands of combinations of genes that we still don't understand.

But someone at Cartaxus must have done it anyway.

The Zarathustra Initiative is a line of knockout kids.

"What was my father's role?" I whisper. But I already know. I can see it in the notes—the passion, the possessiveness about the research.

"Lachlan was in charge of the project," Cole says, confirming my fears. "He started it. He was there from before we were born, up until he quit Cartaxus."

I stand up and sit down again. I want to respond, but I don't trust my voice, and I don't know what to say. I thought I could handle the truth, but I didn't think it would be anything like *this*. This isn't the work of a scientist—this is the work of a monster.

"You haven't asked why he did this," Cole says. "Lachlan always had a good reason for his work."

"A good reason to torture children?" I stand and pace to the sink, bracing my hands on the counter. "To experiment on them? To cut them open and see what they looked like inside?"

"That was part of it," Cole says, stepping up behind me. "But he was looking for something specific, something he could only figure out by mapping the parts of us that make us human. Think about it, Catarina. What separates humans from animals?"

I let out a bitter laugh. "We're the only species who would do this to children, for one thing."

"No," Cole says, his voice gentle. He reaches for my shoulder. "Right now, what's the biggest difference? You've been out in the wild. What have you seen?"

I close my eyes, thinking of the flocks of passenger pigeons, the way they blacken the skies for days when they fly overhead. I think about deer growing fat on abandoned crops, of the blast craters littering the empty, trash-strewn cities.

I open my eyes. "The biggest difference is, we're *dying*."

"That's right. Hydra only affects humans." Cole takes my shoulder, turning me to him. "Your father had a reason for his work, Catarina. He was trying to make a vaccine."

My heartbeat slows. "No, Hydra wasn't discovered yet. . . ."

But that's more naivety. More willful ignorance. I'm standing in a bunker that holds eighty thousand people, perfectly designed to keep them safe from an airborne pandemic. It opened just a few weeks after the outbreak.

"You're telling me . . . ," I breathe. "You're telling me they *knew*."

"For thirty years. Cartaxus has been studying Hydra since before you were born."

"Thirty years?" I press one hand to my forehead, my head spinning with the weight of everything I'm hearing.

"Just come and sit down." Cole gestures to the bunks.

"I don't want to sit down."

"Please," he urges. "I can't relax with you hurting yourself like that."

I drop my eyes. One hand is in a fist, my fingernails digging half-moons into the skin of my palm. I unfurl it slowly, and a thin line of blood runs down my little finger.

Cole sits down on the lower bunk, and I perch myself on the edge beside him, my head dropped, my elbows on my knees.

"It started thirty years ago," he says. "Researchers found a body frozen in the Arctic permafrost. It was prehistoric, and when it thawed, it gave off a cloud of gas. The researchers got sick, the CDC moved in, and then the sick people started blowing. That was the first outbreak. The world's governments controlled it, but they recognized the threat Hydra posed. A research group was formed to study it, and that was how Cartaxus started. Your father joined when most of the work was genetic research, but Cartaxus eventually split into two groups: those who were trying to make a vaccine, and those who were preparing for the inevitable outbreak. They started building airtight camps and decided that all ethical considerations needed to be put aside."

I rub my forearm where the bandage over my panel is starting to itch. "So the Zarathustra Initiative, the knockout kids . . ."

He nods. "They were an attempt to find a vaccine. It had been ten years, and they still weren't any closer, so they were ready to try anything."

"And it worked?"

Cole nods. "Leoben's genome was the basis for the vaccine's code. If it wasn't for your father's research, we'd all be doomed."

I let out a slow breath, scratching my arm, dropping back to my knees to pick up Leoben's file. His young face has dark skin, shaved black hair, and stitches winding up his neck. His genome is like none I've seen before.

My hands are shaking, but somehow my mind is steady. Everything is starting to make a twisted sort of sense.

My father hated Cartaxus because he hated himself. He knew the work he'd done for them on this project was wrong. Did he tell me to stay away from them for my own good, or was he just afraid of what I'd think of him if I found out the truth?

"I know this is a lot to accept," Cole says.

"I don't know why he never told me," I say. My arm is starting to burn, and I rub it against my thigh.

"What's wrong with your arm?"

My vision grows dark for a moment, then blurs before snapping back into focus. "The guard said my panel was regenerating. I didn't think it could, but I guess it can. I think my ocular tech is restarting."

"Let me look at it."

"It's fine," I say, but he reaches for my arm, his movements unnaturally fast. He rips back my sleeve, revealing the bandage underneath.

The breath leaves my lungs in a single, terrified gasp.

"What?" Cole's hands fly back as though I've burned him. "Did I hurt you? What happened?"

"Oh shit," I whisper, ripping at the bandage, unwinding the blood-stained gauze. Underneath, my skin is pale around the incision, where ugly black stitches trace a three-inch line along my arm.

The incision is healing nicely. The wound is neat and clean.

But there are *twenty-four* cobalt dots glowing beneath my skin.

I look up at Cole, my heart racing. "Get the medkit. Hurry, Cole. I need you to cut out my panel."

# CHAPTER 21

COLE STANDS UP, HIS EYES WIDE. "WHAT THE HELL are you talking about?"

"This isn't a hypergenesis-friendly installation. This thing is going to kill me."

The flashing stripe of cobalt light on my forearm casts an eerie glow over Cole's face. The way it's flashing tells me it's installing, which means the hypergenesis protocols have already been overridden. Marcus must have done something to it while I was unconscious. Corroded it, added new code—I don't know how he screwed it up this badly. I close my eyes and see a flash of Amy's twisted mouth and scabbed, disgusting horns.

Marcus's code is inside me right now, rampaging through my cells. I clutch one hand over my mouth, fighting the urge to vomit.

"Can you turn it off?" Cole asks.

"I don't think so." I close my eyes, trying to focus, but none of my mental commands are working. I can't control my ocular tech or even pull up my comm. It's a brand-new system—it could take weeks to set up, to monitor my brain patterns until it knows how to respond to my thoughts. Trying to turn it off like this is going to be impossible.

The only way to stop it is to cut the whole thing out.

"Shouldn't it check for hypergenesis?" Cole asks.

I grab my backpack and pull the medkit from it, flipping it open on the floor. Scalpels, stitches. I'll need a tourniquet. "It's supposed to, but this thing is already installing. It's flashing, can't you see that?"

"So stop it."

"I *can't*," I say. "I told you, it's installing. It's not responding to commands. By the time it does, I'll already be dead."

Cole still doesn't seem to understand. He's looking at me like I'm a child jumping to an extreme solution without thinking it through. Normally, he'd be right. Panels have dozens of layers of security to stop this kind of thing from happening, but mine must be broken. I can't explain it. The only thing I can do is pick up a scalpel and start this myself.

"Whoa," Cole says, his eyes widening as I slide a gleaming blade from the medkit. "The nanites aren't deploying yet. We can find a doctor."

"You're not listening to me," I snap, yanking my navy Homestake shirt off. I hurl it across the room and spin around in my bra to show him the patchwork of crinkled scars along my spine. "The last time I hacked my panel, it took thirty-seven seconds for this to happen. There were holes in my skin, you could see my *spine* through them, and that was just from a single app. I have twenty-four in my arm now. Even if we cut this out, there's still a good chance I'm going to die."

Cole's face pales, but he doesn't respond. I have a sudden urge to punch him. It's hard enough to keep myself from panicking, I don't have the energy to argue with him about this. I step to him. "You *have* to do this. I can't cut it out of my own arm."

"I-I can't," he says. "I can't hurt you, the protective protocol . . ."

"Your protective protocol is a pain in my ass." I unfurl a roll of gauze from the medkit and squat down on the floor, holding my arm out.

"Okay, we'll start at the base. Use the incision Marcus left, that's a start, but it's still going to hurt like hell when it opens up."

I look up to find Cole leaning against the wall with his eyes closed, his hands bunched in fists at his sides.

"You learned how to do this, right? Cartaxus had to teach you panel maintenance."

"No . . . yes," he whispers. "I don't know. There has to be another way."

"We're running out of time. We need to do this *now*."

"But I can't," he breathes, his eyes flicking between my arm and the scalpels on the floor. "Catarina, I'm sorry, I just can't. . . ."

"Get Dax, then—he knows how to do this."

"Crick isn't responding. I think he's in the airlock."

"Jesus, Cole!" I shout, launching myself from the floor. I thrust my forearm across his neck and shove him back against the wall. The bunk beds shudder with his weight, his eyes perfect circles of surprise. "Get Dax!" I yell into his face. "I'm *dying*, do you not understand that?"

He blinks, an unreadable expression on his face, then throws the door open and bolts down the hall.

I drop back into a crouch, sucking in a breath. The stitches I can handle, but maybe it's better to use scissors. I find a tiny, razor-tipped pair in the medkit and sit cross-legged on the floor. My hands tremble as I force one blade under the closest stitch.

Okay, this is hurting a lot more than I thought it would.

A trickle of blood runs down my arm, curling around to drip from my thumb. I kick away the Zarathustra files and pop the next stitch, breathing deeply to clear my head. Two down, ten to go. And I still need to pull them out. The curled black thread is hanging from one side of the cut, glistening with blood. I snip the next five as quickly as I can, snagging the scissors on my skin, adding more trickles of blood to the spatter on the floor.

I close my eyes, fighting a surge of nausea, a throbbing pain radiating from my forearm. The memory of the flesh on my back bubbling and splitting rears up through my mind, and I force my eyes open. If Cole doesn't hurry, we won't have time to do this properly.

Maybe we should just amputate my arm.

I pop another stitch, and the thin film of new tissue along the incision tears apart with a rush of sparkling pain. The wound stretches open, revealing bloody bubbles of fat in a three-inch diamond along my arm. I bite my lip and work through the rest of the stitches, my eyes brimming with tears, when something *shifts* under my skin.

A humming starts up, and the lights on my forearm flicker off. The incision stretches wide like a bloody, unseeing eye. I wince, gritting my teeth against the pain as my forearm bulges, the panel vibrating under my skin.

It's auto-ejecting. The panel has realized that I'm trying to get it out, and it's decided to *help* me.

A dozen tiny black wires wriggle through the wound, coiling and squirming like snakes, dragging the soft pink plastic of my panel into the air. It squelches, wires flicking and coiling, shoving a scarlet-streaked flap directly out of the wound.

The walls spin around me. I gag, managing to lurch over to the sink, spitting out a mouthful of acid and bile. My body shakes with adrenaline as I sink to my knees on the concrete, staring breathlessly at the wound.

An army of squirming black wires fans out across my skin, stretching the wound open, trying to lift my panel out. But they can't. It's stuck. The incision isn't long enough.

I glance at the door. No one's coming. I'm going to have to do this myself.

"Okay, okay, okay," I whisper, groping on the floor for the scalpel I pulled out of the medkit. My fingers are shaking, slick with blood. They slide over the cold steel handle twice before I manage to pick it up. My hand shakes dangerously as I bring the blade to my forearm, trying to figure out the best way to open it. I could make it longer, or cut across it, or turn it into an L shape. I don't remember which way is better, and I don't want to cut a vein.

"L shape, L shape," I mutter, dredging up a distant memory of some kind of training with holoscreens, practicing on other kids. I close my eyes, pressing the tip of the scalpel to my skin, and draw in a deep breath.

But I can't do it.

The invisible hands of fear are locked around the scalpel, keeping it frozen in midair.

"Come on," I growl, throwing my head back. I press the blade into my skin until it stings, but I can't make the swift, clean stroke that could end this.

So it can't be swift, then. I grit my teeth, jabbing the blade into the edge of the wound. Blood wells up and my fingers clench, but I've started. Now all I have to do is drag it two more inches across my skin.

The panel's lights flash as I suck in another breath, steadying myself. It shivers and hums, the black wires writhing like a thousand tiny snakes, coiling closer to the panel's body. They wrap around the strip of plastic, enveloping it completely.

It shifts back into my arm.

"No!" I shout. It's changed its mind. It doesn't think I'm trying to get it out—it thinks I'm hurt, and now it's installing *faster* to help me. "No, no, no, please!"

The lights blink on, racing up my arm, and I scrunch my eyes shut and drag the blade across my skin.

The pain is like a firework. I feel it whistle as it rises, promising heat and light and fury, until it finally detonates. It shatters across my skin, and I let out a strangled cry, buckling, clutching my arm to my chest. The warmth of my blood trickles down my stomach. The panel is humming again, shifting, changing back to its ejection protocol. A fresh cry rips from my throat as it slides, warm and slick, straight out of the wound.

I let out a gasp, shaking with relief. Tears drip from my cheeks, forming clear patterns in the sheen of blood that covers the concrete floor. I drop my arm, grabbing the warm bundle of wires that is my panel, but feel a tug of tension all the way up my arm. A single cable stretches into the wound, jutting from the back of the panel, the same thickness as my little finger. It's black flecked with gold, marking it as one of the network of cables that pumps nanites through my body. Most are no thicker than a human hair, but this is the primary distribution cord. It runs to a socket in my shoulder that must have locked and stopped it.

But that's okay. I've bought myself a few more minutes before the panel tries to turn itself on again. This butchered thing is still hooked up to the cabling inside my body, but at least it's out of me.

I wipe my mouth with the back of my hand and find myself swaying, a rush of heat creeping up the sides of my neck. The room blurs, and I throw my hand out for the wall, but manage only to slide down it, leaving a scarlet streak on the concrete.

Somebody shouts outside, their voice punctuated with footsteps. The door whooshes open, and a hand slides around my head, cradling my face. I blink, expecting to see Cole but instead find bright green eyes, rogue strands of red hair plastered to a freckled forehead.

"Dax," I whisper groggily. He's soaked, stinking of disinfectant. "You found me."

"Yes, Princess. It's okay, I'm here." He turns me to my back on the floor, pushing the hair from my face with his pale, slender fingers. I'm still just in my bra, but it doesn't matter. Nothing matters anymore. Dax found me, and now everything is going to be okay.

"You did it," he breathes, lifting my wounded arm carefully. "Oh, good girl, you got it out."

Cole appears like a ghost behind him, every muscle in his body tense, his eyes wide and haunted as he stares down at my arm. "I . . . ," he whispers, his eyes flashing to black. "I can't be here. I'm sorry. . . ." He stumbles back out of the room.

"Some hero," Dax mutters, turning the panel's body in his hand. "What's wrong with the primary cord?"

"Shoulder socket. It's jammed, like when I hacked my panel. The cord won't retract." I clench my good hand into a fist, trying to draw my mind back into focus. If we can't disconnect the panel in the next few minutes, its emergency fail-safes will try to turn it on again. That might prompt a surge of emergency healing tech to race up the cable and into me. With my hypergenesis, that's a death sentence.

"We have to get it out, Dax," I say. "We need to yank it."

"I'm not yanking anything. That socket branches into your spine. It's too dangerous."

"But the cord is graphene coated—we can't cut it." I glance at the blood-streaked mess of the panel and force my eyes to the ceiling. "We'll have to reboot the socket."

Dax's face darkens. Rebooting the shoulder socket is risky. It means turning the panel on again, which is what we're trying to avoid. But once it's on, the shoulder socket's clamps will unlock for a split second, giving us a chance to pull the cable out. If we get it out in time, I'll be safe.

"I don't know about this . . . ," Dax says.

"It's our only chance."

"I know, but I'm not sure if I can code and pull it out at the same time."

"I can do it." I roll to my side, my arm angled awkwardly behind me. "You pull when I tell you to. I'll run the command."

Dax grabs the genkit and unfurls its reader wire, jabbing it into the bloodied mess of my panel. Silver connectors emerge to grab it, clicking into place. The genkit's screen flashes, and Dax holds the gold-flecked cable tight. I can feel the tension of it underneath my bicep, running all the way up my arm.

"Okay," I whisper to myself, navigating through the genkit's files. One-handed typing has never been my strong suit, but I still manage to tap out a few commands, leaving bloodied smudges across the keyboard. I navigate through the panel's installation system to the scripts controlling the shoulder socket and force a clean reboot. The screen flashes, code scrolling rapidly as it relays the commands.

"It's rebooting," I say, wincing as it burns in my shoulder. "Get ready to pull. Once the clamp unlocks there won't be much time."

Dax nods. Code flashes across the screen, and something clicks inside my shoulder.

"Now!" I yell, and Dax yanks the cable out.

# CHAPTER 22

I LET OUT A SCREAM, ARCHING ON THE FLOOR. THE cable tears through my shoulder, then twists and curls out of my arm. Dax drops the wire-covered, bloody strip of my panel on the concrete. The gold-flecked cable attached to it retracts, coiling up like a snake.

It's out.

I tilt my head back, letting out a cry of relief, my body still shaking with adrenaline.

"That's it," Dax gasps, reaching out to grip my blood-smeared fingers in his own, staring at me. His face is as white as the disinfectant-soaked lab coat hanging from his shoulders. The relief pounding through me is so intense it makes me giddy. I want to laugh; I want to scream. I want to grab the lapels of Dax's lab coat and drag him down to kiss me.

But my limbs feel like they're made of stone. I'm so exhausted I can barely move. The sound of my breathing fades, and my vision starts to swim. Something hot trickles down my arm, pooling in my upturned palm. I look down and swallow. "Dax, I'm bleeding."

"Oh shit. Hang on." He unhooks his belt. He slides it from his pants and slips it around my shoulder, cinching it tight enough to cut off the flow. Pain lances through my arm, but the trickle slows, and my vision starts to clear. Dax rummages through the medkit, pulling out a roll of black thread and a curved needle. "Let's get this closed up so I can bandage it."

I look away as he pulls through the first stitch, glancing at the mess of my panel on the concrete. The dripping heap of wires is still twitching and squirming, a few stray black coils searching blindly for somewhere to plug themselves in.

"It's so ugly," I whisper.

"It's out, that's all that matters." Dax tugs on my arm, tying off the first stitch. "You were brilliant, Princess. God, I've missed you."

"I've missed you too, Dax."

He pauses, one hand on my arm, the other holding the needle. "You're probably wondering why I never called."

I look up at him. His face is tight. He can't even look at me. "I'm wondering a lot of things, but that's definitely one of them."

He pulls through another stitch, hunching over my arm. Drops of the airlock's disinfectant drip from his hair, falling on my arm in stinging drops of fire. "When Cartaxus came to take us from the cabin, I was so relieved they didn't find you. They were awful. They shot Lachlan, and I thought I was going into hell, right up until we got to the lab."

I close my eyes. He tugs on my arm again, tying off the second stitch.

"When we got there, they took Lachlan into the medical ward, and I met the rest of the team. There were thirty of them, all coders. They were brilliant, though you would have blown most of them out of the water, and everyone else was happy to be there. They'd all brought their families. We were safe and comfortable. I realized Lachlan had it wrong. I couldn't believe that we'd left you behind."

He tightens another stitch. "I went to the medical ward to tell Lachlan we needed to get you. The virus was in California, the infection rate was soaring, and we were working on a draft vaccine that Lachlan had written years before. You knew Lachlan's code better than anyone, so you should have been second-in-charge of the work, but he told me you could never come. He made me *swear* not to contact you."

My heart stills. "Why?"

"He was adamant that you would die if they ever took you, that it would be a catastrophe, but he wouldn't tell me why. He was so firm about it that I believed him. I've never seen him so deadly serious about anything in his life. The only theory I could come up with was that maybe you had a condition, something fatal he'd cured with nonstandard tech. I thought it might have something to do with your hypergenesis."

A fatal condition? My hypergenesis? My head swims with the thought. Marcus's daughter, Eloise, flutters into my mind. Her blond eyelashes and soft cheeks. The nucleatoxis disease destroying her brain, held at bay by nonstandard code.

If I *did* have a condition like that, something my father had cured with nonstandard code, it would make sense for him to hide me from Cartaxus. He'd make me promise to stay out of the bunkers. He wouldn't send anyone to find me.

If they did, they might wipe the code from my arm and kill me.

"But that can't be right," I say, opening my eyes. "He never mentioned anything, and he'd never keep something like that hidden from me. It doesn't make any sense."

This time Dax meets my gaze, his emerald eyes troubled. "None of this makes any sense, Princess, and that's what frightens me. Whatever Lachlan was planning, whatever his motivations were, I think we need to figure them out if we want to unlock the vaccine."

I look down at my arm, blood-smeared, swollen, raw. Dax ties off the last stitch and spins the genkit around. The reader wire is still plugged into the ruins of my panel, which has ceased twitching and now lies in a limp mess on the floor.

"The first thing to figure out," Dax says, "is why your panel just broke through five layers of hypergenesis security protocols. I'm going to run a full scan of the architecture, and see if I can find out what the hell just happened."

I nod. His eyes glaze over and the genkit's screen flashes as he logs in wirelessly, using the VR connection in his panel. The genkit starts to hum, and Dax's face goes slack as he shifts his focus into a virtual space I can't share.

The genkit's screen flickers with a constant blur of text and equations, showing the files he's calling up with his mind and reading through at a dizzying speed. I prop myself up on my good elbow and watch his glassy eyes skip back and forth as he works.

Of all the apps I wish I had, VR is the most painful to be without, especially since I already have most of the implants required to use it. Like practically everyone with a panel, I have a basic skullnet—a web of microscopic wires fanned out in a lattice across the inside of my skull. The net picks up the electrical activity of my brain, translating my thoughts into commands that my panel's processors can read and understand.

I also have an optic feed—a coil of wires leading from the graphics chip in my panel into my optic nerve. Together, those implants should have been enough to let me use VR, but the graphics chip in the custom-coded panel my father gave me is ancient and clunky. It can't keep up with the computations required to run VR—it could barely handle the text in my vision when I sent comms to Agnes. All it could do was run built-in filters and draw text and icons. I spent months researching ways to upgrade it, but every other chip I found needed a different power source, a more sophisticated operating system, and a heat-transfer chip to stop it burning a hole right through my arm. None of the code I found was hypergenesis-friendly, so eventually I gave up, but I never stopped wishing that I could launch myself into an immersive VR world.

Lying here, watching Dax, I want nothing more than to join his session and code with him side by side. There's no denying that his face holds an austere beauty, but it was never his looks that attracted me to him. It was this—his concentration, the flitting of his eyes as he casts his thoughts effortlessly into blocks of perfect code. When I'm working, I need to type each word letter by letter, but Dax throws down whole blocks of logic in every thought. My code grows like a house, rising slowly from foundations, each brick laid carefully before the design becomes clear. But with Dax, when he codes through his panel, entire rooms and structures fly together in a whirlwind. I can see it on the genkit's screen—a hundred files open, multiple pages selected and transformed in a heartbeat. With a single thought, he can summon algorithms and rules, rearranging them in a flurry before snapping them into place. It's magical to watch the way his mind spins pages of code like puzzle pieces, splitting and weaving them together with the merest thought.

His eyes bounce back and forth, his breath quickening. The urge to join his session is so strong I can barely hold it in. I want to entwine my consciousness with his, let our minds meld together, and turn blocks of code into towering masterpieces. Together, we'd be twice as fast. Two minds working in harmony.

Dax and I would be something *special* if we could work together.

I reach out for him instinctively, tracing my blood-spotted fingers along the side of his face. They leave tracks of scarlet across his pale, freckled skin, but he doesn't flinch away. He doesn't even seem to feel it. I draw my hand back again just as he snaps out of his session, yanking the cable from my ruined panel.

"What the hell?" he gasps. He reaches for my arm. "I need a tissue sample, something live. I need to run a scan."

"What's wrong?" I hold my arm out, and he slides the needle-tipped cable straight into the freshly-stitched wound in my arm. I hiss as the metal pushes into the incision, producing a fresh trickle of blood. The cable twitches, drawing back a sample of my cells for the genkit to run an analysis on. He pulls it back out, his eyes glazing briefly.

"Dax, what's happening? Is something wrong?"

"You have a backup chip." He looks stunned. He looks *terrified*.

"No, I don't. That's why I was so worried when it was damaged."

He shakes his head. "I don't know what to tell you, but you have one in your spine. It's masking its access, but it looks like a standard setup. I don't understand this."

I stare at him, my head spinning. If I had a backup chip, I could regrow my old panel instead of getting budded with a new one. All my hypergenesis-friendly apps would be back and functioning in a matter of days instead of the weeks it normally takes to grow a panel from scratch. But I've never seen anything about a backup in my panel's code. If Dax has found one in my spine, that means my father put it there and never told me about it.

A cold feeling settles in my stomach, and then the rest of Dax's words catch up with me.

"Wait, did you say a *standard* setup? Like a normal panel?"

Dax nods, his eyes glazed again. "I can't see what's in it, but it's definitely not hypergenesis-friendly. I'm checking the tissue sample."

"What do you need the tissue sample for?"

"I'm checking, but . . ." The blood drains from his face. "But it's the same result."

"What's the same result? Dax, what do you see?"

His eyes refocus, and he looks down at the stitches in my arm, swallowing. "I don't know how to say this, but I don't think you have hypergenesis."

# CHAPTER 23

THE AIR STILLS. DAX'S WORDS ECHO THROUGH MY mind.

*I don't think you have hypergenesis.*

"That's ridiculous." I push myself up with my good arm until I'm sitting cross-legged on the blood-splattered concrete. The movement makes my vision blur. I rub my eyes, shaking my head. "I was born with hypergenesis."

Dax just stares at me. "I don't know what to tell you. These results are all coming up negative. Here, you can see for yourself." He turns the genkit's screen to me. A bright green banner glows at the top, and the words are there, as clear as day.

*Hypergenesis not detected.*

Every time I've plugged my panel in, the same banner has flashed red. I must have seen it a hundred times. This can't be happening.

"But my *back*," I say, my voice shaking. "Dax, you were there that night. I hacked my panel, and half my back bubbled off."

"I know. Trust me, Princess, this is freaking me out as much as it is you."

I doubt it. My stomach is clenched like a fist, my heart pounding. I punch a command into the genkit, running the scan again. The green flashing banner reappears. I try another scan, running deeper this time, testing the behavior of every component of my cells.

The result comes back. A jagged line, representing the way the sample Dax took from me responded to an array of test nanites. A hypergenesis-positive reading would look like wild, patternless static, and a negative reading would be almost flat. My line is like a ridge of mountains. Not flat, but not chaos, either. I stare at it, a chill creeping across my skin.

It tells me I don't have hypergenesis, but it doesn't say that I'm *normal*, either.

"Dax, look at this. I don't know what it means. I've never seen a result like this before."

He leans in, then turns to me. "Didn't your mother have hypergenesis?"

"Yeah, that's how she and my father met. He was running tests on her blood."

Hypergenesis is rare, with only a handful of known cases in the world, but samples from people with the condition are in high demand. Their cells don't behave like they're supposed to, and when that happens in science, there's always something interesting to be learned. When my father was starting out at Cartaxus, my mother was the only living hypergenesis donor in the country. She saw him so often and for so long that she joked that they should get married. When he ran out of code to test on her, he proposed.

She lived another five years, until a well-meaning doctor gave her a syringe of healing tech after a car crash. Most people with hypergenesis die young. The condition is a curse—something that nobody would ever wish upon their child. I haven't thought about my mother since we left the cabin, but Dax is right to mention her. Hypergenesis is a non-Mendelian trait—it isn't passed down by a parent's chromosomes, but it is hereditary. Every child who's ever been born to a mother with the condition has inherited it too.

But none of them had Lachlan Agatta as a father.

"Jesus, Dax. He *did* something to me, didn't he?"

Dax nods, staring at the jagged line on the genkit's screen. "It appears so. He must have found a way to suppress the condition, but it isn't gone completely. I don't know what these readings mean, but they're weak. I wouldn't expect foreign code to even give you a rash, so I'm not sure what happened to your back. There must have been something else going on that hurt you when you hacked your panel that night."

Dax and I both turn to the mess of my panel at the same time. He jams the genkit's wire into its side. It connects with a wet click. His eyes glaze over, flitting back and forth. "Here," he says. "There's something in one of your old modules."

He tilts his head, pulling it up on the genkit's screen for me. It's my healing tech's code—four hundred pages of my father's unique notation. From the installation log beside it, it looks like this was the app Marcus cut out of me. He thought it was neural code and that it could help his wife, but that's ridiculous—this slow, clunky code took days to heal anything worse than a scratch.

I flick my finger across the genkit's touchpad, reading the commands. I've never sat down and actually read through most of this code. Back in the cabin, my father didn't want me messing around with it, and ever since I hurt my back, I've been too scared to even jack into my panel. The code is complicated, but I find myself reading it easily, the way I've always done with my father's work. But a few pages in, I hit a section that isn't like the rest. I frown, scanning the comments.

*Unregistered code . . . Analyze . . . Epidermis . . . Corrode . . .*

My heartbeat slows. "This code was written to attack my *skin*."

Dax nods. "It would have run if you used any apps that weren't registered to your panel. It's vicious, but it wouldn't have killed you. I think your father wrote this to make it *look* like you have hypergenesis, but you don't."

The crinkled scar tissue along my spine prickles. I stare at the code. "But my father wouldn't have—"

I stop myself, digging my fingernails into my palm. He wouldn't have hurt me—that's what I was going to say, but now it sounds impossibly naive.

Of *course* my father would hurt me. I've seen what he did to Cole. He cut open five children and ran experiments on them. What made me think he wouldn't hurt me, too? How could I have missed this? I scrunch my eyes shut, blocking out the evidence on the genkit's screen.

"Princess," Dax says.

He touches my shoulder, but I flinch away. I don't want to be comforted. I don't want his sympathy. I want to break out of here, drive back to the cabin, and burn the whole place down.

I open my eyes and stare at the genkit's screen. The pain gripping me is shifting into anger, making my breath come fast, blurring my vision. My blood pressure is still low, and I should get an IV. I should lie down or bandage my arm, but I can't focus on anything else right now.

"But don't you see?" Dax asks. "Whatever your father did to cure your hypergenesis, he's gone to great lengths to cover it up. It must have been something illegal. This has to be why he left you behind. He needed to hide it from Cartaxus."

"I don't care about Cartaxus," I spit, stunned by the anger in my voice. "He hid it from me, too, Dax. He *lied* to me. He made me think I had hypergenesis, and hid code inside my arm . . ."

My head snaps up, my blood freezing. I grab the genkit and yank it to me.

"What is it?" Dax asks.

The colors seem to fade from the room. My concentration shrinks my world down to the blinking cursor on the genkit's screen. I jump through the folders of my panel's operating system, kicking off a handful of scans.

"Cole told me how Cartaxus started," I say, still typing. "My father was trying to make a vaccine *before* the outbreak, wasn't he?"

"He'd been trying to make a Hydra vaccine for over twenty years."

"That means he had decades to think about how to release it, and make sure Cartaxus wouldn't control it. He saw them encrypt the Influenza code, and he knew they'd do it with Hydra. He wasn't going to let it happen again." I punch a string of commands into the genkit with my good hand, setting off another batch of scans. "This plan we're all following, I can see it now. It just goes back further than I thought."

Dax's brow furrows. "What are you checking?"

I look up at him. The movement makes my head spin. I pull in a slow breath, forcing myself to stay upright. "I've been thinking about this all wrong. I thought my father cared about me—"

"He did, Princess. He loved you more than anything."

"Let me *finish*," I hiss.

Dax looks stunned for a second, then nods swiftly. I set off a scan on the genkit and meet his eyes. "I thought he loved me like most people love their children. But he didn't, Dax, because he wasn't *like* most people. When Cole showed up at the cabin, he didn't want to follow my father's plan, but I used his feelings for Jun Bei as leverage. I thought that was what my father wanted me to do, and I'm pretty sure it *was*, but it made me feel sick to manipulate Cole like that."

Dax nods slowly. My vision blurs in and out. I shift on the floor, trying to keep myself steady.

"But that's what my father did all the time. I see it now, Dax. He manipulated people, and used them as tools. This whole plan to release the vaccine is like a game of chess, and he's still moving the pieces around, even though he's gone. My only mistake is that I thought I was playing the game with him." I swallow hard. "But I'm not. I'm just one of the pieces."

"What do you mean?" Dax's voice is low.

My eyes drop to the genkit's screen. The last scan is still running, searching through the contents of my panel. "In his message, he told me to use the notes he left with me, but I don't think he was talking about *paper*. He left a hidden note in Cole's panel, and he left one in yours, and Leoben's. But I never once thought of checking my own."

Dax freezes. I see the realization come over him as clear as day—he sees it now, what I've seen for the last few minutes. I've never checked my panel for hidden files. I had no reason to. But if my father's plan goes back years, there's no reason he couldn't have left me with something—a password, a backup, a key. Something he would remember to build into his code when he finished the vaccine.

That way, if Cartaxus forced him to encrypt it, he would have someone beyond their control waiting to unlock it. Even if they tried to withhold its release. Even if they killed him.

He left me in the cabin because he needed me for *this*.

The genkit's scan returns, and the screen flashes to black with a list of hidden files in blazing white text. I expect to see the system logs and lists of updates, but not a giant procedural file stored in its own repository. It was saved to my panel on the morning of the outbreak, the last time my father ran a software update for me.

*PROCEDURE_NOTES.txt, 184MB*

The words glow, white and cold. This is the key to the vaccine. I feel it as an itch in the base of my skull. My hand shakes as I click on it, and the screen flashes, bringing up the first page of text. At first it looks like pure, unreadable quaternary, but as I scroll down, I realize it's my father's code. The file is thousands of pages long, but a quick search brings up all the comments, and I lean closer, fighting my swimming vision to read them.

"This is a *program*," Dax says, reading it wirelessly through his panel. "But I don't know what it's doing."

The air hangs still as the math and chemistry spin through my mind, weaving into a single algorithm. This code wields a million variables, a million cell types and separate genes, all unfolded and then sewn together in a staggeringly complex dance. It's a genetic ballet, with each dancer part of a larger, massive pattern, so beautiful and elegant that I can barely breathe.

"I do."

The logic snaps together in my mind. I scan through the code, stunned by what my father has created. I expected a decryption algorithm—something to unlock the source code that's hidden in Cole's panel, but this ignores the panel's architecture completely. Instead, it's aimed at the vaccine's synthetic DNA—the ribbons of proteins swimming in Cole's blood.

I've never seen anything like it. The nanites that run gentech code are designed to build strands of DNA that are coiled up in complex knots, like balls of twine. Those knots are shaped so they can only ever uncoil and wrap around specific parts of your natural DNA. We could take a sample of Cole's blood and distill it down to the knot of DNA that is the vaccine, but it would be almost impossible to untangle and sequence it. Too small, too soft, too unpredictable. The calculations could take years.

But that's exactly what this code is doing.

It uses a clonebox to draw the vaccine out of Cole's arm, making a copy of the encrypted code like his panel does when backing up his apps. That's still useless on its own, but then the procedure branches into something new, and the equations ignite, tracing fractured lines of logic through my mind.

It's wonderful and terrible. It's my father's masterpiece. He's used my DNA as the key to the vaccine—my own body as the object that will break the encryption. We need only to hook me up to the clonebox and run the procedure in this file, and then the vaccine will bleed through my cells and unfurl like a flower, one petal at a time.

*Catarina can unlock the vaccine.*

That's what my father was saying all along.

"It's *me*," I breathe.

"You're right." Dax's face pales. "It's *you*. You're the key."

I nod, staring at the screen, my vision blurring in and out. My muscles are growing weaker, and I know I should lie down. We should call a doctor and bandage my arm. There are a dozen things we should do, but I can't stop staring at the endless lines of code my father left for me.

I've never seen anything like it. If this procedure's code is right, then the password that's being used to encrypt the vaccine is its *own* synthetic DNA. All we need to do is untangle the knot. This code will drag the vaccine out of the clonebox and force it into every cell in my body. The procedure will use my DNA to unravel the tangled coil of the vaccine, but a sample of my blood won't be enough. This needs to be run through my skin, my muscles, my blood and neurons, all living and working in unison. Every cell in my body is part of the key. Each will unwind the knot a little more, and when it's fully unraveled, we can unlock the source code, and we'll be able to release it.

The code will be free to broadcast. People will be able to live without fear. They'll come out of the bunkers; they'll rebuild the world.

But I won't be around to see it.

The realization pushes the air from my lungs. There are too many entry points in this procedure's code. It's not just using my cells to unravel the vaccine—it's tearing them apart, shredding my DNA to pieces. A few minutes after this code starts running, my body will *disintegrate*.

The vaccine will be decrypted, but this code is going to kill me.

My vision dims. I rub my eyes and feel a trickle of heat weave down my arm. Blood is still running from the stitches where my panel used to be. I've been bleeding this whole time. My blood pressure is plummeting, and now I can barely keep my eyes open.

I should have made Dax bandage my arm. I should have gotten an IV, but we both got swept up in the secrets hidden in my arm. Now it's too late. I feel myself swaying. The floor is opening up and swallowing me whole.

"Dax," I breathe. He doesn't hear me. He's pacing the room, coding, his eyes glazed over. He's about to read what the code will do to me, and I know he'll turn to me when he figures it out, but I need his help *now*, before I pass out. "Dax . . . ," I say louder, but he doesn't even blink. I'm slipping to the floor, drifting into the darkness, and either Dax can't hear me or is too distracted to care. There's only one person who can help.

I just pray he's close enough to find me in time.

"Cole," I cry out with every ounce of strength left in me. A chill is creeping across my skin, my teeth starting to chatter. I try to prop myself up with my good arm, but my hand just slides over the bloody puddles on the floor.

My head falls back. The room goes black. The door whooshes open.

"Crick!" Cole yells. "Dammit, she's going into shock!"

Strong arms lift me from the floor, a warm chest against my side. "I'm here now," Cole whispers, lowering me to the bed.

My eyes flutter open. Dax stands behind Cole, staring. "Shit," he whispers. "Oh shit, I'm sorry. I didn't notice . . ."

"What the hell were you doing?" Cole grabs the medkit.

"Here, use this." Dax pulls a vial from his pocket. It's filled with glistening silver fluid—emergency healing tech—raw nanites that don't need a panel to run them. It's not hypergenesis-friendly, but that doesn't matter anymore.

Nothing matters anymore. I'm just a chess piece in my father's plan.

"She can't use that," Cole says. "Have you lost your mind?"

"No," Dax says, uncapping the vial. "It's okay, she can use it." He presses the silver canister to my neck. Cole watches, stunned, as the nanites surge into my body. They spread down my neck and into my chest like slivers of ice scratching through my veins.

I feel them hit my heart. It skips a beat, then my back arches on the bed as they explode inside me, racing through my cells.

"Why can she use the tech?" Cole asks, his eyes wide. "Crick, what did you just do?"

"I healed her," Dax says. "She doesn't have hypergenesis. Lachlan faked it, and she's going to be fine, but we need to keep working. She's the key to the vaccine—we found the procedure to unlock it. I need to get samples, and run tests, to figure out the rest of the plan—"

"No," Cole says, cutting the air with his hand. "We don't need to figure anything out right now. Catarina needs to rest."

"But the *vaccine*," Dax says. "We're supposed to leave in a few hours."

"It can wait until morning."

"You don't understand," Dax urges.

Cole's head snaps around, and he stands fluidly. A steel spring coiling. A blade drawn from a sheath. "You're the one who doesn't understand," he growls, the very air around him rippling with his anger. "She was on the verge of death when I came in, while you were standing right beside her. You say she's the key to the vaccine, and you talk about this plan as if it's something separate, something intellectual. But it's not. *She* is the plan, and Lachlan sent me to protect her. My job is to make sure she doesn't get hurt, and I intend to do it. That means she's going to rest now, and you're going to leave."

Dax glares at Cole. "You can't tell me what to do."

"No, I can't," Cole snarls, "but if you don't get out of my sight, I'll break your neck for letting her bleed out like that."

Dax and Cole stare at each other, the air humming with anger, and then Dax's eyes cut to me, hard and cold. He gives me a sharp nod, then sneers at Cole and turns on his heel to stride out of the room.

It takes a full minute until Cole's hands unclench, and then he turns back to me, dropping to his knees beside the bed. "Are you okay?"

I shake my head. I don't have the strength to list all the ways that I am *not* okay right now.

"I'm tired" is all I manage.

He pulls a blanket over me. "Then sleep, Cat. You're safe now. I'm not going anywhere."

# CHAPTER 24

HOURS LATER, THROUGH SNATCHES OF SLEEP AND half-remembered dreams, I find myself back at home, standing in the cabin. It's cold, but I'm sweating. I don't know if it's night or day. My father must be here somewhere, but I can't hear him.

"Hey, Princess."

Dax catches my arm, spinning me around. His hair flickers between long and short, his face both young and old. "Aren't you happy to see me?" He brushes the hair from my face. "What's wrong, Princess?"

"I don't know."

"You're bleeding," he says, pulling his hand away from my face, holding his fingers up to the light. His skin is dotted with blood that splits into smaller and smaller drops, like water on a sheet of glass, spreading across his hand.

"Nanites," he murmurs, staring at the blood that is now barely more than a scarlet mist. "I always knew there was something wrong with you."

I clutch my face where he touched me, feeling wet, scabbed skin that comes away under my fingers, sloughing off my neck. "I-I'm sorry," I stutter, backing away. "I need to go."

He just watches me, disgust etched in every line of his face.

I turn and run. I need my father. If I don't stop the reaction soon, it'll spread down my back. This is my hypergenesis. If I don't get help, I'll bleed out like my mother did.

But that's not right.

I skid to a stop. I don't have hypergenesis—that was just an app in my panel. So why is my skin splitting apart?

I turn around, finding myself outside my father's door. Part of me knows I need to open it, but I'm gripped with a rush of dread.

Something lurks on the other side of this door. Something I'm still not ready to face. Something dark and powerful that rises up like a long-forgotten memory.

I close my eyes, drawing in a breath, and swing open the door.

My father isn't here. One wall of the room is blown out, the books and shelves covered with streaks of dried pink foam. Outside, a million-strong flock of passenger pigeons changes direction, racing for me. Their eyes are black. Their wings are flames. They shriek as they swarm into the room and surge over me.

I jolt awake, my heart pounding, staring wildly around me. Concrete walls. A bunk above me.

It was just a dream.

I'm in Homestake, in my little room deep underground, and my empty, wounded arm is aching. It's wrapped in gauze, so Cole must have bandaged it, but I slept right through it. I roll slowly to my side on the bunk to look around.

The room is dark, but a bar of pale light in the ceiling traces out the lines of a mattress on the floor. The mess of my panel and the pools of blood have been cleaned away, and my genkit and the Zarathustra folders are stacked neatly in the corner. Cole is lying silently on his side on the mattress, but two twin points of light in his eyes tell me he's awake.

Watching me.

As if in a dream, I push myself up and drift across the floor until I find myself standing above him. I don't know what I'm doing here, and I don't know what I need from him. All I know is that I need *something*, and that something is Cole.

His eyes meet mine, his arms bare above his blankets, the first rows of scars on his chest gleaming in the muted light. I open my lips, but I don't know what to ask him. I don't know why I'm standing above him in the middle of the night.

Then he opens his arms as if he was expecting me, as if it was the most natural thing in the world that I would come to him tonight. I drop into the blankets, and his arms fold around me, warm and secure.

I curl into his chest and fall into a dreamless sleep.

# CHAPTER 25

I WAKE UP NEXT TO COLE AGAIN, BUT THIS TIME there is no awkwardness, and I don't force myself to sit up and turn away. He rolls to his back, I roll to mine, and just like that we're awake, and it feels normal. It feels right.

I don't know if what's growing between us is romantic, or if this is just the kind of bond two people forge when they go through something like this together. It feels like gravity is shifting, swinging us infinitesimally closer. But in another way, it feels like we've always been this close.

"So you don't have hypergenesis?" he asks.

"No. Well, I think I must have had it, once. But not anymore."

"How does that work?"

"I don't really know." I lift my arm, turning it slowly. I can feel the difference in weight now that my panel is gone. "It's not a genetic condition, but my father must have created a treatment. It was probably after my mother died. He would have tried to save me from dying the same way."

"And he didn't tell you?"

I let my arm drop. "No. He hid it, from me *and* Cartaxus. Dax thinks that's why he told me to stay away from the bunkers."

Cole scratches his chest, staring at the ceiling. "That's messed up."

"Tell me about it. I could have had a real panel this whole time."

He looks over. "But you can get budded with another one, and get real apps this time, right? Would that be safe for you?"

"I think so. But I don't need to get budded. It turns out I have a backup in my spine, and it's growing me a new panel right now."

Cole sits up, grabbing a T-shirt, and pulls it on. "If you're growing a new panel, you're going to need a lot of calories. How about I run to the cafeteria and get us some breakfast?"

I sit up beside him, pulling my sleep-tangled hair into a ponytail. "What are my choices?"

"Scramble, beans, congee, toast, waffles, burritos—"

"They have waffles here?"

Cole grins, pushing himself to his feet. "Two servings of waffles coming right up. I'll be back soon."

He steps into his boots and slips out the airlocked door, shooting me a smile I can't help but return. I get up and walk into the bathroom, stopping short the moment I catch a glimpse of myself in the mirror.

The healing tech's nanites have been working overnight, and they haven't just been sealing the cut in my arm. My skin is still scarred, but it looks bright. My lips are smooth instead of chapped, and the heavy shadows under my eyes are all but gone. In a few days, when my panel finishes growing, I could look as good as anybody else in this bunker. Fresh-faced, healthy, clean. Two years of misery and horror, wiped away. It would make me look like a new person.

But that isn't going to happen.

I decided in the night that I would do the decryption. Some part of me knew that I would agree to it as soon as I read the code. It doesn't mean I'm ready, and it doesn't mean I'm willing, but the world can't wait for Cartaxus to unlock the vaccine with brute force. People are dying. The virus is evolving. This is the only way to save humanity from this nightmare.

The apartment's door whooshes open. I turn as Dax walks in, looking at Cole's mattress with a furrow in his brow. His tech can probably read heat signatures. He'll know I shared Cole's bed. My stomach lurches into my throat.

"Princess," he says. His face is unreadable. "How is your arm?"

I step out of the bathroom. "It's . . . fine."

"Good." He glances around the room, his eyes lingering on the hardened mess of my panel in the sink. "I had time to read more of the procedure's code. I'm not sure if I'm reading it right, but—"

"It's going to kill me."

He swallows, meeting my eyes. His red hair is disheveled, and his emerald eyes are bloodshot. He's probably been up all night reading the code, trying to figure out what it would do to me. I understood since I first saw it, but I haven't thought about it from Dax's point of view. He's the one who's going to have to get the equipment ready, to jack me in and run the code.

This is the task my father left him: killing me.

"There'll be another way," he says, his voice tight. "Your father left this as a last resort, but that doesn't mean we have to use it."

"Of course we do. We can't wait any longer. The virus will evolve."

He stares at the floor, his shoulders hunched. "There has to be another way. I don't understand why he's used *you*. Why not someone else? Millions of people would be happy to die for this."

My eyes drop. The same question has been circling through my mind since I first read the code. How could my father leave this task to me? Why would he sentence me to death?

Did he even love me at all?

I don't think I'll ever know the answer. Even though we lived together, I never truly felt as though I was a central part of my father's life. He was protective, and I knew he cared for me, but he would lose himself in his work, forgetting to eat, hacking his metabolism to keep himself awake for days at a time. I wouldn't hear a word from him, or he'd stare right through me while he spoke, lost in a gentech puzzle more compelling than his daughter's face. His work was the burning star of his life, and I existed as a minor planet, visible only in transit, a periodic dimming of light.

But sometimes I was not his daughter—sometimes I was his coding partner. We would sit side by side in the basement, working together as equals. I knew his code better than anyone. I knew what it meant to him.

That's why I'm going to do the decryption.

"The vaccine was my father's life," I say, "and I am the only person he trusted its decryption with. This isn't a punishment, Dax. It's an honor. He chose me because he knew that I would understand what's at stake. He knew I'd see the truth—that releasing this vaccine is worth more than my life."

Dax runs one hand through his hair, bunching it into a fist. For a moment he looks younger, like the boy I knew before the plague. "Princess," he says, but his voice breaks. He covers his mouth with his hand.

I step across the floor and pull him into a hug.

His arms slide around me. His body is trembling like it was when he first stepped out of the Comox. He smells of soap and laboratory-grade disinfectant. The scent fills me with memories—coding in the basement, falling hard for the kid who showed up on our doorstep. I remember fighting over algorithms and swimming in the lake. Listening to my father read us poetry in the evenings.

Dax holds me tightly, his face pressed to my hair. "Are you sure?" he whispers. "You don't have to do this. I can wipe the code. We can say that the instructions were destroyed when we cut out your panel."

I freeze. "No." I step back. "No, we can't. The virus will evolve—"

"Forget the virus. We'll stay in the bunkers." He grabs my shoulders. "You and I can strengthen the vaccine ourselves. You don't have to walk into an execution just because Lachlan left one waiting for you."

Dax's words are pure madness—there's no way we can just *hide* from something like this—but his desperation drags up every doubt I have about my father's plan. My eyes stray to the Zarathustra files, piled neatly on the floor. I trust my father's code, but I'm still handing my life to a man who cut open children.

But he always had his reasons. Cole said he trusted my father more than anyone on the planet, even after what he'd been through. My father was a complicated man, but he wasn't wasteful. He wouldn't have written a procedure like this unless he had no choice.

"*No*, Dax," I say, fighting to keep my voice level. "We're doing the decryption, and we have no time to spare. We can do it tonight if we can get out of here with the clonebox and make it to the lab."

His emerald eyes blaze, but I can see the fight in him fading. He knows there's no walking away from this just as well as I do. Finally, his shoulders drop and he paces across the room. "I always thought we'd get married one day," he murmurs, "after this was over."

"Dax . . ."

"It just seemed like the way it should go. We'd live together, we'd code together, but now . . . we won't." His eyes drop to Cole's mattress again.

"It's not what you think," I say, even though I don't know what Dax thinks, and if I'm honest, I don't know what's happening between Cole and me. "I was shaken—"

He waves a hand. "You don't need to explain yourself. I should have read the code faster. I should have understood."

"It was in quaternary."

"Yes." He gives me a sad smile. "You and your father seem to be the only ones who can read it like that."

I hold his gaze. There is a sadness in his eyes that opens a crack of fear in me. Somehow it's worse than his anger. He's already *mourning* me.

A day from now I'll be gone from this world, and he'll have to live with the knowledge that he was the one to kill me. It won't be clean, and it won't be painless. I've pushed that aspect of the decryption to the back of my mind, but seeing grief etched into Dax's face brings it into focus. That crack of fear widens into a chasm, until I find myself teetering over it, a breath away from free fall.

I will die. There will be no return. My body will dissolve, and I know that death is inevitable, but I'm not ready for it yet. If I believed in something beyond this world, maybe I could clutch at it like a rope, but I don't, and all I see after this life is cold, infinite darkness.

Dax's eyes narrow in concern. I draw in a slow breath and hold it, wrenching my focus back under control. The fear shrinks inside me, folding in on itself, yielding to my will.

I blow out a breath, steeling myself. "Just tell me what I need to do."

Dax looks me up and down, his eyes still narrowed, then turns and scans the room. "Pack your things. I'll get the clonebox and set off the kick to get us out of here. When I do, you and Lieutenant Franklin just need to get up to the garage where your jeep is waiting. Leoben and I will take another one." He glances back at Cole's mattress. "You can't tell him about this, Princess."

"Cole?"

He nods. "He's a black-out agent who's been tasked with your protection. I don't know how he'll react to this. He might be fine, or he might go rogue and try to take you away. He might sabotage the procedure. It's not a risk we can take."

I close my eyes. The thought of lying to Cole sparks a war inside me. Cole deserves to hear the truth, and I don't want to lie to him, but Dax has a point. I don't know how Cole's protective protocol will deal with my impending death.

He might flip out and try to protect me. He might lose control during the procedure.

He might inadvertently destroy any chance we have of unlocking the vaccine.

"Okay," I say, "I won't tell him. How soon can we leave?"

"Within the hour. I can get started now." He steps to the door. It slides open, and he stands with one hand on the frame. "Are you ready?"

I wrap my arms around myself. "Am I crazy for doing this, Dax?"

He looks me up and down, his face softening. "No, Princess. You're not crazy at all. I think you're very brave."

*Brave.* The word is steadying. I let it roll back and forth in my mind, quieting the sparks of fear in my chest. Maybe my father didn't just choose me for this because he knew I'd be dutiful and follow the plan he left for me. Maybe he chose me because he knew I'd face it.

Because I'm strong. Because I fight. Because I'm not afraid to do the right thing.

My father left this task to me because I am *brave.*

"Okay," I say. My voice is firm, unwavering. "Let's do this now. Set off the simulation."

Dax nods once, his eyes lingering on mine, then turns and strides from the room.

\* \* \*

By the time Cole returns with a tray of waffles, I've packed our bags and am pacing back and forth, chewing my fingernails nervously. It's a habit I've found myself picking up the last few days, though I've never done it before. The stress must be getting to me.

My genkit is safely stowed in my backpack, along with the Zarathustra files, and I've left my bloodstained blue Homestake clothing in a pile by the bed. I'm wearing the tank top and cargo pants Cole brought for me, my hair pulled up in a ponytail. I keep wondering if this is the last outfit I'll ever wear.

"Hey," Cole says, setting the tray down. "Are you okay? Crick commed me, said we're leaving now. What's going on?"

"He's getting the clonebox and setting off the kick simulation. We're going to the lab."

Cole's jaw tenses. My intuition spikes.

"What?" I ask. "Is there something wrong with the plan?"

Cole meets my eyes, but he doesn't say a word. My mind rolls back to the morning before, when Dax and Leoben arrived. Dax said the simulation would get us out of here. Leoben said it was written by Jun Bei. . . .

The girl he thought was responsible for the hack that killed my father. The girl who stabbed a nurse with a pair of scissors.

"Oh," I whisper. "I forgot. The kick is Jun Bei's code."

He nods. "It's a computer virus. It runs a simulation that'll make it look like the bunker is under cyberattack. Which it is, I guess. It'll infect every system and cause temporary chaos. It's how Jun Bei escaped from the lab."

Chaos? My stomach clenches. I don't know much about Jun Bei, but everything I've heard has made her sound terrifying. Which is understandable, I guess. I can't imagine what kind of horrors the Zarathustra subjects lived through. If Jun Bei is dangerous now, it's probably because my father made her that way.

But the idea of using her code to break out of Homestake still chills me to my core.

"Cole, this simulation . . . Nobody is going to get hurt, are they?"

He opens his mouth to reply just as the lights flicker, and an alarm wails through the speakers in the ceiling. An automated voice starts up, reciting instructions on a loop.

*"Warning. Lockdown in progress. Proceed to your quarters."*

Cole's eyes glaze over. "Crick has the clonebox and just kicked off the simulation. He and Leoben got into a scuffle with some guards, but they're okay. They're making their way to the parking levels now. It's time to leave." He swings his backpack on, then lifts mine up so I can slide my arms through the straps. I shift it on my shoulders nervously.

"You haven't answered me, Cole. Is anyone going to get hurt?"

He gives me a quick, false smile. "Of course they won't."

# CHAPTER 26

COLE HURRIES INTO THE HALLWAY, WHERE A WAVE of civilians are running to their rooms, swarming through the corridors. "We're going to the elevators," he says, pushing through a crowd of people. "I've got the route mapped out. Stay close to me."

I jog after him, clutching the backpack's straps, a twinge of pain flickering in my bandaged arm. I use the pain to sharpen my focus. Cole leads the way, following some virtual map in his panel that I can't see, guiding me through a seemingly endless series of hallways. All the apartment doors are open, showing me the tiny rooms inside. Hand-knitted blankets are tossed over bunks, and the occasional dog watches us from behind a knee-high gate. The families inside are huddled together, their eyes glazed over, probably waiting for more instructions to tell them they're safe.

But I don't know if they are. Cole's tone has driven a splinter of fear through me. I don't know anything about the simulation we're running. It could be harmless, but from what I've heard about Jun Bei, it sounds like safety was the least of her concerns.

And I don't want to put these people in danger just to get us out of here.

"Almost there," Cole shouts, finally turning into a hallway I recognize. At the far end I can see the faux sunlight and greenery outside. Cole picks up his pace, running now that our path has cleared, with most of the residents already back in their rooms. A little boy at one of the doors gives me a plaintive look as I pass. He's trying to push his door closed, but it won't budge.

It suddenly occurs to me that *all* the doors are open.

The lockdown must have opened them so people could get back into their rooms. But that can't be right. These rooms are designed to be airtight to keep the civilians safe. Surely the most important thing to do in a lockdown is *seal* the doors, right?

"Just two more blocks," Cole calls back.

I jog faster to keep up with him, glancing nervously at the doors. They're still open, and now more people are pulling on them, calling out to one another. They must have run lockdown drills before, and they obviously expect their doors to be closed by now. There must be a delay, some conflict with the simulation. Any minute now the system will surely override it.

We jog out of the building and into an empty street. Tables and chairs lie on their sides outside a café, food splattered across the cobblestones. Everything has been knocked down and tossed aside in the stampede of people running back to their rooms. Cole waves his arm, leading me down the street, past a recreation center where families dressed in gym gear are streaming out.

"Make way!" Cole yells. We turn into the square with the wall of elevators that Leoben and I first came through. A crowd has formed, waiting to get back to their floors. Cole must be sending out some kind of virtual message, because they move back instantly when they see him, clearing us a path.

"Is this a drill?" someone asks

"Please stay calm, sir." Cole pulls me into an empty elevator. He presses his hand to the side, and the doors slowly begin to slide shut. "Proceed to your quarters and seal the doors."

"But my door won't seal, sir There's somethi—" a woman shouts, but the elevator closes, cutting her off.

I turn to Cole. "The apartment doors weren't closing."

"They're on a redundant system. These floors have a dozen levels of airtight security."

"And exactly how many of them are we breaching to get out?"

"It'll be okay, Cat. We'll be out in a few minutes, and this will all be over."

I bring my hand up to chew my thumbnail. It's not us I'm worried about. It's the eighty thousand Homestake residents living here without immunity. The airlock system is the only thing keeping them safe, and I have a sinking feeling that Jun Bei's simulation has compromised it.

The elevator shudders to a stop, and the doors ping open, letting in a puff of warm, humid air. A woman and a little boy rush in from what looks like an aquaponics floor. Shelves of plants stretch out as far as I can see, built above glass tanks filled with tiny, iridescent fish.

"Ma'am, you need to—" Cole says, and curses as the doors close.

The woman pulls off a pair of rubber gloves, wiping her forehead. "Is there a problem, sir?"

"I've commandeered this elevator."

"Oh," she says. "Sorry, I didn't know. We were in the hothouse. My son was helping me with the tomatoes."

"It's not your fault," Cole mutters. "We weren't supposed to stop."

I shoot him a worried glance. It sounds like there are some holes in this plan. First the residential doors won't seal—now the elevators are glitching.

"Where are we going?" the woman asks as we keep rising. "That was my floor. Why aren't we stopping?"

Cole doesn't reply.

"What's happening?" The woman's voice grows frantic as we rise beyond the residential floors. "We can't go up—it's not safe. These elevators aren't even supposed to go this high."

"They do in an emergency, ma'am."

The woman's grip on her son tightens, and they back into the corner. I shoot Cole a questioning glance, but he just shakes his head. We rise for what feels like an eternity, at least another thirty floors, until the doors finally slide open to an underground parking lot. The walls and floor have red diagonal stripes painted across them, with signs warning that this floor is exposed to untreated air. A massive Wash-and-Blast airlock lies between us and the rest of the floor, complete with the space-grade circular doors.

But they're open.

The lights are off, and the airlock doors are wide open. A gust of cold wind blows straight into the elevator. At the far end of the parking lot a ramp leads up to the ground, where I can make out a hint of daylight. The woman clasps her hands over her son's mouth, letting out a scream.

They just got hit with a gust of wind from *outside*.

"What the hell?" I grab Cole's arm, staring through the gaping Wash-and-Blast at the parking lot. "Why is this airlock open? This elevator goes right down to residential."

"We're still safe," Cole says to both me and the mother, gesturing to a green light on the wall. "This air is clear."

"But it's *open*! There are eighty thousand people here, Cole. This isn't safe."

The mother nods, her face pale. "We can't go back down, sir. It's against protocol. We need to be quarantined."

236

Cole sighs, pinching the bridge of his nose. He grabs a panel in the elevator's side and wrenches it open, revealing a glowing red button underneath. "Hit this once we're out, and it'll take you to a safe zone."

"Are we under attack?" the woman asks. "Will my family be okay?"

Cole pulls me out of the elevator, a muscle twitching in his jaw. "Just stay calm. I'm sure everything will be fine." He punches a button on the wall, and the elevator doors close, taking the woman and her son away.

I run through the Wash-and-Blast corridor to the parking lot and spin around, covering my mouth in disbelief.

Our airlock wasn't the only one. Twelve massive Wash-and-Blasts are open, all leading to elevator shafts that go down to the residential floors. The fail-safes have been overridden. The whole compound is compromised. Below me, eighty thousand people are still trying to seal their doors.

But they won't be able to. The kick simulation has broken every layer of Homestake's security, just to get us out of here.

"Wait here," Cole says. "I'll get the jeep. Leoben and Crick have already left with the clonebox. Are you ready?"

"No," I spit, whirling on him. "All the airlocks are open, aren't they? That was Jun Bei's escape plan, wasn't it? She opened everything to get out faster. Cole, there's *dozens* of second-stagers on the perimeter, and nobody here is immune."

"Why are you angry at me?" he snaps. "You're the one who wanted to come here, remember? I wanted to stay away. *You're* the one who agreed to this plan."

My cheeks burn. He's right. I'm the one who made the decision. I chose to come here and steal a clonebox instead of finding one on the surface. The thought just makes me more determined to stop this. To make it right and keep these people safe.

I drop my backpack, dragging out my genkit. "I'm shutting this down."

Cole shakes his head. "Cat, these people are safe. Homestake has a mile-wide buffer zone."

"And that's not enough, not anymore. The virus is evolving, and the clouds are getting bigger. If those people on the perimeter blow while these airlocks are open, the cloud could make it inside, and then there'll be no stopping it. I need to kill the simulation."

I set my genkit on the concrete floor, flicking up its wireless antenna. One of the viruses I've written to hack Cartaxus for the Skies should be able to force an emergency closure. The screen flashes as it boots up, connecting to Homestake's network, logging in automatically. The genkit still has Dax's login details from when he scanned my panel. That's going to make this a *lot* easier.

"Cat, we don't have time for this. We need to get out of here."

"Then go and get the jeep." I keep my eyes glued to the screen, navigating into Homestake's security systems.

He lets out a growl of frustration. "Okay, you have two minutes and then I'm dragging you out of here before the guards arrive."

"That's fine," I say. "I don't need long."

He drops his backpack and runs through the parking lot toward a row of gleaming vehicles. My fingers are a blur on the keyboard as I search through Homestake's systems. Dax's login is like magic; he has top-level clearance. His password ushers me into every server, every database. My genkit's fan hums as I navigate into the airlock system and load up the list of emergency protocols. The screen flashes, showing me a dozen different fail-safes I can trigger to close the airlocks. I pick the simplest one and start running it. If my intuition is correct, then the airlocks would be designed so that opening them is difficult, but *closing* them should be almost trivial.

Almost.

A few commands in, I find myself fighting against what must be part of Jun Bei's kick simulation. It's a virus, that's for sure. It's the most sophisticated piece of malware I've ever seen. Dax must have dumped it somewhere clever, because it somehow got instant access to *everything*. Not just the elevators and the airlocks—it's in the ventilation systems, the lighting, the communications grid, even though it looks like the servers for those systems are separated by firewalls. It's shorting out circuits and wreaking chaos and confusion in every system I can see, and I have no idea how it got to them so fast. My hacks sometimes took hours, and I'd do preparations for days.

This code has taken over Homestake in *minutes*.

I throw a handful of commands at the airlock sensors, but the simulation smacks me down before I finish typing. My genkit's screen flashes, the text blurring before my eyes as the simulation morphs, spinning around to attack my connection.

It knows I'm here. This thing is smart, and now it's coming for *me*. I yank out the genkit's antenna, but I'm a heartbeat too late.

The screen dies.

"No!" I shout, jabbing the power key. The genkit boots up again, but it won't be safe to use the wireless connection anymore. From outside, I hear the distant sound of gunfire, followed by a resounding *crack*. It might have been a grenade, or it might have been one of the infected people on the perimeter detonating. Either way, I'm running out of time. I turn around to look for Cole, and the glow of headlights splashes over me.

He found the jeep. He's coming back.

"Okay, think," I mutter, closing my eyes, trying to remember the list I pulled up of the ways to trigger an airlock closure. There were a handful of options that bypassed the networks, that Jun Bei's code can't possibly stop. A switch near the guard station. A lever in the lookout tower. Explosions in the Wash-and-Blasts . . .

An explosion. That'll do it. If I can crack one of the glass panels in a Wash-and-Blast, it'll trigger the lockdown the guard warned me about. I don't know if it'll jerk the whole system back to life, but it's worth a try. I don't have time for anything else.

The jeep races across the parking lot, screeching to a stop behind me. Cole's door flies open. "Time's up, we have to go. They're coming for us."

"I need a bomb," I say, turning to him, still crouched beside my gen-kit. "Or a grenade, anything. I need to trigger one of these airlocks."

"Are you kidding? Get in the jeep, Cat."

"I'm not leaving until these are closed. I'm serious. I need a bomb to blow up one of the airlocks."

Cole jumps out of the jeep and grabs his backpack. "I'm not blow-ing *anything* up, Catarina. We need to get out now. There'll be soldiers swarming through here any second."

"Please, Cole!"

He tosses his backpack into the jeep and comes back for mine. "It's over, Cat. You tried. Now we need to *run*."

He picks up my backpack, striding around the jeep to throw it in the back, and I look down at my trusty, beat-up genkit. The keyboard is full of crumbs, still crusted with my dried blood, and the duct tape holding the screen together is starting to peel off. It's a wreck, but it's *my* wreck. Without it, I can't hack or code. It's my sidekick, my lifeline.

But if I can get it to self-destruct, it's also a tiny bomb.

Before I can give myself time to hesitate, I yank out the genkit's needle-tipped wire and jab it into the side of my knee. It flies out of my grip, burying itself in my skin, squirming into the socket buried under my kneecap. My leg twitches as the needle tip locks into place with a *click*. The genkit's screen flashes.

*EMERGENCY CODE ONLY.*

There's no panel in my arm, which means there's nothing to check the code I'm about to send into my system. A panel isn't just a computer; it's a *gatekeeper*, stopping toxic code and nanites from being dumped into my body. Without a panel, I have no safety checks. I could send myself nanites that'll chew the flesh right off my bones, that could swarm through my body and devour my cells.

And that's exactly what I'm doing.

A few keystrokes are all it takes to prime the lasers, to make sure that when the genkit detonates, it'll go off like a rocket. I tap out a dozen commands, sourcing malicious code from my stored files, wrapping them up into a virus I can send into my knee. A butchered, weaponized piece of code that will attack my cells in the same way my father bubbled the skin off my back. I don't know how far it will spread from my knee, but I know it's going to hurt. It'll open up a gaping wound in my leg, but that doesn't matter.

Tonight, after we get to the lab and unlock the vaccine, I'll be dead. A busted knee will be the least of my concerns.

The needle-tipped wire vibrates as the commands chug through the genkit, dumping a stream of nanites into my knee. It only takes a second until the genkit's internal safety checks realize what I'm doing, and the emergency system kicks in.

*ILLEGAL OPERATION DETECTED. SELF-DESTRUCT SEQUENCE INITIATED.*

*HALT OPERATION TO PREVENT SELF-DESTRUCT.*

That's the thing about genkits—they're not weapons, and they're not designed to be. If the machine thinks you're trying to kill someone with it, it'll blow itself up. Years of lawsuits, judges, protests, and hastily written laws led to the manufacturers burying tiny bombs inside every processor. Rather than run illegal code, it'll explode with a puff of smoke.

Hopefully the blast will be big enough to close the Wash-and-Blast.

The genkit's screen flashes. White-hot pain flares in my knee. The reader wire tries to eject from the socket, but I hold it in, gritting my teeth. The pain grows, spreading to my calf. Just a few more seconds . . .

*THIS MACHINE WILL SELF-DESTRUCT IN 10, 9 . . .*

"Finally," I gasp, yanking the wire out, crawling on my good knee, shoving my genkit into the gaping Wash-and-Blast.

"What are you doing?" Cole shouts. "Get in the jeep. We need to get out of here!"

"I will," I murmur. "I just . . . I don't think I can walk."

"What have you done?" Cole stares at the genkit, his eyes flashing to black.

*SELF-DESTRUCT IN 5, 4 . . .*

Cole's arm slides around my waist, yanking me from the floor, and the parking lot spins as he throws me into the passenger seat. The genkit's screen flashes red. Cole races around the hood to the driver's side, and then everything seems to happen at once.

My genkit detonates in a flash of light, belching clouds of smoke, and a deafening roar cuts through the air. The concrete floor beneath us shakes. Cole hurls himself into the driver's seat, slamming the door shut behind him. I grab the side of my seat, twisting around to stare back as the jeep surges forward, bouncing up the ramp and outside. That was a *hell* of an explosion for a laptop genkit, but it worked. The steel, circular doors of the Wash-and-Blasts are slamming shut.

"I did it," I breathe, still staring back as we burst into the wasteland, my entire leg throbbing with pain. "It closed the airlocks, Cole."

He doesn't reply. He's probably still angry, even though he gave me no choice. I've just destroyed my knee because he wouldn't use a damn grenade. I turn back, starting to yank up my pant leg to see the damage, and freeze.

The roar I heard wasn't from the genkit. It wasn't my little explosion that made the bunker's floor shake. That was something else, something bigger. It's rising as a cloud on Homestake's perimeter, but it can't possibly be what I think it is.

It's too tall, too powerful. It looks like a *tornado*. A solid plume, fifty feet across, spreading once it hits the clouds. I scrunch my eyes shut and open them again, hoping it's a trick of perspective, but it's not. It's more than twice the size of any plume I've seen before. It rises like a rocket, the color of misted blood.

There's no denying it. It's a Hydra cloud.

# CHAPTER 27

COLE'S EYES ARE GLASSY AND BLACK, HIS FOREHEAD beaded with sweat as he wrenches the steering wheel, swinging the jeep around. It sways as we hurtle away from the lookout tower, bouncing through the rubble and dust of Homestake's buffer zone. The cloud billows behind us, a wall of red mist, racing in from the perimeter. Far above us, three peaks of gas rise like crimson mountains. My breath catches as the weight of what I'm seeing hits me.

Three blowers just detonated at exactly the same time, forming a single cloud, bigger than any I've seen before. They always go in groups—sometimes minutes apart, sometimes hours—but I've never seen them blow like this, creating a single, towering cloud. This plume will spread for miles. Homestake's buffer won't be enough. The cloud is too tall, too strong.

Without its airlocks, Homestake would be doomed.

I twist in my seat to stare out the window as we skid through the wasteland, speeding toward the concrete perimeter wall. The mist is a living thing, heaving through the air, billowing out across the ash-strewn ground. It swallows the bunker whole, engulfing the lookout tower, an unstoppable wave of hot, rolling scarlet.

"What the hell is that thing?" Cole shouts.

"It's a Hydra cloud."

"It can't be." Cole jerks his head to look. "It's too big."

"It's three blowers," I say, turning back to the front, gritting my teeth as pain shoots through my leg. "Three times as strong."

"The airlocks . . ."

"I closed them."

"How?" Cole wrenches the wheel, swerving through the rubble. A pair of gun-bots lie on their backs, their laser scanners splashing the ground. Their arched steel legs flail like overturned insects. Jun Bei's simulation must have destroyed every layer of Homestake's security.

It's the most impressive code I've ever seen.

Jealousy flares through me. I haven't encountered many other viruses that were better than my own code, and Jun Bei's made mine look like a joke. Cole said she and my father used to code together at Cartaxus.

Maybe that was why he was so distant at the cabin. Because I didn't measure up to her.

I bite back the thought, reaching for my backpack hauling it into my lap. The pain in my knee is spreading down my calf.

"How?" Cole repeats. "How did you close the airlocks?"

"I kicked off a lockdown." I flip open my backpack. "I had to make my genkit self-destruct."

We reach a checkpoint on the perimeter, littered with more flailing gun-bots. The steel barricades are bent and smoking, blackened with scorch marks. Leoben and Dax must have blasted their way through before us. Cole floors the accelerator, and we screech through and onto a highway, leaving Homestake and the billowing Hydra cloud behind us. I rifle through my bag for the medkit, pulling out a vial of healing tech.

Cole's jet-black eyes grow wide. "What have you done, Cat?"

"I did what I had to. I told you—I needed a bomb." I hold the vial in my teeth and pull my pant leg up to expose my knee. The fabric catches on the wound, and I gasp at the sudden rush of pain. A trickle of blood runs down my calf. The flesh is swollen, the fabric tight. I grit my teeth, closing my eyes, and yank the fabric back.

The pain is an avalanche. It roars in my ears, drenching my senses. Silver crystals spin in my vision. I blink them away, staring down at what's left of my swollen, ruined knee.

It's worse than I thought. The skin is purple and cracked, revealing deep pink fissures that run like claw marks across my leg. The swelling forms a dark, violet bruise along my calf, snaking through my veins, reaching all the way to my ankle.

The only sign of hope are blisters that have risen like drops of silver in a ring around the spot where I jacked myself in. My body is trying to eject the nanites wreaking havoc in my cells. That'll help, but it won't stop the damage from spreading. There's no way to stop this without a genkit and some seriously brilliant code. These nanites will keep rampaging through me until they die—maybe in minutes, maybe hours. All I can do is bear the pain and pump myself full of healing tech, trying to keep the wounds under control.

I uncap the healing tech vial with shaking hands. Cole looks over and stiffens.

"Oh, no, no," he whispers. The jeep's tires screech. We plow off the side of the highway and into the trees. Leaves smack against the windshield, branches scraping against the doors, and then we burst into a clearing and shudder to a stop.

"No, no." Cole's seat belt flies off him. His voice is frantic, his eyes inky pools of blackness. "Why, Cat? What did you do to yourself?"

"I did what I had to," I say, bracing myself through a rush of pain. "I

*told* you we needed to close the airlocks. Eighty thousand people, Cole."
I jam the healing tech into the ruined flesh of my knee, ignoring the stab
of pain, the way my flesh gives way like rotting fruit.

"Dammit, Catarina!" Cole flinches, turning away, the tendons in his
neck taut. "I didn't want you to hurt yourself."

"I didn't have time to do anything else." I glare at him. "I made a
decision, and you disagreed. *This* is what happens when you don't listen
to me."

Cole scowls, then kicks open his door and marches around the front
of the jeep, making his way to my door. The veins on my leg grow darker,
rippling as the healing tech races into me. Some of the deeper cracks in
my skin tighten, weeping tracks of pink, dilute blood down my calf. The
flesh is starting to repair itself, and with enough healing tech, I should
recover completely.

Not that it matters. Come nightfall, we'll be at the lab, running the
decryption. No amount of healing tech will save me then.

Cole swings my door open and stares at me, his shoulders tight, his
eyes slowly retreating to blue. He scrapes a hand over his face. "I'm going
to carry you to the back and dress the wound. I don't know if I can stop
the damage, but I want to try." He reaches out to pick me up, but I push
him away.

"Don't touch me. I can walk." I slide down to the ground and land on
my good leg, but the movement sends a jolt through me.

"No you can't."

I close my eyes, breathing through the pain. He's right, but I'm angry,
and the last thing I want is for him to carry me.

"Cat, let me help you."

"No."

"*Please.*"

I open my eyes. Cole's face is strained, his hands stretched out, hanging in midair. He looks frustrated, like he's ready to snap and pick me up over my protests, and it just makes me angrier—that he wants to help me now, but he wouldn't lift a finger to help Homestake's civilians.

"I can walk," I growl, taking three painful steps to the back of the jeep, holding its dust-caked side to keep myself upright. Every movement brings a burst of pain, but I grit my teeth and shuffle forward, ignoring the way Cole stares at me.

When I reach the back doors, they swing open automatically, and I manage to haul myself up so I'm sitting in the back, leaning against the side. The effort leaves me shaking. Lines of silver-tinted blood trickle down from the cracked skin of my knee. Cole follows me like a shadow, silent and tense, and stares at the wound on my knee for a long time.

Without a word, he reaches past me and grabs his backpack, sliding out a medkit full of bandages and syringes. Some look like healing tech, but others are red and black, marked with glyphs I don't recognize. Probably some ungodly Cartaxus tech. He pulls out a thick, wet-looking bandage and sprays it with something before wrapping it around my knee.

It's like *ice*.

I gasp, arching my back, stunned by the sudden mix of cold and pain. Goose bumps shoot across my arms. After a second the chill fades, and the pain in my knee starts to soften, slowly dropping into numbness.

"You did this to make your genkit self-destruct?" he asks.

I nod, chewing my lip. My little trusty, beat-up genkit. It did me proud for three long years, and now it's gone. The thought brings a flash of grief.

"You should rest for a couple of days before the decryption," he says. "Your body needs to heal before you put it through something like that."

My head snaps up. How does he know what the decryption will be like? Surely he can't know that it's going to kill me.

He raises an eyebrow. "I'm not an idiot, Catarina. I know you're scared, and I've been on the end of enough genkit cables to know that Lachlan doesn't write painless code. It's going to hurt you, isn't it? You're not telling me because you're worried I won't let you go through with it."

I can't answer. I don't know what to say, and I don't trust my voice to remain steady.

He sighs. "Look, you can do whatever you want, okay? But Lachlan was the one who gave me the protective protocol, and I like to think he did it for a reason. I'm trained for this, I can assess the risks—"

"Is that why you left Homestake's airlocks open? Because you were *assessing* the risks?"

"Yes, as a matter of fact," he says, his jaw clenching. "Those parking levels weren't designed to withstand a blast. They were designed to cave in to protect the bunker if a blower got inside and detonated. If I'd blown the glass with a grenade, it could have brought the ceiling down and crushed us both. Do you have any idea what would happen if you died?"

"If *I* died? There were eighty thousand people in there." I gesture to the sky, where the plume has spread into a muddied smudge. "That cloud could have infected them all."

"And you're the key to the vaccine," he snaps. "If you die, we're all doomed. My job is to protect you, and that's what I was doing. Do you think I *wanted* to risk those people's lives?"

"I don't know, did you?" My voice is sharper than I intend it to be. I know I'm lashing out, but I can't stop myself. I'm frustrated, my knee is ruined, I've lost my genkit, and there are only a handful of hours left until I die.

"Of course I didn't want to hurt them," Cole says. "Dammit, Cat, what kind of monster do you think I am? I didn't even want to leave Homestake. I felt better in that place than I have in years. I wanted to stay there with you, I thought we could—" He cuts off, drawing his hands back from my knee.

My breath catches.

Did he just say he wanted to stay there with me? Does he mean he wanted to stay there *together*?

"What . . . what do you mean? What about Jun Bei?"

He drops his eyes. "You saw her code, how ruthless it was. She killed fourteen people when she escaped from the lab."

I suck in a breath. Fourteen people. Who the hell *is* this girl? What did my father's research turn her into?

"That's what she was like," Cole continues. "I used to be like that too—we all were. All we wanted to do was hurt people after what they did to us." He turns his forearm so his panel faces up, revealing the black leylines snaking up his arm. "I let Cartaxus turn me into *this* because I wanted to forget. I wanted to be a weapon without feelings, but I'm not. I see that now, and I don't want to hurt people anymore. I want to help them, like you do."

"Cole . . ."

His ice-blue eyes lift to mine, and he swallows, stepping closer. This time I don't push him away. I can barely even breathe. For a second I think he might kiss me, and with a jolt I realize that I *want* him to.

I want his lips on mine. I want to grab his shirt, to pull him to me, to close the distance between us and fold myself into his chest. I want to feel the way I did this morning. Safe, warm, secure.

But that can't happen. I can't let it.

It's not safe to sit here and let Cole look at me like this, sparking something inside me that feels like a window bursting open. Not when he's driving me to my death. He can't give me a rush of hope.

Cole can't look at me like this and make me want to *live*.

"We can't," I say, turning my face away. I don't need to say it, to give a voice to the energy crackling between us. Both of us can feel it. Both of us know it's there, but I have to find a way to crush this before it grows any stronger.

"I know you feel this," he urges. "I know it's not just me."

I close my eyes. He's right. There is something flowing through my veins, some magnetism tugging me to him, dragging me by the heart. It's all I can do to brace myself against the jeep's side, trying not to hear the softness in his voice, to feel the way his scent is curling into my senses.

I'm a heartbeat away from pulling him closer, from turning my face up to his. I need to stop this madness, and I need to stop it now.

I open my eyes. "Where's Dax?"

The question is a slap. I hate myself for asking it, and I hate the pain that flies across Cole's face. It only lasts a moment before a wall slams down and he steps away again, wiping any trace of vulnerability away.

"He's with Leoben. They're north of us, on the highway."

I nod, biting down hard on my lip. "We need to tell them about this plume if they haven't already seen it."

He turns to the cloud on the horizon. "They'll be fine. They're both vaccinated."

I shift my weight, gingerly sliding out of the back of the jeep. A dull ache shoots through my knee, but the worst of the pain is gone. "It's not them I'm worried about—it's the virus. I've never seen multiple people blow at the same time like this, but I should have anticipated it. This changes everything."

"Why?"

I swallow, putting weight on my leg, wincing through the pain. "Because it means the virus is evolving, and it's doing it fast. I can't rest, not even for a few days. It's not safe. We need to hurry, Cole. We need to unlock the vaccine."

# CHAPTER 28

WE DRIVE FOR THREE HOURS WITH BARELY ANY TALK between us until we hit an empty stretch of highway near the Montana border. We met up with Leoben and Dax just north of Homestake, and they're now following us, carrying the clonebox in their jeep. According to our dashboard, we've been skirting around a cyclone cell, but the storm has shifted direction, and we're now driving through its center. Rain thuds against the windshield, then flies off reflectively, repelled by the glass's ultrahydrophobic coating. Walls of rain and angry clouds stretch as far as I can see, forming a canopy above the eerie desolation of Wyoming's wide, abandoned plains.

My eyes are locked on the horizon, scanning for more Hydra clouds, even though my nonenhanced vision is too poor to see through the rain. There's a twinge of a headache in the base of my skull, but it's nothing like the full-blown migraines I usually get. That might have something to do with the healing tech pulsing through my veins, working constantly on my knee. It's still aching, but the worst of the pain has passed.

I keep running my fingers over the gauze wrapped around my forearm, searching for a hint of silicone growing beneath my skin.

It's too swollen to feel much, but I don't think there's anything there yet, and there might not be for at least another day. When Marcus cut out my healing tech, my panel only had to regrow a tiny part of itself. Now the backup node in my spine is regrowing an *entire* panel. I already have the network of gold-flecked cables stretched throughout my body, so I only need to regrow the silicone and reinstall the apps. Still, if we keep to the schedule we're on now, I won't live to see it turn back on.

*Brave,* I tell myself. This is my mantra. I will be strong; I will be brave. All I have to do is let Cole drive, let Dax set up the equipment, and find a way to say my good-byes. Not that I have many people left to say good-bye to. Only Agnes, and now I can't even comm her anymore. She might have tried to call, or sent me a text, to tell me what happened to her. I won't be able to check until my panel is grown.

Which means I'll probably never know.

Cole glances over, watching me prod at my forearm. "Are you sure it's safe for you to grow a normal panel?"

I shrug. "I think so. I mean, my father was the one who gave me the backup node that's growing this. He probably thought I'd find it myself. I *should* have, really. I was just too scared to do anything with my panel after Cartaxus took him. He probably expected me to jack in as soon as he left, and hunt around in the code. I would have figured it out eventually. It wasn't very well hidden."

Cole nods, looking doubtful. "Why would he have hidden this from you?"

I drop my eyes. "I have a theory about that, too."

"Oh?"

I chew my lip. "Well, he came up with a treatment for my hypergenesis. I don't know what it was, but I think that's what he was hiding.

And since hypergenesis is only seen in humans, which means it's probably part of the anthrozone, I was thinking . . ."

Cole's hands tighten on the wheel. "You think he developed the treatment based on the research he did in the Zarathustra Initiative."

I nod, closing my eyes. Silhouettes of the five children flicker through my mind, along with scraps from the experimental notes in their files. Surgical examinations. Toxicity tests. Extended sensory deprivation. Cole said my father developed the Hydra vaccine based on the research he did on Leoben, but what if the treatment for my hypergenesis came from that work too? He couldn't have explained it to me without telling me the truth.

I would have learned what he did to Cole and the others. I would have *hated* him.

"What did you mean earlier?" I ask quietly. "When you said you wanted to become a weapon because of what Cartaxus . . . what my father did to you."

He shifts. "Let's talk about that after we get to the lab."

"I want to know. It's important. What happened to you and the other kids?"

He blows out a sigh. "It was different for each of us. We all had different mutations. Your father called them gifts."

"Like superpowers?"

His lips curl. "Not even close."

I pull my leg up slowly so my foot rests on the seat, keeping my wounded knee straight. "What were they?"

"Well, we weren't told what they were explicitly. Your father wanted to make sure that the experiments were *pure*, so we weren't supposed to understand what they were testing us for. But some of us figured it out. Lee's was obvious. They took blood and tissue samples from him for years, and after a while they started locking him in a room with Hydra doses and letting them blow."

I close my eyes, stunned by the brutality. I swallow it down. "So Leoben was naturally immune?"

"Completely. He doesn't even have the vaccine in his arm like Crick and I do, but your father was probably the only man in the world who could tell you how his immunity works. All we know is that it took almost eighteen years for him to translate whatever he found in Lee's DNA into a vaccine."

"What about the others?" I lean down to grab my backpack and slide out the mold-spotted manila folders. Cole stiffens, but he doesn't stop me. I open one folder to a picture of a little girl with shaved blond hair. Anna Sinclair. Her skin looks unusual—as though it's covered with tiny bumps—but it's hard to tell from the photograph. Her eyes are narrowed, staring at the camera as though she'd like to hurt whoever is behind it. "What about her?"

Cole glances over and smiles. "Ah, Anna. She'd approve of that trick you did with your genkit to blow the airlocks. Anything with explosives, and Anna's on board. We didn't know what her mutation was, but she had a thing when she was younger where she'd get growths all over her. Her skin cells wouldn't stop growing. You can see it in the picture. She couldn't eat, either. She spent a lot of time in the medical ward, until Lachlan came up with an app that seemed to clear it up overnight. She's down south now, in another Cartaxus facility. A civilian bunker. They firewalled us, and we've barely been able to talk for the last few months."

"Why is she there?"

Cole looks surprised. "I don't know. They don't tell us that kind of thing in the black-out program."

"She's in it too?"

He nods. "Me, Anna, and Leoben. Anna probably has the most training. She was into the military stuff even when we were little. She wants to run Cartaxus one day."

"What about . . ." I flip through the files, opening the one with the bald girl. Her skin is so pale I can see the veins across her cheeks. She looks like a doll made of glass. "What about Ziana?"

"Ziana . . ." Cole sighs. "Ziana's gone. She escaped during the outbreak. She told us she was going to, and that she didn't want us to find her. I still check for her every week, but I can't get through. She was only really close to Jun Bei."

"Did you know what her mutation was?"

"Yeah." Cole's voice goes hard.

A chill creeps across my skin. "What was it?"

"Are you sure you want to talk about this?"

I tighten my grip on the folders. "I need to know, Cole."

He lets out a slow breath. "Ziana has . . . she has another sense."

"What, like . . . magnetoreception?"

He shakes his head. "She can *feel* some of her body's systems. They're connected to her brain like our nervous system is. When I got shot, I felt pain, because that's what my nerve endings were telling me. Ziana would feel that too, but she'd also feel her blood and her hormones, and a hundred other things just as clearly as the pain. She has too many neurons in her body—at least that's what Jun Bei thought, but it took us a while to figure it out."

Too many neurons. My head spins with the implications. Every panel has a handful of blunt monitors to read data from its user's body: blood sugar levels, histamine releases, hormone balances, the number of cells being shed inside your stomach every hour. The monitors add a feed to most people's VR dashboard, but seeing the stats in your vision is different from actually *sensing* them. Someone like Ziana could grow up knowing more about the human body than any scientist ever had, just by listening to her own.

"That's amazing."

"Lachlan seemed to think so. He worked with Ziana a lot, but she didn't get along with the rest of us. She was always . . . strange. She barely spoke, and she spent most of her time in the medical ward."

"Why?"

Cole doesn't answer, and it suddenly hits me why he didn't want to tell me about Ziana. The easiest way to test someone's awareness of their body's functions would be to hurt and disrupt them. To push them to their limits. To bend them until they broke.

The best way to test someone's ability to survive is to try to *kill* them.

I close my eyes. I've seen the scars on Cole's chest, but I hadn't really let myself think about how he got them. My father's research wasn't just brutal; it was intentionally brutal. He was trying to push these children as far as he could, to see what he'd learn when they fell apart.

I open my eyes, fighting the rage coiling inside me. "What about Jun Bei's mutation?"

Cole glances over, but I don't flip open Jun Bei's file. I don't want to see the look in his eyes when he sees her photograph. I'm in a storm right now—of anger, of disgust, of fear. I don't need to add jealousy to that mix.

"We didn't figure out what her mutation was. Or, at least, she never told me. It wasn't obvious, whatever it was."

"What about you?"

He presses his lips together. "I have a mutation that makes me respond strongly to neural gentech."

"What, like memory blockers?"

"No, like *real* neural gentech. Code that runs inside the brain."

"I thought we were still decades away from that kind of tech."

"Well, I guess Lachlan was just ahead of his time."

"Wow." I lean back, watching the rain bounce off the windshield. Code that can affect people's brains has been the obsession of conspiracy theorists since panels were invented. They figured that if you could change people's skin, you could also change their minds, which meant our thoughts could someday be controlled.

But after years of work and countless primate tests, scientists explained that it was just too *hard.*

The problem is, the brain isn't like any other organ. Our thoughts and memories are stored as billions of tiny circuits. which means it's the *structures* of the cells that are important, not just the cells themselves. It's the way they're organized, the way they link up to one another. The rest of the body is far easier: If you tweak the gene for melanin, then your freckles fade. You want bigger muscles? Just grow some more muscle cells. Most gentech apps are as simple as that. The art of coding lies in finding the safest, most elegant way to do those tiny tweaks.

But the brain is a mass of billions of neurons, and their structure is unique to every person. If you wanted to change someone's brain, you'd need to map it first, and we can't even do that. Mapping every neuron is a task that's just as hard as *building* a brand-new brain, and I didn't think we were even close to doing that.

"So what are you saying?" I ask. "Do you have code controlling your *thoughts*?"

Cole laughs. It's a deep, full laugh, and the sound is jarring after the tense silence that's stretched between us for the last few hours. "No, it's not like that."

"What is it, then?" I shift, angling myself toward him, moving my wounded knee carefully. "Is there code for neural restructuring? How do they handle the computation?"

"There's no thought control," Cole says. "Nothing like that. It's pretty blunt. It started when Lachlan tweaked the unmapped parts of my genome and noticed some changes in my behavior."

I close my eyes, trying not to think about the risk my father took using code that focused on the unmapped parts of Cole's DNA. It could have killed him. It could have driven him insane. It's the genetic equivalent of testing random chemicals by feeding them to a child.

"So what did he find?"

Cole looks over at me, and for the first time since we started driving, we hold each other's gaze. "Tell me why you jacked into your knee to close those airlocks."

I run my fingers across the bandage on my leg. "It seemed like the right thing to do."

"Did you think about it for a while, and weigh up the pros and cons? Or were you following an instinct?"

I think back to Homestake, to when I jammed the wire into my knee before I could hesitate, to stop myself from backing out. "I guess it was mostly an instinct."

He nods. "You wanted to protect the people in that bunker. That's instinctive, Cat, and it's as deep as it gets. Protecting others is a universal instinct, and it can be overwhelming when it kicks in. We're all born with it, which means that it's coded somewhere in our DNA. Our conscious thoughts and memories are built up throughout our lives, but instincts are different. Instincts are *genetic*. And that makes them susceptible to coding."

I chew my lip as I start to see what Cole is getting at. If our instincts are genetic, one day we might be able to rewrite them. But first we'd need to *find* the genes that control our instincts, which could be impossible. Even knockout kids could only take you so far. If a child was afraid of the dark, would that be because of a hard-coded instinct, or because they'd had experiences that made them afraid? Splitting apart the influence of genes and experiences on our personalities—nature versus nurture—has been a problem in science for centuries.

"So your protective protocol, is that an instinct?"

Cole nods. "Protection was the first instinct Lachlan noticed in me. He activated one of my genes with a piece of code when I was eight years old, and I tackled a nurse who was trying to sample Jun Bei's blood. The code didn't change anyone else's behavior, but it made my brain light up like a firework. He figured out that if he tweaked genes that were associated with instincts in me, I would *feel* those instincts in response. He activated a set of genes in the cells inside my brain, and I was suddenly afraid of water. He deactivated them, and the fear disappeared. It didn't work on anyone else, but for me it was like flipping a switch. He could make me feel fear, or protectiveness, all by running a few lines of code."

"Remotely controlled instincts." My head spins. "That's incredible. But . . . that means he could use you to build a map, to figure out which genes controlled which instincts. Nobody's been able to do that before. You're like the Rosetta stone for the human brain."

A brief, unreadable look crosses Cole's face, like a cloud drifting over the sun. "That's exactly what he used to call me. He mapped out hundreds of instincts in my DNA, everything from protectiveness to cravings for sugar. The urge to hunt, to kill . . ."

It suddenly hits me. "He made you *feel* all those things? But how did he test them? You were a child, you couldn't explain what you were feeling properly, and he'd have to test them in different settings, with

EMILY SUVADA

different environments, different strengths. He'd have to make sure you weren't faking. . . ."

Cole drops his eyes.

"He made you kill people, when you were just a child?"

He nods. I stare at him and then force my eyes away. A tear drops from my nose before I know I'm crying, and I bite down on my lip, trying to hold it in.

"Cat, please don't cry. It was a long time ago. I've dealt with it."

"But it was wrong," I say. My voice is thick, and the effort of keeping it level hurts my throat. "He was my father, and you were a child. He treated you like lab rats when he should have been looking after you."

"If it wasn't him, it would have been someone else. Maybe a few years later, maybe decades, but it was inevitable."

"No," I whisper, though I know he's right. If my father hadn't done it, another scientist would have eventually. That's the problem with animal testing. It's so easy that it becomes the only thing people know how to do. When they learn all they can from rats, there's only one way to move on—to rabbits, dogs, monkeys, bonobos. It was inevitable they'd turn to humans.

But that's still no excuse for what my father did.

Cole sighs. "Look, Cat, I've been through a lot, but so has everyone. You think the kids who've lived through Hydra are happy? Some of them have *eaten* their parents. This a hard world, and your father made me hard enough to survive it."

"Stop defending him." I wipe my eyes with the back of my hand. "He was looking after me while he was *hurting* you. It's not right. He locked you up—"

Cole cuts me off. "He created the vaccine. That's all that matters. There's no such thing as right anymore—that ended when the plague

262

hit. Sometimes we need to do awful things to stop worse things from happening. You're still thinking in terms of right and wrong, but this is war, and the rules have changed."

"I know," I say, rubbing my eyes again. I know what he's saying, and I felt the same way myself when I read the vaccine's decryption code. He gave up his childhood, and I'm giving up my life, but that doesn't mean I want to. It doesn't make any of this okay.

The jeep's dashboard flashes red all of a sudden, and I'm so angry and confused that I don't see the girl until we're almost on top of her.

# CHAPTER 29

"STOP!" I SCREAM, WRENCHING THE STEERING WHEEL, sending us flying off the road. The jeep bounces through a barbed-wire fence and slams into a tree. Momentum carries me forward until an airbag hits my chest, bringing up a burst of shimmering stars in my vision.

"Catarina!" Cole shoves the airbag away. His eyes are black and terrified. "What the hell? Are you okay?"

"The girl!" I yank my seat belt off and kick the door open, jumping out into the rain. The dark storm clouds above us make it look like twilight, even though it's the middle of the day. The ground is muddy and slick, and the air smells like lightning. Every time I blink, I see the girl's emerald eyes in my mind, her ash-black hair flying across her face, lifted high on the wind.

What was she doing in the middle of the road?

"We didn't hit her, did we?" I shout, squinting, one arm held above my eyes to block the constant assault of the rain. "What happened to the jeep?"

Cole just stares at me from his seat. "What are you talking about?"

"The dashboard, Cole! It went red, and we almost hit her. I have to find her—she might be hurt."

I crouch down to search under the jeep, wincing as pain shoots through my knee. Part of me knows we can't have missed her. I didn't see her until it was too late, and if we hit her at that speed, there's no way she's still alive. I limp around the jeep, scanning the hood. The black metal is slick with rain and barely scratched, though the tree we hit is now a splintered wreck. There's no sign of blood on the bumper, no hint of the girl at all.

"Cole, I need your help. I can't hear anything without my tech."

His door swings open, and I turn in a circle, squinting through the rain. All I can see are empty wheat fields stretching into the haze of the storm. We're miles from civilization, deep in abandoned farmlands.

That doesn't mean there aren't families still hiding out here, though.

"Maybe she's okay," I say. "Maybe we didn't hit her." My boots sink into the mud as I limp back along the skid marks and up to the road. The highway to the north is empty, the asphalt glistening in the rain, and the only movement to the south is the distant headlights of Leoben's jeep.

"Catarina . . ."

"She was *here*," I say, staring into the rain. But there's no sign of her anywhere. No footprints, no blood. Just empty fields and shuttered houses. There's nowhere to hide, nowhere she could have run to. "Doesn't the jeep have a recording or something?"

Cole frowns. "It's not responding. I think the crash rebooted it."

"Well, I saw her, I swear, but it's like she just disappeared."

Cole watches me carefully, the rain trickling down his arms, glistening on his eyelashes. "There are no human life signs or bodies around us. Maybe you saw a bird."

"A bird?" I choke out. I scrub my eyes. I only saw the girl for a second, but it was enough to know she was real. Standing like a statue in the road, staring at us as we hurtled closer.

"There's nobody here, Cat." Cole looks more troubled than I've seen him, like I'm hurt and he doesn't know how to protect me. "What did she look like?"

"I don't know," I say, shivering in the rain. "She was little, just a kid with green eyes and black hair, and she was wearing a white . . . gown, or something. Like a . . ." I trail off. A hospital gown. That's what I was going to say. But that sounds completely insane. What would a child in a hospital gown be doing in the middle of the road? A jolt runs through me as it comes together in my mind.

Cole is right. She wasn't real. The little girl wasn't a child lost in the rain; she was a hallucination of Jun Bei, looking just like she did in my father's file. I was thinking about the Zarathustra kids just before the crash. I can't believe I just *hallucinated*.

"Oh shit," I whisper, bending over, pressing my hands to my mouth. I'm losing my grip on reality. I'm starting to see things.

We're in the middle of nowhere, and I just crashed us into a tree. How am I going to hold it together long enough to unlock the vaccine?

"Maybe we should take a break," Cole says. "You've been through a lot."

I scrub my hands over my face, scanning the road. Maybe I did see a bird, something my brain caught hold of and turned into one of the Zarathustra kids. But there's no sign of an animal. Just a face burned into my mind that's quickly joined by the other four children. I rub my eyes again, over and over, until all I see is the empty road. Just the rain, the fields, and Cole's troubled eyes.

"I'm okay," I breathe, straightening.

Cole's brow furrows. In the dim light of the storm the leylines curled around his face look like slivers of pure darkness cut into his skin. Water trickles from his close-cropped hair, weaving down the planes of his face.

I can't stop staring at every pore, every drop of rain on his skin . . .

I blink. "I think my ocular tech is waking up again." I pull back the gauze wrapped around my forearm. A single dot of cobalt smiles up from my bruised skin. It blinks once every two seconds. That means the first wires have grown, linking up to the tech from my old panel. There's still no battery, no function cores, no operating system, but it might explain why I just saw Cole's ex-girlfriend in the rain.

"It must have been a glitch in my tech when the wires connected," I say. "I'm sorry, I screwed up."

He sighs, relieved. "Don't worry about it. Let's just get you out of the rain." He takes me by the shoulder to guide me off the road just as Leoben's jeep screeches to a stop behind us.

"What's happening?" Leoben yells out his window.

"Nothing," Cole calls back. "Let's keep moving. Catarina thought she saw something, but it was a mistake."

"I don't think it was."

Cole stiffens, turning around. "Why not?"

Leoben's door swings open, and he climbs out of his jeep with a rifle in one hand. "Because I didn't hit the brakes. The jeep stopped on its own, and now it won't start again."

Cole's grip on my shoulder tightens.

Dax jumps out into the rain. He stalks to the side of the road, sniffing the air. "Do you smell that?"

Cole draws in a slow breath, narrowing his eyes. "Ozone. I thought it was the lightning."

Dax shakes his head, scanning the road. He drops to his knees, swiping one finger across the asphalt. It comes up coated with silver. His eyes glaze over for a second before cutting to me. "This is triphase. It's all over the road."

I swallow, bringing up my own mud-streaked hands, inspecting them in the glow of the headlights. My fingers are shaking, dotted with rain, but there's a strange glint to my skin that shouldn't be there—tiny, iridescent specks of silver. A sheen of nanobots, just like the ones genkits and panels build, but these aren't coded for healing.

They're coded for *killing*.

Triphase is built to destroy, to chew up every organic molecule of every living thing it comes in contact with. I look at Cole and Leoben, seeing the same silver sheen on their feet, their hands, their necks.

We're all covered with it.

"How did this get here?" Cole asks.

"It's in the air," Leoben says, grimacing. "Shit, it's everywhere. Why aren't the little bastards eating us?"

"They haven't been activated yet." Dax's voice is distant. "They're coded, waiting to be set off, and they haven't been here long. It's like they've just come down in the storm."

Cole and Leoben both freeze and lift their eyes at the same time. I follow their gaze up into the rain, squinting through my fingers. Dark clouds cover the sky, still dropping rain in lashing sheets, but through the storm I can make out a hint of something else.

Something dark, moving in a loose formation.

Drones.

Leoben steps instantly closer to Dax, shouldering his rifle.

"I wouldn't do that if I were you, Lieutenant," a voice booms from the sky. Sharp, female, cocky. I know the voice from somewhere, but I can't quite place it. "In the event of their destruction, these drones are programmed to send out a pulse that will activate the triphase. Our scientists estimate that it will take you approximately fourteen seconds to die."

"What do you want?" Cole shouts up. "We don't have anything of value."

"Quite the contrary. You have an end to this hideous nightmare." Spots of light flicker on across the sky, revealing a network of at least a hundred drones hovering above us. They drop slowly, until I can pick up the whine of their propellers, then pause and splash down pinprick beams of light onto the road.

The beams dance through the rain, catching the droplets as they fall, gradually intersecting to form the life-size shell of a woman. She floats in midair, her torso dropping away into vectors of light that glitter on the silver-sheened road. Her face is distorted, rippling as the rain rushes through the rudimentary hologram, but I'd still recognize that trademark smile anywhere.

My hands curl into fists. "Novak." The leader of the Skies. The woman I've spent the last two years working for. "What the hell are you doing?"

She spreads her hands. "We're here to help you, Catarina. You've had a difficult journey, what with Lieutenant Franklin being shot. We've been impressed by your determination, but we think it's time you got the help you need to complete this mission."

I shiver, staring at her, my clothing soaked through. How does she know Cole was shot? How does she know anything?

It suddenly hits me. "Marcus." I turn to Cole. "Marcus put them onto us."

"Yes indeed," Novak says. "It seems that his wife spontaneously developed hypergenesis after installing an app from your arm. Unfortunately, her body was already running a considerable amount of code. From what Marcus told me, it was a miracle they were able to save her."

My breath rushes from me. Amy. I hadn't even thought about her. I was so angry that I didn't realize the code he took might do the same thing it did to me: bubble the skin off her back. It would only have taken a few hours to install; it must have kicked in just after we left.

"Marcus was furious, naturally," Novak continues, "so he sent me everything he'd downloaded from both of your panels, to make sense of what had happened."

My stomach lurches. Cole stiffens, his eyes darting to mine.

"What we found in your panel, Catarina," Novak says, giving me a cold smile, "was so complex that it would take our best coders years to unravel. But the message in your arm, Lieutenant, told me everything I needed to know. It looks like Miss Agatta is the key we've all been waiting for."

# CHAPTER 30

NOVAK'S HOLOGRAM DOESN'T LISTEN WHEN I TELL
her that we need to get to the lab in Canada, to use the equipment my father
left for us. She doesn't understand that the procedure we're going to run is
so complex and specific that it could go wrong countless different ways. She
doesn't believe Leoben when he tells her that Cartaxus is monitoring the
Skies network, that even *talking* to her has now given them our position.

She doesn't listen at all, and since she's the one controlling the triphase on our skin, there isn't much we can do about it.

"We're screwed," I say to Cole as we climb back into the jeep, our
clothes soaked through from the rain, glittering with the triphase. It's
all over us, and there's no scrubbing it off. It's in our lungs now, wedged
between our cells. The faintest blip from one of Novak's drones will
activate it and chew us into dust unless we follow her demands. We
have to follow a route she gave us to Sunnyvale, the secret Skies HQ
I've heard about but have never actually seen. The drones will follow
us. They will watch our every move, ready to send a signal on Novak's
command and activate the triphase. When we get to the Skies base, she
wants to unlock the vaccine live, in one of her broadcasts.

Of course she does.

I pull my door shut, shoving the wet hair from my face. "If Leoben's right about Cartaxus spying on the Skies, they probably heard that whole conversation. We just stole one of their cloneboxes. They're going to come after us."

"I'm sure they will." Cole's voice is low, furious. He grips the steering wheel until his knuckles bloom white.

"We could run," I whisper, glancing through the window at the drones. "We could call their bluff."

"No." He shakes his head, starting the engine. "Not like this. We can't do anything until we get this stuff off our skin." We roll back from the splintered tree and swing back onto the highway. Leoben's jeep follows us, a few car lengths behind, its headlights forming coronas of light in the rain. "Besides," he says, "I'm not so sure they're bluffing."

"They won't *kill* us," I say. "They need the copy of the vaccine that's in your arm, and they need me to decrypt it."

Cole's eyes lift to the rearview, his jaw tightening. "It's not us I'm worried about."

I follow his eyes, gripping the side of the seat to turn around and stare back through the rear windows. Behind Leoben's jeep, a handful of drones remain hovering above the spot on the road where we just stood. One of their lights flashes red. I can't see the pulse it sends, but the effect on the triphase is instantaneous.

Sparks of light rise from the ground, forming glittering silver clouds that rise and spread, swallowing the road, coming dangerously close to Leoben's jeep. The cloud rolls over the grass, consuming everything in its path, leaving only black, charred earth in its wake.

Leoben's jeep speeds up until it's almost touching us. I can't see Leoben or Dax through their windshield, but I'm sure they're terrified.

Novak's message is clear: The triphase is real, and the Skies aren't afraid to use it. Not on Cole or me, perhaps.

But they'll use it on our friends.

I turn back, falling into the seat, my hands bunched into fists. I'm already frightened enough about the decryption, and now I'll be doing it at gunpoint. The thought makes me want to scream. I'm giving up my life for this. At the very least, I want to die on my own terms.

But maybe I still can.

My eyes slide to the handgun holstered at Cole's belt. We don't have much leverage here—not with triphase on our skin and drones above us—but there is one final card I can play. My father's code made it clear that whoever wants to release the vaccine is going to need me *alive*. I can't turn a gun on a hundred drones, or a troop of Cartaxus soldiers, but I can turn one on my own head and hold myself for ransom. I don't know what I'd ask for, or what good it would do, but it'd give me some semblance of control over the last hours of my life.

"You should give me a gun," I say.

Cole glances over. "For what?"

"To . . . protect myself. This might turn into a firefight between Cartaxus and the Skies. What if you get hurt again?"

"Can you shoot?"

"I got that Lurker in the head in the mines."

"At five yards, sure. I'm asking if you could take him down with a nonlethal shot at twenty yards, while it's raining, and he's running in zigzags."

I blow out a frustrated sigh. "Of course I couldn't."

"Then a gun isn't going to help you, but I can give you something better. I just need a few minutes to get it out."

Lightning crackles in the distance, revealing the silhouette of mountains on the horizon. "Sure," I say. "It's not like I'm going any-where."

Cole checks the rearview, his eyes glazing over momentarily. The jeep's headlights glow brighter, and a warning flashes up on the dash. telling me that it's switching to full autodriver mode. Cole turns and reaches over the seat, dragging his backpack closer, and digs around in a zippered compartment. He pulls out a knife.

I roll my eyes. "Are you kidding me? A knife is clearly not better than a gun."

"I never said it was. Just give me a minute."

He tilts his seat back, letting the jeep drive on its own, and pulls the bottom of his shirt up over his chest. The gunshot wound from the mines is now a tiny silver dot on his taut, muscled stomach, beside a trail of black hair that dives down to his belt. Heat prickles on my neck at the sight. I fight it down, forcing my eyes away.

"What exactly are you doing?" I ask.

Cole has the knife clutched in one hand and is prodding around his ribs with the other. "Looking for something."

"For what?"

He spins the knife so the blade juts toward his chest. "For this." He stabs the blade between his ribs.

I fly back against the window, my heart pounding. "What the *hell* are you doing?"

He twists the blade, wincing. "Uh, it's tight. Haven't used it in a while."

"Used what?" I throw one hand over my eyes, squinting between my fingers. "Oh shit. It's in your chest, isn't it?"

He nods, grunting, dragging the blade back out. It scrapes against something inside him, letting out a metallic shriek. The incision is clean and strangely bloodless. He presses his fingers to it, and a swarm of white wires unfurls from his chest, dragging something out with a *squelch*.

"Oh hell no." I turn to the window, pressing my forehead to the glass. Heat is rushing up my neck again, but this time it's because I'm going to be sick. "You did *not* just do that."

"These wouldn't be very useful if they were outside my body. The whole point of these vials is that I can't lose them in an emergency."

He drags a little black pendant from the incision between his ribs, slick and capsule shaped, like a polished stone. The wires in his chest shrink back inside him, dragging the incision closed as they recede. He digs around in his backpack, pulls out a silver chain, and slips the black pendant onto it, then hands it to me. "This is *nightstick*. Keep it around your neck at all times, and just twist the ends to use it. Since you don't have a panel yet, it's probably the best weapon you could have."

I take the pendant carefully and slide the chain around my neck. It's *warm*. Warm from being inside Cole's chest. The thought should disgust me, but for some reason it doesn't. "What does it do?"

He presses a blue bandage to his ribs and pulls his shirt back down. "It knocks people out, probably the same way you knocked me out in the cabin. It'll work on anyone with a panel in a twenty-foot radius, including the person who sets it off. It's good for hostage situations, or when you know you have backup coming. It only lasts a few minutes, but that's plenty of time for you, because you'll be immune to the effects."

"Because I don't have a panel."

"Exactly."

I nod, impressed. "That's actually brilliant."

He smiles, raising his seat, taking the steering wheel again. "I have my moments."

I sink back into my seat, my fingers sliding over the black lozenge.

275

It won't help me hold myself for ransom, but it might end up being more useful than a gun. The spark of an idea is forming in my head—not something I can use to protect myself, though. Something bigger. Something I can't quite understand. "How does this work on every panel? Does it use an EMP?"

"I don't know. The code is top secret. Actually . . ." Cole's eyes glaze over briefly. "Since you unlocked my panel, we have access now. You can read it for yourself."

The smooth curved glass of the dashboard flashes. Lines of white text appear on it in a mix of languages: backslash and DNAssembly. Gentech code. I lean forward, running my fingers across the dash to scroll, unfolding the algorithms in my mind.

The code is precise and devoid of comments, military style, but I'd recognize the attack pattern it's using anywhere. It kicks off a wireless blast to throw itself at the power management system of every panel in a twenty-foot range. It's exploiting a weakness in gentech batteries that's almost identical to the code I wrote to break into panels. That's how I hacked into Cole's arm—I focused my efforts on that one, microscopic weakness. I've never targeted it as precisely as the nightstick does, but the general method is the same: smash the power connection, wedge yourself into the cracks, and hurl commands through.

This code sends just one command. It uses another notation, but it has the same effect as when I knocked Cole out with recumbentibus.

I look up. "Are you sure this works on every panel?"

"Yeah, why?"

My eyes drop back to the code. "Because it's exploiting a weakness in gentech batteries. If Cartaxus wrote this code, that means they know about the weakness. Why wouldn't they fix it?"

"Maybe they want it there, like a back door."

That makes sense—every panel in the world is built on the same basic Cartaxus framework, and I'm sure they'd want a back door to control people's panels without their permission—but this weakness isn't big enough. It's not even a door. It's a window, a crevice. Hardly enough to send one command through.

But still, it's so elegant, so simple. It's hard to believe more people haven't tried to exploit it.

Or maybe they have.

I turn to Cole. "Do you have a copy of Jun Bei's kick simulation?"

"I think so, but it's built for Cartaxus systems. It's not going to help us get out of a Skies base."

"It's not for getting us out. I just need to see it."

Cole gives me a dubious look but flicks it to the dash. I strain against my seat belt, rubbing my wounded knee as I read through Jun Bei's code. It's beautiful. Full of comments, full of wild variable names and references to her own library of custom apps. It would have taken years to write. My stomach twists with jealousy. She's smarter than me. She's ruthless.

She's completely *terrifying*.

And just as I suspected, Jun Bei has used the same attack method as the nightstick code. I couldn't understand how she took over Homestake so quickly when every server was protected, and every system was firewalled. It should have taken hours, but she did it in minutes. But that's because she wasn't hacking the systems.

She was hacking the *people*, instead.

Jun Bei's kick simulation is boosted wirelessly, just like the nightstick, but it reaches every panel in a mile-wide radius. She's given the tiny hidden entry point a name: the *trapdoor*. Just the sight of the word makes me shiver. A tiny, hidden portal that her code, my viruses, and the nightstick all exploit. Her simulation slips two lines of code through the trapdoor—two perfect, flawless lines that take root and give her access to the user's panel.

From there, she has their files, their comm-link, their logins. Why hack through a firewall when you can get the password straight from an engineer's arm?

"This is amazing," I say. "Jun Bei, she . . . she's incredible. Most viruses act like grenades. This is a goddamn *sniper rifle*."

Cole nods silently. Beneath the jealousy and shock at what I've heard about Jun Bei, I'm reluctantly amazed. She's vicious but brilliant. The girl is a stone-cold genius. She might even be a better coder than my father.

If I wasn't driving to my death, I think I'd like to meet her.

"This code," I say, "it means that everyone in the world is vulnerable. Every panel has this same weakness that can be exploited. It's incredible. People would freak out if they saw this."

"So what are you going to do with it?"

I stare at the screen. "I honestly don't know."

"Well, you don't have much time to figure it out. We're almost there."

We swing off the freeway, taking a leaf-strewn exit ramp. The road dives into a valley, over an old bridge, and into a thick, wild forest. Through the trees I can make out the faintest hint of structures in the distance. The glow of a window. A wisp of smoke.

We've reached Sunnyvale.

The outskirts of the town are dark. It looks like an old mining hub, probably abandoned decades ago, judging by the state of most of the houses. As we get closer to the center, the yards grow cleaner, and the windows shine with airtight epoxy. I'd heard Sunnyvale mentioned on Skies forums, and I assumed it was some kind of shantytown, but it's nothing like I pictured. This place is clean and pretty. We drive past suburban streets filled with flower beds and vegetable gardens. It's like we've been transported back to a time before the plague. I didn't even know places like this existed anymore.

We roll past the town square and up to a warehouse, where guards in full hazard suits are waiting for us. Cole pulls the jeep inside and kills the engine. The guards wave their arms, ordering us to get out.

Cole reaches for his door handle but pauses, his eyes landing on the black pendant around my neck. "The range of that thing is twenty feet. Remember that, Cat."

I nod. "Let's just stay calm until we know what's happening."

We climb out into the warehouse, our hands raised above our heads. The space is empty, except for two massive coils of steel cable suspended from the ceiling at either end of the room.

Leoben's jeep pulls up alongside us, its windows dark. Dax and Leoben climb out, their clothes still wet, their skin glittering.

"I've gotta say," Leoben says, looking around, stretching, "I thought you Skies guys were a bunch of idiots. I'm kind of impressed."

"We do our best." One of the hazard-suited guards steps forward, and the warehouse's doors roll shut, locking us in.

Cole stiffens. His eyes flash to black.

I grab his arm. "Hey, it's okay. They have to kill the triphase."

"How do they do that?"

"With an electromagnetic—" My voice cuts out as a humming fills the air. It's coming from the massive loops of wire hanging from the ceiling, growing deafening, morphing into a towering wash of nonsound. It vibrates in my chest, then cuts out abruptly, leaving me shaking. "With . . . one of those."

Cole doubles over, coughing. Leoben lets out a hoot. Dax stands with his arms crossed, glowering at the guards.

I swipe my finger across my arm. The dust on my skin is still silver and glittering, but it's growing slowly clearer as the triphase gathers into harmless clumps.

The guard who stepped forward pulls off his visor and unzips his hazard suit. He's young, with alabaster skin and long black hair with a single streak of white at his temple, just like Dax used to have. He gives us a broad smile, revealing curved white incisors. Vampire enthusiast. I wonder if he's had his stomach lined so he can digest blood.

"Welcome to Sunnyvale," he says. "We're sorry to have brought you in like this, but we couldn't risk letting you go, not with such precious cargo. We've set up quarters for you all, and you're free to move about the town as you like. You're not prisoners. We just want your help with the vaccine, and then you'll all be free to leave."

"Gee, thanks," Leoben mutters. "Very generous of you."

"You'll want to shower and change," the man continues, flashing his fangs. "My people can help you settle into your quarters now, but Miss Agatta will have to come with me to HQ."

Dax steps forward, his face paling. "You can't just *take* her." He thinks they're going to do the procedure now, that I'm about to die. He doesn't realize that the Skies don't have the kind of programmers who could take my father's file and translate it into a procedure this quickly. That's what Dax is here for. That's why my father made him part of this. He's one of the few people on the planet with the skills to run the decryption.

"What's happening?" Cole asks, narrowing his eyes. He turns to Dax. "Is something wrong?"

"No, it's fine. I'll talk to them," I say, giving Dax a meaningful look. "I mean it. I'll be okay."

Dax nods reluctantly, and Cole gives me a suspicious, lingering stare as I follow the guard.

I *hope* I'll be okay.

# CHAPTER 31

THE GUARD TAKES ME THROUGH BLOCKS OF QUIET, tree-lined streets filled with rows of clean, pretty houses. Some have gardens bursting with beans, herbs, and perfect-looking tomatoes that are probably genehacked to hell and back. We stop outside one of the larger houses, which looks normal except for the grid of metal welded over its walls. It forms a building-size Faraday cage that should stop any wireless transmissions from coming into or out of it. The guard leads me up the worn stone steps, through an iron door, and into the beating heart of Novak's network.

Inside, the floor is covered with wires snaking between banks of computers, with glazed-eyed technicians jacked into them. Almost everyone is clearly running a serious amount of what Cartaxus calls "nonstandard" code. Some of it makes the guard's vampire teeth look tame. One woman has a lion's mane that stretches down her back, another has three glossy lenses embedded in the back of her head, and a man carrying a roll of wire has a tail that twitches when he looks up and sees me.

"Catarina." Novak smiles and strides across the room, dressed in the uniform I recognize from her broadcasts: black pleather with glowing cobalt stripes across her shoulders. She looks younger in person, early thirties at most, and there's something eerie about her eyes. One of them has a too-bright sheen that means the eye is probably synthetic—a tiny camera wired up to let her see in extra wavelengths. It's sure to be useful, but it's creepy as hell to look at.

In fact, everything about her is kind of creepy.

"I'm so happy to meet you after all this time." She reaches out to shake my hand. A silver stud glints on the side of her nose, and a tattoo of a double-helix curls up her neck, disappearing into her scarlet hair. Her grip is firm, but her fingers are cold, matching the steeliness of her gaze. "I've been worried about you ever since you broke off our conversation last week."

I look down at the dead triphase still dusted across my skin. "You have a funny way of showing your concern for my safety."

She just smiles. "You're my best hacker, Bobcat. Of course I was worried. I sent Agnes over to check on you, but I didn't hear back. I thought about sending a search team, but we received an anonymous tip-off that you were traveling across the country with an encrypted copy of a vaccine. When we heard from Marcus, we decided we had to do everything in our power to find you. I'm so glad you agreed to join us."

I frown. An anonymous tip-off? It must have been Agnes. But if she got in touch with Novak, why didn't she contact me?

"I'm happy to help release the vaccine," I say, "but I do have some demands."

Novak blinks. "Demands?"

"I'm sure you've read the code that explains the decryption?"

She nods, and something in her expression tells me my guess was right—she's read the code, her people know it uses my body to unlock the vaccine, but they don't know much more about it than that. Only Dax and I are familiar enough with my father's style of coding to understand the intricacies of the procedure so quickly. That gives me an edge. If I play my cards right, I might be able to bluff my way to some kind of leverage.

"Then you'll know that the vaccine won't be properly decrypted unless I allow it," I say. "My father wrote it that way, so Cartaxus could never force me to decrypt it. I'll only allow it to be decrypted to my specifications, and only if it's going to be distributed freely, to every survivor on the surface *and* in the bunkers."

Novak's eyes narrow.

Everything I just said is a lie, but it has enough of a ring of truth to make it believable. I don't need to be willing to decrypt the vaccine—I don't even need to be awake. My cells are all that matters, but Dax and I are the only people who know that.

"Yes," she says finally, "I'm aware of that. But there are some things *you* should be aware of, Miss Agatta."

"Like what?"

She raises an eyebrow. "Things that your father, perhaps, should have told you long ago."

Novak says she needs to prepare something, so she leaves me to wait in a room filled with photographs documenting the last two years. One image is blurred at the edges, taken from an ocular implant, showing a riot in a busy downtown street. I've seen the picture before. It was taken when a bus carrying a dozen second-stagers to quarantine broke down in Chicago. Someone panicked and opened the door, and the scent washed into the street, triggering one of the largest documented occurrences of the Wrath. The madness gets worse in crowds. Normally it drives you toward the infected, but in a crowd, the hysteria grows, and people turn on each other blindly.

By the time the Wrath wore off that day, more than a hundred bodies littered the streets.

I chew my thumbnail, staring at the wild eyes of the people in the photograph. There's no worse feeling than catching the scent and knowing you're slipping into the Wrath—that you're about to hurt people but can't stop yourself. I can't help but wonder if it's the same way Cole feels when his protective protocol kicks in.

"Miss Agatta?"

I jump, spinning around. A leylined guard is waiting by the door. "We're ready for you. Just this way."

I nod, dropping my hand from my mouth. I've chewed my thumbnail down to the quick, which I don't think I've ever done before. I force myself to keep my hands at my sides, following the guard down a stairwell at the rear of the house.

We reach the basement, and pass through a hissing airlock into a room with soundproofing spikes lining its walls. Novak is waiting inside with two people—a man with bright yellow hair, and a woman with slick, transparent skin that looks like it's been hacked with frog DNA. I've never seen anything like it. The glassy layers of skin show patches of muscle and dark streaks of veins.

The glass-skinned woman stares blankly as I enter, one side of her mouth twitching up. The yellow-haired man is drooling, his head tilted to one side. I look between them warily, raising an eyebrow at Novak.

"These are two of the world's leading experts on the Hydra virus," she says. "Or at least, the best we could do on short notice."

The man gives me a slow, deliberate nod, and his whole face twitches.

"Wait," I say. "You're using *puppets*?"

The puppet connection is one of gentech's most dangerous apps, one of the few that the UN agreed to make explicitly illegal. It uses a map of thousands of tiny wires grown throughout its user's nervous system to allow a *puppeteer*, a person in a distant location, to remotely take over the puppet's body. Anyone can be a puppeteer; they don't need any special tech. Their brain activity is captured like it always is, by their skullnet. That activity includes the mental commands that control their voice and movements, and that's what gets transmitted directly into the puppet's muscles.

Usually, it works quite well. Most people's brains and bodies are similar enough that a puppeteer's mental command to nod their head should work on the puppet's muscles too. It's not perfect, though. Puppets tend to twitch, and sometimes their speech is garbled, but it's still the most secure connection possible. Anyone hacking your transmission will just see a stream of unintelligible muscle impulses. Translating them into words would require a machine almost as complex as the human body.

But it's dangerous. Puppets have been known to go into cardiac arrest when their hearts were hijacked by leaked signals from the puppeteers. Sometimes the wires don't grow properly and paralyze the puppets. Sometimes they're forced to do things they don't want to do. The puppets are supposed to be conscious, and able to cut off the session at will, but I've heard of hacked versions of the code locking people inside their minds. Keeping them trapped inside a body that moves with another's will, unable to escape. I can't imagine anything more terrifying.

I never thought I'd see the app in action, and looking into the strange, blank eyes of the two puppets, I hope I never do again.

"This is the safest way for us to talk," Novak says.

"Who are we talking to that requires this level of secrecy?"

Novak raises a scarlet eyebrow. "Cartaxus, obviously."

I blink, looking between the scientists and back to Novak. "*Car-taxus?* Are you crazy?"

"You have to understand," Novak says. "Even though our methods might be different, both the Skies and Cartaxus are trying to defeat the virus and save as many lives as possible. We've fought each other in the past, there've even been casualties, but we know when to put aside our differences and work together."

"You're *working* together?"

"Of course we are. Without the vaccine, humanity is doomed. Your father was the only person capable of writing code like that. Maybe some of our younger generation would eventually grow talented enough, but by then the virus could have wiped out everyone on the surface."

The yellow-haired man coughs. "And now that the virus is growing stronger, the bunkers aren't safe either. No airlock is foolproof, and our buffer zones are all but useless now, as you saw when you left Homestake."

I shift uneasily. "So if you're working together on this, why did my father think you were going to hold back the vaccine?"

The glass-skinned woman smiles. "Because we were."

Novak flicks a strand of hair from her eyes. "Honestly, Catarina, I thought you would have figured this out by now."

I look between them, lost. The female Cartaxus scientist smiles. "You may have noticed, Miss Agatta, that we haven't been securing our servers as well as we could. *Your* attacks were quite marvelous, but very few of your friends in the Skies shared your talents, and they were still able to steal our medical code. That's because we *let* them. When we designed the bunker system, we knew the population would inevitably split into two factions—those in the bunkers, and those on the surface—and that if we broadcast medical code on our satellites, very few people on the surface would trust it."

It starts to make sense. "But if it was stolen . . ."

Novak smiles. "Exactly. If Cartaxus gave away code, people wouldn't trust it, but if it was stolen and decrypted by us, they would. The same goes for the vaccine. If Cartaxus were to broadcast it freely, it would make people suspicious, and they might not download it. Nobody wants a repeat of the Influenza tragedy. However, if *you* stole it and released it to the Skies, they'd snatch it up in a heartbeat."

My head spins. "So this whole time we've been running from you . . ."

"When all we want to do is help you unlock the code," the yellow-haired man says.

My suspicion flickers. "Then why won't you let us follow my father's instructions? We're supposed to go to a lab—"

"Yes, and run a procedure. We know," Novak says. "But what then? How are you going to release the code? How are you going to convince billions of people to download it? There are no clinical trials, no long-term studies. Your father was the only person who could even explain how the vaccine worked, but now he's gone. You're asking billions of people to download a mystery. How are you going to do it?"

I shift my weight from my aching knee. I'd barely even thought about releasing the vaccine. All my focus had been on how to unlock it. "I . . . I don't know," I say. "My father didn't mention that in his notes. I thought people would just *want* it."

"You'd think so," the man says, "but Cartaxus watched millions of people die of Influenza X after your father's vaccine was freely released. The Hydra code is brand-new, it's been rushed through testing, and some people are going to want to wait and see how it works. If that happens, we're doomed. The virus is evolving dangerously fast. You saw the blowers detonating at the same time outside Homestake—that's a three-gene mutation. This code could be obsolete within weeks if we can't get everyone on the surface vaccinated."

"Well, we'll never get everyone," Novak mutters. "Not everyone out there is still rational. There are people who roam around in packs, eating each other."

I swallow. The Lurkers. She's right—they're insane. I doubt they're even lucid enough to control their download settings.

"So what do you want me to do?" I ask.

"That's the thing," Novak says, sighing. "We don't know how to do this. We were hoping your father had figured it out."

"But you both have satellite networks," I say.

"Yes," the glass-skinned woman says, "and we control the panels of everyone in our bunkers for this very reason. We can simply *give* them the vaccine without asking their permission. But we can't do that with the people on the surface."

I nod slowly, bringing my hand absently to the black lozenge hanging around my neck. An algorithm is forming in my mind, the spark of something wild and terrible. Something that might just explain why my father left Dax a copy of Jun Bei's kick simulation.

"We'll do a broadcast," Novak says.

The man groans. "That's your answer to everything."

Novak tosses her head. "This will be different, though. We'll put Catarina and Crick in it. We'll come up with a story about us breaking him out of Cartaxus . . ."

"Oh, I like it," the woman says.

The three of them start planning out some kind of giant broadcast, but I barely hear them. Jun Bei's simulation is spinning through my mind. My father didn't leave it to break us out of a bunker; it was another backup plan—something he knew that I would see and understand. Jun Bei's simulation hacked into *every* panel in Homestake, using the same trapdoor mechanism the nightstick around my neck relies on. It's the one crack in the security of every single panel.

I think I can use it too.

I look up sharply, meeting Novak's gaze as the final jigsaw piece of my father's plan slides neatly into place.

"I can do this," I say, interrupting their conversation. "I can get the vaccine into every panel, but you're going to have to do exactly as I say."

# CHAPTER 32

"IT'S BEAUTIFUL," NOVAK SAYS, LEANING OVER MY shoulder as she reads the code I've written.

"It's evil," I reply.

She just smiles, turning her steely gaze to me. "We live in evil times, Catarina. Sometimes we need to embrace that to survive."

I sit back, crossing my arms, staring at the terminal's screen. It took me less than an hour to write the code that will download the vaccine into every panel. Novak found me a server terminal with a screen and keyboard, and I sat and built a weapon out of Jun Bei's trapdoor code. I wove elements from my own viruses with lines from the sparse precision of Cartaxus's nightstick, blending them into something terrible.

An abomination.

While I was working, Cartaxus and Novak were scrambling to set up a joint satellite network—a formal alliance to share gentech code and information. That was one of my demands, and they met it. They're preparing their people for a unified world.

"So what happens now?" I ask. "Are you ready to run the decryption?"

"Not quite yet." Novak steps away. "I always said I was going to put you on one of my broadcasts. I'd like you to stand beside me while we announce the vaccine to the world."

My stomach clenches. I've forced myself to write this code, and I'm ready to give up my life for the vaccine, but I don't know if I can pretend to be *happy* about it. "I-I don't know what I'd say."

"I'll handle that." Novak's eyes roam over my face. She lifts a strand of my tangled hair, frowning. "But first, we have to get you cleaned up."

Three hours later, I'm led into an igloolike dome with cameras covering its walls and ceiling like a thousand black, unblinking eyes. Novak's daily broadcasts are recorded in VR for people to watch through their panels, so it looks like she's standing in their homes, speaking directly to them. Most virtual reality segments are filmed by just two or three cameras, whose footage is fed through animation engines that build a 3-D image, but the result is never perfect. Sometimes it messes up. The only way to get a perfect image is to film each actor in a VR dome, but they're expensive, and rare. The Skies, as it turns out, has a few of them.

A dozen lights have been carefully positioned between the cameras to light up my hair and face. A makeup artist frantically dusts a final layer of powder across my cheeks before ducking out through a rubber hole in the side of the dome.

I stand awkwardly, shoving my hands in my pockets. Novak's team dressed me in slim-fitting black jeans, a white tank top, and knee-high boots. Three makeup artists worked on my face for an hour before throwing up their hands and declaring that they'd done their best with what they were given. My scarred skin has been smoothed out with a temporary nanofiller, and my hair has been washed, treated, and blow-dried into rippling waves. My long-neglected eyebrows are sharp, and my eyes are lined with black, my eyelashes miraculously multiplied.

Catching my reflection in the lenses is like looking at an alien creature. I still look like *me*, but it's a version of myself that I never imagined was possible. I look smart, refined. It's the perfect mask to hide the nerves jumping inside me.

"On in five," a familiar voice says, crackling from the speakers embedded in the dome's ceiling. A red light above me grows brighter, and a handful of tiny, palm-size screens tucked between the cameras flicker on. One to my left shows Dax tilting his head back and forth, looking at himself in his cameras. The screen to my right shows a stylist fixing Novak's hair.

We're going to stand together—a Cartaxus scientist, the leader of the Skies, and Lachlan Agatta's daughter—and recite a speech Novak's team has written. It talks about how important it is for everyone to download the vaccine, and how safe it is, how thoroughly the code has been tested. I'll tell the world how Dax and I communicated secretly for years, like star-crossed lovers. That the two of us convinced the Skies and Cartaxus to finally work together.

It's all lies.

The speech makes no mention of the fact that Dax only joined Cartaxus because they took him away at gunpoint. It doesn't explain that none of us except for Dax has even *seen* the vaccine, let alone tested it.

That the only person who understood the code is gone.

But that doesn't matter. The broadcast is merely serving as a distraction from the true nature of what the satellites are sending. While we're talking, my trapdoor code will be beamed into the feeds of every satellite in orbit and then crawl silently into the arm of every person on the planet. No one will have a choice. People won't even know it's happened. It's hidden by the same firewall that concealed Cole's black-out code from him. Later, when the unlocked vaccine is broadcast, this trapdoor code will automatically download it. The vaccine will run in secret until some hacker eventually discovers it, but by then the virus will be dead.

Everyone will be safe, and humanity will survive, but that doesn't take away from the fact that this is a violation on a fundamental level.

"Stand on the mark, Agatta," the voice in the speakers says.

I shift until I'm standing on a piece of tape, then look around at the cameras. "Leoben, is that you? Where are you?"

He chuckles. "Yeah, it's me. I'm in Novak's command center, helping them hook up to Cartaxus's network. I'll be running your code. I see you've borrowed some of Jun Bei's handiwork."

I cross my arms uneasily. "I didn't think we had much of a choice."

"No arguments from me. Anyone crazy enough not to download the vaccine probably shouldn't be in control of their panel anyway."

I nod, chewing my lip. He's right; I know he is. This is the only way to beat the virus. So why does it feel so *wrong*?

A long beat passes. When Leoben speaks again, his voice is softer. "So, Dax told me about the decryption."

I freeze, glancing at Dax's screen. He's still turning his head back and forth, looking at himself. He can't hear anything we're saying. Hopefully, wherever he is, Cole can't either.

"What did he say?"

"He told me everything, said I should know what's going to happen in case Cole, well . . . in case Cole does what he's trained to do."

"Oh." I scratch my neck nervously, unsure of what to say.

"I misjudged you," Leoben says. "I thought you were just like Lachlan, but you're not. I'm sorry. And don't worry, I'll handle Cole."

I swallow. "Cole and I, we're not . . . I remembered what you said before. I've been trying not to let us get too close."

Leoben sighs. "Yeah, well, maybe you shouldn't have listened to me."

"What do you mean?"

Before he can reply, the red light above me flashes again, and the feed to the speakers cuts out with a hiss of static.

The broadcast is starting.

On their respective screens, Dax and Novak are staring straight ahead, poised and still, waiting for us to go live. They're ready, but I'm not. I still don't know how I feel about this. I don't know how I'm supposed to stand, or look, or smile. My reflection is that of a stranger, and my speech is a stranger's lies.

The speakers start playing a song I recognize as the Cartaxus anthem—a series of strong, bracing chords. It merges slowly into the trumpets that mark the start of every one of Novak's broadcasts. The introduction finishes, and the dome is suddenly filled with white, blinding light. I try not to flinch or cover my eyes. For all I know, we're live, and there are currently three billion people staring at my face.

On her screen, Novak gives her trademark smile. "Good evening, everyone," she says. "Thank you for watching, for coming together to share this very special broadcast with us. As you know from today's announcements, we will soon be broadcasting the Hydra vaccine. To discuss it, we have two important people here today. On my left is Miss Catarina Agatta, daughter of the late Dr. Lachlan Agatta, and the Skies hacker known as Bobcat."

I force myself to smile and give a stilted wave. The dome's lenses seem to pulse, as though transmitting the world's attention to me instead of the other way around.

Novak turns to her right. "And this is Dr. Dax Crick, the man himself. Our hero, ladies and gentlemen. The author of the Hydra vaccine."

My smile freezes. I stare at Dax's screen. He should be correcting Novak. He should be explaining that my father is the author, and that he was only his assistant. He should say that he doesn't even know how the vaccine works, but instead, Dax just shoots Novak a smile.

"It was a group effort," he says. "Dr. Agatta's work was crucial in coding the vaccine, as were the efforts of the rest of my team."

*His* team? My stomach twists. What the hell is this? How can he be lying so smoothly about something so important?

"You're being too modest," Novak says. "I read the reports of the recent glitch at the Homestake bunker where the airlocks jammed during a routine lockdown. You logged in and closed those airlocks, putting your life on the line to save those people, and you've dedicated the last two years to writing a vaccine that will save us all. I think it's only right to recognize you as the hero that you are."

My heart slams against my ribs. No. That wasn't Dax. I used his login and password at Homestake, but it was *me* who closed the airlocks. Dax is the one who suggested the kick simulation in the first place.

Now he's taking credit for everything. For my father's work. For mine.

And there's absolutely nothing I can do about it.

Discrediting Dax live on air means discrediting the vaccine. I can't say anything that could raise doubts with the survivors watching this broadcast. But if I just stand here like this and let Dax and Novak lie, then everyone is going to read my silence as a confirmation.

It shouldn't really matter. I don't need credit, and I know my father wouldn't care whose name was on the vaccine as long as it reached the people who needed it. But that doesn't make it any easier to stand here and listen to lies coming from the mouth of the man who's going to jack a cord into me in a few hours and kill me.

I'm about to let these people take my *life* away, and they're lying about me with smiles on their faces.

My head spins. Dax and Novak keep talking about the vaccine, about Cartaxus and their labs, about the new joint network. All I can do is stand and stare, until Novak says my name, and everything goes silent.

"Catarina?" Novak's brow creases. "Isn't that right?"

I just stare at her. I don't even know what she just asked me. I couldn't hear a thing through the shock and betrayal drowning my thoughts. I want to tell the world the truth—that Dax didn't save the people at Homestake, that he didn't write the vaccine, that he doesn't even know what's in it. None of us do, and we're about to shove it into everyone's arm without so much as letting them *read* it.

This isn't how it's supposed to be. My father had a plan for us, and this can't possibly be the way he wanted it to end. This plan has crashed and burned into a tangle of lies, but there's no turning back now, and my hands are far from clean.

The teleprompter's screen grows brighter, flashing the speech I agreed to give. The deceit that I'll be remembered for.

I take a deep breath, stare into the wall of black lenses, and say what I've been told to.

I won't have to live with it much longer.

# CHAPTER 33

AS SOON AS THE LIGHTS IN MY DOME DIM, I PUSH
through the rubber door, bumping into a camera-wielding bot, sending
it skittering across the concrete. Dax's dome is next to mine. His pale
hand slides through his door, but I push him back in, shoving my way
through, slamming him against the wall.

His eyes fly wide. He stumbles, his head knocking against a lens in
the cramped, curved space. The polished black glass shatters instantly.
A streak of blood blossoms on his brow. He touches it, then stares at me
in shock. "Princess, what the hell?"

"What the hell?" I repeat, practically snarling. "What the hell was
*that*, Dax? You lied about everything."

"Whoa, whoa," he says, grabbing my wrists, pulling my hands off
his shirt. "I had to. Novak and Cartaxus agreed that the vaccine needed
a face."

"My *father* was the face," I say, yanking my hands away. "It's his
code, his legacy. You can't take credit for something you don't even
understand."

"Your father was tainted." Dax wipes the blood from his forehead, scowling. "He screwed up Influenza and then turned into a recluse. The vaccine needed a fresh face, somebody more appealing than him."

"More appealing? Like the guy who saved the poor people at Homestake? You're the one who almost killed them, Dax. How could you lie like that?"

"Because I had to." His voice grows sharp. "You think I like taking credit for Lachlan's work? I'm going to spend the rest of my life being celebrated for something I didn't do. I lied about it because it's what the people needed, because Cartaxus and Novak asked me to. I lied so that *you* didn't have to."

"But you made me *complicit*. I had no choice but to stand there and agree with you. You made me erase my father's legacy in front of the whole world."

"What does his legacy matter to you?" Dax looks genuinely bewildered. "How can you care about him when his code is going to kill you in a few hours?"

The words are like a knife. I stare at him, not breathing, unable to turn the pain inside me into words. Deep down, I know I'm angry with my father and I'm swinging that onto Dax. I know I'm terrified about the procedure, and I'm lashing out at him.

But that's not all—he's right. I'm going to die tonight, and I cannot see a single hint of pain on Dax's face.

"You don't care," I breathe, stepping away. "You never cared, did you? It was all a lie. You just flirted with me because I was his daughter. Anything to get closer to him."

"That's not true—"

"Of course it is. That's why you never contacted me, isn't it? Two years surviving alone, and I heard *nothing* from you. You could have found a way to call, to tell me the truth."

"Your father wouldn't let me, Princess."

"Don't call me that! Don't you dare call me that after what you just did."

"What I did?" Dax asks, his eyes flashing. "I'm not the one who left you behind, and I'm not the one who designed an encryption that used your *life* as the key. I didn't experiment on children while my own daughter was growing up alone in boarding school. Your problem isn't with me, Catarina, your problem is with your father. Don't take it out on me because you hate your own goddamn DNA."

My breath catches. I step back and stumble into the wall of cameras. The dome is suddenly coffinlike and stifling. I have to get away from him. I turn and force my way through the rubber door, leaving Dax behind me, ignoring him when he calls after me.

I'm not going back. I don't care where I'm going, as long as it's away from him. I run past the line of VR domes, dodging a group of workers. Tears blur my vision. I veer around a corner and stumble right into a wall.

Only it's not a wall, though he feels a lot like one.

"Hey, Agatta?" Leoben asks, steadying me. "I was looking for Dax. Are you okay?"

The mention of Dax's name makes me want to lash out at Leoben, too, but instead I meet his worried eyes and find myself crumbling.

"Cole," I whisper, my voice breaking. "Please, Leoben, I need to find Cole."

Leoben looks me up and down, then nods and takes my arm, leading me through a corridor and outside. We cross a park, and he swipes me into a hotel with a broken neon sign and dim hallways that stink of genehacked weed.

"He's in room forty-eight, upstairs," he says, pointing to a stairwell. "I'll send someone over to get you when we're ready for the decryption."

"Th-thank you," I say. He leaves without another word, and I run up the stairs. When I reach Cole's door, I grab the handle and push it open without knocking. I don't want Cole to see me like this—fighting back tears, breathing so hard I can barely stand—but I need him so much right now I can't stop myself.

The door swings open into a tiny room with a boarded-over window. Cole, still dressed in his silver-dusted clothes, is sitting on the edge of a steel-framed bed. His head is lowered, his sketchbook held open in his hands, but he drops it and stands the moment he sees me. My heart is pounding from running up the stairs, but the sight of the sketchbook makes it skip a beat.

"What's wrong?" Cole is beside me in two fluid strides. "Cat, you're shaking. What happened? Did someone hurt you?"

I glance down at the sketchbook and back to him, my resolve wavering. He was looking at his drawings of her. Of Jun Bei. He's still not over her, and I'm still not over Dax, judging by the way his words have shaken me.

But the more I think about it, maybe that's okay. Cole and I are both broken, but maybe we're broken in the same way. Fractured along the same axis, two halves of a whole, both hurt by people who left us behind and never once looked back.

Maybe it's time we turned away from them, too.

"I saw the broadcast. You did so well. . . ." Cole's ice-blue eyes are creased with concern. It seems to hit him suddenly. "They didn't tell you, did they? You didn't know. You didn't agree to be part of that farce."

I shake my head, biting my lip. I don't trust my voice enough to speak.

Cole's hands curl into fists. "They're using you, Cat. That's what these people do. They use you, and they don't care. But you don't have to let them. We can leave here, right now. Just tell me what you need me to do."

"No . . . ," I start, not knowing what to say. I don't even know why I'm here—why in my darkest moments my first instinct is to run into Cole's arms. All I know is that there's something inside me that feels like it's hanging by a thread, that swings toward him every time he's standing by my side. I know he's the only thing that's felt *right* in this plan, and that if I don't tell him now, I won't get another chance.

"Cat, what do you need?"

I chew my lip, summoning the courage, then step to him, letting my hands slide up his chest.

"I need you."

A beat passes in silence, then understanding flickers in his eyes. He searches my face as though trying to decide whether I'm serious or not. A flash of something passes through him—a hint of doubt, of concern— then his gaze finally locks on mine.

It's like lightning.

This is nothing like the awkward, fumbling moments Dax and I shared. This is power, raw and fierce, crackling in the air. My whole world shrinks and warps, racing down into a point that dances in the light reflected in Cole's eyes.

He's just watching me, so close, so still, waiting for me to cross the gaping chasm that lies between us. Gravity tilts again, nudging us closer, and I let the force fling me across the abyss. My hand trembles as I slide it behind his neck, close my eyes, and press my lips to his.

For a heartbeat it's like kissing stone. He is immovable, a statue of pure resistance. I'm hit with a flare of horror—I was wrong; he doesn't want me. The shock grips me like a fist, until he melts suddenly, his arms snaking around my waist.

His lips part with a low sound of yearning and desire, crushing against mine as he kisses me back, hard. He tastes like salt and sweat. His scent curls through my senses, reducing my circling, frantic thoughts down to a background hum.

This is *right*.

The touch, the taste, the very smell of him folds into a space in my heart that is his perfect size and shape. His chest against mine. His fingers pressed to the small of my back. The way my shoulders fit neatly inside the circle of his arms.

I break off the kiss to drag in a breath, and he brings one hand to my face. "Cat—" he starts, but I don't want to talk. We don't need words right now. All I want are his lips on mine and his hands on my skin. I grab his shirt and pull him to me, forcing his lips open with mine.

He yields for a moment, stunned, then lets out a growl in the back of his throat. He pushes me with his hips, guiding me to the bed, and we tumble into it together, my fists bunched in his shirt.

"I want you," I whisper, tugging at the fabric. His shirt comes off in a blur, showering us with a cloud of sparkling nanites. The scars on his chest gleam, and I shove him onto his back, bringing my lips to each cruel line slashed into his skin.

A moan rises from his throat. He pulls me up to kiss him again, his hands sliding underneath my tank top.

"You're so beautiful, Cat." He drops onto the pillow, staring up at me. "You have no idea how beautiful you are."

I close my eyes, arching my back, hooking my fingers under the hem of my top to pull it off just as a knock sounds on the door.

I freeze.

Cole is up in a blur, shirtless and flushed, sending me tumbling onto the bed. He has a gun in his hand and has angled himself between me and the door before I can even scramble to sit up.

A second knock sounds and then a flap at the bottom of the door swings open, and a paper-wrapped package slides through a metal slot. Footsteps echo down the hallway, disappearing slowly, and Cole sets his gun down on the desk and picks up the package.

He turns it over in his hands, then rips the paper open and scans the contents briefly before handing it to me. "It's for you."

"For me?" I take the package. A white cotton bathrobe and slippers fall into my lap, along with a silver slip of fabric that feels like water when I touch it. A handwritten note is clipped to the back.

*Wear this for the procedure. Change in the bathroom unless you want us watching.—Novak*

My head snaps up, my eyes searching the corners of the ceiling. "Cole, are there cameras in here?"

He shifts uncomfortably. "Uh, yeah."

"Why didn't you tell me? I was about to take my shirt off!"

He scratches his neck. "Well, I was a little distracted by the fact that you were . . . you know, taking your shirt off."

I just stare at him. I want to be angry, but there's a flush on his cheeks, and dead nanites in his hair, and I've never seen anyone look so beautiful.

"Jesus, Cole." I stand up from the bed, clutching the fabric and the bathrobe, my skin still tingling in the places he kissed me. A second ago this felt so right, but now all I feel is a lurch of confusion. I don't know why I'm here or what I'm getting us into.

I'm about to die, and he's about to lose me. Coming to his room was a mistake. I shouldn't have let my weakness get the best of me.

"I should go."

"Cat, wait." He takes my arm. "I'm sorry. I should have told you about the cameras. I was going to, I swear."

I shake my head. "It's not that. It's the procedure, my father, everything. I can't think straight right now. I shouldn't have come here. This was a mistake."

"It didn't feel like one to me." He steps closer, bringing his hand to my face.

My eyes drop to the sketchbook on the floor. "Really? Then why were you looking at your drawings of Jun Bei when I came in?"

"I wasn't." He bends down and picks up the sketchbook. "I wasn't looking at her, at least."

He flips open the book to a page near the end, where a girl's face with bright, sharp eyes stares back at me. Her mouth is tilted slightly, her jawline curved up elegantly into a mass of long, swirling dark hair. She looks beautiful and strong. But this face doesn't belong to Jun Bei. This is a sketch of *me* during the broadcast. Every curve and plane of my features has been drawn so perfectly, so carefully, that it takes my breath away.

I tear my gaze from the drawing and up to Cole. Something trembles inside me at the look on his face.

It's pure vulnerability. Pure, unrestrained emotion breaking through from a man built and forged to be a weapon. The look sends a jolt through me. A rising voice, an answer. A feeling so powerful it makes my hands shake.

He's right. This is *real*. I can feel it between us like a shift in time and space, a distortion of the very laws of nature. There's no turning back from this. We've already gone too far. I promised Leoben that I wouldn't hurt Cole, but now he's opened up his heart just in time to see me die.

I've lied to him. I'm still lying. He's going to hate me for it.

There's nothing so dangerous as an Agatta's best intentions.

"Cole," I breathe, my voice breaking. I want to leave, to run, to wind back the clock and give us more time together. Instead, all I can do is step into his arms and let him pull me tight against his chest.

This time when he kisses me, it's not with the fire that was driving us before. It's soft and gentle, the kind of kiss that makes the world shrink down. We hold each other, and somewhere in the sound of his heartbeat, I find myself circling a tentative kind of peace.

If this is how I get to spend the last afternoon of my life, then maybe everything is okay.

Maybe I'm ready to die after all.

# CHAPTER 34

NIGHT IS FALLING BY THE TIME A GUARD KNOCKS on Cole's door, telling us the Skies are ready to run the decryption. We're led outside and into a black-windowed car to take us to Sunnyvale's research laboratory, where Dax and Novak are waiting. Cole sits beside me in the back of the car as we roll across town, with one hand on his knee, the other in my lap, his fingers laced through mine.

"You look beautiful," he says. "I like this outfit a lot."

I roll my eyes. I'm dressed in a cotton bathrobe, but underneath I'm wearing the silver slip of fabric Novak sent me. It turned out to be a *pressure suit*, a swimsuit-shaped outfit made from a micron-thick layer of fabric designed to transfer nanosolutions into my skin. It feels like I'm wearing air, and it looks like it too, but it took some work to get into. The fabric is flexible and stretches almost infinitely, but I still needed Cole's help to get it on.

At least, that's what I *said*, loud enough for anyone spying on Cole's room to hear before we retreated into the tiny bathroom. It was cramped and musty, but when Cole checked for cameras, his sweep came back clean. He helped me pull the silver fabric over my skin, and the embers of the fire between us sparked back into flames.

"I'm just saying you look good." He gives me a low smile that makes my stomach prickle with heat. "I like what you did with your hair."

"It isn't as neat as Agnes does it." I reach my free hand up, touching the fishtail braid I've knotted my hair into, just like Agnes used to do. I still haven't heard from her. I sent her an email from a terminal when I was working on the trapdoor code, but it just sat in her inbox, unread. Part of me knows it's naive to think she's still okay. She'd never ignore me like this. Logically, I know something bad must have happened to her.

But just for now, I'm forgoing logic. It isn't enough to get me through this. I'm sitting in a car that's taking me to my death, about to submit my body to lethal code my father crafted for me. I have no guarantee that it will work, or that it's even the right thing for us to do.

Instead of logic, I'm choosing the light I see in Cole's eyes whenever he looks at me.

I'm choosing *hope*.

Every touch from Cole, every glance and smile is a burst of warmth that chases the shadow of the decryption from my mind. When he looks at me, I can almost believe that I am the girl in his drawing, with her head held high and her eyes ablaze. He is like a drug, and a powerful one. The strength of my feelings frightens me—I don't know how my heart entwined with his so quickly. Maybe it's what we've been through, or maybe we really are broken in the same way, our jagged edges aligning perfectly. I wish we had more time together. I wish I could tell him the truth.

I hope he'll understand, after I'm gone.

"They're making a bonfire," I say, looking out the window as we get closer to the lab. A pile of logs has been set up in the high school's football field. A crowd has formed around it, coming out to witness history. I can feel their excitement, and I can sense it in Cole, too. The thrill of knowing that we're just hours away from ending this nightmare, from defeating the virus, and rebuilding the world.

For the price of one life, I can give these people a future again.

How many people get to say that?

The car pulls into a parking lot beside a three-story building that was once a school but is now a research lab. Silver snakes of ductwork hang haphazardly from the windows, and the lawn is overgrown, littered with trash.

"You sure these guys can handle this?" Cole asks. "This place looks like a dump."

I smile. "That's what you said about my father's lab, remember?"

He snorts. "I guess I did. Are you ready to do this?"

I nod, squeezing his hand. "Yeah, let's go."

Cole and I keep our hands locked together as a guard leads us through the school's rubber-lined airtight doors and into a long, dimly lit hallway. The doors along it open into old classrooms that I peer into as we walk. There are chalkboards on the walls and chairs stacked haphazardly. I expect to be hit by nostalgia for my time at boarding school, but all I can think about is Cole.

His fingers are laced through mine. His scent clings to my skin, and I can't stop glancing at him to see if he's looking back at me. I should be terrified, but I feel brave as long as I'm beside him.

This isn't just a crush. This is more.

It might be love.

I squeeze Cole's hand as we turn a corner, and he squeezes it right back, bumping his shoulder into mine. A rush of heat prickles my cheeks.

I can't believe I'm falling in love on the last day of my life.

The guard leads us through a pair of scuffed double doors and into the school's gymnasium. Cluttered lab benches stand in rows across the floor. It smells like disinfectant—the same sharp vanilla scent that I've come to associate with Cartaxus. Dozens of white-coated scientists mill around the lab benches, tending to humming genkits, checking the equipment. The walls are covered with screens and charts, maps and genetic reference tables, and a snake pit of power cords is duct-taped to the floor. It's just like the cabin's lab—haphazard, messy, organic. The thought is strangely comforting.

"Novak sure likes cameras," Cole says, dropping his hand from mine.

I follow his eyes up to the ceiling and pull the bathrobe tighter around me. At least a thousand minicopter drones are swarming through the rafters, most no bigger than a fly. They swoop through the air like passenger pigeons, moving in a flock across the room. Each one carries a tiny, black-eyed camera. Now that I've seen them, the high-pitched whine of their propellers is all I can hear.

The doors click shut behind us. Novak's voice cuts through the air. "Cameras, sound check. Clean language, people. Future generations will study today's footage in school."

I frown. That's unsettling. I shuffle closer to Cole as the ceiling lights grow brighter and the swarm of drones falls like rain. They whiz past my face, looping in frantic circles around me, building a three-dimensional map of my body.

"Welcome, Miss Agatta," Novak says, striding across the room to greet us, speaking in the warm, confident tone she always puts on for the cameras. The drones dart around her as she walks, but she doesn't seem to notice. Her scarlet hair has been pulled back into a Mohawk-like braid, and she's swapped her uniform for mirrored stilettos and a lab coat. Leoben and Dax are standing across the room with a team of scientists beside the clonebox. Dax is watching me through the whining cloud of drones, but I ignore him.

"We have everything set up for you, Catarina," Novak says. "I've followed the decryption procedure's code right down to the letter."

"Have you?" I ask, raising an eyebrow. I know she's lying. I doubt she's even read the code. If she had, she wouldn't be so excited about filming this. Once the vaccine hits my cells, my body is going to *dissolve*. That's not exactly appropriate footage for humanity's future schoolchildren.

"We've made every preparation," she replies. "We'll be using a chamber to keep you comfortable." She gestures to a shoulder-high vat made of thick curved glass. It's filled with a blue liquid, the same color as a cloudless sky, that casts an eerie, rippling light on everything around it. An immersion chamber. I've seen them in movies. The fluid is laced with nanites that will help my body accept the decryption procedure. It'll have painkillers, beta-blockers, and a hefty dose of healing tech, but it won't be enough to keep me alive, not by a long shot.

I step closer, looking the chamber up and down. This bubbling glass box is where I'm going to die. In this room, surrounded by cameras and people I don't know. It's suddenly *real*, it's right in front of me, and there's no avoiding it anymore.

"Are you okay?" Cole asks.

I look up, realizing that I've frozen mid-step. I try to move, but my feet are glued to the floor, my voice trapped in my throat.

"Cat, what's wrong?" Cole asks, concerned. "Is everything okay?"

"I-I'm fine," I say, swallowing the panic, trying to push the fear from my mind. *Be brave,* I tell myself, but the words ring hollow. I search for the warmth I felt just minutes ago, but I can't find it.

Cole's eyes aren't shining anymore; they're cold and worried. He's frightened, and his fear is forming a feedback loop with my own. I'm scared, and he can see it, and there's nothing I can hold on to. I've been keeping the decryption in the back of my mind, but now it's here, and it's *real.* The last minutes of my life are ticking down, and I'm still not ready.

I'm not ready to die.

I close my eyes, forcing the panic down. I'm stronger than this. I'm brave, and I don't need Cole's light to see it. I've fought, *survived* for two long years in this nightmare of a world. I've been strong, and now that same strength of will is going to help me die.

"It's just the disinfectant," I say, clearing my throat. "I always hated the smell."

Cole nods, searching my face. He knows something is wrong, but there is no waver in my voice, no sign of the storm raging inside me.

Novak looks between us. "Okay, let's get started. Lieutenant Franklin, since we'll be cloning the vaccine's core from your panel, there's a chance that your tech might glitch."

Cole nods, his eyes still on me. "I'm willing to take that risk."

Novak smiles, revealing a row of bright, sharp teeth. "It's not the risk to *you* that I'm worried about. I've seen your panel's code, and it's my understanding that a minor glitch could be quite . . . problematic." She gives him a meaningful look and gestures to a chair a few yards away, with white leather restraints riveted to the arms.

Cole glances at it, then back to me. He looks reluctant, but he nods. "That's probably a good idea. Okay, Cat, let's do this."

"I'm glad I met you," I blurt out. "Whatever happens, I want you to know that."

His brow creases. "You'll be fine."

"I know, I just . . ." I trail off. I don't know how to say good-bye. After all we've been through, he deserves much more than this. The drones must sense the emotion in my voice, because they rush to capture the moment, swarming around us, buzzing between our faces like moths around flames.

Cole steps closer to cut them off. "I'll be right here, Cat."

"I know you will."

He takes my hand and squeezes it, then pulls away, and in a moment of desperation, I clutch his shirt and press my lips to his.

It is a simple kiss. There are no tears, no roaring flames. We are two people coming together, joined for the briefest moment. Even so, it's enough to slow my heart and bring the warmth of his smile back into me.

He pulls away, grinning. "Okay, enough of that," he murmurs. "Get in your glowing tub and save the world."

I let his hand drop, my cheeks aflame. "Wish me luck."

He winks. "You don't need it."

"I'll see you on the other side."

# CHAPTER 35

A NURSE GUIDES ME TO THE IMMERSION CHAMBER and helps me out of the bathrobe. I cross my arms over my chest, self-conscious in the silver pressure suit. I try not to notice the stares from people around the room, but there's no getting away from the buzzing cloud of drones. My face is still made up, still perfectly smooth and even-toned, but there's no hiding the pale scars on my leg or the scabbed bruise on my knee. People don't have skin like this anymore, not with gentech. They don't have hair on their legs or skin discoloration, not unless they want it.

Now that I know my hypergenesis was a lie—a cover to hide whatever treatment my father designed—I can't understand why he didn't give me an aesthetic suite. He knew how miserable I was with bad skin and rough hair, having to brush my teeth and stockpile old-fashioned deodorant when everyone else had apps. I can almost understand him hiding the hypergenesis treatment from me, but to give me such a rudimentary panel just seems *cruel!*

I don't know what would be more shocking to the people around the world watching the feed of tonight's events: the heavily hacked enhancements of some of Novak's scientists, or my complete lack of them.

The nurse gestures to a metal staircase leading into the vat. I kick off my slippers and climb up it quickly, eager to get into the cover of the blue liquid. It's thick and warm like honey, but it's not really *wet*, and forms a strange, convex meniscus around me wherever I touch it. It's deep enough for me to stand comfortably with the liquid around my shoulders but dense enough for me to lift my feet and float without sinking to the bottom.

Dax strides across the room, pushing a rattling steel trolley topped with an array of surgical instruments. He's in a white lab coat, his hair perfectly styled, his skin made up to be even paler than usual. He looks nervous, and he should be. He's probably wondering if I'm going to shout at him again and make him carry that for the rest of his life.

Honestly, it's tempting.

Most of the drones have followed Novak and Cole over to the chair with the restraints, but a handful are whining around us, circling the tank. I could make a scene right now, in front of the cameras, and there's nothing Dax could do to stop me. A few pointed words about how he was the one who set off the kick simulation at Homestake should be enough to shatter his golden reputation.

But I won't do that.

Deep down, I don't hate Dax, and I don't want to hurt him. He's unfeeling and ambitious, but I think part of me always knew that. Maybe that's even what drew me to him in the first place. I liked him for his mind and his potential, because those are the parts of myself that he brought out too. I know he felt the same way. *I always thought we'd get married*, he said when he learned what the decryption would do to me. *We'd code together.* Most people would have mentioned children, or love, or growing old, but Dax knew that any future between us would center around our work.

Our bond was intellectual, and that was what made it strong.

But when you love someone for their mind, you can't expect that their heart will belong to you too.

He stops beside the tank. "I've checked everything about a hundred times, and the procedure is ready to run. I'm sorry about before."

I slump into the glowing liquid, blowing out a sigh. "You're an ass," I mutter. "And it's your loss. I hope you know that."

He rests his pale, slender fingers on the edge of the vat and flicks a sharp glance back at Cole. "I do, Catarina. More than you know."

Something in his tone rings true. His emerald eyes are as unreadable as ever, but I catch a hint of sadness in them. I look away, across the room at Cole. A doctor is working on his arm, and Novak is making one of her speeches to the cloud of cameras.

"Tell me Novak knows what's going to happen," I whisper.

"Disturbingly, she *does*. She wanted cameras in here from the start, but when I explained . . ." He drops his voice. "When I explained the procedure's effects, she ordered a whole swarm. I think she's making a film. Don't worry, though. Nothing will be live. The broadcast is delayed, and it's mostly footage of her and her team. People won't be watching *you* when the decryption is happening."

"Well, that's a relief." I kick in the liquid, leaning back against the vat's curved side. The painkillers and beta-blockers are already working. I'm still terrified about the decryption, but the ache in my knee is gone, and the edges of my terror are bleeding into calm.

"I have some bad news," Dax says. "Since you don't have a panel, we'll need to do a spinal jack to hook you up to the clonebox."

I wince. Spinal jacks are a last-resort procedure using a socket buried in the back of your neck. It grows there in case people lose their arms and need emergency treatment, but it means cutting through muscle and screwing a cable into your spine. I should have realized that we'd need to do one, but I guess I've been trying not to think about it. I pull the fishtail braid over my shoulder. "Are you going to do it?"

He waves his hand across the steel trolley he brought over, where a row of scalpels glitter in the liquid's blue light. "I think that's best. Are you ready?"

I glance around the room, trying to prepare myself for what's about to happen. Cole's already jacked in, with his eyes shut, his head tilted back. A thick cable juts from an incision in his forearm, coiling into the clonebox that stands humming in the middle of the room. It's waist high and cube shaped, built of glass that shows a jungle of internal tubing, where ninety liters of gray liquid is pumping constantly. That's approximately the same volume of liquid you'd get if Cole were to melt into a puddle on the floor, and that's precisely the scenario the clonebox is designed to replicate. Every cell in Cole's body needs to be duplicated so the soupy liquid inside the clonebox is recoding itself to match Cole's DNA. If that were to happen inside a living person's body, their cells would break apart in the same way mine are about to do. But inside the frothing liquid of the box, they'll be recoded from scratch without affecting Cole at all.

His panel will see the clonebox as an extension of his body, and it will send his apps, including the vaccine, in to protect it. That's when we'll jack me in. Another thick black cable is jutting from the clonebox, curling across the gym's floor to the side of the vat. Dax will hook it into my spinal socket, and if the procedure's code works like it should, the gold-flecked cables in my body will pump the vaccine's code into every limb. Every muscle, every nerve. My own DNA will decrypt it piece by piece, and my body will send the decrypted code back, ready for release.

I stare at the humming clonebox, at the cable in Cole's panel, at the whining clouds of drones spiraling through the air. I'm still frightened, but I made up my mind about this the moment I found the procedure's code in my panel. The only thing I can do now is choose how I want to face it.

I look up at Dax, steeling myself. "Yeah, I'm ready. Let's do this."

I let Dax pull my head forward so the back of my neck is exposed, my chin resting on the curved rim of the vat. His fingers prod along my spine, and I feel a flash of pain as he slides a syringe of anesthetic into the muscle.

"Okay, here we go," he says. A scalpel clinks beside me, followed by a quick slash, a hint of pain, and a sharp tug on my neck. The cable vibrates as it connects with the socket, locking itself into my spine with a wet, metallic crunch.

My vision flashes. The power running through the cable is bleeding through my wiring, glitching out my ocular tech. "It worked."

"Good." Dax's fingers slide from my neck. "I'll kick off a biometric scan."

I nod, slowly straightening my head, blinking through the sudden blast of noise in my vision. It's not just my ocular tech that's glitching. All my implants are starting up in a rush, flooding my senses, turning the whine of the drones into a roar.

"This scan looks clear," Dax mutters, his eyes glazing over. "Your levels are within acceptable limits, and . . . Ah."

"What?"

His forehead creases. "That backup in your spine we found, I can see more information now. It's not masking its access anymore, and it's growing a panel in your arm again, like we thought. It has a hard drive, and it looks like there's data on it. Maybe it was backing up everything from your genkit."

"Maybe . . . ," I say, confused. "Can you see anything else about the hypergenesis treatment?"

"I'm taking a look now. I can't see anything obvious except a lingering dose of ERO-86 in your blood. It looks like it was being synthesized by your old healing tech code. I'll send a command to bring the levels down to trace, then we should be good to go."

The cable in the back of my neck vibrates, and a jolt races down my spine.

"What . . . ," I breathe, suddenly dizzy. "What's ERO-86?"

"It's a post-traumatic-stress treatment," Dax says. "It suppresses memories. They use it in black-out training, but it's probably a false reading. With your panel growing back, there'll be all sorts of chemicals in your blood. I wouldn't worry about it."

"M-memory supp-ess-nt?" I slur, my lips going numb. Whatever command Dax used on me, it's left me barely able to speak. But he has to listen to me. He can't just ignore a memory suppressant reading, not after everything we've found. If the backup node in my spine has a hard drive with data on it, maybe there's something in there about the decryption. Something important that my father expected me to find.

What if it's a way to unlock the vaccine without killing me?

"Okay," Novak says. Her stilettos click across the floor, and the drones swarm back around me. She stands beside the vat, resting her mirror-fingernailed hands on the rim. I force my eyes open, struggling to stay upright. My voice is barely a breath when I try to speak, and my arm doesn't move at all when I try to grab Novak's sleeve.

She raises an eyebrow at Dax, oblivious to me. "It's time to make history, Dr. Crick. The clonebox is running. Is she ready to go?"

"All clear," Dax says, his eyes still glazed. "We can start decryption on your command."

I shake my head. "St . . . ," I murmur, my lips shaking. I try to shout, but nothing comes out except a sigh.

"Cloning now," Novak says, staring intently at me. The drones whiz around us, a cloud of thousands of eyes trained on me, but not a single one of them can see that I want this to stop. Novak raises a scarlet eyebrow, giving me a sharp-toothed smile. "Hold tight now, Catarina. Transferal on my word."

"St . . . ," I breathe, closing my eyes.

The cable in my neck vibrates.

"Installation starting in three . . . two . . . one."

# CHAPTER 36

THE LABORATORY DISAPPEARS. THE VAT, THE DRONES, and Novak's synthetic eye blink out, replaced by an infinite stretch of black. I spin around in the darkness, searching for a light, and find myself standing on a tiled floor beside a floor-to-ceiling window.

Outside, three mountains rise like sentries, shrouded in fog, their jagged peaks tumbling down into thick, verdant forest. The sky is slate gray, and fingers of frost lace the edges of the window. I feel the cold right down to my bones. I turn, scanning the room, but all I see are bare walls stretching into shadow. The window is unmarked, and a single triangular fluorescent light glows on the ceiling above me.

"Okay, darling," my father says. I spin around to find him behind me, dressed in a white lab coat, his dark hair combed and parted on the side. He has a white, gleaming genkit on a trolley beside him, with a cable curling out of it and into my arm.

"Let's try this again," he says.

I look down. A cobalt bar of light shines from my forearm—a full panel with thousands of apps. It's blinking a Morse signal, telling me it's accepting a new app from the genkit's cable. I look back up at my father, smiling.

"Remember to focus on your breathing," he says. "I won't let you get sick. I'll be listening closely."

"But when it hurts too much, I can't talk." My voice is younger, frightened.

He smiles. "I won't be listening to your voice, darling. I've had your heartbeat patched into my feed since you were a little girl."

He points above him. A chart appears, hovering in the air. A jagged green line, matching the beats of my heart. They are strong and steady, quickened by fear.

"Are you ready?" he asks.

I nod, my hands in fists. My fingernails are bitten down to stubs. "I'm ready."

My father turns a dial on the genkit, and the cable jutting into my panel vibrates. Pain bleeds up my arm to my shoulder and across my back. I swallow down a gulp of air, biting back my fear, trying to focus on my breathing . . .

But this isn't right.

I'm not here. I'm in a laboratory at Sunnyvale with a cable jacked into my spine. Is this the memory my father suppressed with the ERO-86? Dax cleared my system, so maybe it's coming back. My head snaps up, searching the room for something familiar.

But I don't remember this place—I don't remember *any* of this. The panel in my arm, the genkit, the code my father was running. I scan the room but see nothing except the jagged, three-peaked mountains looming outside the window.

*"Catarina?"*

Cole's voice. I spin around, but all I can see is my father, coding with his eyes glazed.

*"Cat, are you okay?"*

321

"Cole?" The room is growing blurry. The memory is fading, but I still don't know what it means. I don't know what my father did to me.

And if I don't remember it now, I won't get another chance.

*"What the hell is going on? Can't you see that she's in pain?"*

The scene wavers. Cole's voice is dragging me back to him. I fight the pull of it, searching for a clue, something to help me remember what happened here.

*"Cat, talk to me!"*

The mountains rumble, and the memory flickers in and out.

*"Cat!"*

I close my eyes and blink into a world of bright, sparkling pain.

# CHAPTER 37

MY BODY THRASHES IN THE GLASS VAT. DAX IS NEXT to me with Novak, each holding one of my arms, keeping my head above the surface. I gasp, kicking out, my feet sliding over the bottom. Jolts of pain race down my spine like sparks along a fuse.

This is the decryption. I don't know why I'm still alive, but judging by the pain, I won't be for very much longer.

"What about a sedative?" Novak asks.

"N-no," I gasp. I don't want to be sedated. If this is the end, I want to see it.

Dax's eyes snap to me. "You're back." He sounds surprised. "What do you need, Princess? Painkillers?"

"I need . . ." I gulp. "I need to stop talking."

He nods. "Fair enough."

Novak turns to shout over her shoulder. "Let's dim the lights, people! Get some tech syringes out. And stand down, Lieutenant. Nobody's hurting your girl."

My head snaps up. Cole is standing behind Dax, his eyes black, the cable to the clonebox still jutting from his arm.

"C-Cole," I whisper. He shouldn't be up. He should be strapped down in that chair. If he breaks off the decryption, we won't get another chance.

Cole's eyes fade to blue as I speak. He steps closer. "Catarina, are you okay? What's happening?"

"I-I'm just . . . uncomfortable."

"It's okay," Dax says. "I'll adjust the nanites." The vat's liquid glows brighter, and the pain ebbs away.

"Something's still wrong," Cole says. "Her heartbeat is too high. It's hurting her."

"I'm fine," I manage to choke out, my legs kicking out involuntarily. But I'm not—the pain is back already, and I can barely focus enough to speak. It laps at me like the sloshing liquid in the vat, drenching my senses, taking my breath away.

I try to crawl inside myself and block it out, but it's like forcing water back through floodgates, and it just rushes over me.

"Forty percent decrypted," a voice says.

"What?" I gasp. That can't be right. I should have died by now. Something sparks in my neck, and my head flies back, my body shuddering.

"Hold her still!" Novak yells.

Gloved hands grab my head and arms. My chest thumps against the glass. The liquid splashes out in glowing waves that shatter into droplets when they hit the floor.

"Her blood pressure is rising!" Cole shouts, pushing his way to me. "Dammit, Crick, we have to stop!"

"Don't listen to him," Dax snaps. "It's working, we're sixty percent decrypted."

"Novak!" Cole roars. "She's *dying*, kill the code!"

I want to reply, but I can't form the words. My jaw is clenched tight, my ocular implant cycling through random filters.

"Seventy percent!"

The world blinks to blue, then green, then black-and-white as my head slams against the glass, my lips parting in a scream.

"Get off her!"

A shriek cuts the air, and one of the lab counters crashes to the floor. The crowd around me scatters as the room bursts into motion.

The lights flicker on and off. Cole is at my side, his eyes black, reaching into the liquid to haul me up. I jerk back in a spasm, trying to tell him not to touch the cable, that it's too late, but he disappears again.

Another crash echoes through the room. Above me, the ceiling is spinning, thick with drones, zooming in and out of focus as the pain thunders through me. I look down in time to see Leoben fighting Cole, their fists blurs in the strobelike, flashing lights. They topple backward, sending another lab counter to the floor, and I slump into the liquid.

The pain has a voice, and a scent, and a mind. It's racing through my nerves, leaving nothing but smoke and ash behind it. I scrunch my eyes shut, and in the darkness behind my eyelids I see the towering silhouette of the three jagged mountains. The image warps and bubbles like a photograph in flames, growing brighter until it's blinding; then the pain surges into the base of my skull.

My mind is suddenly rising, jettisoned from my body atop a blistering plume of heat that feels like death itself. The world seems to shrink below me, fading to a speck, taking my body and my screams with it.

Then it's over.

The pain drops away as sharply as it started, and I sink into the liquid, drifting beneath the surface. The strength is gone from my limbs. The image of the mountains still hovers in my vision, tugging at my memory like a long-forgotten song.

"Get her out, now!"

Gloved hands drag me back above the surface. I choke up a mouthful of sour liquid, my throat raw from screaming. Voices rise through the room, and the drones swarm around me like birds of prey circling a dying animal.

"Get her some tech!" one of the nurses shouts.

My head rolls to the side. Cole is straining against Leoben on the floor, and Dax is standing beside me, his emerald gaze locked on me.

This is it. I can see it in his eyes, and I can *feel* it. The lights are dimming, the frantic voices around me falling silent. Across the room, Cole kicks Leoben away and races to me, his eyes black and frightened.

But he won't make it. There's no stopping this. I know there's no escape. If the pain is ebbing now, it's because most of my nerves are already dead. I try to yield myself to it, but my heart rate hitches higher. Maybe this would be easier if I truly believed that there was something waiting beyond this world. But I don't, and that terrifies me. The world was here before I was born, and it will keep spinning after I am dead. The universe is continuous; I am the anomaly. I am the thread that begins and ends, the flame that sputters out. A chance collection of proteins and molecules that perpetuates itself, bound by the electric fire of my mind.

That fire is fading now. The knitted proteins of my body are unraveling, and I will soon be gone. I've known this for days; I stepped into this room knowing it.

But I'm still not ready.

"Tech boost!" a nurse shouts, plunging a syringe into my chest, sending a fresh burst of pain jolting through me. My limbs straighten instantly, smacking against the glass.

So much for most of my nerves already being dead.

I choke, writhing in the liquid as Cole shoves the nurse aside and wraps his arms around me, keeping my face above the surface.

"Cat," he breathes through the walls of pain toppling down on me. "Stay with me. Just hold on—you're going to be okay."

I blink, my vision shuddering, my limbs thrashing against him, sending glowing droplets of the liquid flying across his face. The silhouette of the mountains flashes back into my mind, then vanishes like smoke in the wind.

"Cole," I breathe. "I remember . . . I remember something. I don't understand."

But he isn't listening. His eyes are glazed over, his arms still locked around me. A look of amazement is spreading across his face, and the room has fallen quiet.

"Fully decrypted," Novak announces on a speaker, breaking the silence. A hum of voices begins to rise. "First batch test . . . complete. Second batch test . . . complete. Tests from Europe and Asia coming through now. They're complete too. Four hundred ninety-three permutations tested, with zero trigger penetration. It's official, everyone. We have a vaccine!"

The room erupts into a roar. The drones scatter into frantic spirals, circling the crowd, capturing the moment.

"That . . . that's it?" I whisper. Nobody listens. The nurses are laughing and crying, hugging one another. I want to tell Cole that this is wrong, that they need to check again, but he suddenly pulls me from the vat, holding my dripping body to his chest. He crushes me to him and kisses me while the crowd circles around us, raising a cheer.

"You've done it," he whispers, his lips on my ear. "It's over, you did it."

My body is shaking, but it's just exhaustion—my vision is clear, and my heart is pounding, but it's steady and strong.

Dax stares at me through the crowd with a haunted look in his eyes. He knows what I know, but I'm too weak to say it.

There's no way I should have survived that kind of procedure.

It's impossible. It's insane.

I should have died in that vat.

# CHAPTER 38

THE NURSES UNSCREW THE CABLE FROM MY SPINE, then rub me down with a sponge that soaks the blue liquid away. Novak disappears with Dax to launch a broadcast announcing their success to the world.

That isn't all they're broadcasting. The code I wrote is now running from the new joint network of satellites, installing the vaccine on the panels of everyone on the planet. The people in the bunkers will be expecting it, and most people on the surface will download it willingly. Those who refuse to download it will still have it running secretly in the background of their panel's operating system. We're violating their rights, but at least they'll be protected from the plague.

A cheer rises from the corner of the room, where some people are lifting their panel arms in celebration as the vaccine installs. The movement catches on, and the drone cameras circle the crowd, capturing the rising sea of cobalt light. The cheer spreads like a wave until the gymnasium is a pandemonium of tears and laughter. People drop their arms, hugging one another, crying.

It's over. The vaccine is released. It's *done*.

It's too much for me to take in. I stand mutely, my fists bunched in the bathrobe's fabric. The crowd around me is starting to sing, but I don't raise my voice to join them. My thoughts are turning in on themselves like paper curling as it burns.

I'm *alive*.

It makes no sense. It should be impossible; my body should have crumbled into a slick, watery mess. Instead, I'm merely tired, my muscles humming with the healing tech the nurses plunged into my chest.

Cole stands watching me, his eyes wide with wonder, as though I'm glowing in a wavelength known only to him.

"You saved the world," he says. His hand slides to the small of my back, and he leans in to kiss my temple. I don't know how to react, so I just close my eyes. I should be happy, but all I can think about are the flashes I saw during the procedure. The three mountains. The conversation with my father. They must be memories, and they must explain how I survived, but trying to remember them now is like grasping at handfuls of smoke.

I want to tell Cole, but I don't know how to say it.

*Sorry I didn't tell you, but I was supposed to die today?*

When I open my eyes, Leoben is pushing through the crowd, holding a foaming bottle of champagne. He thrusts a glass into my hand and tilts the bottle to fill it.

"You look like someone who needs a drink, Agatta."

"Leoben . . . ," I start, unsure of what to say. He knows I was supposed to die in the decryption. Dax told him so he could hold back Cole if it came to that, which it *did*. A patch of Leoben's white-blond hair is wet with blood, and the front of his shirt is torn open.

"Yeah, whatever," he says, giving me a meaningful look. "Not supposed to mix alcohol with healing tech, I know. I think we can let that slide for tonight. It's time to celebrate. We can pick our way through the code tomorrow."

I look down at the glass of champagne in my hand. He's telling me to forget about it, to enjoy the fact that we've done what we came here for.

The vaccine is out. It *works*. It's over.

But how can I celebrate when I'm standing here like this, unscathed and whole in a body that should have shattered like glass?

"To the great Lachlan Agatta!" Leoben shouts, holding the bottle aloft. "May he continue to confound us!"

The crowd around us echoes the toast, confused but enthusiastic. I stare hard at my glass, then drain the champagne in one gulp.

"Attagirl!" Leoben yells, slapping my shoulder.

Cole laughs, snatching the bottle from him, tipping it up to take a gulp. Someone opens the doors to the football field, where the bonfire is already raging. Music pulses through the air. The crowd begins to drift outside to celebrate around the fire.

Leoben grabs the bottle and ducks down to see his reflection in the vat's curved side, pouring the champagne over his head to wash the blood from his hair. "I'm gonna get you for that, brother."

"You can try," Cole says. He squeezes me to his side, trying to snag the bottle back. Leoben shakes it, capping the mouth with his thumb, then sprays both of us with foam. I can't help but laugh, shrinking into Cole. His grip on me tightens, and he gives me a smile I thought I'd never see again.

It suddenly hits me that this is *real*. I'm standing next to Cole in a world that's ablaze with hope. The vaccine is out, and I'm going to be alive to watch the world rebuild. The thought makes my head swim.

It's hard to believe I have a future again.

"You think they're going to open the bunkers now?" Leoben asks, looking around for somewhere to put the empty champagne bottle. He drops it into the blue liquid of the vat.

"I guess so," Cole says. "They might wait a few weeks, but I think a lot of people are ready to go back outside."

The Cartaxus anthem chimes, and the screens on the wall blink, showing video feeds from around the world. There are fireworks over survivor camps and people praying in circles. Crowds in the bunkers are swarming into the common areas, holding their children. Two years of nightmare. Two years of plague.

I keep telling myself that it's finally over, but it still isn't sinking in.

Outside, a *crack* tears through the air. I flinch instinctively, staring out at the football field, expecting to see the plume of a blower detonating. Instead of a rising cloud of mist, I see the glow of a firework, casting a brilliant white light over the crowd's upturned faces.

"Come on, let's go find Dax," Leoben says, waving us out into the night, swiping a bottle from a girl beside him. Another two fireworks whistle into the air and erupt, blue and scarlet. I know what they are this time, but the sound still makes me flinch.

The crowd is singing, the music pounding. The bonfire is ablaze. The screens on the wall are flashing with a million happy faces, and suddenly I can't breathe. I blink and see three mountains draped in pure white snow. I see my father's piercing gray eyes locked on mine.

Cole steps forward, but I stay frozen.

"You okay, Cat?" he asks.

It's too much for me to take in. Too much joy, too much confusion. We've done what we were trying to do—we've released the vaccine—but I still feel like I'm teetering, standing on shifting sands.

"Cole," I whisper, "can we go somewhere quiet?"

"Are you okay? Do you want a nurse?"

"No, I'm okay, I'm just . . . overwhelmed." I clutch the bathrobe around me. "I could do with a shower, and some clothes."

Cole's eyes glaze briefly. "They put some clothes in a room for you. There's a bathroom you can clean off in, and a bed, too."

"Now now, soldier."

He grins. "That's not what I meant, but I like the way you think."

I send an elbow into his ribs. He laughs, grabbing my arm, hooking it around his waist.

"I'm taking Cat to shower and get changed," he shouts to Leoben.

"Too much information!" Leoben yells back. He tilts the bottle of champagne upright over his mouth, then tosses it deftly, sending it in a perfect arc behind him and into the vat.

Cole slides his arm around my shoulders, guiding me through the thinning crowd. Hands reach out for mine, high-fiving, faces lit up by the bonfire's flickering light. A dozen people try to stop us, wanting to talk about the decryption, but Cole weaves me past them expertly, ducking into the hall.

The doors swing closed behind us, dulling the sound of the fireworks, of the raucous crowd out on the field around the fire.

"Is that better?" Cole asks, guiding me down a dimly lit hallway.

I sigh, leaning into him. "You have no idea."

He leads me through the school, past rows of empty classrooms, finally stopping to push open an unmarked door. Inside is a tiny room that must have been the sick bay, with a few cots arranged along the gray cinderblock walls. An outfit of fresh Cartaxus clothes is folded neatly on a table by the door, beside a pair of boots, a hairbrush, and a packet of wipes. The light in the room is already on, and Dax is waiting inside with an unreadable expression on his face.

Cole's eyes narrow. His arm grows tight around my shoulders. "What are you doing here, Crick? I thought you and Novak were busy making one of her broadcasts."

"We're done. We prerecorded most of it earlier. I need to talk to Catarina in private, and you should probably go and check on Leoben. He just commed me—he's already drunk. The fireworks are running out, and he asked where the jeep was. He mentioned something about a rocket launcher."

"Ah, that's not good," Cole mutters. "I should probably . . ." He turns to me.

"It's okay," I say. "Go. I need to talk to Dax anyway."

"Are you sure?"

My stomach tightens. I need to talk to Dax about the decryption, but I'm not so sure I'm ready for whatever he's come to say.

"*Go*," I say, pushing Cole's chest. "I'm fine, honestly. Go stop Leoben before he blows something up."

Cole squeezes my hand and jogs back down the hallway. Dax stays silent, watching me impassively. Once Cole's footsteps fade, I step into the room. My body sighs with relief as I sit down on one of the steel-framed cots.

Dax's emerald eyes never once leave mine. He looks like he's trying to read something written on my face, something he can't understand.

"What color are your eyes, Catarina?"

I frown. Of all the things I expected to hear, that's not one of them. "They're gray, like my father's. A polymorphism on OCA2, you know that."

"Yes, I do." He sits down on the cot beside me, staring with an intensity that makes me want to shrink away. "What did you do during the decryption?"

"I don't know how I survived. There's a lot going on that I don't understand, like—"

"That's not what I'm talking about," he says, cutting me off. "What did you do to the vaccine?"

I blink. "The vaccine? What are you talking about?"

He stands and paces across the room. "You're a genius, Catarina. Don't play the fool, it doesn't suit you."

My breathing quickens. "Dax, I swear I don't know what you're talking about. Is this something to do with the ERO-86?"

Dax pauses mid-step. "The memory suppressant. Of course." He turns, his face softening as he looks me up and down. "You really don't know, do you?"

"Know what?" I stand and stride across the room to him, clutching the bathrobe around me. "Dax, I'm losing my mind here. Tell me what's going on."

He swallows. "I analyzed the readings from the clonebox, and I found what was generating the ERO-86. You have a neurochemical-producing implant buried in the base of your skull. It used to be controlled by a subfunction in your healing tech code, but it went offline when your panel was damaged."

The air grows still. I search Dax's face for a hint that he's joking, but all I see is fear. I reach one shaking hand up to touch the back of my head. The base of my skull. That's where my migraines come from.

"Did you say my healing tech?"

Dax nods, and I draw in a breath. That's the function core that Marcus cut out of me because he said it had *neural* code. I didn't believe him, but in a way he was right. It wasn't neural code, but it *was* producing neurochemicals. Memory suppressants. Maybe that was why Amy seemed lucid afterward.

But why the hell did my father give it to me?

"Okay," I say, my voice wavering. "What does that have to do with the procedure?"

Dax presses his lips together. "The implant switched on again during the decryption, but it wasn't generating ERO-86 anymore. I didn't realize what it was doing until I saw the feedback from the clonebox."

"What was it doing?"

Dax laces his pale, slender fingers together. "It added four million lines of code to the vaccine."

I step back. "No. I thought you *checked* the code. I thought it was working."

"It is, but the vaccine was supposed to have roughly five million lines, and the version that came out of you had nine. I have no idea what the new code is doing, but it looks like it's acting as a daemon—running independently, without instructions. I've never seen anything like it before."

I stare at him wordlessly, the roar of celebrations outside drifting into a wash of static. There are four million lines of untested, unchecked code in the arm of *every single person*.

And I'm the one who put it there.

"How did this happen?" I breathe. "Why wasn't it picked up?"

"Novak pushed the testing. She wanted the vaccine to be broadcast as quickly as possible, and Cartaxus signed off on it. The vaccine is still working against the virus, but this code is running too, and I don't understand it. I can barely even *read* it."

I close my eyes, my heart pounding. Four million lines of rogue code, sent by my own trapdoor into every family, every child. The thought makes me want to be sick. It could be lethal; it could be toxic. I can't *believe* Cartaxus didn't check the code before they let Novak send it out.

"Maybe it's just administrative junk from the decryption," I say. Meaningless filler code that shouldn't interact with a person's DNA. "You can clean it up in a patch, right?"

"Possibly." Dax's voice is solemn. "All I know is that this code has gone out to everyone with *my* name on it, and I have no idea what it does."

I push my fingers through my hair, bunching it in my fists, trying to get my head around everything that's happened. I survived the procedure. I had a memory suppressant in my system, generated by an implant which added a four-million-line daemon to the vaccine.

"That's not all," Dax says. "I asked about your eyes because according to the clonebox, they're supposed to be green." He pulls a pen-size swabber from his pocket, chrome finished with a needle point on one end, and a pad for swabbing on the other. "Do you mind?"

I hold out my arm. "They're gray—you can see for yourself. Maybe there was something wrong with the readings from the clonebox. Maybe everything is fine."

"Maybe," he murmurs, running the swab across the crease in my elbow. He flips it deftly to press the needle point to my wrist. I barely feel it pierce. Dax's eyes glaze over, and he points the pen at the wall, shooting out a flickering projected display. A report appears. The first sample is the one from my elbow—dead skin cells, grown days ago, shed before the procedure. The second sample is platelets from my blood—fresh and constantly renewed. Biological summaries of both samples glow on the cinder-block wall. They detail every gene, from the mutation that lets me digest dairy to the family of genes that control the size and shape of my teeth.

Dax blinks, and the summaries disappear, leaving a single result remaining. My eye color.

*Sample 1: Female. 16–18. Eyes: gray.*

*Sample 2: Female. 16–18. Eyes: green.*

I feel myself begin to sway. This scan isn't checking for apps; it's measuring the immutable, unchanging DNA inside my cells. Gentech can't change that. It's supposed to wrap around the genes like paper around a present, leaving my natural DNA untouched.

But if this report is right, my *underlying* DNA has been changed. It's like wrapping paper around a present and somehow changing what's *inside* the box.

"This is impossible," I breathe, but the proof is glowing right in front of me. According to this scan, I stepped into the vat with gray eyes and stepped out with green. It's a violation of everything I've learned about coding. It's a breach of the fundamental laws of gentech. It should be impossible. But then again, I should be dead.

I have no idea what to believe anymore.

"What the hell did my father do to me?" I spin to Dax. "This has to be linked to the hypergenesis code we found. The implant, the vaccine, the way I survived the procedure. He did something to me, and he made me forget it."

I close my eyes and see a flash of the mountains I remembered during the decryption, but the image blurs as soon as I try to focus on it. It was a place I knew. I was *there*. A drum starts up at the back of my mind, but I still can't hear it clearly enough to drag the memory out.

When I open my eyes, Dax's face has paled. The light above us blinks out, and the music outside dies away, leaving only the crackle of the bonfire. The cheering and singing of the crowd morphs into a swell of confused voices.

"Power outage?" I ask, groping for the light switch on the wall. "Dax, pull up your sleeve. I need some light."

But he doesn't reply.

My fingers brush the door handle, and I swing the door open, letting in a slice of light from the windows on the other side of the hallway, where the bonfire is raging. "Dax? Are you okay?"

He's standing like a statue, his lips moving slightly, the way he looks when he's deep in a coding session. The freckled curves of his cheekbones glow orange, lit up by the bonfire's flickering light.

No, not the bonfire. The light is coming from his panel.

It's suddenly glowing bright *orange*.

"What the hell is happening?" I ask.

"It's the vaccine," Dax whispers. "It's incredible."

"What's incredible? Why is your panel orange?"

"It's an attack." Dax's brow furrows with concentration, his body growing rigid. "But I can't stop it. You need to get help, Princess. Quickly, *run*."

My stomach lurches. I want to ask more, but the urgency in Dax's voice sends a knife of fear through me. I back out of the room nervously and scan the hallway. It's empty, with no sign of Cole or Leoben. Beyond the windows, the crowd is wild and raucous again, the sound of firecrackers echoing in the air. The celebrations are back in full swing.

"Cole?" I call out, jogging down the hallway. I reach a corridor and glance down it, but it's empty. Everyone is outside at the fire. Cole must still be talking to Leoben.

A *crack* rings out behind me, and one of the windows shatters. I drop instinctively into a crouch. Squares of broken glass ricochet off the walls, skittering across the tiles, making me suddenly aware of my bare feet. With the window broken, the sound from outside rushes in—the roar of the fire and a frenzy of wild, shouting voices.

Adrenaline kicks through me. The sound I heard before wasn't fire-crackers, it was gunfire. The people around the fire were cheering just a few minutes ago.

Now they're *screaming*.

I push myself up, inching higher until I can see out the closest win-dow. Dax said this was an attack, but he didn't say who was behind it. If it's Cartaxus, I'd expect copters and drones, but the sky is empty. In the flickering light of the bonfire all I can make out is a writhing mass of silhouettes.

I creep closer, dodging the broken glass, staring into the night. There are no trucks, no gun-wielding troops rounding people up. There isn't any order to the fighting at all, but the people in the crowd are all screaming and fighting with one another. It looks like a mass attack of the Wrath, but that makes no sense. There are no second-stagers here, no hint of the scent to send the crowd into a frenzy. It's like everyone has suddenly just gone *crazy*.

And all their panels are blazing a bright, neon orange.

I suck in a breath, dropping back into a crouch, panic rising inside me. This isn't an attack—there are no soldiers out there, no drones dropping bombs. This is worse. It's the *vaccine*. The daemon code that was added to it in the decryption must be affecting these people somehow. It's sent them all into the Wrath, and now they're killing one another like animals.

And it's all my fault.

A door creaks back down the hallway. I turn my head, tensed. Dax steps from the school's sick bay, his shoulders hunched, his movements jerky. His panel still glows orange, and he has something in his hand. It looks like the swabber, but in the dancing light of the fire it might be a gun.

340

"Going somewhere, Princess?" Dax asks, tilting his head. His voice is off, eerie and low.

"Dax?" I ask, my voice wavering. "Dax, what are you doing?"

He lifts his hand toward me, his shadow leaping across the walls. The bonfire's light shows his face twisted in a snarl. I realize a heartbeat too late that he's lost his mind too, and I push myself to my feet and run.

That's when the bullet hits me.

# CHAPTER 39

THE COLOR BLEEDS FROM MY VISION. THE DOORS set into the hallway blink into black-and-white smudges as I fly from my feet. I land hard on my side and roll to my back, gasping for air. The ceiling must be dark, but right now it's a sheet of pulsing, throbbing white.

Dax shot me. I know this even though there's no pain yet. I felt the bullet. I heard the sound.

I still can't believe he actually *shot* me.

"Dax," I gasp, rolling to my side, sucking in a lungful of air. The wound in my shoulder erupts like a fireball. I try to push myself to my knees, but the pain licks through me, and I fall back to the floor.

Footsteps echo down the hallway. I pull myself into a ball, waiting for another bullet. Instead, Dax just stands above me, pale and wide-eyed. He stares in confusion at the gun in his hand.

"P-Princess?" He unloads the gun, hurling it down the hallway, then drops to his knees beside me. He presses his hands to his face in horror.

"Dax," I cry. This is *him* again. Maybe the attack has passed. I grit my teeth, grabbing the wall, forcing myself up. The crowd outside is still fighting, screaming, roaring. Gunshots pepper the air. Dax seems to be himself again, but everyone else still sounds insane.

He takes my arm to help me up. "You have to run, Princess. I'm losing control. I can't fight it much longer."

"But I need your help. We need to stop this—I can't do it without you."

His eyes glaze over. He's fighting whatever the hell this attack is. "I don't think this is happening anywhere else," he whispers. "It's just Sunnyvale. Cartaxus, they . . . they don't believe me." His voice breaks. "Princess, I *shot* you. You need to run before it comes back and I hurt you again."

"No," I say, grabbing his collar. "Just *listen* to me, Dax. I know you can fight this. You have to try."

He shakes his head. "It's too late. I can't stop it. I can feel it—I want to hurt you, I want to . . ." His voice rises into a growl.

"No," I cry, stepping away as he doubles over, struggling for control. "Dax, listen to my voice. Fight it, please! I can't do this on my own!"

"No!" he shouts. He grips his hair in his fists and screams, every muscle in his body rigid. A shudder passes through him, and his eyes snap up to mine, wild and empty.

The snarl is back on his face. Every trace of my friend is gone.

"Oh shit." I stumble backward, finally remembering the nightstick. I jerk my hand up to my neck, searching for the pendant. Dax is on me in a blur, his hands whipping out to grab both my wrists, slamming me back into the wall.

My shoulder erupts with pain, the back of my head bouncing off the concrete. Pinpricks of light dance in my vision. Dax's hands fly to my neck. He wrenches the silver chain away and waves the pendant in my face.

"Nightstick, Princess? Very sneaky."

His voice is low, eerily calm. He tosses the pendant to the floor, and it slides across the tiles, slipping underneath a row of lockers. He brings his hand back to my face, gentle at first, then slides his fingers around my neck.

"I know you're still in there, Dax," I gasp, trying to claw his hand away. "I know you care about me. You don't want to hurt me."

"Oh, but I do," he says, his eyes shining. "You don't know how much I want to hurt you, Catarina. I want to cut your skull open and see what Lachlan left inside you."

I close my eyes, panic thrashing in my chest. This isn't Dax; this is something that's taken over his body—some dark and twisted version of my friend. I don't know how to bring him back. All I can think to do is keep telling him the truth and pray that wherever *my* Dax is, he's able to hear me.

"Dax, I need you," I plead, staring into his eyes. "You're the only one who can read the vaccine. I can't fix it without you."

For a heartbeat, something flickers in his face. A hint of doubt, just the slightest sign that my words are reaching him. His gaze wavers, his hand growing loose on my neck.

Then his eyes go hard, and his lips curl back.

"Liar!" he yells, shoving me into the wall. My wounded shoulder smacks into the concrete, dragging a scream of pain from me. "Do you think I've forgotten how you were always better than me? Always reading Lachlan's code like it was a goddamn picture book?"

"No!" I cry, my vision blurring. "Please, Dax! Stop it!"

He draws his hand back, curling it into a fist. Using a strength I didn't know I had, instincts I've never felt, I clutch his shirt and drag him to me, smacking my forehead into his nose.

He roars, clutching his face, blood spurting between his fingers. I push off the wall and try to run, but I'm not fast enough. He grabs me by the hair, jerking me back. I fall hard to the floor, my scalp burning, the hallway spinning around me.

"You're dead now, Princess!" He drives a boot into my ribs.

I gasp, spitting blood, trying to curl into a ball. He drives another kick into my side, knocking the wind from me. I choke for air as he rolls me over, flipping me to my back, and straddles me, pinning me to the floor. My shoulder is a raging, howling sea of pain. My strength is fading from me, my muscles growing shaky.

"That's right," he mutters as I shudder, my hands clawing uselessly at the floor. The ceiling is a spinning mess of shadows, my lungs clenching like fists.

"P-please!" I manage to cry out as he wraps his hands around my throat. "Dax, please! You don't want to do this! Listen to me!"

But he's not listening. He's not *there*. His nose is bent and bleeding. He lifts his hands to wipe it, and time slows down to a crawl.

The world grows silent. He's going to kill me. I can see it happening so clearly that it plays like a film inside my head. His hands will drop back down, stronger than mine, tech enhanced, and they will slide in a cruel ring around my neck. He'll hold me down and squeeze my neck until I stop fighting, until my lips are blue and cold.

There's no bringing him back from this. There's no reasoning or begging. The man above me is no longer my friend.

"I'm sorry, Dax," I breathe, in the heartbeat of time when his hands are off me, in the fraction of a second I'm able to move. "I really am sorry."

His eyes grow wide as I lunge up, every muscle in my body aching, and tear his ear off with my teeth.

# CHAPTER 40

DAX SCREAMS, RECOILING BACKWARD. I SPIT HIS ear out, the metallic taste of his blood filling my mouth. It's so horrible and intimate it makes my stomach turn. I force down the urge to vomit and scramble to my feet.

My shoulder is a fireball of pain. I lurch to the row of lockers, searching frantically for the little black pendant. A glint of silver catches my eye as Dax staggers across the hallway, blood streaming down the side of his neck.

"Come on," I breathe, grabbing the chain, sliding the pendant out from underneath the lockers. I twist the two ends between my fingers like Cole showed me. A jolt of electricity prickles across my skin, filling the air with the scent of burned plastic.

Dax draws one hand back to punch me, and then his panel blinks off and he falls to the floor.

I let out a cry of relief, dropping the pendant, standing over Dax's crumpled body. His nose is broken, his ear is gone, and his face is streaked with blood. He looks so pitiful that I don't want to leave him, but I don't have a choice. Cole said the nightstick would only work for a few minutes. I need to get outside, find the jeep, and get myself to safety.

I'm the one who ruined the vaccine, and now I need to find a way to fix it.

I turn and careen down the hallway, stumbling into the lockers in a daze. Gunfire cuts through the screams outside. My shoulder throbs, the back of the bathrobe wet with blood as I run blindly past the classroom doors, searching for the exit.

There. The airtight doors. I haul them open with my good arm, scrambling into the street outside. The air is thick with smoke, ringing with gunfire. The bonfire casts a flickering light across the people in the road, and my breath catches in my throat.

Their eyes are wild and inhuman. Every face is a bloody snarl. Their forearms are all glowing the same orange as Dax's panel. They're fighting, biting, clawing one another apart in front of my eyes, and I'm the one who did this to them. This is all my fault.

I'm the one who crafted a piece of code to force the vaccine into each of their arms. I just wanted to help them.

Instead, I drove them all insane.

Gunfire echoes in the street. Chips of concrete hit my legs, sent flying by a hail of bullets that slams into the curb behind me. I stumble back, searching wildly for the source, and spot armed figures leaning out of the windows of a nearby building. They're roaring with laughter, shooting everyone below them, and there's nowhere in the street to hide, no safe path to follow.

I'm going to have to run.

I bolt into the road, dodging the crowd, trying to remember the way to the jeep. A sudden light flashes through the windows of the shooters' building, and a blast rips through the air like a thunderclap. My eardrums pop, the ground trembling. Flaming rubble flies up from the building, arcing parabolically through the night. A billowing cloud of smoke rises in a plume as the roof falls inward, the building crumbling into dust.

"Oh, no, no, no," I breathe, stumbling back. Debris rains from the sky. The wild-eyed people around me scatter, scrambling for cover. I turn and run, my ears ringing from the blast when I hear a voice, distant and faint.

"*Catarina!*"

It's Cole, calling out for me. Fierce, alive, and sane.

The sweetest sound I've ever heard.

"Cole!" I scream, spinning around, sprinting back down the street. Clouds of ash and dust are spewing from the explosion. There's glass on the road, and my feet are bleeding, but I'm so close. We're going to make it out of here. "Cole, I'm coming!"

The air sings with gunfire as I run. More bullets whiz past me, hitting cars parked on the side of the road, shattering their windows.

"Take cover!" Cole shouts. "I'm coming for you, but I need to set off another blast!"

I lurch off the road, pulling myself behind one of the cars. A second explosion rips through the air, making the night flash into day. A building near the school explodes, sending bricks and bodies flying in a mushroom cloud of smoke. My ears ring, whining in the aftermath as rocks and rubble fall like rain, the air thick with gray, chalky dust.

"Cole," I choke out, clambering to my feet, gaping at the devastation around me. Cole is the one blowing up the buildings—he's doing it to protect me. Smoking debris stretches out as far as I can see. The ruins are strewn with bodies, littered with patches of fire and chunks of twisted metal.

Cole stands in the middle of the road amid clouds of swirling ash, his eyes twin pools of perfect blackness. He has a rocket launcher on one shoulder, his rifle in his other hand. The panel on his forearm is a sweet, brilliant blue.

"Cole, you have to stop!" I cry.

"They're trying to kill you."

He swings his rifle in a clean arc, letting off a round of bullets. A group of people fighting near me fall to the ground, screaming. I lurch out from behind the car. "Stop, Cole, it's not their fault—it's the vaccine! We need to get out of here. We need to stop this!"

"Stay in cover!" he shouts.

"No!" I cry, running into the street. If I stay in cover, he'll keep killing anyone who poses a threat to me. But that's *everyone*, and it's all my fault. "Stop shooting them! Cole, please, we have to go!"

The gravel in the road bites into my feet as I run for Cole. Everywhere I look, I see carnage. Dust-coated bodies are sprawled on the street, their orange panels slowly blinking out. Countless more lie among the ruins. Cole has blown apart two buildings and sent the crowd scattering, killing anyone around me.

But there are more of them coming.

I hear them before I see them. I turn my head back, my breath catching. A mass of snarling, shouting people is swarming down the road, running straight for us. They must have seen the flashes of light and heard the blasts of the explosions. Now there are hundreds of them, charging for us, stampeding down the street.

There are too many of them to fight, even with a rocket launcher.

"Cole," I cry, coughing in the dust. "We need to run, now!"

As if in response, the jeep hurtles around the corner, its horn blaring. The headlights splash over me as it screeches to a stop. It swings around, skidding across the rubble littering the street, its doors flying open as it turns.

"Get in!" Cole roars, his gun aimed at the crowd.

I race forward, shots ringing out around me, and lunge headfirst through the open door. Cole launches himself into the driver's side, reaching over to yank the door shut behind me; then the jeep plows back down the street.

"Are you okay?" Cole shouts, flooring the accelerator. Gunshots thud against the windows. "Did they hurt you, Cat?"

I shake my head, seeing blood and bodies every time I close my eyes. "Just a . . . a flesh wound."

"What?"

"Nothing," I say. The jeep's dashboard is a mess of warning symbols. "Do you know what's going on? Is this happening everywhere?"

"No," Cole growls. "This is an attack. Cartaxus wouldn't believe us until Lee sent them footage from his eyes."

"Leoben's okay?"

"He's fine. He's gone looking for Crick. Novak wasn't affected either, along with half her scientists. Whoever's doing this is picking and choosing who they target."

"This is the vaccine, Cole. There was extra code added to it. . . . And I gave it to everyone."

"Whatever's happening, this sure as hell isn't your fault."

I just shake my head. We speed past the visitors' center, bouncing across the bridge. I grit my teeth, blood trickling down my back as the odometer ticks higher. We need to get away from here. I want to be miles from this madness before we even think about stopping.

Two minutes pass, then four. We hit the freeway and screech up the exit, skidding onto the leaf-strewn road. My shoulder is a white-hot kernel of pain. I try to dig my fingernails into the palms of my hands, but nothing happens, and I realize that for the first time in my life, I've bitten my nails down to stubs.

Cole eyes the blood on my face, my hands. "What happened to you, Cat?"

I lean forward to show him the wound on my shoulder. "Sh-shot," I stutter.

Cole slams the brakes, cursing. He flies out of the jeep and is at my door in a blur, carrying me around to the back.

"Shh," he whispers, flipping the doors open, lowering me to my side on the crumpled sleeping bags. "It's okay, just breathe, Cat. You're going to be okay."

Cold air hits my back as he slices through the bathrobe, lifting the blood-soaked fabric away from the wound. He peels back the air-thin layer of the silver pressure suit, climbing into the jeep, straddling me in the tight confines. "Easy now. I'm going to give you some tech, and then I'm going to get you patched up."

I twist my neck to look up at him. When I had to cut out my panel, his protective protocol kicked in and he could barely look at me. Now there's a bullet in my shoulder, and his eyes are a clear, soft blue. "Are you . . . are you okay to do this?" I ask. "With the protective protocol?"

He pauses, watching me. "Yeah," he murmurs. "I think I am." He uncaps a healing tech vial and presses it to my back. A prickle of heat runs down my spine, and the pain starts to ebb away.

"That's good," I breathe.

He leans down to kiss my hair. "You might not think so in a minute. The bullet's lodged in your scapula. I need to get it out."

I nod, clenching my hands tight. "It's okay, I can handle it."

"I know you can."

When he leans back again, he has a palm-size yellow plastic box in his hands with a crank in the back that clicks when he winds it. The plastic is covered with deep scratches. I know what this is. It's a golden retriever. An electromagnet. It's going to yank the bullet out of me.

"Are you ready?" he asks, holding the box to the wound in my shoulder.

I nod, gritting my teeth, burying my face in my hands.

The box lets out a whine, and the bullet hits it with a *crack*. Pain races through my back, arcing along my ribs.

"It's out, it's out," Cole whispers, spraying something icy on my back. It heats up once it hits my skin, hardening like plastic. "This'll keep the wound clean until it closes on its own. The healing tech is starting to kick in."

I nod, shaking, my breath whistling through gritted teeth. The pain flares up before subsiding slowly. Cole's gaze trails down my face to my neck. "Your neck is bruised, and your face. Cat, what happened to you?"

A lump forms in my throat. "Dax . . . He was like them, Cole. He tried to fight it, but he couldn't. He's the one who shot me."

Cole's face blanks. He turns to stare back down the highway, his eyes blinking instantly to black.

"No," I say, sensing his thoughts. "No, I need you here. We need to figure out how to stop this."

"It would only take a minute." He stares down the road. "I have a sniper rifle. I could do it from the hill."

I close my eyes, pushing down the memory of Dax's hands on me. His fingers around my neck, digging into my throat. A ball of rage spins in my chest, but vengeance isn't what I need. That wasn't Dax who hurt me; it was something else. The daemon he found, the four million lines added to the vaccine. I saw the change come over him as clear as day. It happened to everyone with the orange panels. It's *still* happening to them.

We need to stop it.

"I need a genkit," I say, pushing myself up, reaching for the side of the jeep. "If I can read the vaccine's code, maybe I'll understand what's happening. Maybe there's a way to turn this off."

"That's a good idea—" Cole starts, then freezes. "Lee just commed me. He couldn't find Dax, and he's on his way here. He said Cartaxus . . . Oh shit, they're sending drones."

"Why?"

"I don't know." Cole throws a sleeping bag over me. "Lie down, stay low. I need you to hang on to something."

"Cole?"

He pulls the doors shut and climbs into the front.

"Cole, what's happening? They're not going to attack, are they?"

He doesn't reply. The jeep surges back down the freeway, and a high-pitched whine starts up in the distance. I scramble to my hands and knees, staring out the rear windows as points of light fly in over the mountains. Drones. Thousands of them, in a cluster-blast formation.

Enough to blow all of Sunnyvale to oblivion.

"Wait, Cole!" I yell. "Tell them to stop! You have to explain!"

The jeep races forward, screeching along the freeway.

"They're not listening to me," Cole calls back.

I grab his backpack to steady myself. "You have to try again. Dax is down there—they can't kill him!"

We race around a corner, and I'm thrown into the window, staring in horror at the sky. The drones are hovering now, a thousand points of light in a geodesic dome above Sunnyvale's ruined town center. I open my mouth to shout to Cole, but it's too late. The formation scatters, and I know it's over.

I see the detonations before I hear them—brilliant streaks of light and a blinding flash that illuminates the midnight sky. Thousands of lives blink out of existence in the space of a heartbeat, blown into a cloud of dust.

The jeep races up the freeway, tires screaming on the road.

Five seconds later the shockwave hits us and throws us into the air.

# CHAPTER 41

WHEN THE DARKNESS CLEARS, I'M IN A LABORATORY looking through a window at three mountains that rise in the distance, carpeted in verdant green forest. I can't remember how I got here. I'm dressed in gray, my hands are small, and my fingernails are bitten down to stubs.

"Careful, honey."

I turn around to find my father behind me. He's in a white lab coat with the Cartaxus antlers embroidered on the pocket.

"You're going to mess up the replication if you don't watch those proteins." He points to the glowing desk in front of me, where the hologram of a curled strand of DNA hovers beside a few lines of code. The DNA spins as I brush it with my hand, zooming in until I see the flaw in my work.

"Is this better?" I focus until the image ripples and changes.

My father nods, resting one hand on my shoulder. "That's perfect, good girl."

Pride swells in my chest. I've been working so hard to please him, and I'm finally getting this right.

"There's something I want to talk about," he says, sitting beside me. He waves a hand, and the hologram blinks and disappears. "It's about the Hydra virus. You know about it, don't you?"

I nod. The scent, the detonations. I've been studying it for months.

"So you know I'm working hard to find a vaccine, don't you?"

"Uh-huh," I say with a child's voice. "I know you'll make one. You're so clever."

The skin at the corners of my father's eyes crinkles as he smiles. "There's something I need your help with, but it's going to be long and difficult. You'll have to be very strong."

"I can do it," I say eagerly.

He smiles. "I know you can."

"What do you need me to do?"

"Nothing yet. This is a special project. It will be hard, but we'll be saving everyone if we get it right."

I clutch my hands into little fists. "We'll beat the virus. I know we will."

"Oh, we'll do so much more than that, darling. We'll be saving people from *themselves*."

My father reaches for the glowing panel on my arm, but his fingers feel like fire where he touches me. The skin on my forearm splits and peels off in burning, brittle flakes. I jerk my arm away, clutching it to my chest, but the flakes are spreading fast, like cracks racing through glass.

"What did you do?" I gasp.

My father simply laughs as the cracks in my skin race up my neck, sending glowing flakes into the air like scraps of burning paper. My face blisters, burning away. I let out a scream, but my father just smiles down at me.

"That's my good girl."

# CHAPTER 42

I JOLT AWAKE, STARING AROUND WILDLY AS THE dream fades away. I'm on my stomach in the back of the jeep, wrapped in a silver thermal blanket. I can hear the steady sound of Cole's breathing nearby, but I have no idea where we are.

We were leaving Sunnyvale; that's the last thing I remember—the daemon, the orange panels, the fighting. We got on the road to escape it, and then . . .

Then Cartaxus bombed the valley.

The memory hits me like a punch. I close my eyes, seeing the pin-prick lights of Cartaxus's drones. So many lives, gone. I thought releasing the vaccine would bring the world back to normal.

Instead, I've made it worse.

I lift my head to look around, wincing as the movement sends a jolt of pain through my wounded shoulder. We're parked in the forest, and the jeep's back doors are open, the air heavy with the scent of pine and wood smoke. It's just before dawn. A layer of mist is curling in from the trees, wafting across the dew-spotted grass. We're in what looks like an old national park campsite, complete with a stained cinder-block restroom and a few blackened fire grates.

Cole is asleep on a mat beside the embers of a fire, his breathing steady and slow, his arms crossed over his chest. He looks cold, as though he lay down beside a warm fire and fell asleep before he could gather the energy to get a blanket. His eyes are lined with shadows, and a rash of dark stubble on his jaw tells me I've been unconscious for more than a few hours. At least one day, maybe two.

My eyes lift to the horizon for a sign of where we are, and my breath catches in my throat.

On the other side of the lake, three rocky peaks rise from the forest into a blanket of low-hanging cloud. I *know* these mountains. I saw them during the procedure and in my dream, and looking at them now tugs at something in my memory. Did my father bring me here? The thought crystallizes for a heartbeat before splintering, spinning back out of reach. It's like a name on the tip of my tongue. A song at the edge of my hearing. Every time I think I catch it, it ripples away.

I crawl to the back of the jeep to get a better look, pushing away the silver blanket. Cole's eyes blink open, instantly black. He sits up in a blur and grabs the rifle lying beside him.

"Cole, it's okay. It's just me."

His eyes snap to me, his pupils contracting. "Cat," he breathes. "How are you feeling?"

"I feel like . . . I feel like I got shot in the back."

"That's a common side effect of getting shot in the back." Cole stands up slowly, stretching. His movements are stiff, and I can tell that he hasn't had much sleep since we left Sunnyvale. He's still in the same dust-strewn, wrinkled clothes, and there's a bandage on his arm that wasn't there before.

His eyes are bloodshot, like he's been crying. My stomach clenches. "Did Leoben make it out?"

"He's fine," he says, rubbing his face. "He's not far from here."

I let out a sigh of relief. "You look awful."

"You're not looking so great yourself." He rolls his head from side to side, cracking his neck. "You got pretty beat-up. Some of the bruises rose while you were sleeping."

"Oh," I say, bringing my hand up to my face. My cheeks and eyes feel swollen from where Dax hit me. "I was hoping that was just a dream."

"I should have gone back and killed him."

I drop my eyes. He means it. His voice is like ice, but it's not the violence in his words that shocks me. It's the flash of Dax's snarling mouth, his elbow in my face, and the little voice inside me that says *Maybe I should have let you.*

I swallow. "Well, I guess Cartaxus's drones did that for you."

"No, Crick's not dead. Novak got the bastard out, and he's back to normal somehow. They've been all over the VR channels, taking interviews, talking about the vaccine."

"What?" I push myself up to my knees, clenching my teeth against the pain. "So who triggered the orange panels? What are the Skies saying?"

"That's the thing—they're not saying anything. It's like it never happened. Novak and Dax are setting up a new joint HQ for Cartaxus and the Skies. Everyone's still working together. They say the plague is over. It's been two days, and there haven't been any new infections. They're even talking about opening the bunkers up."

I press my hand to my forehead, swaying. This news is everything I've wanted to hear, but it doesn't make any sense. Why would the Skies help Cartaxus after their drones blew Sunnyvale to hell? *One of* them must have set off the orange panels. Someone drove everyone crazy . . .

But maybe it wasn't either of them.

My pulse slows to a crawl. Cartaxus and the Skies wouldn't maintain their truce like this unless someone else was behind the orange panels. Someone they couldn't fight alone. Someone capable of manipulating them, who could construct a plan that would plant malicious code into every panel on the planet.

Someone like the *great* Dr. Lachlan Agatta.

"It was my father," I breathe. "Dax said an implant inside me added four million lines to the vaccine's code, but that was what he wanted all along, isn't it? That's why he needed me to unlock it. He wanted to get that code into everyone's arms without Cartaxus seeing it." I cover my mouth. "Cole, I made them send it out to *everyone*."

"This isn't your fault. Don't think like that. This was Lachlan's doing and his alone. Leoben and I think he has to be the one behind the attack on Sunnyvale."

The realization takes a moment to settle in. "You think he's still alive."

It isn't a question. I see the answer in Cole's eyes, and the thought knocks the air from my lungs.

"We don't know for sure—"

"But there's a chance?"

Cole nods. "There wasn't much left after the explosion in his lab. I checked the report. They found a few traces of blood and tissue that matched his DNA. He could have been the one behind the hack that blew up the lab in the first place. It wouldn't be easy, but Lachlan's smart enough to leave tissue behind as a decoy."

*Smart enough.* I let out a short, bitter laugh. Of course he's smart enough to fake his own death. He's smart enough to manipulate us into releasing his abomination of a vaccine to everyone.

And he's still going. Whatever his plan is, it certainly isn't over. Driving a town full of people crazy isn't a big enough goal for a man like my father. Any minute now he could use the vaccine to turn on the orange panels across the world.

He could kill us all. But *why*?

"We need to find him," I say. "Whatever he's trying to do, he's not finished."

"I know. That's why Lee and I came up here. We're near the lab he wanted us to go to, the one he mentioned in the notes he left us. It took us a while to find it, but we spotted some landmarks last night. Lee's gone down there on foot to check it out."

Landmarks. The lab. Something itches in the base of my skull—the same feeling I get before a migraine, but it's different this time. I stare at the mountains on the horizon. They're the landmarks Cole is talking about—I know it. I must have seen them when I was a child, but I still can't remember *when*.

There's a wall in my mind I can't punch through. A memory locked away, rattling deep in my subconscious. It draws closer every time I look at the mountains, every time I think about the flashes I saw during the procedure. Something happened to me in that vat. Something I can't explain.

"Cole, there's something I need to tell you." I take his hand, climbing out of the back of the jeep.

"What is it?" He takes my elbow to steady me, then looks into my eyes, and a jolt passes through him. He steps away suddenly, his face paling, staring at me like I just pulled a gun on him. "Why did you do that to your eyes?"

"What?" I bring my hand to my eyes, meeting bruised, tender sk_n. "What are you talking about?"

"The upgrade. They're green—you changed their color. Why did you do that?"

"I didn't do anything." I turn to the side of the jeep, peering at my reflection in the mud-strewn windows. My face is bruised, one eye swollen, and my hair is full of dust from the explosions. My cheeks look hollow; my lips are chapped . . .

And I have bright green eyes.

I blink. "My new panel must have . . ." I drift off as I look down at my forearm, seeing three lights flashing beneath bruised, dirty skin. It's still growing. It hasn't started running yet. There's no way it could have changed the color of my eyes.

Then I remember what Dax said.

After the procedure, he told me that my gene for eye color had mutated during the decryption. It should have been impossible, but he kept insisting that it happened. One tiny gene, which controlled the color of my irises, had flipped. I'd walked into that vat with gray-eyed DNA and walked out with green.

"Cole," I whisper, still staring at my eyes in the window. "I lied to you about the procedure. It was supposed to kill me."

"What are you talking about?"

"The decryption, it was supposed to destroy my cells when the vaccine passed through me. Dax and Leoben knew, but nobody else did, and we didn't know how you'd react, so Dax made me promise not to tell you."

Cole grabs my good shoulder and spins me around, searching my face. "Are you kidding?" He backs away. "You're serious, aren't you? You thought you were going to die? Is that why you came to my room? Jesus, Cat. You weren't even going to say good-bye?"

"I couldn't risk your protection protocol kicking in." It sounds like a flimsy excuse, as if I don't care about him at all.

He just stares at me. "What the hell, Catarina? You were just going to let me watch you die?"

"You don't understand what I'm saying, Cole. I should have died. A normal person would have died as soon as that code started running."

Cole freezes. "What do you mean *normal*?"

I swallow, rubbing the back of my head. There's an ache starting up there, but it's not like any migraine I've ever felt. This feels like there's something sparking, burning inside me. Something scratching at my skull from the inside, trying to get out. "I don't know. I don't know anything anymore. I think my father did something to me and made me forget it."

"And your eyes?"

I look down at my arm, at the bruises on my skin that will fade as soon as my panel starts working. "That's what doesn't make any sense. Something happened during the procedure. Dax said my DNA just . . . changed."

Cole's breath catches. "So it's not an upgrade?"

"No," I say. "I mean my *underlying* DNA, the thing that's supposed to be untouchable, is different than it was before. It's impossible, but it happened. It should have killed me, but I'm still alive. I don't understand how my father made me like this, but I'm starting to remember things."

Cole stands frozen. I don't know if he's even breathing. "What do you remember, Cat?" he whispers finally.

I turn to the mountains, lifting my good arm to point at them. "Those. I've been here before, but it's not clear. . . ." I close my eyes, trying to dredge up the memory. It's like trying to remember falling asleep—you know it happened, but the details turn into fog when you focus on them.

It doesn't help that the closer I get to remembering, the more my head pounds, until I can barely breathe through the pain.

When I open my eyes, Cole's face is white. "What else?"

"My father and I were arguing. We were in a . . . a lab like the one in the cabin. I was younger, and I was wearing gray. I could see these mountains through the window."

"No," Cole says, staring at me with wide, haunted eyes. The intensity of his gaze is starting to frighten me. "There was nobody else here, no other children. The lab in this valley is where I grew up. It's where the Zarathustra program was based. There were ten guards, eight nurses, two doctors, and your father. That's all. I knew every heartbeat. I remember every visitor."

"This is where you grew up?" I turn to the horizon, the edges of my vision blurring. The fog has rolled off the mountains, drawing the memory closer. It's sharper now. More insistent. The base of my skull is aflame. "I remember a hologram. I was young. I was biting my nails. . . ."

I look down at my fingernails, shaking. They're bitten. I've been chewing on them for the last few days, ever since Marcus cut the healing tech out of my arm. No, not just the healing tech—the *memory suppressant.*

I don't think I ever bit my nails before that.

When I look up, Cole is staring at me like he's seen a ghost. "Oh God," he breathes. "Oh no. Oh *no.*"

My throat tightens. "You're scaring me."

"He changed your memories," Cole says, grabbing my shoulders, his fingers digging into my skin. "He blocked them, and your DNA, it *changed*, so it's possible. It's possible . . . Jesus, I nearly lost it when I saw your eyes. They're the exact color I remember."

I blink, confused. "Cole, you're hurting me."

"Oh God." He swallows, tears filling his eyes. It's like he can't even hear me. "It's true, I can see it. You came into my arms that night, and I think part of me knew. She always came to me like that. Always in the middle of the night when she had nightmares, curling up beside me, since we were kids. I held you that night and I felt *her*, I could smell her, but I thought it was crazy."

"Cole," I cry, struggling against his grip. The pain in my skull is flooding down my spine, into my limbs, burning lines of fire through me. I choke back a cry, my chest shuddering. "Cole, what are you saying?"

"It's you," he breathes. His arms slide around me, crushing me to him. His body is a rock, but his shoulders are shaking.

"It's you," he whispers, his lips at my ear. "You're *Jun Bei*."

# CHAPTER 43

BLINDING SPARKS, LIKE CROSSED WIRES, RACE THROUGH my brain. Cole's voice echoes in my mind.

*You're Jun Bei.*

"No," I spit, shoving him away. "Do you know how crazy you sound? I'm Lachlan's daughter. I've *seen* my DNA."

"What if he changed it?"

"That's impossible. That would kill me, it would—"

"How do you explain what happened in the decryption?" Cole cuts me off. "What happened to your eyes? Shouldn't that have killed you too?"

"I don't know." My voice is trembling. "But she was a completely different person, Cole. It's not possible."

"She bit her fingernails," he says. "She had your height, your frame. She used to code with Lachlan all the time, using a holographic display down in the lab."

"No." I step away, rubbing the heels of my hands into my eyes. "I'm not her, I can't be. I went to boarding school. I *remember* my childhood. I had a room full of books, and I spent all my time coding. The school was in the mountains, in Canada."

"That's exactly where we are now." Cole's voice breaks. "Don't you see? That's how you make false memories—you build a story on top of something true and tell it to a person over and over until they believe it. They did it to me, to all of us. Why do you think I kept the scars? They're the only thing I can trust."

"My memories aren't false!" I whirl on Cole. Part of me wants to hit him, to stop these accusations that feel like nails being driven into my skull. "I remember the food, the clothes I wore, the goddamn soap I had to use."

I freeze. The soap. The sweet-sharp vanilla scent I've smelled so many times in the last few days. In the cleaning wipes Cole gave me back at the cabin. In the Wash-and-Blast at Homestake. In the Skies gymnasium. It's a disinfectant, a Cartaxus brand. I've always *hated* the smell.

"You're starting to see it," Cole whispers. "Your memories are blurred, aren't they? There's nothing you can grab hold of and know for sure it's real. Try to think of something specific. What were your birthdays like? When did you get your first period?"

"I don't know," I say. "Just *stop* it, stop talking."

His questions feel like arrows in my side. I don't remember my birthdays, but they've never meant much to me anyway, so I probably just spent them in my room. My first period, though—a physical change. I would have been intrigued; I would have jacked myself into my genkit and analyzed my hormones. I close my eyes, searching my memory for the day it happened.

But there's nothing. No memories at all.

My breathing hitches higher, making my throat burn. I open my eyes and find Cole watching me with his hand over his mouth. He reaches for me and I stumble away, scrambling to the jeep to yank out my backpack. I turn it upside down, shaking it until the Zarathustra folders slide out. I drop to my knees and grab Jun Bei's file. Her eyes glare up at me when I flip to the black-and-white photograph clipped to the back.

Bursts of pain, like firecrackers, pop in the base of my skull.

Jun Bei. The girl I saw on the road. Small, scarred, fierce. The wild, murderous genius who was in love with Cole.

I blink and see her eyes in the mirror. Crying. Afraid. For a moment it feels impossibly real, but I shake the thought away. I'm not her—I'm *Catarina*. I have my father's skin, his face, his hands, his genes written into every inch of my bones. I've seen my DNA, I've sequenced it, and I would have noticed something like this. . . .

Only, that's not true.

I never had hypergenesis, and I didn't figure that out. My father made me too afraid to touch my own panel. I flip the pages in Jun Bei's file, turning away from her photo, reading the notes my father left in her sequencing report.

*Rapid uptake. Whole-body regeneration. Cellular anomalies.*

I flip the pages frantically, until a comment stops me in my tracks.

*Jun Bei is a blank canvas waiting to be painted over. She's just a child now, but she could be a masterpiece.*

"Oh no," I breathe, rocking back on my knees. "No, it can't be. He's my father. . . ."

"Then how do you remember the lab?" Cole drops down beside me, a file clutched in his hands.

No, not a file. A sketchbook. His drawings.

The throbbing in my skull rises into a storm as he opens it, turning the pages, flipping through the sketches. Each one hits me like a bullet. Those eyes. That smile. The tear tracks on her cheeks.

"No," I gasp. "Stop it, please. . . ."

Cole's shoulders heave, tears pooling in his lashes. "It's you, it has to be. The first time I saw you, it took my breath away." He chokes back a cry. "I've loved you all along."

The wall in my mind parts with a roar.

Bright green eyes, black hair falling in my face. My skin is pale and my knuckles are bruised, and there's a stranger's face in the mirror. I feel her tears and her anger, feel her hands turning DNA models in the air, solving puzzles deep inside a white laboratory. I've been kept here as long as I can remember. I see bars and concrete cells. I see scalpels and arterial spurts of my own blood.

And I see Cole.

I see him as a child. I see him smiling, laughing, screaming. Bandaged and broken, I see him with every beat of my heart. The memory of Cole's smile hits me like a bolt of lightning, shattering the pain and confusion, splintering the walls in my mind.

He is my friend and my confidant. My soul mate and guardian. I am a girl called Jun Bei, and I am in love with Cole.

This truth detonates inside me, crackling across my skin. My memories of boarding school fall away, crumbling into dust.

"Cole," I gasp, blinking away tears. "Cole, I remember."

His arms curve around me, folding me into his chest. "It's you," he breathes, his voice thick with tears. His lips find my cheek, his hands shaking as they tangle in my hair. "It's you, it's *you*."

I let out a cry, a thousand points of pain aching in a body that is not my own, that has been changed and twisted into something else. Tears stream from eyes that belong to a stranger, hands and limbs and lips and teeth that are wrong and changed and desecrated.

This is not my body.

"Who am I?" I cry. My mind curls in on itself, the fragments of who I *was* and who I *am* splintering apart. "Who was I?"

"You were wonderful," Cole says, pressing his lips to my forehead. "You were clever, and brave, and stubborn, just like you are now."

"We were . . . together," I choke out.

Cole lets out a strangled sound, something between a sob and a laugh. "Yes," he breathes. "Yes, we were together."

Pressure rises in my throat. I close my eyes, blinking away tears, and see a dorm room with gray blankets, a patch of gauze taped over Cole's chest. He was always bandaged, always coming back from surgery and limping to my side. I see his fourteen-year-old form, already too strong to be strictly human. His eyes burn in the darkness as he tells me we'll run away. We're alone, his arms are around me, and there's power in his breathing. He kisses me, tells me he loves me, and I promise we will always be together.

"I love you," I gasp, touching his ribs, his arms, his beating heart. I know them. I love them. I press my face to his neck.

Then his lips find mine, and I pull myself into him, clutching him as he kisses me. Something roars inside me as his lips crush mine. A deep, aching cry that rises from my chest and bursts from me as I throw my head back, screaming into the sky.

*He* did this. The man who is not my father. He took me apart, cell by cell, and remade my body in his own, twisted image.

Cole presses his head to my chest, his arms circling my waist as I stare up at the gold-streaked sky, tears running down my cheeks. More memories surge up from my past, itching inside my skull, flashing across my vision like a glitching video feed.

I see trees and highways, a forest and a lake. I'm not in the lab anymore. I'm fifteen, I'm in the cabin, and Lachlan is telling me that this is where we'll live. He shows me the property, he's trying to be kind, but he's weak. He can't rip Cole from my mind no matter what he does to my

DNA. I see myself running into the mine shafts, hiding a box of stolen files behind an orange kayak, promising that I will return to look at the photograph of Cole and never let myself forget, even though my memory is already in broken, blurry pieces that fall through my hands like water when I try to grasp at them.

I see Lachlan finding me, shouting, dragging me back into the cabin. I see his eyes grow wide as I smash the windows and cut my hands on the glass, trying to scramble through and run. I see him fighting me, wrestling me away as I suck my hand to spit blood at him, screaming for Cole.

Then he locks me away, and there are no gentle arms to keep me from the darkness. I am alone with the monster who changed my face, and he tells me that I will not remember.

But I do.

# CHAPTER 44

"ALMOST THERE," COLE SAYS. "HOW ARE YOU DOING?"

"Okay," I say. "As long as I'm with you."

He smiles, glancing over at me. We're in the jeep with the windows rolled down, following a dirt road into the valley at the base of the three-peaked mountains. It's midmorning, and the sky is a deep, stormy gray, the air ringing with the percussive cries of a flock of passenger pigeons.

I'm sitting twisted in the passenger seat to protect my wounded shoulder, one hand stretched out to rest on Cole's leg. I haven't left his side all morning. I'm afraid I'll fall apart without his touch. My mind is still a storm, but Cole is my anchor to reality.

Now that we've found each other, I won't let anything break us apart again.

"Any more memories coming back?" Cole asks, nodding at my lap, where I have the photographs from each of the Zarathustra files arranged in a rough line.

Every time I look at them, I remember something new. Ziana singing tunelessly. Leoben chasing me down the halls. Anna climbing into the lab's ductwork and making it all the way to the roof before the guards dragged her down. Little fragments of memories keep coming back to me, but they're scattered and incoherent, rushing away before I can take hold of them. I don't know if that's a side effect of the ERO-86 wearing off, or if it's how my memories are going to stay.

"I still can't remember anything properly," I say. "It's all bits and pieces, like I just don't have a past anymore."

"What about your memories of boarding school?"

"They're even worse. They're like . . . black-and-white photographs. I don't know how I ever thought they were real."

"That's how the brain works." Cole looks out the window, scanning the trees. "If you suppress memories, it'll build a story to take their place. I've had it done to me. I spent two weeks away from the lab, just after the outbreak, but I don't know where. My black-out tech kicked in and stopped me from remembering. When I got back, Lachlan showed me photographs of me in Los Angeles. He said I'd been extracting a scientist from the city, getting them away from the riots. He told me what the weather was like, and what I'd eaten, and I started *remembering* it all."

"So were you really there?"

"That's the thing. I took one of the photographs and ran it through an image checker. It was faked. That didn't stop me from remembering being there, though. Memories are weak. They're fallible. That's why I kept my scars."

My hand rises instinctively to my chest. The skin there is smooth and unscarred, and I have no memory of it looking like Cole's. But in Jun Bei's photograph, there is a network of stitches and puckered lines stretching all the way to her neck.

Scars can be healed easily enough. Skin color can be altered. Hair, facial structure, eye color can all be changed with enough time. But there shouldn't be a way to edit what's *inside* my cells.

I pick my file up from the pile on the floor and flip it open, scanning the contents, itching for a genkit cable to jack into my arm. I could figure this out so much faster if I could do my own analysis. The sequencing reports in the moldy file are in a format I'm not familiar with, and some of the experimental results are so bizarre that I can barely understand what Lachlan was testing for, but there's something here that just might explain what he did to me.

"What do you see?" Cole asks.

I flip back through the pages, chewing my thumbnail. "I think I might know why I survived the decryption. It looks like my cells are *flexible*, but I don't know how. Most people's cells can't handle changes to the natural DNA inside them. They reject it, which tends to destroy the cells, too. But it seems like my cells just . . . adapt. They change to suit whatever DNA is inside them, but I don't know how."

"Does that mean you could change your body back?"

Cole's words hang in the air. I've been asking myself the same thing for the last few hours, but it feels strange to hear it asked aloud. I wear Lachlan's face and skin, I have his eyes and hairline. His genes are written in the shape of my nose and the taper of my chin. But it's not just his face anymore—it's *mine*. It's the face I've seen in the mirror for the last three years. Through the outbreak, through the desperate winters alone in the cabin. My eyes are so like Lachlan's, but they also belong to me. The fire in them, the strength of my jaw, the tangles of my hair.

When I look at Jun Bei's photograph, I still feel like I'm looking at *her* instead of me.

The thought of wearing Lachlan's face is sickening, but the thought of having to change myself again is traumatizing too. I don't know how I want to look. I don't even know who I am.

"I . . . I don't know," I say quietly.

"I'm sorry," Cole says. "I shouldn't have asked that. It doesn't matter what you look like."

But it does. He's right—it's part of who I am. The way a person looks is based on their DNA, and Lachlan *changed* mine. My chest tightens. "I'm not Jun Bei, Cole, not according to what's inside me. I'm someone else, but I don't know who. I don't know anything anymore."

His hand slides up my back to rest on my good shoulder. "We'll figure it out together."

I nod silently. I feel like I'm drowning, like I'm slipping into a cold, dark sea. Cole's hand on my skin is a life raft, keeping me above the surface, but it's not enough. I need to find something inside myself. A flame of bravery.

I turn my gaze inward, but all I see is shadow.

The jeep slows. Cole's eyes glaze, and he pulls off the road and onto a heavily overgrown trail. "We're close to the lab," he says. "It's just another few miles. Lee went to check it out on foot overnight, but he's got stealth tech running, so I can't hear him."

We bounce over rocks and fallen branches until we pull up beside Leoben's jeep, parked in a thicket of trees.

Cole climbs out, his eyes still glazed. He motions for me to stay, but I'm already halfway out of the jeep. I slide heavily to my feet, wincing as pain flickers in my still-wounded knee.

Overhead, the pigeons are circling, their cries as deafening as hail on a roof, but I still manage to catch a low whistle cutting the air. Three sharp notes that yank at my memory. My head snaps up, scanning the trees. That's the signal we used as children, when we called to one another. I know the reply—a two-note echo. I whistle it without thinking, and somebody behind me lets out a gasp.

I spin around to see Leoben stepping out of the forest, carrying a rifle and a mud-smeared backpack. Dirt and ash are caked into the lines of his face. His shirt is torn open, revealing the scars and thick black tattoos covering his chest. His arms are scratched and bandaged, crisscrossed with smears of dried blood. When his brown eyes meet mine, they hold me frozen in place.

He still doesn't trust me. I have the face of the man who tortured him, who cut him open to see what he looked like on the inside. He said there was nothing so dangerous as an Agatta's best intentions.

But I am no Agatta.

"Lee," I breathe. Fresh memories rise like tiny fireworks, crackling inside my mind. I see Leoben, small and skinny, playing a game in the hallway. I feel him huddled with me, shaking with pain. I see him screaming and running from the nurses, a trail of blood behind him, a shard of broken glass clutched in one small fist.

He's my friend, my brother. We've known each other since we were babies. How could I not have seen it before?

Leoben narrows his eyes, but as I hold his gaze, his expression drops into disbelief. He looks back into the jeep, where the folders are scattered on the floor. "No . . . ," he says, backing away. "No, it's not possible."

"It is," Cole says. "It's her, Lee. It's Jun Bei."

"It *can't* be."

"Lee," I say again, staring at the tattoos that cover his arms. Suddenly I can read the story etched into his skin.

An eagle, bear, wolf, scorpion, and mountain lion trace their way across his arms, one animal for each of the Zarathustra children. Mine is the little mountain lion—small but fierce—and its story ends in a circle tattooed on Leoben's chest.

"You put Jun Bei over your heart," I whisper.

"Of course I did," he says. "She was my sister."

"It's beautiful," I murmur, reaching out to brush the ink-stained skin with my fingers. "But I must have told you a hundred times, Lee. Mountain lions don't have spots."

My words hang in the air for a moment, and then the wind is knocked from my lungs as Leoben slams into me, lifting me from my feet. His arms crush my sides, his face pressed into my hair as he spins me through the air.

"Ow!" I say, laughing. "Lee, my shoulder."

"I'm sorry, I'm sorry." He puts me down but keeps his hands locked on my arms, shaking me as if he's trying to convince himself that I'm real. "I still can't believe it. Jesus, why did he do this to you?"

I touch his face, his chest, his scars. The affection I feel for him is like a light inside me blinking on. "I don't know why he did any of this, Lee. I can't remember."

He swallows, pressing my hand to his heart, tears filling his eyes. He looks between me and Cole. "Then let's go and ask him." His voice trembles. "I picked up a heartbeat in the lab. I can't wait any longer. I want him dead."

# CHAPTER 45

"NIGHTSTICK COULD WORK," COLE SAYS. "ONE OF us sets it off, and the other comes in blazing."

Leoben shakes his head. "He'll be ready for code. We need to come in with steel."

The two of them are in the front of Leoben's jeep, with Cole's following behind on its own. I'm sitting in the back, listening to them make plans, a black holster around my waist and a handgun at my side. We're going to face Lachlan in the lab. We talked about calling Cartaxus or the Skies, or sending in a fleet of drones, but decided it was too dangerous. Lachlan's too smart for that. He'll be watching every blip of communication, waiting for any hint of an attack. If he feels threatened, he can turn on the orange panels anywhere in the world, just like he did in Sunnyvale.

He has the whole world hostage. We don't have a choice. We have to convince him to let us get close to him, and then we have to kill him.

The thought is like the shadow of a hurricane on the horizon. I know it's coming, but I can still turn my eyes away. I can pretend for just a few minutes longer that we're not planning the murder of the man I called Father until a few hours ago.

If I let myself think about it too long, I might lose the nerve to follow through on the plan I'm formulating.

Cole and Leoben keep talking as we drive, speaking in military shorthand, noting firing angles, guns, traps, and contingencies. Their anger ripples in the air like heat, growing more focused by the second. It's something to behold, seeing them work together. Two majestic, crafted weapons thrumming with power, planning an assault I know they'll execute with surgical precision.

At least they *would* be able to execute it, if it wasn't an attack on Lachlan Agatta.

I stare through the jeep's rear windows at the three-peaked mountains in the distance. If Lachlan is in the lab we're driving to, that means he's been here all along. This is where he told us to go in the note he left in Cole's panel, and I can't help but wonder what would have happened if Novak hadn't forced us to go to Sunnyvale.

Would we have driven here and found him waiting? Would he have told me the truth about my past?

Somehow, I don't think so. Lachlan's plan is more complex than that. I still don't know what his endgame is, but I think he wanted everything to happen exactly as it did.

While we were at Sunnyvale, Novak said she'd received an anonymous tip-off—that I would be traveling across the country with the vaccine. At the time I thought it was Agnes, but she wouldn't have known where we were going. It could have been Dax or Leoben, but something tells me it wasn't.

That leaves Lachlan.

I'm starting to think he *wanted* us to end up at Sunnyvale. He wanted Novak in charge, unable to stop herself from broadcasting the decryption live and rushing the vaccine's testing. He wanted me in a vat with a cable in my spine, and my body acting as a conduit for the four million lines of his daemon code.

If that's true, then the whole plan is brilliant, and he's played us like a song. I shouldn't expect anything else from a man like Lachlan, and that's why I'm terrified.

Because if he's planned everything that's happened until now, that means he's still in control.

A light rain starts to fall, echoed by a roll of thunder. Cole turns around in his seat to look back at me. "You ready for this? We're going to drive straight up to the lab and go in there unarmed. The more normal we act, the closer he'll let us get."

"Yeah, that sounds smart," I say, still looking out the window, fiddling nervously with the zipper of one of the bags beside me. Both Leoben's and Dax's sleeping bags and gear are still piled in the jeep from when they were traveling together.

"You don't even need to come in with us," Cole says.

That makes me look up. "Are you *kidding*? I have more reason than anyone to want to see him dead."

Leoben grins. "Told you she wouldn't like that."

Cole's brow tightens. "I'm just saying, it isn't going to be safe. There could be traps. He might have weapons we have no defenses for." He nods at my arm, where a handful of cobalt dots are glowing from beneath the bruised skin of my wrist. My new panel is starting to initialize, but only a few apps have finished installing. "Are any of your other apps working yet?"

I look down. "No, but there's a rough interface. The healing and VR modules should be starting soon." I blink, summoning a few lines of black text into my vision, reading the scrolling log of installation messages. Within an hour, maybe two, I'll be able to use a full VR interface, to code without a keyboard, to plunge myself into VR worlds. And soon, according to the text in my vision, I'll be able to access all the data Dax found backed up inside my spine.

Those terabytes of data aren't backups from my genkit. The dates I see scrolling across my vision are from years ago. The names and file types are clear—these are personal files. I'm still carrying everything that Jun Bei once kept stored inside her arm.

Every scrap of code. Every stored recording. Lachlan didn't wipe it when he changed my DNA. He left it all in there, waiting to be found. Jun Bei's life, stored in comms and documents, is still locked inside me.

Cole doesn't know about that yet.

If I tell him, he might realize what it means. He might think it through and see the full scale of Lachlan's plan, the same way I've been seeing it since we started driving. He would see that we're still just chess pieces being pushed around a board.

If Cole knew what I was planning to do once we get to the lab, he would leave me behind.

Leoben veers us off the road and along a muddy driveway that rolls down a hill and through a winding creek. A single memory flutters through my mind—the chill of water splashing up my legs as I run in the dark—but it's lost as we pull through a patch of trees and into a grassy field.

The breath rushes from my lungs. The lab looms before us—a square, three-story building jutting from overgrown grass. The whitewashed concrete walls are stained with rust and mold, and the flat concrete roof is lined with cracks that have sprouted weeds. The windows are broken, most of them covered with iron bars, and there's a peeling Cartaxus logo painted above the door.

I wrap my arms around myself, staring at it. Vague memories filter back—of dimly lit hallways, wooden bunks, and scratchy gray blankets. Of laser scanners, dead bolts, and snarling, genehacked dogs.

This is a place of nightmares.

"Home sweet home," Leoben mutters. He pulls the jeep up on the gravel remains of a parking lot and kills the engine. Behind us, Cole's empty jeep trundles across the grass and circles around to the other side of the lab to form a two-point perimeter.

"There's one person in the back of the lab," Leoben says. "I'm pretty sure it's him. He's badly wounded, from what I can tell. He's having trouble breathing. There's a shitload of satellite data beaming up from here. I think this is where he's controlling the crazy-people code from."

"So how do we block it?" I ask. "He could turn it on the moment we get inside."

"That's my job," Leoben says. "You two are going in on your own at first. I'll stay out here and use the black-dome chips in the jeeps to block his connection. He'll be cycling his frequency, and the jeeps suck at matching it. I'll help them out, but I need to maintain physical contact. I think I can hide the fact that I'm blocking him for five minutes, maybe ten, but eventually he'll figure it out, and once he does, I won't be able to stop him. You need to get in there and blow whatever he's using to control the code—could be a server bank, could be a bunch of genkits, which is kind of Lachlan's style. Once you disable the connection from inside, I'll come in and we'll deal with the old man himself."

"Can Cole stay out here and block the connection instead?" I ask.

"Negative," Leoben says. "Cole sucks at this stuff even more than the jeep. You and I were the only ones with any *real* skills."

Cole turns to me. "Why do you want me to stay outside?"

"Because I think he's going to use you against me somehow. He could have killed me during the procedure, but he didn't. He could have run away, but he's still here. He left a backup of my old panel inside me, even though he must have known I'd find it in the decryption."

"You think he *wanted* you to remember?" Cole asks.

"Of course he did," I say. "Why else would he have sent you to find me? This is all part of his plan."

Leoben snorts. "It's a stupid plan, then. He's going to get himself well and truly murdered."

"No," I say, "it's a *genius* plan. I still don't know what Lachlan is trying to do, but I'm almost certain that he needs my help. I think Sunnyvale was some kind of test to see if he could control people with the vaccine. That's why he didn't activate the orange panels in everyone. But his plan will be bigger than that—Lachlan didn't do this to drive everyone crazy. You think you're in control right now, but we're all still pieces on his board, and he's moving us around. Whatever his real goal is, he's been waiting for us to get here, and I'm pretty sure it's because he needs my help."

"But there's no way you'll help him now," Cole says. "Not after what he did to you."

"I don't *want* to help him, but I might not have a choice."

"But he has no leverage, not once we block his connection. He can't make you do anything."

"Don't you see?" I whisper. "He's made me remember *you*. Your body is full of his code—I saw that when I hacked your panel. I've seen it every time your eyes go black. If you walk in there with me, he's going to find a way to hurt you, I know it. Then I'll do whatever he says. He made me remember my past so that he can use my feelings for you to control me. That gives him all the leverage he needs."

Cole stares at me, his brow pinched. There are shadows around his eyes, and his cheeks are hollow. He looks weaker and more exhausted than he did when he was shot. I can't bear the thought of losing him again. I won't watch him get hurt. He's spent every minute since he arrived protecting me, and now it's my turn.

He stiffens as he realizes what it is I'm planning. "No, you're not going in there alone, absolutely not."

"You have to let me do this."

"There's no way in hell." Cole's eyes blaze. "I just got you back. I won't risk losing you again."

"It's not up to you."

Cole freezes. He can read it in my face before I say it, and he throws his hands out, reaching for my mouth.

But he's too late.

"Recumbentibus."

The word hits him like a bullet. He slumps, coughing, then falls back in his seat.

"Jesus," Leoben says. "What the hell did you just do?"

I crawl to the back of the jeep and push open the rear doors. "I knocked him out. He'll be down for fifteen minutes. I'm going in there alone—don't try to follow me. Wait out here and block his connection."

"Yes, ma'am," Leoben says, stunned. "Welcome back, Jun Bei."

I nod, turning to stride to the lab, not sure how I feel about hearing that.

The steel door set into the front of the lab is unlocked. I push it open to a shadowed waiting room I'd expect to find in a doctor's office. Dust-covered chairs are arranged beside an empty reception desk, with the Cartaxus antlers printed on a sign behind it. Triangular lights on the ceiling blink to life the moment I step inside, creating a glowing path leading to a hallway across the room.

Lachlan knows I'm here. Of course he does. He's probably been tracking our movements all the way from Sunnyvale. The lights pulse, urging me to follow them. Lachlan is guiding me through the lab.

"Okay, then," I mutter. "I'll come to you."

I let the door swing shut behind me and limp down the hallway. The overhead lights flicker as I walk, guiding me past dusty rooms that tug at my memory. I've run down this hallway before, and I've been dragged down it by my hair, kicking and screaming, with wires in my arm.

The lights stop at an unmarked door, but even without them, somehow I know this is where I need to go. I can *feel* it, deep down. An itch in the base of my skull. I grit my teeth and turn the handle.

The door swings open to reveal the gleaming laboratory I've seen so many times before. The room from my dreams, and the flashes during the decryption. The tiled floor and wall of glass looking out at the three mountain peaks. They loom beyond the window, shrouded in mist.

Lachlan sits across the room, watching me with a smile.

"Hello, darling," he says. "I've been waiting for you."

I freeze. I've been preparing myself to see him for the last two hours, but the sight of him still takes me by surprise. He's badly wounded. The skin on his face is scabbed and raw, and he's sitting back in a mechanical chair that looks like it belongs in a dentist's office. One hand is bandaged; the other is a blistered mess. His wrists and neck are wrapped in layers of blood-spotted gauze.

But it's *him*. Lachlan. The man I once called Father. Meeting his gaze brings back a flood of jumbled memories. I see our days together in the cabin mixed up with the years spent as a prisoner in this nightmare of a lab.

I was his experimental subject. His victim.

But for the past three years I was his *daughter*, too.

"It's really you," I say, stepping into the doorway. Lachlan's bloodshot eyes drop to the handgun at my side. Something attached to the door starts humming.

I look down just in time to see two electromagnets tear the socket out of my wounded knee.

# CHAPTER 46

I FALL TO THE FLOOR, LETTING OUT A SCREAM AS twin arcs of pain burn through my legs. Blood splashes the tiles. My lungs contract and lock like fists, sending me sliding to my side.

My right knee seems intact. It was farther from the door when the magnets turned on.

My left knee, the one I destroyed at Homestake, wasn't nearly so lucky.

The black fabric of my pants is torn open, revealing a gaping wound in the flesh of my left leg. It stretches from mid-thigh down to my calf, exposing dark muscle, beating veins, and the white glint of bone.

Lachlan put electromagnets inside the door. That's *my* trap, my own goddamn trap. How the hell did he know?

The handgun at my side is gone, ripped from its holster by the magnets. It bounces off the door frame and skids across the tiles, coming to a stop just out of my reach. The metal socket from my left knee is embedded in the side of the doorway, and the end of the gold-flecked cable that ran down my leg hangs from the wound. It flips about on the tiles, broken and sparking, trying to reach the socket again.

"Use your belt, quickly."

I look up, woozy. Lachlan sits motionless in the chair, watching impassively as my blood forms a dark, gleaming pool on the tiles.

"You're going to need to cinch your thigh, or you'll bleed out. That's an artery, darling. You'd better hurry. You'll be unconscious soon."

I yank my belt off with blood-soaked fingers, fumbling as I wrap it around my thigh.

"Tight, now."

I gasp, wrenching the belt tight, gritting my teeth against the pain.

"That's good. I'm sorry to have to hurt you, Catarina, but I wanted to make sure we had time to talk before you try to kill me."

I tie the belt off, holding the end to keep it tight, but the wound is still pulsing with thick, hot blood. The tissue in my knee is new and fragile after I hurt it at Homestake. The magnet ripped it open like a knife slicing through fruit. I grit my teeth, yanking the belt tighter. "I'm not going to have much time to talk if I keep bleeding like this."

Lachlan watches me for a moment, then nods. A steel drawer beside me shoots open with a hiss of refrigerated air, revealing a row of silver syringes.

"Healing tech," he says. "Straight into the wound, that's the fastest way. It's the latest generation. I designed it myself."

I pick up a syringe, biting my lip. I don't trust Lachlan, not by a long shot, but the puddle of blood around me is growing by the second. The bleeding shows no sign of stopping. I can feel my blood pressure dropping. I don't have any choice but to do what he says.

I drive the needle into my shredded flesh, scrunching my eyes shut.

"That's my girl," he says. "Well done."

Almost instantly, the pain ebbs away. I drop the blood-smeared syringe on the floor, gasping with relief. The blood flowing from the wound slows, then turns into a trickle. I shift my weight, pushing myself up shakily until I'm sitting against the wall, my leg splayed out in front of me.

Lachlan watches me, his expression still impassive and unreadable. Part of me is flung back to when Cole first told me he was dead. I cried for this man. I *loved* him. Maybe part of me still does. That would explain the tightness in my throat, the pounding of my heart. I came here today with a gun and every intention of using it, but sitting here now, looking into Lachlan's eyes, I don't know if I could.

He coughs wetly. He looks seriously wounded. Bandages cover his ankles and feet, and what skin I can see on his hands and neck is blistered and scabbed.

"You're hurt too," I say. "It looks like you could use one of these syringes."

His eyes drift down to his bandaged hand. "Unfortunately, that isn't possible. I miscalculated the time I'd need to get out of the lab at Cartaxus when I blew it up. The genkits corrupted my panel when they detonated. I can't risk using healing tech until my system is clear."

"That's not like you. You're normally so careful."

Lachlan shrugs, then winces at the movement. To my horror, part of me still aches to see him in pain.

"Another hacker had already weakened our systems," he says, "and the genkit's self-destruct sequence ran faster than I planned."

I blink, confused. Could he really not know the hacker was me? I consider telling him for a moment but change tack instead.

"You faked my hypergenesis."

"Ah, yes. That was unfortunate. I had to stop you digging too deeply into your panel. You would have found too much too soon."

"What about my mother? Was she . . . was she even *real*?"

A flicker passes across his face. A shadow of something deep and true. "She was very real, Catarina. I loved her very much, just as I love you. But she isn't your mother, as I'm sure you've come to realize."

I just stare at him. I don't need to answer. The anger in my eyes should be all the evidence he needs.

"I assume you'd like to know how I changed your DNA."

I nod, gritting my teeth. The skin around the wound on my leg is starting to blister—but not like it's falling apart. Like it's melting back *together*.

"How much do you remember about the Zarathustra program?" he asks.

I gasp, arching my back as my leg shakes, my nerves aflame. Strings of wet, torn flesh are coalescing, stretching across the wound, slowly pulling the two edges back together.

"N-not much," I stutter, my vision blurring. "Except that you used knockout kids, and you were making a vaccine."

"Close, but not quite. You weren't knockout kids. The genetic recoding that happened in the Zarathustra project was performed by nature herself. She *transferred* her gifts to you."

My head snaps up. He's talking about gene transfer. When two species interact, sometimes they share their DNA. Humans carry genes from plants, bacteria, and even viruses that have made their way into our genome over the course of our evolution.

My breath stills. "You used the virus."

Lachlan smiles. "Indeed. You and the others were grown in tanks in this lab and infected with Hydra when you were just a clump of cells. Most of the samples died instantly, but a handful of you survived. Your cells replicated so quickly that the virus couldn't keep up. Its triggers were destroyed as your cells split and replicated, and parts of Hydra's

DNA intermingled with your own. It changed your cellular structure. It built and shaped your bodies. It's true, you're not my daughter. You're the daughter of the plague."

The air stills. The sounds of my breathing and my beating heart shift up into some harsher frequency. The fog-covered mountains beyond the window shudder in my vision. It seems to shake the very foundations of the building, rattling my breath. But the ground is not shaking; I am.

My identity is splintering like a ship thrust against stone cliffs. I feel the mast of myself snapping, my sails ripped to shreds. I knew I wasn't normal. I knew my cells were changed and twisted—there is no other way I could have survived the vaccine's decryption. I knew Lachlan changed me, broke me, forged me into something else, but I didn't know just how unnatural I was.

I'm not just abnormal. This is more than a genetic tweak. I was created, built, and rearranged by the virus.

I'm not even quite *human*.

"But I've seen my DNA," I whisper. "It's like yours. There's nothing from Hydra in it."

"Oh, there is, you just can't see it. Genkits run their scans on humanity's forty-six chromosomes, with cursory checks for duplicates. They discard anything that looks like a contaminant, which means that your additional two chromosomes don't show up on the average scan."

"I have forty-eight chromosomes?" My stomach lurches. I press my lips together, fighting the urge to be sick.

"Don't get too excited about it. Cole has fifty-four, and Ziana had sixty, but she was barely human at the best of times. Your additional chromosomes can't be changed, but the forty-six I've worked on are incredibly flexible. You're a chameleon, darling. The rest of us can mask small parts of ourselves, but you can literally become anything you want, recoding yourself from your very foundations."

Every word from Lachlan's lips is another wave in the storm in my mind. I press my hands to the cold, tiled floor as though the contact will anchor me somehow.

"That's my *gift*, isn't it? That's what you were studying when you cut me open."

He nods—a short, jerking movement. "That research helped me develop the procedure you used to unlock the vaccine. It would have killed anyone else before it was done. That was why I needed your help, Catarina. I never wanted you to get hurt. I never wanted anyone to get hurt—that's why I set this plan in motion. The vaccine is our last chance, and humanity's survival depends on it. Everything I've done has been to ensure its release."

"But you don't care about the vaccine! I talked to Cartaxus. They were going to pretend to withhold the code and let the Skies give it to everyone on the surface. That would have worked, and you know it. But all you cared about was putting whatever abomination you wrote into it. You know I was there at Sunnyvale. I saw the orange panels and what it did to those people. You *murdered* them. That had nothing to do with humanity's survival."

"Oh, but it did," Lachlan says, his voice rising. "You're so focused on the virus, but Hydra isn't our greatest threat. Why can't you see that, darling? I've gone through so much to make you understand. Ever since the beginning, I've done this all for you. Sunnyvale was for *you*, Catarina."

His eyes are locked on mine, and my hands are pressed to the floor, but I am crashing against rocks, tossed high on furious waves. I close my eyes, seeing drones in the sky. Blood and broken bones. Orange panels glowing from the arms of snarling beasts.

He did it all for me. The monster who is not my father. I'm the one who let him, who paved the way.

It was all my fault.

"But I don't understand," I say. "Sunnyvale was a nightmare. Dax almost killed me."

He just smiles. "There wasn't a person in that town capable of killing you, darling. You might not remember your training, but I assure you it's still there."

"Why?" I cry, my voice breaking. "Why did you make everyone go crazy?"

"You can't make people go crazy with gentech," Lachlan says. "You know this, Catarina. Tell me how I could have controlled those people with a piece of code. Tell me how I could have made them kill each other. The human brain is too complex to be controlled like that. All you can do is encourage or suppress parts of us that are already *there*. That's what Sunnyvale was for, darling. I needed you to see it for yourself."

I blink. The pain in my leg is still crippling, and my breathing is ragged, but my mind is growing clear. I'm beginning to see what he's talking about—what he was trying to show me through the horror of Sunnyvale. It's the same thing I've seen so many times over the last two years, but I've never put it together until now. I close my eyes, shuddering as it falls into place.

The Lurkers. The hordes at Sunnyvale. The response to the virus's scent.

They're all the same instinct, like different notes in the same chord.

"Instincts," I breathe. "That's what you were doing with Cole. You were looking for where our instincts are coded in our DNA, and you found them."

He smiles. "That's right. I found them all through Cole and mapped

393

them out painstakingly in our genome. We like to think we're complex creatures, that our higher-order thinking is what controls us, but in reality we're mostly driven by our instincts. You see their ugly face in every scandal. Every act of war. We try to keep our instincts reined in, but it's like blocking out the sun. They bleed into our lives, into the very fabric of society. I mapped out those instincts, Catarina, but I found one I couldn't ignore. One little gene, deeply hidden, held inside each of us. It's the quintessence of the rage you saw in Sunnyvale."

"The Wrath," I whisper.

"Yes, darling. The Wrath. So many of our violent behaviors can be traced back to that one little gene. The scent of the infected doesn't *change* people's minds, it just switches on a part of them that's been there all along. An ancient part of our reptilian brain, left over from when we were savages. I didn't create the horror you saw in Sunnyvale. I just brought it to the surface."

I close my eyes, seeing the leaping fire and snarling hordes, seeing Sunnyvale's streets erupting into bloodshed. But I've seen it for longer than that. I've felt it for years, heard its voice whispering to me, begging for release. The abyss. The darkness inside me that held the knife every time I killed a second-stager to survive. The beast. I can hear it now, lurking in my cells.

A tiny core of evil, boiled down to a single gene.

"When I found it, I knew we were saved," Lachlan says. "Humanity could finally evolve into a superior race and leave our horrific past behind us. I tried to show Cartaxus, but they couldn't see the bigger picture—that the virus wasn't the real threat to our survival. It was the *Wrath*. It's been controlling us since we were cavemen. We've had one war after another throughout our entire history, all because of this tiny, insignificant gene. We're doomed if we keep going, whether we beat the virus or not. The only way to save humanity is to find a way to change."

"And that's what you're doing?" I ask. "With the vaccine, you're . . . changing people's genes? You're trying to recode the human race?"

"When you pick up an apple with a rotten spot, do you eat the spoiled flesh? No, you cut it out. Humanity has a spot, Catarina. It's tiny, but it's powerful, and it's holding us back, keeping us bound by the obsolete instincts of our ancestors. We needed it once to survive, but we don't need it anymore."

"Can you even hear yourself?" I gasp. "It's not up to you to choose!"

"The choice is obvious!" Lachlan's eyes grow wide. "The human brain has barely evolved in fifty thousand years. It only takes a computer chip a decade to become obsolete. but we're running on fifty-thousand-year-old hardware. Humanity needs to evolve or we will die."

"But you're destroying people," I say, my voice trembling. "You weren't helping the people at Sunnyvale—you were tearing them apart."

Lachlan reaches out a hand to me, his skin blistered and weeping. "It was important that you saw just how dark we are inside. That's why I had to do it. You had to see it up close, with your own eyes, or you wouldn't understand what I'm trying to do. I need you to help me, Catarina, like you promised years ago. I isolated the instinct and used the vaccine to suppress it, but the effect is temporary. With your help, and with your *gift*, we can make it permanent."

Permanent. I close my eyes, my head spinning. He wants to change the DNA of everyone on the planet the same way he changed mine. Recode their underlying genes. The idea is terrifying—but only because it's coming from a man who wants to *force* it on the world. I've seen the Wrath, I've felt it, and I'll always carry the shame of what it made me do. The immunity. The thrill I felt after taking it. If I had a choice, I would have done anything to stop myself from turning into that beast.

And I wouldn't be the only one.

"So why don't you just tell people about this?" I ask. "Nobody *wants* this inside them. Not after Hydra, and what it's done to us. We could decide as a species to stop this, to cut it off with this generation. You already grew a line of plague children inside vats—why didn't you come up with a way for people to choose this for their children?"

Lachlan closes his eyes, sighing. The sound is rough; his throat is burned. "Don't you think I've tried, Catarina? I must have tried a thousand times. The human genome is a perfectly balanced equation with so many terms that we still don't understand. You can't simply pluck a gene from it and expect the result to remain stable. That's why gentech can't change your natural DNA. The core of what makes us human is constant and immutable. I tried growing specimens with the gene for the Wrath removed, but their brains never grew properly. One day future scientists will learn how to cleanly slice that part of us away, but for now we rely on *you*."

Something inside me trembles. I brace myself against the wall, staring into Lachlan's eyes. "What are you talking about?"

"My research with Cole showed me the patterns of our instincts within our genes, and his gift gave me a method of activating or suppressing them. But you operate at a level beyond that. You are the code that writes itself. Your body can take in noise and turn it into a symphony. Your DNA rebalances the equation of humanity in a way I have yet to comprehend. If you join me, Catarina, if we work together on this, we can reproduce your gift and share it with the world."

"I know you want to change them," I whisper. "You want to rewrite their DNA like you rewrote mine. But I don't understand—what does that have to do with instincts?"

He smiles. "You're not seeing the true beauty of your talents, Catarina. When you accept a change to your DNA, it's not just your body that recodes itself. Your mind opens like a flower, mimicking the personality of the person whose DNA you're taking in. Your brain restructures itself with an ease it would have taken us centuries to develop. You can take on the personality, and the strengths, of anyone you choose."

"My . . . my brain?" Ice settles inside me. "What do you mean?"

Lachlan chuckles. "You were always bright, darling, even when you were little. Solving puzzles faster than the others, always remembering what you were told. But the treatments started early. Much of your intelligence came from me. It's not just my face you wear, Catarina. I gave you my mind, as well."

# CHAPTER 47

"NO," I BREATHE. A CRACK INSIDE MY MIND GROWS wide, splintering the last of my hope, the last vestige of my self-control.

Not my mind. My body, I can handle. This is just skin and bone and flesh. Impermanent.

He cannot have my *mind*.

"Don't you think like me sometimes?" Lachlan asks. "Don't you read my code as if you were the one who wrote it, darling?"

My stomach twists. I lurch to the side, gagging. He built his mind over mine. He took everything I am.

Now he wants to do it to everyone else.

Rage blazes through me like a flame along a fuse. Through tears I see the handgun I dropped, lying just out of my reach. I hurl myself toward it, grasping for its barrel, but my hand slips in the pool of my blood and my knee smacks into the tiles. The pain tears a ragged scream from me. My body curls in on itself instinctively.

"There it is!" Lachlan shouts. "The Wrath, Catarina! I can see it in you as clear as day."

I suck in a breath, trying to drag myself to the gun. He's damn right this is the Wrath—I'm summoning it with all the strength I have. The beast is howling, rising through me, painting my vision red, and I'm calling it to me, begging it to take over again.

He needs to die. He's murdered me; there is no other word for what he's done. He's ripped away every shred of the person I used to be.

My hands lock on the barrel, dragging it across the tiles, and I lift it, flipping it into my palm, my finger curling around the trigger.

"What would Cole think if he could see you now?"

I stop, the gun aimed at Lachlan's heart. My eyes slide to the window, and I see my reflection overlaid across the mountains, my face twisted in rage.

My breath catches. I've never seen myself this way, never dared to look into a mirror after yielding to the Wrath. The girl in the window is not someone I know, but there is an echo in her eyes of the child I'm only just beginning to remember.

The girl who plunged scissors into a nurse's throat. Who killed four-teen guards to escape from the laboratory she spent her childhood in. She wouldn't hesitate; she'd pound bullets into Lachlan's chest until the magazine ran out.

But I'm not her anymore.

I scrunch my eyes shut, letting out a scream of frustration. My finger slides away from the trigger. The Wrath raging inside me wants to shoot Lachlan now, but I can't let myself yield to it. I can't kill Lachlan in a fit of rage, and I can't do it for revenge. I want to be the girl Cole watched with wonder in his eyes. The one smiling from his sketchbook.

In his eyes, I am fierce, but I am not a murderer.

I throw the handgun down, my chest shuddering with adrenaline. "I won't kill you, but I won't help you with this plan. You have to stop this madness. People have the right to make up their own minds. You can't decide for them."

"You're defending the Wrath, Catarina! I'm only taking away a part of us we should have bred out long ago. It's an artifact from when the people who survived were the ones who *killed everyone else*. We relied on that instinct then, but we don't need it anymore. It's holding us back, keeping us from our true potential. What did you see in Sunnyvale that was worth saving?"

I close my eyes and see Dax's hands on my neck. The dark gleam in his eyes after he shot me in the back. Sunnyvale was a mass of blood-thirsty animals. There was nothing there I can defend. Not a single thing worth saving.

But that doesn't mean I'm willing to lobotomize the entire human race.

"This choice isn't up to you. It's up to all of us." I grit my teeth, trying to sit up straighter. "I saw Dax drag himself back from the Wrath when he saw what he'd done to me. If he was strong enough to fight your code, then we're strong enough to fight the instinct. We can overcome it on our own."

Lachlan shakes his head. A jerking, pained motion. "As long as the Wrath remains, humanity will never truly be free of it. It will sit at the back of our minds like a sickness, leaching into every choice, every action. It has always controlled us, and it always will. There is a chasm that lies between the savage idiocy of animals and humanity's true potential, Catarina. Civilization has built us a bridge that lies stretched across that chasm, but the Wrath is stopping us from crossing over it. We cannot evolve without shedding our past. We are a flawed beast, and we cannot move forward until we cut this weakness from ourselves. You can't seriously argue for keeping evil inside us, darling. That is madness."

"No," I say, pushing myself up. My bloody hands slip on the tiles, but I manage to grab the edge of the closest genkit and haul myself up. "I'm not arguing for evil—I'm arguing for discussion. People need to see your work, and then maybe they'll choose to do this on their own."

He snorts. "They'll never make the right choice. I spent years trying to convince Cartaxus to take this seriously, but they never saw the value in my work. We can't leave it up to people to decide this for themselves. You don't ask the patients to tend to the sick. This is the only way to save us."

"You're insane." I sway, gripping the genkit to steady myself. My wounded knee is pulsing with pain. "You've lost track of what's right and wrong. I'm not going to help you with this."

"You think it's up to you?" Lachlan's gaze grows steely. "You'll help me, Catarina, or I'll switch the suppressor into reverse somewhere else. How about Homestake?"

"You can't do that. We blocked your connection."

"That's interesting, because I just did it. It should take another minute before Homestake's eighty thousand civilians start killing each other."

My blood freezes. As if on cue, Leoben's voice echoes through the hallway, shouting that the black-dome chips aren't working anymore.

"Eighty thousand lives," Lachlan says. "They're in your hands, my darling girl. Say you'll join me, and they can all be spared."

I stare around wildly. My eyes snap to the gun, but I don't know if shooting Lachlan will save Homestake's civilians. I turn to the humming, industrial-grade genkit I'm gripping for balance. Its wireless light glows a clear, solid blue. He must be using it to control the vaccine. If I want to save Homestake, there's only one option.

I'm going to have to fight his code.

I look down at my arm. My panel hasn't finished growing, but a handful of cobalt lights are blinking beneath my skin. This probably won't work, but it's the only weapon I have left to fight with. I grab one of the needle-tipped cables hanging from the genkit's cable port and jam it into my wrist.

The moment the cable snakes under my skin, my vision blinks to blue, and I tumble head over heels into the first VR session I can remember. Text and images batter my mind, racing across my vision, though I can still make out the vague outline of Lachlan's silhouette.

"What are you doing, Catarina?"

I ignore him, trying to orient myself in the VR interface, fumbling desperately in the mess of menu items. It's hopeless. I need a keyboard. The VR chip in my arm is newly grown; it hasn't yet learned to read my thoughts. It'll be weeks until it can understand the commands I send to it and make sense of the impulses my brain generates.

But that's not entirely true.

This panel is grown from the backup of the one Jun Bei carried, so I still have every file and setting she stored in it. Lachlan may have rewritten my mind, but I still have memories of Jun Bei. There is still some flicker left in me of the girl I used to be. If I can drag back a glimpse of her, just for a moment, I might be able to control my panel enough to launch an attack.

I close my eyes, ignoring the wash of text and color the VR interface throws at me, trying to zero in on my strongest memories. Leoben's smile. Ziana singing in the trees. Anna laughing at the impressions of the nurses that Leoben used to do. Cole's face in the moonlight the first time he kissed me. The night he swore to me that we would always be together.

Something prickles in the base of my skull, and the edges of the

VR interface ripple into focus. It's working. I grasp desperately at more memories, urging them back to me, trying to bond with the girl inside me, with who I used to be.

I see Cole standing beside me, staring out at the mountains through the barred windows of our room, our hands linked together. We were so young and broken, and he was the only thing that could take my pain away. We saw the darkest parts of each other, and we faced them together. He was the brightest light in my life, and I threw myself into him the way someone would hurl herself off a cliff.

Something stirs within me. A presence. A whisper. A keyhole into a dark and hidden part of me. I reach for it, grasping, urging it back to me, and the VR session snaps into focus. Cole's face fades from my memory, but something deeper takes its place.

I hear a voice rising inside my mind that is not my own.

Her words are clipped and sharp. She speaks the way a rifle fires. She is steel and glass and blood fused into a blade. This panel in my arm is her universe. She knows every line of every file.

I open my eyes and let Jun Bei sweep back into me.

The genkit's mainframe unfolds before me, sparklingly clear. Files and commands, links and directories sprawled in a virtual map. A firewall pops up as I tilt myself into it, but I've faced firewalls before, and I have an arsenal of viruses waiting inside my arm. My fingers twitch, my instincts urging me to type a string of commands, but I don't need to code that way anymore. I can work like Dax does, jacked straight into the heart of the machine. I tilt my head back, my consciousness sliding into my panel, searching for something I can use.

"You can't fight this, Catarina."

Lachlan's voice is distant, inconsequential. I ignore him. A dozen files rise before me, forming a wall in my vision. A glance at each is enough to bring its meaning back to me, and I pick and choose between them, selecting loops and subfunctions. Lines of code unfurl like smoke billowing from a fire. A single thought brings blocks of logic spinning together, then coalescing and stretching out into infinite virtual space.

A new virus of fresh, devastating code snaps together in my mind, and I wield it like a knife, stabbing it into the genkit's heart.

The firewall crumbles. It's almost too easy. Lachlan has been holding me back all this time. The hypergenesis wasn't just to stop me from studying my DNA, it was to stop me from turning into *this*. The girl I used to be. A mind too sharp, too powerful for him to control. He gave me his intelligence, sure enough.

It's the biggest mistake he ever made.

The genkit's defenses peel back like blistering layers of paint, revealing the pure, structured programming at the heart of the machine. Lines of code blink into view like strands in a multidimensional spiderweb that stretches out in every direction as far as I can see. Some are black, others white, some are silver and yellow, each running a different task in the genkit's memory. A pulsing strand in the distance is a lurid, blazing orange, and I know instantly that it's the strand I need to break.

It's a satellite connection linking Lachlan to the tower at Homestake, and it's pulsing with a constant stream of information. I angle my consciousness closer, skipping through memory banks like a stone across a lake.

"What are you doing?" Lachlan shouts, his voice half-lost in the wave of code I'm riding.

"I'm fighting you," I whisper.

I trace the strand to a communications port and send every attack, every scrap of malicious code I can remember into its base. Electric shocks. Logic bombs. Every line in the stockpile of weapons I've been developing ever since I was a child. "You gave me your mind," I say as the connection frays and hisses. "Maybe that wasn't such a good idea."

"You won't stop it, Catarina." Lachlan's voice is far too calm. "The connection is linked to the machine's core. Breaking it will trip the self-destruct."

I pause. He's right. Buried at the base of the glowing orange strand is a web of white that's wound into the genkit's power unit. Severing the connection will set off the self-destruct sequence—the same trigger I set off in Homestake, only this machine is a hundred times more powerful. Its blast will take out half the room. I won't be able to run, not with my wounded leg.

It'll kill us both within the space of a heartbeat.

Cole's face flashes into my mind. I just got him back. I have a life and a future. I don't want to die, but deep down I know what I have to do.

"You think we're animals," I say, throwing my consciousness harder into the genkit's architecture. "You think we're controlled by our instincts, that we're just the sum of our genes. But you're wrong. I've faced death, and I'm not afraid anymore. I'm ready to die to stop you."

I blink back into the room as the connection snaps, severing the link to Homestake. Lachlan's bloodshot eyes lock on mine, full of something that looks strangely like *pride*.

"I'm sorry, Father," I breathe as the door to the hallway flies open and the bank of genkits on the wall explodes.

# CHAPTER 48

IT TAKES SIX HEALING TECH SYRINGES TO STOP THE blood pulsing from Cole's back after he threw his body over me when the genkits exploded. His back shredded down to his titanium-latticed ribs, and the skin on my hands is sliced to ribbons as I haul shards of glass and metal from his flesh. Leoben forces bags of saline, then finally bags of his own blood, into Cole's veins.

Cole's heart stops twice. After an hour it grows steady, and Leoben and I stare at each other across the silver-tinted flesh of Cole's back.

We're blood-drenched and shaking. Pale and exhausted.

Brother and sister.

*Alive.*

We didn't have time to save Lachlan. His corpse sits slumped in the dentist's chair, his body riddled with shrapnel. While I was resuscitating Cole, I saw the light fade from Lachlan's eyes and heard him take his final breath.

It almost looked like he was smiling.

When Cole is ready, we carry him outside for no reason other than wanting to get out of the prison we spent our childhoods in. Leoben and

I drag logs and sticks from the forest to build a fire together, and lay Cole beside it to keep him warm. I stretch out next to him until his vitals stabilize and his internal tech takes over.

Hours later, the sun dips below the horizon as the night's first stars blink into an azure sky. Cole breathes steadily, still asleep on a roll-out mattress on the ground, his face bathed in the light from low flames dancing up from the fire. His back is a mess of silver streaks, more nano-mesh than flesh, but I don't care. I just want him to heal.

Leoben waited for a while, then went off hunting. He said he needed to kill something, which part of me understands. We've just lost our father, in a way. We grew up as prisoners and subjects in his experiments, but Lachlan was also the man who raised us. My memories of my child-hood are still scattered—broken moments and snatches of conversations drifting without context in my mind, but I know that part of me cared about him back then, despite everything he did. There is a void where his shadow once fell, and I don't yet know how to rearrange my emotions to fill that space.

Since Leoben left, I've sat for hours with my back against one of the jeep's tires, staring into the flames, unsure if I'm numb or just over-whelmed. Part of me thinks that if I let myself feel anything at all, I'll fall into a chasm inside myself and won't be able to climb out. Or maybe I'll be fine. Cold and dispassionate, like Lachlan. I don't know which reaction would be worse.

The fire crackles, and Cole's hands twitch in his sleep. He shifts to his side, brushing against me, his skin warm and flushed. It takes all my strength not to pull his arms open and curl into his chest, to kiss the soft skin beneath his jaw where his stubble fades away. I still haven't told him what Lachlan said to me. About changing my mind.

I still don't know how to feel about it myself.

If Lachlan's mind was written over mine, then maybe I'm no more than a copy. A butchered, mutant clone with one gender chromosome and a bunch of inhuman DNA separating me from him. I wear his skin; I share his personality—all that's left from Jun Bei are the memories of a girl I barely know buzzing in the back of my mind. I don't know if it's enough to resurrect her, or if I've truly lost that version of myself.

I don't know which option frightens me more.

I glimpsed enough of Jun Bei when I hacked the lab's genkit to know that the pain of her childhood is what defined her. She took that pain inside herself and let it crystallize there, creeping into her heart until it glittered like ice. I thought Cole was a weapon made of steel, but he has softer places hidden inside. He is vulnerable, and gentle.

Jun Bei is not.

Her voice has faded from my mind, but I can still feel the power of it, the echo of her thoughts on the fringes of my mind. To remember her fully, and hear her voice like that again, would mean opening myself to the pain she carried. I don't know if I can bear that. I don't know if I *want* to.

But when I think of the little mountain lion on Leoben's chest, I feel a void inside me.

A log in the fire pops, and Cole stirs, his hand brushing my ankle. "Hey there," he says, blinking awake. He rubs his eyes, bleary. "Where's Lee?"

"Hunting," I say. "Don't get up. I'm keeping watch. He wanted to let off steam by shooting things."

He smiles, his eyes puffy. "That sounds like Lee."

I snort. "How are you feeling?"

"I'm pretty high on meds right now, but I think I'll be okay. What about you?"

I shrug. My hands are bandaged, and my leg barely has any strength, but it isn't my physical wounds that worry me. "I'm not doing so well," I admit.

Cole opens his arms, inviting me closer, but I'm not sure I can let him hold me. I'm not the girl he thinks he loves. How is he going to feel when he finds out the truth about what Lachlan did to me?

"Come here," he says, reaching for me. He slips a hand around my arm, tugging me into him. "I know there's a lot to figure out, but we're together now. It's going to be okay."

I breathe in a lungful of his scent, letting myself curl in closer. There's nothing I want more than to believe those words right now. But I don't know if they're true. I don't know if anything is okay. I don't know who I am, or how I'm going to handle everything that's happened.

Cole pushes the hair from my face. "How's your new panel?"

I rest my head in the curve of his shoulder, lifting up my arm. "It's strange—I can feel apps that I've never used before. I don't even know what they're supposed to do."

He smiles, a playful gleam in his eyes. He takes my hand and turns it gently. "Can I try something?"

"Sure," I say warily.

He slides his hand along my forearm until our panels are pressed together, the way I've seen him do with Leoben. I let my eyes glaze over, waiting to see a comm or a file, but all I feel is a low, prickling heat in my stomach.

"Here," he says, lifting my other hand to his face, tracing my fingers down his cheek. Sparks rise on my skin in the same place I'm touching him.

"Is that . . . Am I feeling what you feel?"

"Mm-hmm," he says, moving my hand, tracing my fingers over his lips. Lines of fire rise across my own.

"Are you feeling what I feel too?" I ask.

"Of course, it's a feedback loop." He grins and pulls me closer, leaning in to kiss me.

The feeling erupts across my skin—my own rapid-firing nerves leaving me breathless, shaking as our lips press together. It's like fireworks—tiny pops of pleasure growing stronger with each moment the kiss lingers until it's so intense I can't take it anymore.

"Holy shit," I gasp, pulling away, breaking the connection between our panels. "Is this what you and Leoben were doing when your panels were pressed together?"

He throws back his head, roaring with a laugh that turns into a wince of pain. "No, but I've got to tell him you said that."

My cheeks flush, my body still tingling. "That's a hell of a piece of code."

Cole grins. "It's supposed to be used to transfer pain for medical diagnoses, but you hacked it years ago."

"*I* wrote it?"

"Yeah, baby. You've been a badass from the start. It wasn't him. You know that, right? It was always *you*."

I let my gaze drift up to his, my heart stuttering. The firelight catches his eyelashes, lighting up the curves of his face.

"I heard everything," he says. "He wanted me to hear. He patched your conversation through to me, but I think part of me knew even before he told you. It's going to be okay, Cat. We'll get through this."

"But . . . Jun Bei," I say. "If what Lachlan said is true, then she's *gone*, and you loved her, you—"

He cuts me off with a kiss. "I did love her," he says when he pulls away, "and I still do. That's something I need to figure out, but we'll figure it out together. People change, and they still love each other. You've just changed a little more than normal."

"A *little*?"

He cups my cheek with one hand, his ice-blue eyes roaming over my face. "You're not as different as you might think. I see a lot of her in you. Her spark, her determination." He grins. "Her continual attempts to kill me."

I roll my eyes.

"But seriously, I see good parts of Lachlan in you too, and there were good parts. You know that. He was brilliant, just like you. But you're not him, no matter what he said. You're your own person, Catarina."

"Cole—" I start, then bite my lip, turning away as tears fill my eyes. Cole pulls my face to his chest, stroking my neck as I cry. He doesn't know how much I needed to hear that. I don't know the girl I was, and I don't know who I'll become, but for right now I'm Catarina. I think I can live with that.

After the tears slow, we lie together silently as the fire crackles and a flock of pigeons swoop and cry above us. Cole's stomach grumbles, and he presses his lips to my ear. "You hungry?"

I nod, my face still pressed to his chest.

"Well, so am I, and I'd cook," he says, "but I'm an invalid and all. . . ."

"You don't want my cooking. I can't tell you how many times I've had food poison—" I pause as an icon pops up in the edge of my vision. It's my comm-link app coming back online. The icon spins as it boots up, hooking into the new joint network Dax and Novak set up for the broadcast. "Comm-link is back." I say. Thousands of messages flood my vision, their text completely covering my field of view. All my old texts are downloading from the network to my new panel. I rub my eyes, fumbling mentally for a way to make them disappear. "Ugh, I think I'm downloading every comm-link message I ever got."

Cole laughs. "You're strobing out."

"Is that what you call it?" I blink again, shaking my head as the words flash and spin. "This is making me seasick, it's . . ." I trail off as Agnes's name pops up. All her messages from the last two years are downloading, scrolling across my eyes so fast I only catch snatches of words.

Got soup . . . You cold? . . . Cartaxus drones . . . up on the highway . . .

"You okay?" Cole asks.

I swallow, nodding. "Yeah, I just saw some old messages from Agnes. I wonder where she is, if she's safe."

A handful of messages scroll by from my contacts in the Skies about the vaccine, and then I see Agnes's name pop up again.

Bobcat, I'm tracking your father.

I freeze, searching for the message, but it's gone. More words flash up so fast I can only catch snippets, but they're enough to send a jolt through me.

. . . in Nevada . . . near the solar farms . . . follow the pigeons . . . plan must be stopped . . . Bobcat, don't trust Lachlan . . .

"What the hell?" I whisper.

"What is it?"

"She's in Nevada. These messages are from the last couple of days. She's been sending texts to my comm, but my panel wasn't working. She's fine, she's alive."

"See," Cole says, rubbing my arm. "I told you I didn't kill her."

I should be relieved, but my stomach is clenching. If Agnes was tracking Lachlan, then what is she doing down in Nevada?

"I . . . I need to check something," I say, pushing myself to my feet. I hurry to the lab, limping on my bad knee.

Cole sits up slowly. "Wait," he calls after me. "Where are you going?"

Part of me wants to stop and explain, but the rest of me is already gone. I push open the lab's heavy steel door and weave through the chairs in the waiting room. The ceiling lights flicker on automatically, triangular fluorescents blinking as I limp down the hallway. The doors to the lab are bloodstained, one swinging from a broken hinge. I draw in a breath, steeling myself, and step into the room.

The shrapnel-riddled body of the man I once called Father sits slumped lifelessly in the dentist's chair. He sat there the whole time we were talking, barely moving even when I hacked the genkit. He could have tackled me and ripped the wire out of my arm. I know he was wounded, but he still made it to the lab somehow. It wasn't like he was *paralyzed*.

So why didn't he get out of his chair?

I replay the moment in my mind, the skin on the back of my neck prickling. For a man who had such complex plans, this suddenly seems too simple.

Something is wrong.

I step closer, reaching for his hand, tracing my fingers across his cold, burned skin. Every line of his face is familiar. His eyelashes, his fingernails, his teeth are all those of a man I once fiercely loved.

But today I learned that looks can be deceiving.

I slide my knife from the sheath at my thigh and jerk it up his pants, splitting the gray fabric open to his knees. The burns around his feet stop a few inches up his calf, and above that his skin is a clean olive. No blisters, and no burns. No injuries at all except for the shrapnel from the genkit I blew up.

This doesn't look like a man who was burned so badly that he couldn't get out of his chair.

I stand, swaying, my pulse thudding in my ears. I look over his face again.

"No," I breathe. "It can't be."

"Cat?" Cole calls out. "Where are you?"

My stomach heaves. I spin around, covering my mouth with my hand, and shoulder my way back through the lab's doors. My eyes well with tears as I run down the hallway.

"Cat, what's wrong?" Cole asks when I burst into the waiting room. He reaches for my arm, but I shove past him and push through the front door.

I stumble out into the grass and double over, my hands braced on my thighs, fighting the nausea rolling through me. Cole's footsteps sound behind me. The lab's door screeches open, and he runs to me, his eyes wide.

"What happened? Are you okay?"

I draw in a ragged breath. "It was too easy. I should have guessed."

"What do you mean? Cat, you're scaring me."

"It wasn't him," I say, my voice shaking. "It was a *puppet*."

He stands and steps back. "No, it couldn't be. . . ."

I swallow, the dead man's face filling my mind. Once I realized what Lachlan had done, the differences were sickeningly obvious. The man's eyes were set too far apart; his Adam's apple was too big. The point of his chin wasn't as pronounced as mine. I should have noticed, but he'd been so artfully burned and bandaged that my mind skipped over those minor details.

I blew up those genkits and killed an innocent man—someone with a panel full of code designed to make him look like Lachlan Agatta. A helpless puppet forced to sit there, trapped in his own body.

"We haven't killed him," I say, choking back a cry. "He's still out there. This is all part of his plan. We're still being played."

Cole's hands ball into fists. "We'll find him," he says with steel in his voice. "We'll hunt him down and make sure he's dead this time."

"But we can't *beat* him. He's too smart."

Cole turns to me. "No, he's not. You beat him here, and you can do it again. You have the mind of the greatest scientist this world has ever seen, but you are so much more than him."

He takes my arm, helping me up. Overhead, passenger pigeons dart across the sky, their cries echoing from the mountains. Cole's touch ignites something inside me—the smallest flicker of courage—and I catch a glimpse of a dangerous feeling I've kept locked away so long.

Hope.

"But I don't even know who I am," I whisper.

"I do," Cole says. His hand rises to my face. "You're strong, and you're brave, and you care about people. You offered your life to release the vaccine, which means you're nothing like him. He's wrong about you. We're more than what our genes dictate we should be. You're proof of that, Cat. He just doesn't know it yet."

I stare into Cole's eyes, feeling the earth tilt beneath me, gravity pitching me into a fight I'm not sure I can win. It's impossible to out-smart a man with a mind like Lachlan's—even with armies and drones, rebels and hackers, we'll never take him down.

But he made one crucial error. One flaw in his perfect plan. He gave me his mind—his intelligence, his cunning.

It's time for me to embrace it.

## ACKNOWLEDGMENTS

To my incredible agent, DongWon Song—thank you, thank you, thank you. From the moment we first spoke, I knew you were going to change my life, and I'm so grateful to have you with me on this roller coaster! Thank you for being my first editor, for seeing the heart of the book when it was in rough shape, and showing me how to make it shine. #TeamDongWon forever! Thank you to Kim-Mei and Howard at HMLA, Caspian, Ben and Sandy at Abner Stein, Heather and Danny at Baror International, and Michael Prevett at Rain Management. I'm so lucky to have such a wonderful team representing me.

To my editor Sarah McCabe, thank you for your constant support and wonderful notes—some of the best lines in this book were written after you encouraged me to dig deeper. To Liesa Abrams, Mara Anastas, Mary Marotta, and the team at Simon Pulse and Simon & Schuster Children's—thank you for making me feel so welcome, and for working so hard on this book! Regina Flath, I *love* you for creating this amazing cover. It's everything I hoped for and more. Thank you, Michael Strother, for championing this book and giving me this chance.

To my UK editor, Tig Wallace, thank you for your humor, your passion and your excellent notes—you helped me tighten and polish this book immeasurably. To Hannah Bourne, Harriet Venn, Rachel Khoo and the team at Penguin Random House Children's UK, thank you for your enthusiasm and continual support. Thank you to my copyeditors,

# ACKNOWLEDGMENTS

Brian Luster, Wendy Shakespeare, and Sophie Nelson, for your admirable patience with my inability to follow basic comma rules, and for catching so many inconsistencies!

To my husband, Edward, who has encouraged and supported me through revisions, rejections, deadlines, and moments of frantic joy—thank you. I am so lucky to have found you, and I'm so lucky to be going on this adventure with you. Thank you for listening to my wild ideas and endless science factoids. Thank you for making me believe I can do anything I put my mind to. Thank you for reading this book approximately twelve million times.

To Lora Beth Johnson. Where do I begin? How can I possibly capture in words what you mean to me? There is a special kind of love that springs up between critique partners whose minds and hearts are perfectly aligned, who encourage and challenge and defend each other, who cry on each other's shoulders and dance excitedly when the good news finally comes. Thank you for always being there, for always guiding my writing to a better place, and for your endless patience and generosity. You make me a better writer, and a better person. I'm so grateful to have found you.

Thank you to my mother, Cate, for filling my room with books, for reading to me and encouraging me to craft my own characters and stories. Your creativity and your talent have always been an inspiration to me. Thank you to my father, Brock, for sharing so many wonderful books with me—Vonnegut, Orwell, Adams—and for letting me ramble about writing and publishing. I inherited my love of words from you, and am grateful for it every day. Thank you to my family—Rachel, Ellie, Rory, Corinne, Leanne, Bev and David, Kate, and the Townsends for your excitement and love, and help along the way. Thank you Debbie, Ed and Jeff for your enthusiasm and welcoming me into your family.

ACKNOWLEDGMENTS

To Karrie Shirou, thank you for your eagle eyes and brilliant mind—this book is so much stronger because of your critique! Thank you Anne Tibbets for your constant support, advice, and friendship. To the incredible writing friends I've made along the way: Matt Wallace, Marina Lostetter, Sarah Gailey, Alyssa Wong, Sara Mueller, Alex Acks, Amal El-Mohtar, Kristin Henley, Imogen Cassidy, Kate Ristau, Brianna Shrum, Chris Randolph—thank you for the signal-boosting and support!

To Toni Fatherley—the best English teacher I've ever met, thank you for always challenging me to do my best, to aim higher, to work harder. I needed it. Thank you Sonya, for introducing me to Roswell, Mélanie for being such an inspiration, and Seti for sharing so many wonderful adventures with me. Thank you Jun Bei, for loaning me your name, and my Macq friends: Murray, Monica, Megan, Serena, Gen, Vidya, Julia, Ben, Anna, Monique, Suhail, and Melanie, for your encouragement to follow my crazy dreams. Thank you David, Jess, Theresa, Kristin, Alison, and all the Reedies who fill my days with math and code and wonder.

# THE POEM IN THE PIGEONS

Cat discovers a sonnet encrypted in the DNA of passenger pigeons. Can you decipher it? Check out emilysuvada.com/extras/the-pigeon-poem for a hint!

ACATGCACTGCGCATGATGTATATTGCATACAACGTGCGCT
GCATGTAACGCGTACTACATATAACGTGTACTGCGTACGATG
TATATTGCATATGATGTATATTGCGTATAACGCATGTTGCACAT
GACGCATGCTGCACGCGACGTGCGTTACATATAACGTACGTTG
CACGCGACGCATGTTACATATAACGTGCACTGCGCATGATG
TATATTGCACGTGACGTGTACTGCACGCAACGTACATTACG
CACGATGTATATTGTATATGATGTATATTGCATACGACGTATACT
GCATGCGACGTACACTACATATAACGTGCGCTGCATGCAAT
GTATATTGCATACAACGTGCGCTGCACGCAACGTACACTA
CATATAACGTATACTGCACGCAACGTACATTACATATAACGCAT
GCTGCACATGACGTGCGTTGCATGTGACGCACGCTACATATA
ACGTACGTTGCACGCGACGCATGTTACATATAACGTGCACTG
CGCATGATGTATATTGCGTACGACGTGCGCTGCGTGTGACGT
GCATTACACGCAATGTATATTGTGTGTAACGTGTATTGCACAT
GACGCATGCTACATATAACGTACATTGCACGCGACGCACACT
GCATACAACGTGCATTGCATGTGATGTGCACTGCACATAAC
GTACACTGCACGTAACGTGTACTGCGCATAATGTATATTGCA
CATGACGCATGCTACATATAACGTATACTACATATAACGTATGCT
GCACATAACGTATACTGCACATGACGTGCGTTACATATAACG

CACATTGCACATAACGTATACTGCGTGTAATGTATATTGCATA
CAACGTGTACTGCACGCAACGTACATTGCGTACGATGTATATTG
TACGTGACGCGTACTACATATAACGCACGCTGCACATGACGT
GCATTGCACGTAATGTGCATTACATATAACGTACGTTGCACGC
GACGCATGTTGCATACGACGTGTACTGCACGCAACGTACGC
TACATATAACGTGCACTGCATGTGATGTATATTGCGTGTGACGT
GCGTTGCATGTAACGTACACTGCGTACAATGTATATTGCACAT
GACGCACATTGCGTACGATGTATATTGCATACGACGTGCGCTG
CACGCAACGCACATTGCGTACAACGTGCGCTGCACGTAATGT
GCGTTACATATAACATGTACTACATATAACGTGCATTGCACAT
GACGCACGTTGCATGTGATGTATATTGCACATGACGTGCGTTA
CATATAACGTACGTTGCACGTAACGTACACTGCGTACGACGT
GTATTACACGTAATGTATATTGCACATGACGTGCGTTACATATA
ACGCATGCTGCGTGTGACGTACGTTGCATGCAACGTACACT
GCGTACAACGTGTACTGCACGCAACGTACGCTACATATAACG
TATACTGCACGCAACGTACATTACATATAACGCACATTGCACG
CGACGTGTACTGCACGTAATGTGCATTACATATAACATACATTG
CGTACAACGTACACTGCATATGACGTGCACTGCACATGACGTG
CGTTGCATGCGATGTATATTGCACGCGACGTACGTTACATATA
ACGTGTATTGCACATGACGTACGCTGCACATAACGTACACTGC
GTACAATGTATATTGCGTGTAACGTGTATTGCACATGACGTGC
GTTGCATGCGACGCATGCTACACGTAATGTATATTGCGCATGAC
GTACACTGCATATGACGCATGTTGCACGCAACGTGTACTGCACG
CAACGTACGCTACATATAACGCACATTGCACGCGATGTATATTG
CATGCAACGTGCATTGCGCATGATGCGTGCTACATATAACACA
CATTGCACGCGATGTATATTGCGTGCGACGCATGTTGCATGT
GACGTGCGTTGCATACGACGTGTATTACATATAACGTGCACTG
CGCATGATGTATATTGCGTACGACGCATATTGCACATGACGCAT
GTTGCACATGACGCACATTACATATAACGTACGTTGCGTACAAC

GTGCGCTGCACGTGATGTATATTGCGTGTAACGTGTATTGCA
CATGACGCATGCTACATATAACGTGCACTGCACGCGACGCAT
GTTGCGTGTAACGTATACTGCACGTAATGTATATTGCATACGAC
GTGCGCTGCACATGACGTGCATTACATATAACATATACTGCACG
CAACGTACATTACATATAACGCATGCTGCACGCGACGTATACT
GCGTACAATGTGCATTACATATAACGCACACTGCACGCAACG
TACGTTGCATGTGACGCACATTGCGTGTAACGTACACTGCGTA
CAACGTACACTGCATGTAATGTGCATTACATATAACGTGTACT
GCACGCAACGCACATTGCACGCGATGTATATTGCACGCGAC
GCATATTGCATGTGACGTGCGTTACATATAACGCATGCTGCA
CACGACGCGTACTACACGCAATGTATATTGTGTACGACGTGC
GCTACATATAACATGTACTACATATAACGCACGCTGCACATGAC
GTGCATTGCACGTAATGTATATTGCGTACGACGCATATTGCACG
TAACGTGTACTGCGTGTAATGTATATTGCGTGTAACGTGTATTG
CACATGACGCATGCTACATATAACGTGTATTGCATGTGACGTG
CATTGCACATGACGCGTATTACATATAACGTATACTGCGTGTAAT
GTATATTGCACATGACGCACATTGCGTACGATGTATATTGCATAC
GACGTGCGCTGCGTACAACGTACACTACGCACGATGTATATTG
TATGTAACGTACACTGCGTACGACGCACATTGCGTACAACGT
GCGCTGCGCATGATGTATATTGCGTGTAACGTGTATTGCATGT
GATGTATATTGCATGCGACGTACACTGCACGCAACGTACACTG
CGTACGATGTATATTGCGTGTAACGTGTATTGCATATGACGCA
CATTACATATAACGTACGTTGCACGCGACGCATGTTGCACGT
GACGTACACTGCATGTAATGTATATTGCGTGTAACGTGTATTG
CACATGACGCATGCTACATATAACGTATACTGCACGCAACGTAT
GCTGCACATGACGTACACTGCACGCAACGCACATTACATATA
ACGTATGCTGCATATGACGTACGCTGCATGTGATGTGCGTTA
CATATAACACATGTTGCATGTGACGTATGTTGCGTGTGACGTG
TACTGCACGTAACGTACATTACATATAACGCACATTGCACATA

ACGTGTACTGCGTACGATGTATATTGCATACAACGTGCGCTG
CATGTAACGCGTACTACATATAACGTGTACTGCACGCAACGCA
CATTGCACGCGATGTATATTGCGTACGACGTGCGCTGCACGT
GACGTACACTGCGTGTAACGTGTATTGCACATGACGTGCGTTG
CATGCGATGTATATTGCACGTGACGTGCGCTGCGTACAACG
TACACTACATATAACACACATTGCACATAACGTATACTGCACG
CAATGTATATTGCATGCAACGTGCATTGCATGTGACGCATGCT
GCACATAATGTATATTGCATATGACGTGCGTTGCATGTAATG
TATATTGCATACAACGTGCATTGCACGCGACGTGCGCTGCATG
TAATGTATATTGCATATGACGTGCGTTGCATGTAATGTATATTG
CACGTGACGTGTACTGCGTACGACGTACACTGCGTACAACGC
GTACTACATATAACGTATACTGCACGCAACGTACATTACATATA
ACGCATGTTGCATATGACGTACGCTGCATGTGATGTGCGTTA
CATATAACATATACTGCACGCAACGTACATTACATATAACGCG
TACTGCATGTGACGCACATTACACGTAATGTATATTGCGTGTAAC
GTGTATTGCATGTGATGTATATTGCACGTAACGTATACTGCGTG
CGACGCATGCTACATATAACGTGCGCTGCATGCAATGTATATTG
CGTATAACGTGTATTGCGCATGACGCATGCTGCACATGACG
TATGCTGCGTACGATGTATATTGCACGTGACGTATACTGCGCAT
GATGTATATTGCGTATAACGCATGTTGCACGCGACGCACGTTG
CATGTGATGTATATTGCGTACAACGTGTACTGCATGCGACGTG
TATTGCGTGTAATGCGTGCTACATATAACATACATTGCATATGAC
GCATGTTGCACACGATGTATATTGCACGTGACGTATACTGCGT
GTAACGCACATTGCATGTGACGCATGTTACATATAACGTATGCT
GCATATGACGTGCGTTGCACGCAACGTGCGCTGCGTGTAATG
TATATTGCGTGTAACGCATGTTGCATATGACGTGCGTTGCGTAC
GACGTACGTTGCACGCGACGCATGTTGCACGTGATGTATATTG
CACATGACGTGCGTTGCGTGTAACGTGCGCTACATATAACGT
GCATTGCACATGACGTACGCTGCACATAACGCACATTACACGCA

424

KEEP READING
FOR A SNEAK PEEK AT THE
THRILLING SEQUEL!

A MORTAL COIL NOVEL

THIS
CRUEL
DESIGN

EMILY SUVADA

IT'S MIDNIGHT, BUT THE SUNSET IS STILL FADING into darkness, the day stretched late by our northern latitude and the Earth's axial tilt. A million-strong flock of passenger pigeons soars above me, the tips of their feathers glowing faintly, like a swarm of fireflies. They swoop and dart between the trees, their movements sharp and agile, a constellation of pinprick lights against the darkening sky. The sound of their calls echoes from the steep mountain slopes, filling the crisp night air with a hurricane of sound.

This flock is nothing like those I remember from the cabin. These birds are a new strain, with their own mutations and quirks. Their cries are shrill, punctuated with complex streams of whirrs and clicks. They're getting smarter with each new generation.

It's almost like they're learning how to speak.

"Lighter on your feet. Eyes on me," Leoben says, prowling in a slow circle around me.

I lift the weight from my heels, dropping my eyes from the flock. My fists are raised, my hair hanging tangled about my shoulders. We're deep in the forest, the grass around us tracked with muddy footprints. There's blood in my mouth, dirt streaked across my skin, and bruises rising on what feels like every inch of my body.

"Keep that guard up, squid."

I tighten my stance. "Did you just call me *squid*?"

A low smile tugs at Leoben's lips, and my stomach clenches. He's going to come at me again—I can see it in his eyes. He's unarmed, and I know he won't really hurt me, but he's still a black-out agent. A tower of finely-crafted Cartaxus weaponry, trained to fight since he was a child. His every movement is precise and lethal, corded muscles flexing beneath the tattooed skin of his arms. He tilts his head, his smile growing into a grin, then pushes off his rear foot and streaks forward in a blur.

There's no time to think. I lurch to the side, dodging the fist he's aiming at my ribs, but his other hand goes straight for my throat. I bring up a knee, sending out an elbow that connects with his jaw, but by the time I can draw back for another strike, his foot is planted behind mine.

That's all he needs. A simple lever to tilt me off balance. Even though I know he's sending me flying, I can't help but marvel at his grace. His fingers stay locked on my neck, guiding my descent as I tip backward and hit the ground hard enough to knock the air from my lungs.

He steps back, rubbing his jaw as I wheeze, curling up on my side in the grass.

"Good," he says, nodding.

I roll to my knees, choking in a breath. "Good? I barely touched you."

He reaches down a hand to help me up. "You're getting better, but you need to be more aggressive. You have to try to bring me down too."

I stand unsteadily, trying to blink away the flecks of silver at the edges of my vision. We've been at this for days, and every session makes me feel like I've been hit by a car, but he's right—I'm getting better. My reaction times are being whittled down, my senses growing sharper, and there are fresh, slender muscles in my shoulders and forearms. I've never felt as powerless as I do when I fight Leoben, but this training is the only thing in my life right now that makes me feel like I'm in control.

"You okay?" Leoben asks, peering at me. "You don't look so good."

I rub my eyes, swaying. "Yeah, I'm fine."

He shakes his head, the streaks of iridescent blue eyeliner traced above his lashes catching the sunset's dying light. "You're a bad liar is what you are. Come on, Cole'll be back from lookout soon. We should stop for the night or he'll kick my ass for beating you up."

"I disabled his protective protocol."

"I know," Leoben says. "But he'll still kick my ass."

He slings an arm around my shoulders, walking me back into our makeshift camp. Our two jeeps are parked in a muddy clearing, a camouflage-printed tarpaulin stretched between them. The trees around us are tall and thick, their trunks coated with moss, the ground at their bases bursting with ferns. We've been here for a week, hidden deep in the forest, an hour's hike from the Zarathustra lab. We camped in its parking lot the first night after I blew up the genkits, but a troop of Cartaxus soldiers arrived and sent us fleeing into the woods. None of us wanted to stay near the prison we spent our childhoods in, but we were too hurt to get on the road, and we had nowhere else to go anyway.

So we've stayed here, resting and healing, eating freeze-dried rations and sleeping in our jeeps. There are still soldiers at the lab, and it probably isn't smart to stay this close to them, but the jeeps' black dome chips are hiding our location. Besides, this flock of pigeons has been growing larger by the day, their cries filling the air, their glowing plumage providing more than enough cover to hide us from the prying eyes of drones.

Leoben swings open the rear doors of his jeep, pulling out two metal flasks. "I mean it. You need to rest. You're not looking so great, squid."

"You can't call me squid," I say.

He tosses me one of the flasks. "So many rules with you. Can't call you 'squid,' can't call you 'potato.' You're my sister, and you're getting a nickname."

"Cole doesn't have a nickname."

He rolls his eyes. "That's because his name is *Cole*."

I unscrew the flask and take a swig of water, swishing it around my mouth to clear out the blood, then spit it into the grass. "And where did you get 'squid'?"

"They can change the expression of their genes, kind of like you. Cephalopods. I read about it."

"Wow." I take another swig, fighting a rush of dizziness as I tip my head back. "I don't know whether to be offended or impressed."

He crosses his arms proudly, a grin spreading across his face. "Definitely impressed."

I snort, lifting the flask to pour water over my face. Leoben and I have spent most of the week together while Cole has been recovering from his injuries. Lee braided my hair when the gunshot wound in my shoulder was healing, and I've woken him from his nightmares, but after a week of living as brother and sister, he still can't call me *Cat*.

Honestly, I don't really mind, though I'm not so keen on squid. The three of us are all coping with my identity in our own ways. Cole's been quiet, Lee's cracking jokes, and I'm doing what I always do—building carefully constructed fortresses of distraction and denial.

That's how I made it through the outbreak—I spent my days hacking Cartaxus, helping Novak's rebel group, the Skies, distribute medical code to the survivors on the surface. The harder I worked, and the longer

I locked myself away in the cabin's basement lab, the less it hurt when I heard people detonating in the distance or had to choke down doses for immunity.

This week I've had no shortage of ways to occupy my time. Cole's tech has needed constant attention while it's regenerated. I've been training with Leoben and reading through the paper files that Cole and I brought from the cabin—barely sleeping, barely eating, barely letting myself think. I'm probably headed for a crash, but it's working so far. I've managed to bend my thoughts away from what's been hurting me the most.

I've barely thought about the green-eyed child with scars curling across her chest.

Jun Bei.

She is a shadow on the edge of my senses, a puzzle left unsolved. All week I've been waiting for more of my childhood memories to return, but they're still blurry and scattered. I don't know if that's all I'll ever remember, or if I'm just afraid of seeing more. My childhood feels like a black hole I'm locked in an orbit around—I can't escape it, but if I drift too close, it could tear me apart. I might spend a lifetime recovering from what's been done to me.

But right now, I have to stay focused. I have too much work to do.

From what we've been able to tell, there haven't been any attacks since Sunnyvale. No more orange panels, no more crowds of people turned into mindless killers by the toxic code that was added to the Hydra vaccine. Cartaxus has hidden the truth about what happened—they're still sending out daily broadcasts from the joint satellite network they set up with the Skies. Every morning, Dax and Novak splash onto the jeeps' dashboards, talking about the success of the vaccine, promising that we're getting closer to a new, unified world. Everyone is still celebrating the end of the plague—there are parties raging in the bunkers and in every survivor camp on the surface.

None of them know that there's a threat hidden inside their panels, and that the real enemy is still out there.

Dr. Lachlan Agatta. The world's greatest gentech coder, and the man I once called Father.

Three years I loved him, waiting desperately for him to come home after Cartaxus took him from the cabin. I still wear his features on my face and his DNA inside my cells. From what he told me when I faced him at the lab, the patterns of his thoughts are carved into my very *mind.*

I don't really know what that means yet, or why he chose to do it, but I know that Lachlan's plan didn't end with changing me. The daemon code he added to the vaccine gave him access to every panel on the planet, and his goal is far worse than turning crowds of people into monsters.

Lachlan's work on Cole showed him the link between genes and instincts, and it let him isolate the gene that controls the Wrath—the instinctive rage that lurks inside all of us, coded into our DNA. A single whiff of the sharp scent of the infected can be enough to trigger it, turning a crowd of people into mindless, bloodthirsty killers. Lachlan thinks he can use the vaccine to make humanity *better.* He wants to permanently recode everyone's minds by forcibly erasing the Wrath from our DNA.

But we won't let him. I know better than anyone how it feels to learn that your mind is not your own, and every minute since I found out the truth I've been researching, planning, and learning to fight.

Because once we're ready, we're going to track Lachlan down.

And then we're going to kill him.

I screw the cap back on the flask and toss it into the back of the jeep. There's a creek a short walk from our camp, and I should go and wash this mud off me before I try to sleep. Not that I have anything clean to change into. We're almost out of soap, food, and healing tech. We'll need to get on the road again soon, but we still don't know where Lachlan is. The best lead I have is the comm message Agnes sent me after the vaccine's decryption saying that she'd tracked him to Nevada. I've tried contacting her every day since then, hoping to hear her voice or just find out if she's okay, but I haven't been able to get through.

I know we'll find Lachlan, though. He told me he needs my help to finish his plan. He can use the vaccine to suppress or trigger instincts like he did with the crowd at Sunnyvale, but he still can't alter them *permanently*. I'm the only person whose natural DNA can be recoded without killing them, and now he wants to use me to recode everyone else—to change their minds in the same way he changed mine. Going after him is dangerous, but as long as he's alive, I'll just be another pawn on his chessboard.

I have no choice but to face him, and I know he'll give me a way to find him. He *wants* me to go to him. He thinks I'll actually join him, though the thought is ridiculous.

We just have to make sure that when we're hunting him down, we're not walking into another trap.

"How's your tech today?" Leoben asks, tugging off his dirty tank top. The brown, scarred skin on his chest gleams in the soft light from the pigeons.

I look down at my dirt-smeared arm. The backup node in my spine has unspooled into a brand-new panel—a blazing stripe of cobalt light that stretches from my elbow to my wrist. I spent the last three years believing that I had hypergenesis, an allergy to the nanites that run most gentech code. I survived the outbreak with six measly apps, but now I have thousands: reflex enhancers, built-in painkillers, even eyebrow management. I should be able to code without a screen or keyboard, and my VR chip is powerful enough to launch me into fully rendered virtual worlds.

But I still can't get any of it to work.

My panel's automated apps are running—my healing tech, sensory filters, even a standard aesthetic suite—but it won't *listen* to me. There's a net of four million nanoelectrodes coiled inside my skull to record the electrical impulses that flit through my brain, so I should be able to *think* about my comm-link and have it pop into my vision, but my panel still hasn't learned the patterns of my thoughts. It can't tell if I'm thinking *comm*, or *night vision*. It was learning faster while I was injured, but now that I'm healed the installation has slowed to a crawl. At the pace it's going, it could be weeks until I have full control over my tech. . . .

Unless I find a way to speed up the installation again.

"It's still not working properly," I say, reaching into the back of the jeep, searching under the piles of clothes.

"I was thinking of deleting your healing tech," Leoben says. "If we freak your panel out, it might speed up again."

"I had a similar thought," I say, sliding out a black handgun, "but my plan was a little more direct."

Leoben's eyes drop to the gun, narrowing. It's a Cartaxus model—silencer screwed into the barrel, a hacked targeting chip wired into the stock. It's loaded with custom ammo—hollow resin bullets filled with beads of healing tech that should cause superficial injuries.

At least, they *should* be superficial if my calculations are correct. I haven't tested them yet.

Leoben just stares at me. "Are you serious?"

"It's totally safe."

He snorts, shaking his head. "Those sound like last words to me."

He takes the gun and turns it in his hands, his eyes fixed on an empty space in the air beside it. His tech will be showing him data from the targeting chip. Muzzle velocity, recoil, impact simulations, all displayed in a virtual interface sketched into his vision. I'd be able to see it too if my panel was working, but when I try to focus on the gun, all I see is a burst of static. My tech has been like that all week—glitchy and strange, messing with my vision. I need to get it running again soon, though. We've been waiting here for Cole's injuries to heal, but now he's better, and I'm the one we're waiting on. There's no point in us going after Lachlan until my panel is running and I'm able to *code*.

Leoben checks the gun's chamber. "What's the plan?"

"Thigh," I say, propping my leg up on the jeep's tailgate. "Close range, more accurate that way." I pull up the hem of my black leggings, pointing to a scarlet targeting glyph drawn on my skin. "I marked a site already—no arteries, no bone. Just muscle fibers and at least five days of recovery. That should be enough to kick my tech's installation into emergency mode again."

Leoben taps the gun's barrel against his palm. "This seems risky, even for you."

"Do you have a better idea?"

He tilts his head, considering. "Actually, yeah. I could shoot you in the hand."

"What?" I step back, pulling my hands to my chest instinctively.

"It's safer," he says. "If this bullet fragments in your leg, it could nick an artery, but your hand will be fine. Those bones heal fast, and your tech will shut down a bleed like that in seconds. Come on, hold out your hand."

I look down at my clenched fists, hesitating. This seemed a lot less reckless when I was planning on getting shot in the leg. An injury in my hand should still speed up my panel's installation, but it feels more frightening, and definitely more painful. Leoben could change his mind any minute, though, and I don't want to have to do this myself.

"Okay," I say, holding out my left arm, the light of my panel washing over the creases in my palm as I unfurl my fingers. "Give me a five-second warn—"

Leoben pulls the trigger.

The shot through the silencer sounds like glass breaking, startling the pigeons in the trees above us. They erupt in frantic spirals of light, their cries filling the air like a hailstorm. I double over, clutching my hand to my chest. The pain hasn't hit me yet, but I can feel it coming. Scarlet emergency messages scroll wildly across my vision. Blood pressure readings, injury monitors, healing tech levels. My tech is kicking into gear, sending a jolt of adrenaline into my muscles, making my vision flicker as it draws in and out of focus. I suck in a breath through gritted teeth, then look down at my hand to survey the damage.

But there's no wound.

Leoben throws his head back, laughing. "You should have seen your face!"

I look up, shaking. "What the hell, Lee?"

"There's no way I was going to shoot you, squid."

I lunge forward to punch him in the arm, but a *crack* echoes in the distance, and the air rushes from my lungs.

Leoben doesn't react, but I stand frozen, listening to the sound as it echoes off the hills. Someone else might mistake it for a gunshot, but I've heard that sound so many times that it's burned into my memory.

It was faint and muffled, mixed with the cries of the pigeons, but it sounded a *lot* like a Hydra cloud.

"What's wrong?" Leoben asks.

"I thought I heard something. Didn't you?"

"These birds are messing with my audio filters. What did you hear?"

"An explosion."

Leoben's smile fades. His eyes glaze, scanning the trees, and another *crack* sounds in the distance.

"I heard that one," he breathes, and I turn and bolt into the trees.

My vision flashes as I race through the woods and up a muddy hill, my tech spinning up emergency filters automatically, trying to brighten the trail ahead of me. Leoben follows close behind, catching up as I reach a switchback, both of us heading for a lookout on the crest of the hill. I've run up this trail a dozen times searching the sky for Cartaxus copters, worried they'd found us, but never to look for a *blower*.

The vaccine is out. The virus is dead.

Nobody should be detonating anymore.

We burst together through a line of trees at the top of the hill and stumble out onto the edge of a cliff. The last rays of sunlight are disappearing over the horizon. From up here I can see the sawtooth silhouette of the three-peaked mountains in the distance, the infinite stretch of spruce forest to the south. I shove the loose hair back from my face, searching for a plume. The flock of pigeons forms a writhing, swirling blanket of light through the tufted canopy. but there's no sign of a cloud.

My vision flickers, and I rub my eyes, willing my tech to switch back to standby, but it doesn't respond. My panel is only listening to my adrenaline levels, not my thoughts. It still thinks I'm in danger.

And maybe I am.

If those explosions were blowers, the victims probably had the vaccine. I gave Cartaxus code to force it into every panel on the planet. There are a few survivors on the surface without panels in their arms, but the likelihood of *two* of them blowing near our camp is low. If those explosions were blowers, it could mean the vaccine isn't working anymore.

But I don't even want to think about that possibility.

"I can't see anything," I say, rubbing my eyes again. "I don't know if it's my tech or not. It still isn't responding to me."

Leoben steps to the edge of the cliff, scanning the horizon. He'll be checking for heat signatures, anomalous air patterns. If there's a cloud, his tech will find it. "Nothing," he says. "That was a detonation, though. Seemed smaller than a blower. Could have been a bomb."

"Why would two be going off right now?"

We turn to each other at the same time.

"Shit," I breathe. "Cole."

Leoben turns so fast he's barely more than a blur, bolting back through the trees and down the trail. I race after him, my heart kicking, fresh adrenaline alerts blinking in my vision. I couldn't tell from the sound where those explosions were coming from—they could have been in a nearby camp, or they could have been at the lab. Cole could be hurt. The thought wrenches at something inside me, as real and painful as a wound.

I try to summon my comm-link to call Cole, but all I get is a burst of static. "Can you call him?" I yell to Leoben.

"He's gone dark," he shouts back, racing into camp. "You drive to the meeting point!" He wrenches the tarpaulin away from his jeep, slamming the rear doors shut. "I'll run the trail in case he's there."

"No," I gasp, skidding down the last stretch of the hill. "I'll run. My panel's still freaking out. I won't be able to control the jeep. You take it."

Leoben's brow furrows, but he nods, climbing into the driver's seat. "He'll be okay, squid. Be safe."

"You too," I say. He pulls the jeep across the clearing and down the muddy tire tracks that lead to the road that loops around the lab. There's a meeting point we set up there, where if anything happened, if there was any hint of danger, we'd meet.

Cole will have heard the blasts, and he'll be waiting there for us. He *has* to be.

I race across the crumpled tarpaulin, heading for a gap in the trees that marks the trail to our lookout point. Leoben and Cole have been taking turns to hike to it every day and watch the lab in case Lachlan shows up. The trail drops sharply once it leaves camp, zig-zagging down a rocky, tree-covered slope. I take the switchbacks fast, bolting through the trees, spotting a figure at the bottom of the hill.

A person, kneeling on the ground. Dark hair, black jacket.

"Cole!" I scream, racing for him. He's on the ground. I should have brought a medkit. "Cole, are you okay?"

I skid to a stop as the figure stands and turns to me.

It isn't Cole. It's Jun Bei.

## ABOUT THE AUTHOR

EMILY SUVADA was born and raised in Australia, where she went on to earn a degree in mathematics. She previously worked as a data scientist and still spends hours writing algorithms to perform tasks that would only take her minutes to complete on her own. When not writing, she can be found hiking, cycling, and conducting chemistry experiments in her kitchen. She currently lives in Portland, Oregon, with her husband.